Though
his music
touched millions . . .
his heart
sang for
only one

# THE ROAD TO LOVE

"I don't know what happened between us today, Holly, or if it means anything." Cole brought his hand up to touch her arm. She backed away as if operating on reflex. "But I'd like to stick around for a while to find out."

Before she answered, she widened the space between them even more. "For a while?" she shot at him. She was suddenly inexplicably angry. "Is staying with me like playing house for you? What do you think I am, a stopping-off place where you can find shelter and companionship and pretend you're part of something you miss when you're on the road?"

"We have to talk, Holly—about a lot of things. And we have to do it over a lot more meals and another rainstorm and while watching at least a dozen more sunsets."

"My mother warned me about poets."

He smiled in relief that she was no longer on the attack. "What did she tell you?"

"That they would either break my heart," she said softly, "or make it soar."

Harper
Monogram

# ALONE IN A CROWD

## Georgia Bockoven

**HarperPaperbacks**
*A Division of HarperCollinsPublishers*

This is a work of fiction. The characters, incidents, and dialogues are products of the author's imagination and are not to be construed as real. Any resemblance to actual events or persons, living or dead, is entirely coincidental.

HarperPaperbacks  *A Division of* HarperCollins*Publishers*
10 East 53rd Street, New York, N.Y. 10022

Cover illustration by Jeff Cornell

First printing: March 1995

Printed in the United States of America

HarperPaperbacks, HarperMonogram, and colophon are trademarks of HarperCollins*Publishers*

❖ 10 9 8 7 6 5 4 3 2 1

*This book is dedicated to Karen Solem and Carolyn Marino for their unfailing enthusiasm, encouragement, and wisdom. They are the best, pure and simple.*

# Prologue

*Cole Webster pressed his fingers* against the bandages that covered his face. Nothing happened. He pushed harder. Slowly, relentlessly, his fingers sunk deeper into the gauze.

According to the surgeon, there were times during the nine hours Cole had been on the operating table that the outcome had been questionable. Several of the bones in his face hadn't just broken, they'd splintered; it was a miracle none of the fragments had penetrated his brain. His leg, broken in two places and put back together with a metal plate, was accorded incidental status when compared to the head injuries. The team of specialists had patched and wired and put the pieces back as best they could, leaving Cole mute until his jaws were unwired, his features something of a mystery until the swelling went down.

Thoughts of an old woman Cole had met in Arkansas when he was a kid working the county fairs with a second-rate bluegrass band came back to him. She'd noticed him looking at her hands—the fingers crippled and turned back on themselves from arthritis. When he'd asked her if they hurt, she'd told him, "Not so much anymore, but there was a time I believed taking a hammer to them would make them feel better."

Having no yardstick to measure such pain, he'd recoiled at her words. Now, almost twenty years later, he finally understood.

His probing fingers broke through the invisible barrier and he felt a sharp, breath-stealing stab to his left eye. He rocked back against the pillows and let out a low moan, for the moment he'd attained his goal, the primary, constant pain was forgotten if only for as long as it took his eye to stop hurting. One of the doctors who'd examined him that morning had told him to think of his discomfort as something positive. After all, when you considered the alternative . . .

The doctor didn't have a goddamned clue. If he had, he would have known there were some experiences that made dying look good. Experiences like having a motorcycle slip out from beneath you and then stopping the free-fall down a canyon by hitting a tree face-first. Worst of all for Cole was the memory. Every detail, both before and after he'd hit the oil slick, was etched in his mind, like individual frames in a low-budget thriller.

The squeak of a door hinge broke through the red haze of Cole's pain. He leaned forward in an attempt to see who had come into the room.

"I found it," Frank Webster announced as he moved toward Cole. His stride matched his triumphant grin. "Couldn't be more perfect if we'd special ordered it. The house itself is one of those god-awful places the Hollywood people used to like to name. The real estate agent called it Casa Blanca. It's miles from the main road. There's even a place for the helicopter, or at least there will be once we get rid of the fence around the tennis courts. I had the pilot do a test run this morning, and the house is less than twenty minutes from the Ventura hospital. We can get the doctors to you or you to them quicker than we could if we were staying at home."

Cole stared at his father through eyes swollen to narrow slits and without their usual crutch of corrective contact lenses. Even with the double disadvantage, he could see the animation in the older man's face. Give Frank Webster a problem to solve and he was in his element.

Coming out of the anesthesia, the first thing Cole had heard was his father's voice, telling him over and over again in a whispered, monotonous litany that he wasn't to worry about being discovered. Only the surgeons knew who he really was.

During the days that followed, Cole couldn't stop thinking about his father's choice of greeting. In his more forgiving moments, he told himself it was only natural that as soon as Frank learned his son had survived, his focus would turn to damage control. After all, that was what managers did. And, as Frank constantly reminded him, it wasn't as if Cole Webster were some John Doe off the street.

Frank moved so Cole could see him without turning his head. "On the way over here I was thinking about what the tabloids would do if they ever got hold of this. It got me in such a state I missed the turn and had to circle back. Took me a good mile out of my way."

Cole closed his eyes against what he knew was coming next. Frank was resurrecting an earlier argument when Cole had snatched a pen from his father's ever-present notebook and had written an angry challenge to the autocratic way he was being treated.

"There wouldn't be any way to put an end to the gossip those people would print short of parading you in front of the cameras," Frank went on. "Given how they operate, I'm not sure even that would do it. The way you look now, we could stick anyone out there and say it was you. Can you imagine what those people would do with that notion? They'd have you dead and us trying to pass off a look-alike. There wouldn't be a thing we could do to prove 'em wrong short of having you fingerprinted."

Warming to his subject, he began to pace. "I know what you're thinking, we could find ways to deal with the tabloids. But there's not a goddamned thing we could do about the critics. If they get a scent of this, they're going to be like buzzards circling overhead the entire time you're down. The longer it takes for you to get up again, the more doubts they'll throw out about your ability to ever come back. It's a given that if you say something often enough, Cole, it becomes fact."

For emphasis, he stopped at the foot of the bed and looked directly at Cole. "Plain and simple, it's like I always told you, critics are paid to criticize. If we let them find out about the accident, they're gonna be writin' that your career's over before you step foot out of this hospital. Then when you go out on the road again and you miss a note or move a little slower, they'll be knocking each other out of the way to get to their computers and say how they were right about you being finished."

Even if his jaws weren't wired together, Cole wouldn't have tried to argue the point with his father. He'd seen what happened when critics made up their minds a singer was slipping. It made no difference whether they were right or wrong or simply filling an otherwise slow news day with idle speculation. Once the match was put to the kindling, there was nothing that anyone, least of all the singer himself, could do to put out the fire.

"I hate to admit it," Frank added with a quick grin, "but I can't help thinkin' what a shame it is that we have to miss out on the publicity something like this would bring. There's not a doubt in my mind that this would be the biggest story to hit country music since Patsy Cline's plane went down."

There was one unwavering truth about his father: His behavior never deviated. He was always the hustler. Always looking for the angle. Frank Webster's warped perception of Cole's accident was nothing out of the ordinary, certainly nothing unexpected. Still Cole couldn't help feeling a stab of disappointment.

"Gotta go," Frank said. "Trevor wants an answer on the new album cover by tonight."

Cole leaned his head back and listened to the door closing behind his father. Alone again, he let his mind drift.

God, he was tired. No, it went deeper than tired. He was worn out. Why else would he care that Frank hadn't once thought to ask his firstborn son how the hell he was feeling?

# 1

*Belinda Hanover shifted position* on the lounge chair, slipped her hand under her cascade of blond hair, and lifted it off her shoulders. The cedars that had been planted to keep photographers' long-distance lenses from prying at users of the Olympic-sized pool also kept any but the strongest wind from reaching her. She let her hair fall back and automatically ran her fingers through the mass to restore its fullness.

After a quick glance to see that the top of her T-strap bikini still covered her nipples, she closed her eyes, laid her head back on the pillow, and tried to remember the details of the article she'd read in *Cosmo* about altitude and the increased exposure to ultraviolet rays.

She'd arrived at Casa Blanca less than an hour ago for her obligatory weekend with Cole, and already she was looking forward to leaving. She hated everything about the place, including the time it took to get here. It didn't matter that Cole hardly noticed her when she came to see him, Frank still insisted she make the weekly sojourn.

Cole had talked to her so little since the accident, it had taken her two weeks to notice when the wires were removed from his jaw. But then it wasn't communication Frank brought her here to provide for his son. She'd considered telling him Cole had no interest in sex and hadn't since the accident, but had thought better of it. Giving Frank that kind of information was tantamount to telling the burglar at the foot of your bed where the guns were hidden.

A bell beside her sounded, indicating that the seven minutes she'd allocated for her left side were over. She reset the timer for another seven minutes and turned to her right side, carefully arranging her body for maximum effect should Cole happen to be watching from the house.

Rhonda Marie Hanover, the consummate stage mother, had taught Belinda well. College was for plain girls. Belinda's face and body would take her further than any degree ever could.

Rhonda had introduced Belinda to the beauty pageant circuit a week shy of her first birthday. Belinda had won, of course, and what had started out as a Saturday time filler for a lonely woman and an uncommonly beautiful baby had turned into an all-consuming passion. The circuit became the focus of their lives. Somewhere in the process Rhonda lost her husband and Belinda her childhood, but both were too busy traveling and preparing for the next contest to give either much notice.

No other girl before or since had won as many trophies as the "Lassie from Tallahassee," Belinda Sue Hanover. When she turned sixteen, Rhonda sent out a press release to announce that her daughter was retiring from competition to concentrate on an acting career. *People* magazine flew a writer and photographer all the way to Florida to help mark the occasion.

The photographer had posed Belinda on the front lawn, surrounded by trophies, her arms in the air like a game show hostess showing off the prizes. Her mother stood next to the photographer, providing encouragement and last-minute instructions.

Rhonda sent a copy of the article to every agent in Hollywood. Three responded. One of them actually sent a contract, telling them Belinda was scheduled to test for a television pilot as soon as she arrived in Los Angeles. Of course there was the small detail of a six thousand dollar processing fee to be paid up front, but the agent pointed out that a girl like Belinda would undoubtedly earn twice that much her first week of work.

Rhonda had been beside herself with excitement. She'd put the check in the mail and the house up for sale the same day the letter arrived.

Admittedly success did not come as easily or in precisely the way Rhonda and Belinda had anticipated. Still, it wasn't the demeaning route those stupid women in the audience at the Donahue show had tried to make it seem.

Belinda was proud of her centerfold layout. It wasn't as if she'd posed with her legs spread or with fingers stuck up her crotch, for cryin' out loud. The photographs were works of art and tastefully done. But the loudmouthed feminists had refused to see that. All they wanted to talk about was the one picture where she'd posed in front of a blow-up of herself winning the Miss Tunturan Mall contest when she was five years old. Those women had missed the point entirely. The magazine was simply trying to show that some little girls do indeed grow up in delightful ways. To say it was child pornography was totally off the wall.

They refused to listen to her when she talked about the contacts she'd made or the important parties she'd been invited to because of her work for the magazine. *How else could someone like her have met Cole Webster?*

"Hey, Belinda," a male voice called. "You about through out here?"

She looked up and saw Randy Webster coming toward her, sporting a lopsided grin. She glanced at the timer. "I've got a couple minutes more. Why?"

"I don't want to go inside by myself," he said. "Frank's going to throw a shit fit when he sees me here."

She brought her hand up to shield her eyes. The return smile that tugged at her collagen-enhanced lips was genuine. She liked Randy. Cole's brother was the bass player for the road band and the only one in Cole's inner circle who didn't treat her as if she were simply a transitory item in his life and therefore not worth cultivating. She propped herself up on her elbow.

"I thought you were supposed to be on display this weekend," she said. It was Randy's marked resemblance to his brother that had successfully allowed Frank to hide Cole's long absence. Or, more accurately, the resemblance they used to bear. Since the accident, Randy actually looked more like the old Cole than Cole did himself.

"I figured if I had to pretend I was Cole," Randy said, "I might as well act the part." He glanced down at the toes of his boots and then up again, a mischievous gleam in his eyes. "So, I called down to the house and gave everyone the day off. If there's no audience, there's no need to perform."

"I'd like to give the people Frank hired to work here some time off, like the next month. Surely your father could have found someone who spoke a *little* English."

"Speaking English has nothing to do with it. He wanted people he could blackmail into keeping their mouths shut. Who better than illegal aliens?"

"He's become obsessed with this thing." In the beginning, she and Randy hadn't believed the switch could be accomplished. Randy had even argued with his father that if the press ever got wind of their subterfuge and decided to play up the secretive angle, it would create the explosion that really could destroy Cole's career. But, as usual, Frank refused to listen.

To their admitted surprise, Randy's assumption of Cole's life had worked. At least it had so far. Randy had even stood in for Cole on a long-distance shot for the inside photograph on the new CD. Luckily, it wasn't the first time he'd substituted for Cole on something like that so no one was suspicious when he told them Cole was tied up elsewhere. A couple of guys in the band had begun to question how long Cole was going to lock himself away to work on new material, but everyone else seemed content to let Frank or Randy act as go-between for whatever business they might have had with Cole. Which was pretty much the way things usually happened when Cole was between road tours anyway.

"The way Frank acts you'd think he really believes Cole's career would be over if anyone found out about the accident," Belinda said.

"As I see it, it's not so much that Cole's career would be over as that he'd have to spend the next five years trying to prove he's as good as he's always been. Critics would lose their jobs if they filled their columns with the same thing all the time. Cole being good and being on top is old news."

"It was the same on the pageant circuit," she admitted. "Girls were the cutest thing going when they were the underdogs, and bitches on wheels when they were winning all the time."

"You were so young when all that was going on. It must have been hard on you."

She never talked about the bad things that happened to her back then. People were always so quick to criticize something they didn't understand. It was better to let them think her years of competition had been everything the promoters advertised. "So, what do you think Frank is going to do when he sees you?" she asked, shifting the focus back to Randy.

"He'll go ballistic." Randy pulled a chair over and sat down. "Which is why I want you to come inside with me, Belinda, my love."

"I'm not sure how I should feel about you wanting my protection." She came up and reached back to adjust the chair to a sitting position. Randy moved to do it for her.

"Consider it the highest of compliments."

She flexed her arm and playfully studied the muscle. "Are you hinting I've been putting too much time in at the gym lately?"

Almost as if he couldn't stop himself, Randy's gaze swept her near naked body, a flush coloring his neck as he did so. "No," he said softly, "that's not what I'm saying at all."

His action pleased her as much as his words. It was nice to be appreciated once in a while. God knew she'd gotten little enough attention from Cole lately.

"Your dad doesn't think either one of us is taking this thing as seriously as we should, and your being here today isn't going to help," she said. Randy's ongoing "job" since the accident was to put on Cole's clothes a couple of times a day and wander around the studio, which was a good two hundred yards from the main house. Frank made sure whoever he brought in for a meeting took a walk around outside before they left so that they could report seeing "Cole" sitting at the piano behind the large plate glass window or outside playing with one of the dogs.

"Hell, Cole isn't even convinced all this was necessary," said Randy.

"When did he tell you that?"

"A couple of weeks ago."

"Then why didn't he put a stop to it?"

"Remember, when it was all going down, his mouth was wired shut. And if you can't outshout Dad, you ain't gonna win."

"I don't think it made any difference. When Frank gets something in his head . . ." Usually she was more circumspect about criticizing Frank to either of his sons.

"Frank convinced himself the plastic surgery would do miracles,"

"But didn't the doctor say it was the swelling that was

causing most of the change and that in a couple of months he would be back to normal?"

"If they got all the bones back where they were supposed to go the way they said they did, then they got a couple of them in backwards. I haven't been able to figure out why, but Cole just doesn't look the same."

"It's that scar over his eye. It's all I can see when I look at him. They should do something about it."

"Cole said he was through with hospitals. Six operations were enough."

The timer sounded beside Belinda. She reached down to shut it off and then motioned to the chair beside Randy. "Would you be a sweetheart and hand me my wrap?"

He held the electric blue garment for her while she slipped her arms through the sleeves. "You ready to go up to the house?"

"What makes you think Frank is going to go easier on you just because you're with me?"

"Can't blame a guy for trying."

She put her arm through his and leaned in close. "Especially not one I'm as partial to as I am you."


Cole stood at the living-room window, his weight balanced on his good leg in an attempt to ease the constant ache in the other, and watched Belinda and Randy as they walked toward the house. They were in deep conversation, their heads almost touching. Randy looked up and Cole saw that he was laughing. He felt an irrational surge of jealousy. No one laughed around him anymore; hell, they hardly talked around him.

Randy stopped to pick something up from the lawn. He examined whatever it was, gave it a toss, and quickened his step to catch up with Belinda.

Lately a feeling of envy passed through Cole whenever he was around his brother. But blaming Randy for being born second and escaping the pressure of fulfilling

Frank's dreams made about as much sense as yelling at the sun for coming up in the morning.

Growing up when they'd had only each other for company, they'd been inseparable. But then Cole's career had exploded and everything changed. In the beginning the demands on his time were flattering and exciting and he tried his best to fill them all. And then one day he realized he'd become so wrapped up in himself he had no idea what was going on in Randy's life. He didn't know the smallest thing, like who his brother was seeing or even if he was seeing anyone. Two kids who'd been raised on the road, isolated from everyone their own age, who'd only ever had each other for friends had turned into adults who at times struggled to find something to say when they were alone together.

Cole heard someone come into the room and glanced up to see his father's reflection in the window.

"How's the view by the pool?" Frank asked.

It was obvious by the coy tone in his voice that Frank didn't expect an answer. To him, Belinda was mind candy, not a serious topic of conversation.

"What the hell—" Frank pressed his face closer to the window. "What's he doing here?"

Confused at the outburst, Cole asked, "Who?"

"Randy. I told him I didn't want him leaving the house this weekend."

Cole turned from the window. "Looks like he thought better of the idea."

"That damned kid can't do one thing he's told and get it right. I should have known not to trust him."

"Jesus, Dad, give him a break. He's been at this over four months now."

"You've been protecting Randy too long, Cole. If you don't cut him loose, he's never going to learn to go it alone."

"Cut him loose? What in the hell is that supposed to mean?"

"Randy doesn't know up from down in the real world. It's about time he learned." Frank put his head back and let out a long-suffering sigh. He was still looking at the ceiling when he said, "Why are we rehashing this same old crap when we've got more important things that need doing?" He purposefully stared at Cole. "You're not working on those exercises the doctor sent over, are you?"

The question caught Cole off guard. "What exercises?"

"That's what I thought." There was a perverted triumph in his voice as though he was pleased that his suspicions had been confirmed. "For your voice," he explained with a show of patience. "I can't hear any improvement. If we're going to pull this off, you've got to do your part, Cole. I can't do it all myself."

Before Cole could answer, Frank switched subjects again. "I have the blueprint Andy wants you to go over for the new stage. He sent the—"

"I don't want to think about that right now." More to the point, he didn't want to be around his father anymore. "If anyone comes looking for me, I'll be in my room."

"Running away again? That's getting to be quite a habit lately."

"What do you want from me?" Cole demanded.

"Nothing you shouldn't be wanting for yourself. I've worked too hard—hell, we both have—to watch everything disappear because you couldn't keep off that goddamned motorcycle. I'm not going to let ten cents worth of oil spilled on some backwoods road destroy the greatest thing that's ever happened to country music." He reached up to put his arm across Cole's shoulders. "Look, I know it seems like I've been pushing you pretty hard these past couple of weeks, but everything I'm doing is for your own good."

"If you only knew how sick I am of hearing that." He was as tired of the for-your-own-good part as the country-music-savior bit.

"It's the truth."

"Then maybe it's time you got a life of your own and stopped living mine for me."

Frank withdrew his arm. "Of all the ungrateful—"

"Give it up, Dad. I've heard it too many times."

"Someday you're going to push me too far."

The dialogue was so familiar, it seemed scripted. This was the point where Cole was supposed to hang his head and say something about being under a lot of pressure and not meaning to take it out on Frank. Then Frank would forgive him and they would go on as if nothing had happened.

Cole crossed the room and dropped into an overstuffed chair. After several seconds, he rocked forward, his elbows propped on his knees. "Why don't you show me the storyboards Steve sent over for the *Single Man* video?"

Cole had been scheduled to go into the studio the day after the accident to do some final work on the title song for the new album. Although Frank had been pressuring him to go with what they already had so that they could meet the announced release date, Cole had refused. The one area of his career where he still maintained any control was in the studio, and he held on to that with the tenacity of a pup defending its favorite teat.

"I thought I told you we decided to make 'A Walk on the Right Side of Town' the first single," Frank said. "Everyone agrees it's a stronger lead."

With seven albums behind him, Cole should have been accustomed to the last-minute changes that came with putting one to bed; instead, he found himself increasingly frustrated at his lack of input and control. As producer, his father handled everything from choosing the songs to the studio musicians. He approved the cover, the cuts to be released as singles, and the location and number of tour dates. Frank Webster was considered a genius by those who knew and understood where the real power lay in the music business.

Who was Cole to argue with genius?

Frank was constantly being asked to take on promising new singers. He turned them all down. Every one of them. His son was the focus of his life. Always had been, always would be. And there wasn't a thing Cole could do about it.

"I wish you'd told me you were thinking about switching 'Single Man' with 'The Right Side of Town,'" Cole said.

Frank hesitated. "I didn't just switch it."

Cole looked up. "What's that supposed to mean?"

Frank grew noticeably uncomfortable. "I probably should have said something to you sooner, but when you were still in the hospital and Tony Klossen started pushing to get you back into the studio to wrap up 'Single Man' I had to come up with something, so I told him you were stalling because you were looking for a way to stop working with Gloria, and dropping 'Single Man' from the album was the best way to do it."

Cole covered his face with his hands. "Tell me you at least had the courtesy to let her know what was going on."

"We'll make it up to her. When all this dies down—"

Cole leaped to his feet, his anger swift and tangible. The sudden movement sent pain shooting through his head. His leg almost gave out on him. He grabbed the arm of the chair to keep from falling. He caught his breath and pressed his other hand hard against his forehead, as if he could contain the pain. "Either you call right now and give her a reason she can live with, or I call her and tell her the truth."

"See what happens when you get yourself worked up?" Frank crossed the room and eased Cole back into the chair.

"I want you to call her, Dad." The pain was making him sick to his stomach. "Now."

"She's probably not even home yet." Frank made a show of looking at his watch. "I'll try in a couple of hours."

Cole brought his arm up to shove his father aside. He moved to get up again.

"Oh, all right," Frank relented. "If it's that important to you, I'll do it now."

Cole waited until Frank was gone before he leaned his head back and closed his eyes. Seconds later the sounds of Frank and Randy arguing drifted into the room.

# 2

*A breeze caught the lace curtain* at the bedroom window. Cole lay stretched out on the bed, a sheet carelessly flung across his hips, his hands tucked under his head. He watched the shadows dance across the textured ceiling and thought about the number of nights in his life the light had come from neon signs instead of a full moon. Even after all this time, the neon still outweighed the moonlight.

The restlessness, the questioning that had been with him during the four months since the accident, had become as familiar and expected as his shadow. He'd go to bed exhausted and still be awake at three or four in the morning. His mind simply wouldn't shut down. If it wasn't the accident replaying itself, it was something gnawing at him about his career. What had grabbed him by the short hairs that night wasn't whether he'd be able to return to the stage and convince the ever-eager critics that just because the "California Cowboy's" face had been rearranged didn't mean his voice or style had changed; it was that he couldn't seem to find it in him to care. But no matter how hard he concentrated, he couldn't seem to remember the joy that came with walking out on a stage and singing for a stadium full of fans who knew the words to every one of his songs.

He just didn't give a damn anymore. About anything.

It was a terrible way to feel.

Beside him Belinda sighed softly as she turned from her back to her stomach and settled into the new position. Earlier that night, when he got up from the dinner table and announced he was going to bed, she'd insisted on accompanying him. He'd protested, but she'd refused to be put off.

Once they were alone, she began to undress him, telling him a massage was what he needed, "to relax you, and help you sleep better," she'd said, both of them knowing what she really meant. Her methods had never failed in the past; there was no reason to believe they wouldn't work now. Especially after so many months of abstinence. When it came to the art of erotic stimulation, he'd never been with another woman as skillful as Belinda. She could do more to bring him to a mind-blowing climax with the tip of her tongue than other women had done with their entire bodies.

Only it hadn't happened.

They'd put the failure down to nerve endings still so sensitive they made him want to scream no matter how lightly she ran her hand over the middle of his back or down his leg.

There were places on his face like that, too, especially the scar at his temple and the one over his eye. At times the glasses he'd been told to wear for the next six months in place of his usual contacts felt as if they weighed ten pounds, and he was forced to slip into a world where he was half-blind to gain relief.

Shaving was torture. He either cut himself where the skin was numb or gritted his teeth as the razor passed over the areas where it felt raw. Which was why he'd taken to wearing the stubbly beard everyone hated so much.

As bored with talk about his condition as he was sure everyone else was, he hadn't bothered telling anyone why he'd grown the beard, only that he'd shave it off when the time came. According to the doctor, it could be weeks before the sensitivity faded, or it might be months, or he could be this way for the rest of his life.

So what if he looked a little different and sounded a little different and walked with a bit of a limp and could hardly stand to have people touch him? He was alive.

How could he say it and believe it and still not feel it?

He closed his eyes to the Rorschach test playing on the ceiling and focused on the sounds drifting in from outside. A cacophony of crickets, frogs, and night birds greeted and surprised him. It was loud enough to wake the dead and he hadn't heard a thing.

A mental smile formed at the ludicrous cliché and the thought that, if true, it was probably because the dead were less self-absorbed than he'd become.

As he listened, a new sound intruded. It was so alien to the others, it took him several seconds to place it. He sat up, grabbed his glasses off the nightstand, and swung his legs over the side of the bed, careful not to disturb Belinda.

When he reached the window he pulled the curtain aside and peered down. Randy, his arm hauled back to throw another missile, looked up at Cole. An eerie feeling washed over Cole. It was as if twenty years had instantly disappeared and he was seeing himself at eleven on the night he and Randy had run away together. Only that time it had been Cole standing outside Randy's room.

Cole lifted the double-hung window the rest of the way and unlatched the screen. He leaned out to let Randy see him better. "Whatever you've been drinking, you've had enough."

"Haven't touched a drop since dinner," Randy protested in a voice just loud enough for Cole to hear. "Come on down, big brother. I'm breaking you out of this place."

Cole glanced at Belinda to be sure the commotion hadn't disturbed her and remembered she'd taken a sleeping pill along with her nightly assortment of vitamins and would likely be out until late the next morning. He said to Randy, "What's the occasion?"

"It's a surprise."

After Randy had gone to the trouble of being there, the least Cole could do was play along. He stuck his head out farther, making a show of seeking a means of escape. There was a decorative ledge just below the window that looked as if it had been put there in an attempt to hide one of the additions to the house. A couple of feet away a rain gutter exited the tile roof and made a jog to accommodate the ledge. Because of the age of this wing of the house, he guessed both were better secured and of stronger material than they would have been if new. "I don't know. . . ."

"For Christ's sake, I'm not asking you to elope. I just want you for one night. Now get your pants on and meet me out front." He tossed the remaining pebbles toward the raised flower bed directly under the window. "And would you please see if you could manage to get down the stairs without waking everybody up?"

Cole tried to focus on reasons he shouldn't go with Randy when the idea of escaping, if only for one night, became irresistible. He started inside then hesitated. Sticking his head back out the window, he said, "Randy, wait there for me."

It took a minute for what Cole was really telling him to sink in. "Are you crazy?"

"That remains to be seen, doesn't it?" Cole ducked into the bedroom and put on a pair of jeans, a T-shirt, and some tennis shoes. He tried not to notice how simply getting dressed left him breathing as hard as when he'd been running five miles a day. Without giving what he was about to do the second thought it deserved, he went back to the window, swung his good leg over the sill, and braced his foot on the ledge.

Randy's eyes became saucers. "Jesus H. Christ, that tree you hit didn't just rearrange your face, it scrambled your brain. Think a minute about what you're doing, would you?"

"That's part of my problem—I think too damn much." Cole slowly shifted his weight to the foot out on the ledge. It seemed solid enough.

"Cole, come on," Randy pleaded. "This is just plain dumb."

"Shhhh." He pointed to the left with his chin, indicating the room nearby. "You're going to have Frank out here if you don't keep it down." Straddling the sill, he brought his other foot out and placed it beside the first. Gradually, he shifted his full weight to his feet, giving the ledge a testing bounce before committing himself fully.

Satisfied, he began edging toward the downspout. As he moved farther away from the safety of the window, a voice from his childhood beckoned to him, telling him he need only move his arms the way he did in his dreams and he could step off the ledge and fly. Although compelling, he resisted the impulse. The memory of the one time he hadn't, when he was seven and believed he only had to want something badly enough and it was his, was embarrassingly and painfully clear.

Fifteen feet below the ledge, Randy paced frantically. "Damn it, Cole, why are you doing this to me?"

Cole looked down and grinned. "Hey, this wasn't my idea. I would never have come up with something this harebrained. I'm the sensible one, remember?" With the tips of his fingers still clutching the window casing, he slid his other hand toward the pipe, but all he found was more stucco. He shifted his gaze to his outstretched hand, trying to gauge how far he had to go. His heart sank. He was still a good six inches away. Prudence demanded he go back. He took a deep breath, thought a minute, and laughed out loud. "Hey, Randy, remember Prudence Esposito?"

Randy thought a minute, and then despite an obvious

attempt to suppress it, a smile formed. "Wasn't she one of the old ladies Dad used to leave us with when we stayed in Nashville?"

"The one with really thin lips and the mole on her eyelid," Cole supplied, "who drooled chew down her chin whenever she fell asleep in front of the TV."

"And drank moonshine out of a pickle jar and said it was iced tea," Randy added.

"We never listened to Prudence then."

Randy's smile faded. "What's the matter with you? You got some kind of death wish?"

"I'm just sick of living like death is the worst thing that can happen to me." Instead of immediately reaching for the pipe, he took a moment to enjoy the sense of freedom that had come over him. "Randy?"

"Now what?"

"Stand a little closer, would you?"

Randy did as he was asked and moved toward the house. "What do you want me to do?"

"Catch me if I fall."

"Screw that," Randy told him. He made a show of returning to where he'd been standing. "You're on your own on this one."

Cole grinned and took a deep breath. He might feel differently in another minute or two, but right then, he felt incredibly, intoxicatingly alive.

One more sliding step and his fingers touched metal; he'd been right, the pipe wasn't aluminum. Instinct took over when his hand wrapped around the drain. He planted his toe and swung around so that he was facing the building and straddling the pipe.

Slowly he began to ease himself down and over the ledge, his long-sedentary muscles screaming in protest at the effort. A searing pain wrapped tentacles around his bad leg. Balancing his weight on his hands and hips, he stretched his good leg out to feel for the bracket that held the pipe to the wall.

"You're shy a couple of inches," Randy called up.

Cole rocked his hips and shifted lower until he reached the makeshift foothold. Then, with a quick push, he was over the edge. Precariously balanced on one foot, he slid the other down the pipe, seeking another toehold.

"You're never going to make it," Randy announced. He came forward, reached up, and touched Cole's heel with the tips of his fingers. "Keep coming. . . . You're feeling for my shoulder."

The muscles in Cole's arms ached with the effort just to hold on. "Get out of the way and let me jump."

"Yeah, right, so you can break something you missed last time?"

"Randy, I'm slipping. Get out of the way." The warning came just as Cole lost his grip and started to fall. He landed on top of Randy, sliding through his grasping arms to the ground. Randy stayed upright for a half second before he toppled into the privet hedge beside Cole.

The frightening silence was broken when Cole let out a deep groan. "I think my leg's broken."

Randy pushed himself up into a sitting position. "Which one?"

"The right one."

Randy gingerly ran his hand over Cole's right leg.

Again Cole groaned. "No, I think it's the left one."

Randy shifted his attention to Cole's left leg.

"No, I'm sure it's the right one."

Randy laughed. "Get away from me, you son of a bitch," he said and gave Cole a shove.

Cole pushed his glasses higher on his nose and sat up. The effort sent a shooting pain through his shoulder and a pounding to his head, but they were nothing compared to the exhilaration he felt at having made it down, however ingloriously.

Randy stood and offered his hand. Cole came slowly, grunting with the effort. He was brushing himself off when he saw the expression on Randy's face change. "What is it?"

"Dad's light just came on."

"Shit. If he catches us . . ." There was no need to finish. Cole grabbed Randy's arm. "Let's get out of here." They took off, Randy at a run, Cole lopping behind.

"He's going to know it was us out here as soon as he sees the bush," Randy said.

"I'm an invalid, remember? How should I know what happened to some bush fifteen feet under my window?" They came around the front of the house and headed for Randy's ancient, beloved truck. Almost as if they'd rehearsed their actions, they wordlessly climbed inside and held the doors rather than risk the sound of closing them. Randy released the brake and the '53 Chevy rolled toward the gate.

Not until they'd cleared the main compound did Randy chance turning on the engine. The lights stayed off until they reached the lower road. Then, as if on cue, they swung their doors open and slammed them shut at the same time, turned to look at each other, and broke out laughing.

"Two grown men should have something better to do with their nights than sneak out of the house and hope their daddy doesn't catch them," Cole said, the pleasure in his voice belying the disapproval in his words.

Randy rolled his window down and let the warm summer air fill the cab. Cole did the same. "So, where're we going?" he asked.

"I told you, it's a surprise. Sit back and enjoy the ride."

It wasn't until Randy pulled to a stop and shut off the engine some time later that Cole realized he'd dozed off. He sat up, stretched, and looked around. The truck was parked on a flat area off a narrow road, a steep hill in front of them, the ocean at their back.

Randy got out and unsnapped the tonneau that covered the truck bed. When he finished, he opened two beach chairs and put them in the truck bed, their backs braced against the cab. Cole came around the open tailgate and saw a large cooler and two rolled-up sleeping bags. He grinned. They were there to party. Just like the old days when they would cut out and let loose, risking Frank's wrath for their illicit night of freedom.

Only this time, all these years later, the escape had been Randy's idea. "How did you know this was what I needed?" Cole asked.

Still standing on the truck bed, Randy stopped what he was doing and lowered himself to his haunches. His gaze swept the ocean before settling on Cole. "I've only been playing at being you for a couple of months now," he said slowly, "but it's enough for me to know there's no way I want what you've got." He opened the cooler and handed Cole a long-neck.

"I'm sorry Dad dumped this on you." Cole took the beer, but hesitated opening it, mulling over the consequences of adding an alcohol headache to his usual one.

"Don't be. Being you has allowed me to see some things I needed to see."

Cole continued to stare at the bottle. Finally, with a snort of disgust over his indecisiveness, he gave the top a quick twist. If there was hell to pay in the morning, it was his hell and he'd pay it. He brought the bottle up and took a long swallow. The cold liquid hit his empty stomach with a jolt.

"Jesus, Cole, take it easy. We've got all night."

Cole hitched himself up on the tailgate, letting his legs swing free over the side. The pain that followed the action was nothing compared to the joy of the seeming normality. "Maybe getting drunk is what I need. Just like the old days. We sure had us some nights to remember."

Randy laughed and settled down beside Cole. "I'm not sure how many of those nights I actually remember, but ask me about the hangovers and I can describe every one of those sons of bitches in full detail."

Cole took another drink, shorter this time. He gazed out at the ocean and let the night take him in. The moon's reflection was like a silver sword laid across the water. "When we're up there onstage you ever wonder what it's like to be those people on the other side of the lights?"

"They're the same as we are. Just a different set of problems." Randy slid the bottle down his thigh, wiping the melting ice off on his jeans.

"How come I'm the one out front and not you?"

"Whoa," Randy said, drawing the word out. "Where did that come from?"

"It's something I've been thinking about a lot lately."

"You were at the right place at the right time. People were looking for a new kind of country singer, one who represented the southern soul buried in people who lived outside the South."

Cole gave him a disgusted look. "You mean a 'California Cowboy.'"

It was his tag, a derogatory term created by a critic who had slammed Cole for supposedly abandoning his roots. With his usual skill, Frank had taken the negative and turned it into an asset, moving them to Los Angeles and retitling the next album, *Country Soul.*

Never mind that Cole had been born in North Carolina and spent the first twenty-five years of his life below the Mason-Dixon Line and was no more at home in California than a Carolina cardinal. Not even knowing the canyon where they'd made their home was a prime target for both fire and earthquake was enough to send Frank east again.

Randy crossed his feet at the ankles and stared at his boots. "If someone knew what put them on top, they'd be able to figure out how to stay there, and that's—"

"Hand me another beer, would you?"

Randy flipped open the chest, took out two bottles, and handed one to Cole. "As I was saying—"

"Don't," Cole said. "I'm tired of talking about me."

"You gotta stop driving yourself crazy thinking you're going to wake up one morning and find all of this gone."

Cole smiled to himself and wondered what Randy would say if he told him anonymity wasn't a nightmare, it was a favorite dream. "You ever talk to Mike or Eric or any of the other guys in the old band?"

"Just Buddy lately. I call him a couple of times a year to see what he's up to."

Buddy Chapman had played mandolin and fiddle in Cole's first official band, the Mississippi Road Warriors. They'd traveled the circuit as a group, going from gig to gig in an old motor home held together with duct tape and bungie cords. It still amazed Cole the difference seven years had made in his life. The bus he used now had cost over half a million dollars and Cole Webster Enterprises had four of them.

Mike had played lead guitar and Eric keyboards. The band stayed together for a while after Frank let them go, but then went their separate ways. Cole's own career was taking off at the time and soon had become all consuming. After a few aborted attempts to get together, they'd drifted out of each other's lives. In the past year, he'd thought about the guys a lot, had even asked some other musicians about them, but nothing ever came of it.

"He still with that bluegrass band?" Cole asked.

"Buddy?"

"Yeah, last time I talked to him—"

"Hell, that was three maybe four years ago, Cole. Where've you been?"

"Has it really been that long? How could that be? It seems like yesterday." Were the conversations he thought he'd had with Buddy only in his head?

"Don't you read that god-awful rambling Christmas letter Suzy sends out every year?" Buddy and Suzy had been married a year before the Mississippi Road Warriors broke up.

"I've never gotten one."

"Sure you have. At least he told me they send you one and I can't think of any reason he'd lie about it."

"It must go to the office." There was a staff of people who did nothing but answer Cole's mail. Only occasionally, if the request was "newsworthy," or Frank felt Cole should see to something personally because it had a human interest angle, were any of the letters brought to his attention. It was another area of Cole's life and his career where he had relinquished control out of both necessity and expediency.

"Or Dad figured it was better if you didn't get it."

"What's that supposed to mean?"

Randy lifted his arms over his head, stretched, then got up and moved to sit in one of the folding chairs. He stuck his legs out in front of him, crossing them at the ankles. After grabbing another pair of beers from the cooler, Cole joined him.

"You better go easy on those," Randy said. "It's been a long time since you had anything stronger than Dad's coffee."

"I know what I'm doing," Cole snapped.

Randy held up his hands in surrender. "No need to bite my head off."

Nothing more was said for several uncomfortably long minutes. Finally Cole leaned back heavily in his chair and let out a sigh. "I'm sorry. It's just that I get so damned tired of being told where to go, what to do, how to do it, and how to feel about it when it's over."

"Not by me," Randy said pointedly.

"What did you mean about Dad not giving me Buddy's letter?"

"He thinks he needs to protect you."

"From Buddy?"

"From everybody he can't control and who doesn't think the way he does."

"That's crazy."

"Does he ever ask your opinion about the people he hires or tell you when he's going to fire one of them?"

"He's my manager. It's his job to handle those things."

"He's scared, Cole, and he's doing whatever he feels necessary to hang on. You've grown too big for him."

"Why would I dump Dad? I'm where I am today because of him."

"And he knows better than anyone else how much shit he put you through to get you there and probably figures it's on your mind every time you look at him. The place you are now in your career you could have your pick of managers and producers. Hell, there's not a one of them in the business who wouldn't fall all over himself for a chance to work with you."

"Dad's family."

"If you're talking about loyalty, it's a concept he doesn't understand. He expects you to act the way he would."

Cole leaned forward, resting his elbows on his knees. He watched the waves roll onto the beach and thought how he and Randy had been raised knowing places, not people. The last time he'd seen any of his relatives had been at his mother's funeral. He'd been seven, Randy four.

Cole finished his beer and motioned toward the cooler. "You got anything to eat in there?"

"As a matter of fact, I do," Randy told him. He set his beer down and made a drumroll with his index fingers on the top of the Styrofoam box. When he finished, he reached inside and brought out a pink cake box wrapped in a plastic bag. "Feast your eyes on this."

Cole stared at the displayed cake. It was covered in the kind of frosting roses he and Randy had fought over when they were kids. The top had been sprayed blue, and there was something written in a darker blue gel that he couldn't make out. "What does it say?"

Randy laughed. "Originally, Happy Birthday Susan. I got a special deal on it because they made a mess trying to change the Susan to Randy."

Cole's heart sank as everything fell into place. "Today's your birthday," he announced softly.

"Don't go getting sloppy on me. I didn't bring you out here for that."

"I'll make it up to you. I promise. I don't know how, but I'll find a way."

Randy set the cake down between them. "I was going to just let it go," he said, "but I knew how bad you'd feel when you figured it out so I decided, what the hell, why not throw my own party? Now dig in." He shoved his hand into the cake and brought up a huge chunk.

Cole only hesitated a second before he, too, stuck his hand into the cake. With a flourish, he held his trophy aloft and tipped his head. "Happy birthday, little brother." As an afterthought he added, "And to Susan, too."

Randy grinned and before Cole had a chance to react, slapped his hand against his brother's in an explosive high-five salute. Cake landed in their hair, on their clothes, and slithered down their arms. "Ain't life grand?" Randy said.

With a quick swipe of his tongue, Cole caught a piece of frosting that had landed in the corner of his mouth. The taste triggered a flood of memories, of a dozen other birthdays he and Randy had celebrated together where they'd shared a store-bought cake. "Thanks," he said simply.

Randy sent him a puzzled look. "What for?"

"Always being there when I needed you."

"I warned you not to go getting sloppy on me." Randy held his cake-encrusted hand threatening inches from Cole's face.

"Go ahead," Cole challenged. "But remember, the payback's a bitch."

With purposeful strokes, Randy wiped one side of his hand along Cole's cheek, the other side on his forehead. "Damn, I didn't mean to do that. It was an accident."

"I can see how torn up you are about it," Cole said. He reached for another handful of cake.

The fight was on.

# 3

Cole yanked the pillows off the bed and threw them on the floor. Next came the bedspread and then the sheet. There wasn't one logical reason for his wallet to be hidden in the folds of the bed, but he'd looked everywhere else.

Frank came into the bedroom. He stepped over a pair of jeans Cole had pulled out of the dresser and pointedly looked around at the mess. "You and Belinda have a fight?"

"I can't find my wallet."

"Did you look in the things we brought back from the hospital?"

"Shit." Of course it would be in there. "Where did you put the bag?"

"Downstairs. In the front closet." Frank followed Cole out of the room. "Why the big panic to find your wallet now?" he asked suspiciously. "You've been without it for almost five months."

Cole hesitated, then figured it was as good a time as any to tell Frank he was going to drive himself back to the house. "I need my driver's license," he said. "Randy told Belinda he would bring her car, so I volunteered to drive his truck."

Frank's reaction was swift and explosive. "There's no way in hell I'm going to let you drive that truck through Los Angeles traffic."

"*Let* me?" Cole said coolly.

"What's the matter with you? One trip down the side of a mountain wasn't enough? You know as well as I do that truck is an accident waiting to happen."

"You don't seem to mind when Randy drives it." He started down the stairs, frustrated that his bad leg kept him from moving any faster.

"Changing the subject isn't going to work. You're not driving Randy's truck and that's it."

When Cole reached the landing, he whipped around to face his father. "Where do you get off telling me what I can and can't do? I'm thirty-one years old, for Christ's sake. I'm perfectly capable of making my own decisions."

"Decisions like sneaking off in the middle of the night to get drunk on some beach? That showed a lot of maturity all right."

"Nothing happened."

"You were lucky."

Cole continued down the stairs. He'd built the bars to his prison with his-peace-at-any-price philosophy. It had taken years to put them up; they weren't going to disappear in a day. "I'm willing to assume that responsibility."

"And what about all the people whose lives depend on you?"

"It isn't their *lives* that depend on me, Frank, it's their livelihoods. Big difference." He found the closet and the bag. His wallet was inside. There was a deep scar on the brown leather. Cole preferred not to speculate how it had gotten there. He shoved the wallet in his pocket and grabbed a Dodger baseball cap Randy had left sitting on the shelf. "I'll meet you at the house in a couple of hours."

"I've got some material in the limo we need to go over before your press conference. If you drive yourself, there won't be time."

"I told you I'd be at the conference, but that I didn't want to talk to the press. Have Janet do it. That's what we pay her for, isn't it?" They'd hired Janet Reynolds away from the top public relations firm in southern California. She handled Frank and his frequent tirades as brilliantly as she handled a hostile press. In four years she'd become an indispensable member of the team, one of three people Frank trusted and the only one not related to him.

"She's going to handle all the official stuff, but you still have to be prepared for the casual questions that will come later."

"Don't worry, I'm not going to blow it for you, Frank." Finally, Frank had admitted that Cole was never going to be able to go back out on a stage without explaining the change in his appearance. Now the trick was to convince a room full of skeptical reporters that there wasn't more story than they were being told.

Cole was resigned to the effect the announcement would have: a round of public appearances to prove he was as good as he'd ever been. He had to let people see for themselves that he might look a little different, but underneath, he was the same Cole Webster.

Randy came strolling down the hall eating an ice-cream bar. Cole rolled his eyes. His brother had a built-in radar for moving in on Frank when he was on the verge of losing his temper.

"I thought you'd be long gone by now," he said to Cole.

Frank's lips tightened to a hard, thin line.

"Another minute and I will be." Cole settled the baseball cap on his head and grabbed Randy's sleeve. "Why don't you walk me out?"

"Glad to." Randy waited, looked at Frank, and took a crunching bite of the chocolate-coated ice cream. He chewed a second and asked, "Something wrong?"

"You know goddamned well what's—"

Cole let go of Randy's sleeve, grabbed his arm, and propelled him toward the front door. "Leave it alone," he said.

"I take it he's not too thrilled with the idea of riding home by himself?"

As soon as they were outside, Cole released his brother. "Why do you do that?"

"What?"

"Bait him."

"I don't know." Randy shrugged. "Probably because it's so easy."

"Well, do me a favor and leave me out of it from now on."

Randy grinned. "Bad morning?"

"I've had better." Cole turned and started down the walkway toward the truck.

Randy followed. "From what Belinda told me, it doesn't sound like it's going to get any better. She said Frank has decided to let the press in on the big secret after all."

Cole stopped dead in his tracks and faced Randy. "Don't you think you could have figured that one out for yourself?" he challenged. "All you had to do is look at me, for God's sake."

Randy held up his hands and backed away. "I get enough of that crap from Frank. I don't need it from you. I'm outta here."

Cole was driving past the gates when it occurred to him the list of people he owed apologies was growing in direct proportion to the number of people he'd talked to that day. Of them all, Belinda was first in line. She'd done the least to set him off and he'd come at her like some spaced-out pit bull.

The really sick part was that after he finished his tantrum, she'd been the one who apologized when she should have told him to take a hike. But that wasn't

Belinda's style. She had her own way of bargaining for peace at any price.

Cole leaned across to the glove box and pulled out a tape—the demo Randy had told him he received in the mail from a new songwriter—and slid it into the player. He propped his arm on the open window and scratched his chin. Even after all this time, the half-inch beard still itched occasionally.

A sudden rush of music filled the cab. Thoughts about the battles he'd already fought that day and those to come faded as the melody insinuated itself into Cole's consciousness. He found himself being drawn in, first by the persuasion of a beautifully played, lone guitar and then the words themselves. The song wasn't about lost love or drinking or thumbing your nose at the establishment, it was about the beauty of a woodland meadow as seen through the eyes of an urban child. The words were profound in their simplicity, the message urgent, but cleverly subtle. It was out of a sense of fairness that the listener became the champion of the meadow and the child's right to bring his own children there one day.

Cole rewound the tape and played it again. And then again. The fourth time he mouthed the words; the fifth, he sang along. He tried to remember what Randy had told him about the writer, but he hadn't paid enough attention for anything to stick.

The miles passed without notice. Traffic increased as the mountain road widened and then fed into a freeway. In his head he heard the music as he might record it himself—the strain of a guitar, the hint of a keyboard, and the rhythm of the bass as they came together for what he'd already started to think of as his song. Knowing the piece was likely being offered around, it was everything he could do to keep from pulling over to find a telephone to call Randy, the one person in Los Angeles without a phone in his vehicle. Reason prevailed when he looked around and realized how close to home he was.

Minutes later he exited the freeway and headed up the narrow canyon that led to his house. Although Frank insisted they formed their base of operations in California because of the California Cowboy thing, Cole and Randy believed it was more his way of getting back at the people on Nashville's Music Row for their years of rejection.

Of the dozens of houses Cole was shown, he'd finally settled on the one that had some land around it, not even bothering to go inside the house itself until after the deal was set. There were the usual pool and tennis court and a spectacular view of the Los Angeles basin at night. They planted heavy and kept everything watered and green, and there wasn't a day that passed one of them didn't say something about how far they'd come and wasn't it amazing. What they always left unsaid was that no matter how beautiful or extravagant the surroundings, California wasn't home, and it never would be.

He was on the long side of a mile from the house when the engine began to sputter and then choke and then die. "Son of a bitch." He slammed his hand against the steering wheel. "You couldn't wait another mile?"

He shoved the gearshift into neutral, steered onto the shoulder, opened the door, and got out, casting a hopeful glance down the road and then at his watch. Since he'd made better time than he figured, it wasn't likely there would be anyone looking for him for a couple of hours. A red BMW came toward him. He waved. The car sped by as through he were invisible. Next came a Mercedes and then another BMW. Both drivers reacted the same as the first.

To kill time, Cole went to the front of the truck and lifted the hood. What he knew about cars and how they functioned was on a level with his knowledge about what went into steak Diane that made it taste so good.

The instant he saw the engine it hit him what was wrong and it had nothing to do with broken or missing parts. With sickening clarity, Cole heard Randy telling him that he would need gas to make it home. He'd even shoved money in his pocket, knowing Cole never carried any of his own.

Cole ran his hand down the front of his right leg trying to gauge how far it would carry him. By the time he reached the brick-pillared iron gate that marked the entrance to his house, he found out. He'd limped more than walked the last hundred yards. He bit back a groan and leaned his shoulder into the metal post that held the intercom, which was connected to the grounds-keeper's office.

A male voice answered the bell. "Can I help you?"

"It's Cole, Marty. Would you send someone to pick me up?"

"Marty doesn't work here anymore. I took his place. . . . Name's Roger."

Frank had been at it again. It seemed the staff lasted only as long as it took Cole to learn their names. "Glad to meet you, Roger. Now would you send someone to the gate? I still need a ride."

"Are you with one of the newspapers?"

"I'm Cole Webster," he repeated slowly, with strained patience. "I live here."

"That's not possible. Mr. Webster came home—" As if realizing he was about to reveal more than he should, he added a quick "Never mind."

Cole had his mouth open to protest he couldn't possibly be both inside and outside the gate when it all began to make a perverted kind of sense. Somehow, Randy must have gotten there first. For anyone who'd been hired since the accident, Randy was Cole. "Call up to the house and let me talk to him."

"That's impossible."

"Why is it impossible?"

"Because Mr. Webster is tied up at the moment. He doesn't have time to—"

*Tied up at the moment?* Where did Frank get this guy? "Then let me talk to Frank."

"He's busy too," Roger said. "You're one of those people from the tabloids, aren't you? Mr. Webster said to tell you—"

Cole cut him off with an abrupt "Is Belinda at the house?"

There was a long pause, followed by a reluctant "Yes."

"Then maybe you could get *her* for me?"

"I'm sorry, but—"

"Goddammit," Cole shouted, "you either get her on the fuckin' phone or—" He stopped and took a breath. The guy was only following Frank's instructions. "I assume you like your job and that you want to keep it?"

"Of course I do."

"Good. And you will—*if* you get someone down here to pick me up within the next five minutes. Think about it, Roger. Can you afford to take the chance?"

There was another long pause. "I'll see what I can do."

Cole released the button and lowered himself to the ground. He massaged his leg and thought that his being stuck there was the result of yet another argument between Frank and Randy, this one over Randy losing the card key that opened the gate. After that, Randy refused to carry a replacement and could only gain entry by calling in.

Under other circumstances Cole would probably think it funny to be locked out of his own house. At the very least, he'd be able to see the humor in fighting to gain access to a place that, less than an hour ago, he'd convinced himself he didn't want to be.

What was funny—peculiar, not the laughing kind—was to discover how easily he'd adapted to a life-style that had been as alien to him as a banjo picker to a rock band. He'd been raised on grits and greens and black-eyed peas. Now, he not only knew the difference between a truffle and a trifle, he took secret pleasure in the knowledge. Somehow, somewhere, he'd bought into the belief that such things mattered.

Until he'd hooked up with Belinda, when he wasn't on the road touring or in the studio recording, he was dating some of the hottest stars in Hollywood, stars whose lives revolved around seeing and being seen. He didn't miss a trendy restaurant or an "in" nightclub. But it got old quick. He found he didn't enjoy dancing with someone who was more interested in looking around to see who was looking at her than she was in keeping up her end of the conversation.

Frank didn't approve of Cole's walk on the wild side, but he kept the complaints to a minimum. Mainly because of the magazines. Janet couldn't fill all the requests for interviews. And it didn't seem to matter if they turned one down; an article would appear anyway. If there wasn't an article, there would be pictures with lengthy captions. For one four-month period, there was something about him every week in every tabloid in the supermarket. It got so bad that at one point, Cole simply stopped reading everything but his favorite science fiction and mystery writers, and then even they let him down when he found his name mentioned as part of an ancient pop culture in *Return To A Silent Planet* and one of his concerts was used as a background for a murder in *The G String Affair*.

A converted golf cart crested the hill that hid the house from the front gate. Cole worked his way back up to a standing position. It was hard to believe that only months ago he'd been running five miles a day and working out four times a week with a personal trainer. He cringed to think how much effort it was going to take to get him back into that kind of shape.

The driver stopped so close to the gate it couldn't be opened without moving the cart again; it wasn't a good sign. A tall, beefy man struggled to extract himself from behind the steering wheel. "Still here, huh?"

"Where else would I be?" Cole answered.

"Figured maybe you would've taken off by now."

"Now why would I want to do that?"

"I thought that maybe since I called your bluff by coming down here that you wouldn't have the guts to stick around."

What kind of game was this guy playing? Couldn't he see whom he was talking to? From a distance someone might mistake Randy for Cole, but not up close.

And then it hit him what was really going on. Randy was pulling another one of his stunts. "Would you just open the friggin' gate?" Cole said wearily.

"I'm sorry, mister. I can't do it."

"I don't know why Randy put you up to this, but the joke's getting old, fast."

"Mr. Webster didn't have anything to do with me coming down here. He warned me how clever you guys from the tabloids can be, and I wanted you to know you weren't going to get away with anything as long as I was on duty."

"You guys from the tabloids?" Cole repeated, incredulous. "Open your eyes, man. I'm Cole Webster. *This is my house.*"

"It isn't going to do you any good to yell at me." He turned and headed back to the cart. "I know you're just doing your job, but I've got a job to do, too. You can tell your boss you ran into somebody a little smarter and a whole lot more stubborn than you expected."

Cole was too stunned to say more than "You don't recognize me at all? Not even a little bit?"

"You look a little like Cole Webster around the eyes, I suppose, but it's not enough to get you where you want to go." He climbed in the cart and turned the key. "Maybe if you'd shaved the beard and let your hair grow some, you could have pulled it off, but nobody's ever going to believe Cole Webster would be out running around looking the way you do."

Cole knew it was useless to argue. Still he couldn't keep from adding, "You're going to be in a shit load of trouble when Frank finds out about this."

Roger smiled and turned to look over his shoulder

before he backed away from the gate. "Trouble's better than the unemployment line," he said, and drove away.

Cole shook his head. Despite the annoyance at being kept out of his own home, he couldn't help feeling a little sorry for the guy. Pressing his hands to the small of his back, he stretched and stared down the road he'd just come up. If it weren't so far back to the truck, he might feel even sorrier.

He could sit outside the gate until someone he knew came along to let him in, but what if that someone was a reporter? Wouldn't that make a charming headline. COLE WEBSTER LOCKED OUT OF HIS OWN HOME—REJECTED BY FAMILY AFTER DISFIGURING ACCIDENT.

The trip down the hill eased the ache in his thigh but made the front of his shin feel as though it were on fire. He was never going to be able to go back on tour like this. People came to see the high energy he put out onstage as much as they came to hear the songs. His show wasn't just a roll call of his hits; it was a "happening."

A loud clanking noise caught his attention. He looked up and realized he was almost back to the truck, just one more corner. He entered the curve and saw flashing yellow lights sweep the trees that lined the roadside. A sick feeling hit his gut when he realized what was going on. He quickened his pace, mouthing a quick prayer that he was mistaken.

But he wasn't.

Dammit—what more could go wrong that day?

# 4

"*One phone call*, that's all I'm asking," Cole said.

The tow-truck operator made an adjustment to one of the chains that held Randy's pickup in place on the flatbed truck. "I keep telling you, man, I can't do it. Boss says I let anyone use the equipment and it's my job."

Cole changed tactics. "I'll pay you double whatever you get for hauling the truck to the shop if you take it up the hill to my house. It's only a mile from here—a lot closer than wherever it is you're going in the city."

The man stopped what he was doing and gave Cole the once-over. "You saying you live in this neighborhood?"

"In the house on top of the hill."

"Right. The way you're dressed I'm gonna believe that."

"What's wrong with the way I'm dressed?" He was wearing what he always wore, T-shirt and jeans and tennis shoes.

"If you really were from around here, your shirt would have one of them horses on it and your jeans would have creases down the legs. I've been working this area for ten years. I know the people who live around here."

"Look at me," Cole insisted. "Don't I look familiar?"

The man gave him a blank stare. "I suppose you're going to tell me you're some big, hotshot movie star."

"Not movie star . . . singer. I'm Cole Webster." Cole dug his wallet out of his back pocket and flipped it open to his driver's license, something he should have thought to do with Roger. He pointed to the picture. "See, that's me."

Taking the wallet, the man studied the license and then Cole. He shook his head and handed the wallet back. "I don't know where you got this thing, but I'd get rid of it if I were you."

"I had an accident. It changed the way I look."

"Uh-huh." He picked up the wrench he'd been using and tossed it into the cab. "I got a piece of advice for you, fella. People who live in neighborhoods like this don't like your type wandering around their streets any more than they like abandoned trucks cluttering up the scenery. I'd hightail it out of here if I were you."

"The truck wasn't abandoned; I ran out of gas. If you'll just take me where I want to go, I can prove I really am Cole Webster." An idea hit, one that should have been obvious. "Check the registration. The truck belongs to my brother, but you'll see that I'm telling the truth about the address."

"I looked. There wasn't any registration."

"Are you sure? Did you go through the glove box? Under the seat?"

"There wasn't anything in the glove box, and the only thing under the seat was an empty bag of corn chips."

Cole sensed it would be a waste of time to ask if he could look himself. "What difference does it make where you take the pickup as long as you get paid?"

"The difference is the cops called this one in. You're gonna have to go through them to get your truck back." He climbed inside the cab, slammed the door, and looked out the open window at Cole. "Hop in. I'll give you a ride down the hill."

Cole hesitated.

"Suit yourself." He leaned forward and started the engine.

"Hold up," Cole said. There was no telling how long it would be before Frank sent someone to look for him. He was certain to have a better chance of getting to a phone in town than he would if he stayed where he was. He walked around the truck and got in. "Thanks, man. I appreciate the lift."

"No problem."

Twenty minutes later, the tow-truck driver dropped Cole off at the base of the freeway on ramp. "It's none of my business," he told Cole, "but like I said before, I'd get rid of that driver's license if I were you. Someone catches you with it and it's going to get you in a whole lot of trouble."

Cole nodded. "I appreciate the advice."

The driver nodded, slipped the truck in gear, and drove off. Cole stepped away from the cloud of diesel exhaust and headed across the street. He was in a section of town he didn't recognize. The streets were lined with warehouses and abandoned buildings. He spotted a convenience store a couple of blocks away and limped off in that direction.

There were four customers inside, two women and a young boy wandering the aisles, and a man at the counter buying a loaf of bread. The clerk was a girl who looked to be in her early twenties. Cole's immediate and automatic reaction was to lower his head and reach for the bill on his cap. When he realized what he'd done, he decided to run a test. He removed the cap and shoved it in his back pocket. After taking the time to run his hands through his hair, he openly stared at the two women coming toward him. Both met his gaze. The first gave him a quick, meaningless smile, the second a dismissive look, as if he were simply another man on the make.

There hadn't been a flicker of recognition, not even a glimmer of possible familiarity. He had to resist the urge to go after the women and question them the way he had the tow-truck driver. He glanced at himself in the convex mirror at the end of the aisle. Was it that he'd changed so much, or that he had somehow managed to run into half a dozen people in the same day who had missed out on what the press had labeled Webstermania. Was it ego, or could it have been his imagination, that had led him to believe he would be recognized wherever he went?

He moved closer to the mirror. Could a couple of scars, a haircut, and a beard make so much difference?

"Hey, mister, you need some help finding something?" the girl at the counter asked suspiciously.

"Uh . . . yeah, I'm looking for a phone," Cole said.

"It's back there by the cooler."

"Thanks."

"You need change?"

Cole shoved his hand in his pocket and brought out the money Randy had given him earlier. "Looks like I do," he told the girl. He gave her a twenty.

With a supply of quarters, nickels, and dimes, he found the phone and called home. Randy answered after the third ring.

"Where are you?" he said, lowering his voice to a whisper. "Dad is—"

"Can you get out of there without him seeing you?"

There was a pause. "I guess so. Why?"

"I need you to come and get me."

A soft groan preceded "What's wrong with the truck?"

"It's a long story. I'll tell you when you get here."

"Dammit, Cole, you didn't get in a wreck, did you?"

"I ran out of gas," he reluctantly admitted.

"I told you that was going to happen."

"Could we discuss it later?"

"You want me to leave without saying *anything* to Dad?"

"I'll take care of it when I get there."

"You do remember there's a couple dozen reporters

due to show up here in—" there was another pause, "another ten minutes or so."

"Dad and Janet can handle them until I get there."

"Where are you?"

Cole queried the clerk, passed her directions on to Randy, then said, "Put Janet on the phone and then get out of there as fast as you can."

Seconds later a female voice came on the line. "This is Janet Reynolds."

"Janet, it's Cole."

She too dropped her voice to a whisper, only hers had a sharper edge than Randy's. "You were supposed to be here an hour ago."

"I'll explain later. All you need to know now is that I got tied up and I might not make the press conference." He'd never missed anything like this before and was counting on Janet knowing he wouldn't skip out on her without a reason.

"Have you talked to Frank about this?"

"Not yet. I thought I'd let you take care of him for me."

"Thanks a lot. Did you have an alligator locked up somewhere you wanted me to wrestle for you, too?" She sighed in resignation. "It would help if I could tell him something more than the obvious. He already knows you aren't here."

"Tell him I'm fine. None of the rest of it matters."

"He's going to be worried."

"So what else is new?" The question sounded insensitive even to him. "I'll be there as soon as I can."

"Could you be a bit more specific? Are we talking an hour?" When he didn't answer, she prompted, "Two?" Still he didn't say anything. "The least you could do is give me a ballpark figure."

The harder she pushed, the more he resisted. "I don't want to be tied to a specific time."

"All right. I'll do what I can . . . with Frank and the reporters."

"I knew I could count on you."

"Just don't make this a habit. Hell hath no fury like a reporter who thinks he's being manipulated."

"I'm sure it's slipped your mind, but you once told me that manipulation was the bedrock of show business. It changed my entire outlook."

"You're too young to be so cynical."

There was a long pause; finally Cole asked, "Is something wrong?"

"It's just that I was looking forward to seeing you again. It's been a long time."

"Thanks."

"I should have told you that before." As if she understood how uncomfortable she'd made him, she added breezily, "I'm off. Facing a roomful of people focused on your jugular is always so invigorating."

Cole hung up and wandered over to the magazine rack where he picked up a copy of *Music Weekly* magazine. Reba McEntire was the featured artist with Vince Gill on the upper left corner and a picture of the pre-accident Cole Webster on the right. Cole flipped to the table of contents, curious to see if rumors about his long absence had begun to surface. He was familiar enough with the magazine to know it was marketed as providing up-to-the-minute news, which meant the lead time on most articles was less than two weeks. Only television and the daily newspapers had more current information.

The article on him was positioned as the second lead and contained photographs from his last concert tour. He skimmed the first couple of paragraphs, looking for something that alluded to his disappearance. There was information about the change in the release date for the new album and about the European tour being put together, standard stuff.

Cole wasn't sure who was responsible, Frank or Janet or both, but they'd done an amazing job of keeping things quiet. It was going to be interesting to see the press's reaction when they discovered how completely they'd bought into the coverup of his disappearance. There were a couple of reporters he could think of who were going to be particularly upset at being duped.

He put the magazine back and went outside. A half hour later Randy pulled up in Cole's Lotus. "How did you wind up in this place?" he asked as Cole got in.

"You got any money?" Cole asked, delaying the telling of his improbable tale.

"Some."

"Enough for us to get something to eat?"

"There's a ton of food up at the house. You'd think the entire southern California press corps was coming."

"I don't want to go back there now," Cole said. "I've been thinking about something that I want to talk to you about."

"And it's so urgent it can't hold for a couple of hours? I hate to keep hammering on this, but there are a lot of people waiting for you up at the house."

"Let them wait."

Randy turned to look at Cole, a spark of mischief in his eyes. "Are you sure you want to do this? Dad's going to kill us when he finds out."

"Dad's at his finest when he has a crisis to manage."

"I think I like this new, improved Cole Webster," Randy said. He depressed the clutch, shoved the car in second gear, and left several dollars' worth of rubber on the asphalt.

"Would I do that to your truck?" Cole grumbled.

Randy laughed. "You're welcome to try."

Later, at the restaurant, Cole put his hand over his cup to let the waitress know he'd had enough coffee. Randy took another refill.

"I don't understand how you think wandering around Los Angeles for a couple of days is going to do anything for you." He dumped a packet of sugar substitute into the black liquid. "Tell me again what it is you think you're looking for."

Cole was afraid that if he tried to explain something he didn't understand himself, it would trivialize what he was feeling and he would lose the drive to see it through. "It isn't something I can put into words."

Randy was quiet for a long time. "So it's a Zen kind of thing you're talking about?"

Cole pressed forward, leaning his elbows on the table. "Have you ever thought about what you would do if you woke up one day and everything you'd come to take for granted was gone?"

"You mean career wise, I assume?"

"One day I was a nowhere country singer doing week-end gigs at bars where they talked so loud no one could hear the music, and the next I was some prophet who was leading a dying industry to the promised land. No one seemed to notice or to care that I was the same person both days."

Randy slid his cup onto the table and shook his head. "If you don't get past this thing, you're never going to be able to walk out on a stage and convince the people who came to see you that their money was well spent."

Cole almost smiled in relief. In his own ass-backward way, Randy had put words to Cole's fears. "So you understand why I've got to get away?"

"I've got the why, it's the how that's still confusing me. How is taking off by yourself going to give you the answers you want?"

The idea had come to Cole on the way to the restaurant and was something he didn't fully understand himself. "Maybe it won't."

"Then why not go at it another way?" The waitress came by and filled Randy's cup again. He caught her eye and smiled his thanks. "Not to put too fine a point to it, but it's damn dangerous for you to be wandering around Los Angeles by yourself."

"Millions of people do it every day."

"But not Cole Webster."

"That's just it. No one recognizes me anymore. I've been given a once-in-a-lifetime opportunity to—"

"You haven't changed as much as you think."

"Look around," Cole insisted. "Do you see anyone staring? Has anyone made a point of coming by? Has anyone even shown they're the least bit interested in us?"

"So they're busy talking." Randy's gaze swept the restaurant. "That doesn't prove anything."

"When was the last time I went anywhere without being recognized?"

Randy thought a minute. "Damned if I can remember," he admitted.

"It's as though I've been given this window of opportunity. Once the press finds out about the accident and pictures of how I look now start appearing, I'll be right back where I started. All I want is a couple of days."

"What are you going to do if the same thing happens to you with this window that happened to you the last time you went through one?"

"What are you talking about?"

"You fell on your ass, big brother."

Cole smiled. "I'm willing to take the chance."

"What about Belinda?"

Somehow she'd slipped his mind. "Tell her I said she should visit her mother for a couple of days."

Randy shot Cole an angry look. "Don't you think you should tell her yourself?"

"It wouldn't do any good. She isn't going to understand."

"What right do you have to expect her to understand something you don't?" he snapped.

"When did you become Belinda's champion?"

"When you stopped. Dammit, that woman's crazy about you, Cole."

"And I'm crazy about her." Somehow the words didn't

ring true. "I just don't always show it." Cole picked up his glass and moved it in quarter-inch increments, making a series of concentric water rings on the table. From the first day Cole brought Belinda home, Randy had looked at her around a blind spot. He was convinced she was the perfect woman for Cole, the one who would give him the nieces and nephews he was aching to spoil. Cole didn't have the heart to tell him that Belinda was so terrified what a baby would do to her body, she'd had a tubal ligation two years before she'd even met him. Actually, it was one of the things Cole liked best about her. He'd decided years ago that fatherhood wasn't in his future. Unlike Randy, Cole was a strong believer in heredity. It worried him what he might pass on to a child. Not one Webster man any of them could remember had known what it was to be a real father. Cole had no illusions he could do any better.

"Then you'll tell her about this yourself?" Randy prodded.

Cole knew when to give in. "I'll call as soon as she gets to her mother's."

"That's not going to work." Randy heaved himself back into the corner of the booth. "I'm never going to get her out of the house without saying something about what's going on."

"And if I call her at home, you're not going to get her out of there in time to miss Frank's explosion."

Several seconds passed before Randy said anything. Finally, he ran his hand through his hair, frowned at Cole, and asked, "Does Dad have any Greek blood in him?"

"What has that got to do with anything?"

"I was trying to remember, weren't they the ones who killed the messengers when they brought bad news?"

Cole dipped his hand in the glass and flicked the water at Randy. "Just stay close to the front door and leave the truck running. You'll be fine."

"What truck?"

A sheepish grin stole over Cole's face. "Oh, yeah, I forgot." He slid across the bench, started to get up, and sat back down again. "Something else."

"Now what?"

"I'm going to need some money."

Randy dug for his wallet. He handed Cole everything he had. "You're not going to get far on that."

Cole fanned the bills and did a quick count. There was less than two hundred dollars. He took out a twenty and handed it back to Randy. "You need this for the cab."

Randy waved him off. "I can take care of it when I get to the house."

Cole stared at the money, trying to figure how long it would last. It had been so long since he'd paid for anything himself, he had no idea how much a motel, food, and a toothbrush would cost. He shot a questioning look at Randy.

"Something wrong?" Randy asked.

"I don't know where my money is."

Randy frowned. "I thought you said you didn't have any."

"The money I have in the bank." Cole reached up and rubbed the back of his neck. He could feel a headache threatening. "I don't know which bank it's in."

"How do you pay your bills?"

"The accountant pays them."

"Where do you get your spending money?"

"I never go anywhere I need it."

"What about a Mastercard or Visa?"

Cole shook his head. "Don't have one."

"How does Belinda get her money?"

"She tells the accountant what she needs and he takes care of it."

Randy looked incredulous. "You like living that way?"

"What's the point of carrying money when I never need it?"

"Because it's what people do." He slid across the seat

until he was sitting directly opposite Cole. "You're living like somebody's damn pet poodle."

"It's not that bad," Cole said without conviction. A thought struck. "Where do you get your money?"

"Do you mean originally, or—"

"Are you paid by check or cash?"

"Check."

"Which bank?"

A look of understanding flashed through Randy's eyes. "Harbor International."

Cole sent Randy a triumphant smile, laid two five-dollar bills on the table for the tip, and stood up. "I think I just solved my money problems."

Randy picked up one of the fives and handed it to Cole. "Just in case," he said.

Cole paid the bill and walked outside with Randy while he waited for his cab. "I almost forgot, there's one more thing I want you to do for me."

"Now what?"

"The song on the demo?"

"Yeah?"

"I want it. I like it better than I've liked anything in a long time."

"It's not your standard stuff." Randy shoved his hands in his pockets and rocked back on his heels. "You're going to have a hard time getting it past Frank."

"You do your part and I'll do mine."

A yellow cab pulled into the parking lot. Randy held up his hand to the driver and stepped off the sidewalk. He turned to Cole. "Take care of yourself, big brother."

Less than three hours later, Randy was in yet another vehicle, on yet another road, heading in yet another direction.

"Are you sure he's all right?" Belinda asked for the third time as they hit the Pacific Coast Highway.

"He just needs to get away by himself for a while to do some thinking," Randy said. She'd been so upset when he told her Cole wasn't coming home right away that he decided to drive her to her mother's house in Long Beach himself. They'd no sooner gone through the gate when he realized he couldn't pass the whole trip pretending he didn't know what was going on with Cole. Not only wasn't it fair to Belinda, but once she discovered he'd known everything all along, she would never trust him again. He'd chosen the long route to give her plenty of time to question him.

Belinda turned to stare out the side window of her Corvette. "There has to be something more," she insisted. "He's had plenty of time alone. He could have done all the thinking he wanted."

"You know Cole. He doesn't always do things the logical way."

She turned and pinned him with a stare. "You're hiding something."

"I wouldn't do that to you," he said simply, honestly. He'd expected her to be worried, but this went deeper. "Cole is like a kid with a new toy. It's just that this toy happens to be his face. He can't wait to try it out."

"But why did he have to go alone? I would have gone with him."

A flippant, easy answer played itself out and remained unspoken. She deserved more. "This has nothing to do with you. You know how moody Cole can get sometimes." She dropped her chin and her hair fell forward, hiding her face. It was everything he could do to keep from reaching over to brush the silken wave back over her shoulder. Far too easily, he could imagine how her hair would feel as it slipped through his fingers.

"I don't know what I'd do if something happened to him."

"It's just a couple of days. All you have to do is pretend he's still at Casa Blanca and he'll be back before you've had a chance to miss him."

"Is it me?"

The traffic started to pick up, forcing Randy to give more

attention to his driving. He looked for a place to pull over. Settling on a tree-lined residential street, he stopped in front of a pink stucco house and turned off the engine. "Would you please explain what you meant by a question like that?"

She didn't look at him. "Is he tired of me?" she asked softly. "Is this just some way to get rid of me?"

The question took him by surprise and made him wonder if there was trouble between Belinda and Cole. "All I know is what he told me," Randy said. "He was afraid if you didn't leave, Frank would take his frustration out on you." Randy took her hand in his and gave it a reassuring squeeze.

She peeked at him through a cascade of hair. "I don't know what I'd do without him, Randy. He's my world."

Randy swallowed hard. How could Cole be so wrapped up in what was wrong with his life that he couldn't see what was right? "He knows how lucky he is to have you, Belinda." He gave her an encouraging smile. "And if he ever forgets, I'll remind him."

Her fingers tightened around his hand. "I'm so lucky to have you for a friend."

At that moment, he would have done anything for her. "Once Cole gets past this thing and is back to his old routine, it'll be like none of it ever happened."

"Do you think I should offer to meet him somewhere?"

Randy became acutely conscious of the feel of her hand in his. The contact had taken on an intimacy he'd never intended. He didn't know how to free himself without it seeming he, too, was anxious to get away from her. Finally, in an exaggerated and comically grandiose gesture meant to put them back on a casual level, he brought her hand up and kissed each knuckle. He was caught unawares at how unbelievably soft her skin felt and how wonderful she smelled. "It's up to you," he said and cleared his throat. "But I got the impression he wanted to do this alone."

"Are you telling me that because you're afraid I'll get my feelings hurt if he doesn't want me to come?"

"He's looking for something, Belinda, only he doesn't know what it is yet. He's not going to be much good to himself or anyone else until he figures it out."

"You know what it is, don't you?"

"What makes you say that?"

"Everyone thinks you're the easygoing one, but I've watched you when you thought no one was looking. You don't miss a thing. I'll bet you know Cole better than he knows himself."

"You'd lose. Cole is always surprising me." He wasn't sure how he felt about being watched, even by someone he liked. There was only one thing Randy had of value that had been denied his brother, and that was privacy.

"I should probably get to my mother's before too much longer," Belinda said. "I think I should be alone when Cole calls, don't you?" She smiled coyly.

Unbidden, an image of Cole and Belinda making love came to him. What he saw was stimulating and incredibly erotic, but it was also sadly devoid of any real passion. He was disturbed that he had invaded his brother's bedroom, however unintentionally.

Without saying anything more to Belinda, Randy started the car. Instead of heading back toward the Pacific Coast Highway, he turned inland to pick up 405.

When Belinda realized what he was doing, she said, "I appreciate the effort, but another half hour isn't going to make much difference."

"It wasn't that. I just remembered all the stop signs between here and Long Beach." She looked so disappointed he wished he'd made up something less pragmatic. It was easy to forget how insecure she could be and how desperate for reassurance. With all that was going on with Cole, it was reasonable she would be even more unsure of herself than usual. From now on he would have to be more careful to consider her feelings.

# 5

*Cole sat on a bench* opposite the Pirates of the Caribbean ride in Disneyland, fighting a dark oppressive mood, oblivious to the people passing in front of him. The day had started out better than he'd anticipated. Belinda had been far more accommodating about being moved to her mother's house than he'd had any right to expect. As usual, she'd been understanding and sympathetic and in tune to his needs even when he didn't understand them himself. She was perfect, as always. And, as always, he'd come away feeling he owed her something, not knowing what it was, just that he was in her debt.

He'd been to the bank earlier that day and learned that he did indeed have several accounts with Harbor International, or more accurately, Cole Webster Enterprises had them. Even after showing his driver's license, no one would tell him the exact figures, only that all of the accounts were solvent and reasonably funded and that he couldn't access any of them. For once it didn't matter whether anyone recognized him or not; his name was everywhere it should be except on the signature cards.

Until a few years ago, they'd never been far enough ahead to bother with a checking account. Then, when they'd finally gotten beyond the hand-to-mouth stage, Cole had been complaisant about his father's willingness to continue controlling the money. Why not? For everything Frank wasn't, he was scrupulously honest.

Cole rubbed his wrist where his Rolex watch had been. Even though he'd never liked the thing, it stuck in his throat that he could get no more than twenty-five hundred for something his record company had paid twenty-five thousand for less than a year ago.

Cole stretched and got up to leave, acknowledging that coming there had been a mistake. Despite his need to be by himself, he wasn't the solitary man he liked everyone to think he was. There were some places that were meant to be appreciated alone, and others that merely pointed out how alone you were.

He pulled onto the freeway and was headed back to the motel when it hit him that it wasn't more time to think that he needed, it was less. When he was working he didn't care who kept the money or signed the checks. He didn't question the people around him and he didn't question himself.

But first things first. He had a long-standing itch that only a night in LA's raunchiest honky-tonks would scratch—and he wasn't going alone.

Cole automatically reached for his flip phone and remembered he'd left it at the motel. He took the next exit and stopped at a grocery store. The public phone was located next to one of those kiddie pony rides. There was a boy with a terrified expression riding up and down in time to ice-cream-truck music. Cole waited for the horse and music to stop before he dialed.

Frank answered. "Hello."

Cole almost hung up.

"Who is this?" And then, "Cole? Is that you?"

"Yeah, it's me," he finally admitted.

"Where the hell are you?"

"I'm fine, thanks for asking."

"Do you have any idea the trouble you've caused everyone with your disappearing act?"

Cole leaned his shoulder into the building. "No, but I'll bet you'd be willing to tell me if I asked."

"If it hadn't been for some quick thinking by me and Janet, those reporters would have crucified you."

"I didn't ask, Frank."

"You ungrateful—" Frank caught himself. "I should have told them the truth and let you dig yourself out of the hole."

Cole would not lose his temper. With Frank it was the same as losing the argument. "I realize it's probably insensitive of me to point this out, but isn't handling the press part of your job?"

There was a long, black silence. "I'm your father. How dare you talk to me as if I were one of the hired help?"

The timing was rotten, but Cole couldn't let the moment pass without comment. "When I get back there are some things that we need to get straightened out between us."

"What's that supposed to mean?"

"I really don't want to get into it now."

"Fuck that. If you think I'm going to sit still while you criticize the work I do for you, you've got another think coming. Don't you ever forget that I was the one who made you. Everything you are and everything you have you owe to me."

"Take it. It's yours. I don't want any of it anymore." A stabbing pain shot from temple to temple across the back of Cole's eyes. He grimaced and pressed the palm of his hand to his forehead realizing as he did that this was the first full-blown headache he'd had since leaving Casa Blanca.

"What's the matter with you? Are you on something?"

Cole sighed. "I assume you mean besides the drugs the doctors have been feeding me?"

"I'm not the idiot you obviously think I am. I know you

stopped taking that stuff a long time ago." There was another long silence. "When are you coming home?" Frank's voice had turned suspiciously calm.

"In a couple of days," Cole said, surprised that he'd hedged the truth.

"Why did you call now?"

"I want to talk to Randy."

"He isn't here," Frank answered a little too quickly. "I think he's outside. Give me your number and—"

"I'll call him back later."

"When?"

"What time is it now?"

"Where's your watch?"

The man didn't miss a thing. "I discovered the only way I could get my money out of the bank was to rob it. I let a pawnbroker rob me instead."

"You should have told me you needed money."

"Why should I have to ask for something that's mine to begin with?"

"Is that what this is all about? You want more spending money?"

Anger and a deep frustration swept through Cole. "Tell Randy I'll get back to him."

"Wait a second, he just came in."

"What's up?" Randy queried, his tone at odds with the innocent question.

"I was thinking we could hit a couple of bars tonight, if you don't have something else going."

"That's probably not a very good idea."

"Oh?" Cole said, puzzled. "Why not?"

"It's kind of hard to say."

"Something's wrong. Should I try to guess?"

"You couldn't, not in a million years."

"What do you want me to do?"

Randy was silent for several seconds. "I'm not going to do this," he said, his voice muffled as though he'd covered the receiver to talk to someone else.

Cole tensed. "Randy? What's going on?"

"Dad seems to think you've gone off the deep end. He's talked to the doctors and they want him to admit you to some private hospital out in the valley where you can be observed for a couple of days."

"He wants to have me committed?" Cole could hear his father in the background. The words were garbled, but the tone was clear. Plainly, Frank was furious with Randy.

"Cole—I'll talk to you later."

Frank's voice broke in. "Get out of my sight. Get the hell out of my house. I don't want you—" The rest was indistinguishable. "I'm sorry you had to listen to that garbage, Cole," Frank said. "I never meant for—"

"Are you telling me Randy had it wrong, that you haven't been talking to the doctors about me?"

"It isn't the way he made it sound."

"Then why don't you tell me the way it really is."

"I've been worried about you. You have to admit you haven't been yourself lately."

"If I thought you had any idea who I really am, I might believe you knew what you were talking about." He paused and then said, "I'm going to hang up now."

"Wait, you haven't said when you're coming back."

"I don't know."

"When are you going to call again?"

"I don't know." He had the receiver from his ear before he remembered there was something else he wanted to say. "Oh, by the way, Dad, that house you just tried to throw Randy out of? It's mine. If there's any throwing out to do, I'll be the one to do it." He didn't wait for a reply.

Cole got into his car and sat with his hands locked on the steering wheel. A new, strangely compelling restlessness came over him. It was as if Frank's behavior had freed him somehow, letting him know that burying himself in work was not the answer.

And then it came to him.

His decision made, he bristled with impatience at the

traffic on the freeway. When he hit the desert it was everything he could do to keep from opening the Lotus up. Reasoning helped him keep it at eighty, a speed he figured might get him a ticket but not a night in jail.

The beauty of false dawn coming to the mountains Cole crossed in northern New Mexico barely registered as his mind remained consumed with his driving and the passing road signs that told him how far he still had to go to reach Taos. The mountains gave way to a high plain, deceptively flat and uneventful until he came to an enormous chasm created by the Rio Grande.

He was close now. A peculiar nervousness hit him. He had a hollow feeling in the pit of his stomach, much like the one he'd had sitting in the audience at the Country Music Artist's Awards waiting to see if he would be named entertainer of the year for the fourth year in a row.

The first time he was nominated had been a breeze, his excitement centered around finally getting to meet the people he'd idolized all his life. Not even in his most private dreams had he imagined he would actually win.

The second year was even easier. There was no way he was going to win two years running, so why bother getting excited? He went to have a good time and with any luck, to pick up an award or two for his fourth album. He'd made a real fool of himself when his name was announced, and he just sat there thinking that for some reason, they were going over the list of nominees again.

The third year drove him crazy. He kept telling everyone he wouldn't win and everyone agreed, but to a person, they couldn't resist adding, "But then, you never know."

He'd won. And then the damnedest thing happened. On the way to the podium, his IQ dropped fifty points. He was convinced that no one in the history of award ceremonies had ever made a dumber acceptance speech.

This past year he'd been nominated again and had again told everyone he wouldn't win. He finally got one right.

God, he hated awards.

Cole looked ahead and saw that he was approaching the edge of town. Out of habit, he glanced at his wrist. Finding it empty, he shifted his gaze to the dashboard clock. It was only 6:45. Too early to be knocking on someone's door unannounced. He calculated how long it would take to find a phone book, look up the address, and ask directions. Not long enough. Maybe he should stop at a restaurant first and kill some time over breakfast.

A smile stole over his face. There was no way in hell he was going to sit in some restaurant watching the clock knowing he was minutes away from his destination.

Propriety be damned.

Buddy Chapman answered Cole's knock wearing a red-and-green plaid bathrobe. He'd put on a few pounds in the years since Cole had last seen him. The weight had softened the angular lines of his face and, despite the silver streaks in his black hair, made him look younger. Tucked under his arm, he had a squirming two-year-old girl dressed in a pink pajama top and a diaper. "What can I do for you?" he asked, stifling a yawn.

Cole saw no reason to be coy. "As I see it, you can either ask me in for breakfast or tell me to go to hell. You've got every right to do the last, but I'm hoping it will be the first."

Buddy eyed Cole more closely as he leaned over and set the two-year-old down on the tile in the entry. She immediately ducked behind his legs. Seconds later, she popped her head out to peer around his knees. She looked up at Cole with aggressive curiosity. Buddy gave him the same look. "Cole? Is it you?" he said, plainly not believing what he was seeing.

Cole grinned with relief. "Yeah—a little the worse for wear, but it's me all right."

"Well I'll be. . . . You're just about the last person I ever expected to find standing on my porch."

"Does that mean you want me off?"

Buddy hesitated. "I would be lying if I said there weren't some hard feelings."

"You've got every right to them."

Again, Buddy hesitated. "Oh, hell," he finally said, "hard feelings can't buy me a cup of coffee, so what good are they?" He came forward, threw his arms around Cole, and gave him a bone-crushing hug. "You're welcome for breakfast." He took Cole's arm and brought him inside. "And for lunch and dinner if you're gonna be around that long. I just don't want you thinkin' Suzy's out to poison you 'cause she's still carrying a grudge. She never did learn to cook worth a damn."

"I heard that," Suzy said. She was standing in a doorway at the end of a long hall, her arms crossed, a wooden spoon in one hand.

"Come here and see if you can guess who this is," Buddy said.

"I don't have to guess, I already know who it is—the famous Cole Webster."

Cole flinched at the hostility in her voice.

"Now how did you know that?" Buddy asked.

"I saw his car. Nobody else we know would drive something like that."

Buddy shot a questioning look at Cole.

"It's a Lotus," Cole informed him.

"Jesus, don't you remember me telling you that you had to have a pickup truck to make it big in country music? No wonder you're still struggling."

Cole laughed. It was either that or make a complete fool out of himself crying. "I've missed you, Buddy. I had no idea how much."

"He hasn't been all that hard to find," Suzy said.

The two-year-old decided Cole wasn't to be feared anymore. She stepped on the toes of his tennis shoes and wrapped her arms around his legs. "Gotcha," she squealed.

Cole had no idea what to do with her. His experience

with kids her size would fit in one of his boots and still leave room for his foot. His confusion must have shown, because Buddy quickly reached over and rescued him.

Lifting his giggling daughter high in the air, he gave her several loud kisses on her neck before setting her back down on the floor. "Now scoot," he said. She took off for Suzy.

"She's beautiful," Cole said. "What's her name?"

"Darla," Suzy replied.

"I didn't know you had a daughter."

Suzy let out a snort of disgust and went back into the kitchen.

"Then you probably don't know she's got an older brother," Buddy told him.

"And another one on the way," Suzy informed him from somewhere in the kitchen.

The ice in Suzy's voice let Cole know her anger was cradled in a deeper and more secure place than Buddy's and she wasn't about to let it go as easily. "Maybe it would be better if I came back later."

"She's only mad at you 'cause she thinks she needs to protect me," he said softly. "Once she sees there's no need, it'll be all right." He put his arm across Cole's shoulders and led him down the hall toward the kitchen. "So, tell me, how is it that you're out roaming around on your own?" He grinned. "I've got a feeling this is going to be one interesting story."

Only then did Cole fully realize how deeply he'd missed Buddy. The logical, the obvious, first question should have been how Cole had come to look the way he did. By leaving the why and how of what had happened to Cole until later, Buddy was saying it didn't matter.

"The story's longer than it is exciting," Cole said. "And to be fair, I should tell you straight out, it's not real pretty."

"I've got lots of time." He moved behind Cole when they came to the doorway. "And it's obviously what you came for."

He was right, of course, but saying it out loud put a self-serving spin to Cole's reason for being there that made him question whether it was right to stay. He was still wrestling with how he should handle the situation when he looked up and saw Suzy staring at him, her hand over her mouth, her eyes wide in disbelief.

"My God, what's happened to you?" she asked.

"Leave him be," Buddy said before Cole could answer. "He'll tell us when he's ready."

"It's all right," Cole told him.

Suzy came toward Cole. When she was within touching distance, she reached up and ran her finger across the scar over his eye. "I couldn't really see you before. . . . I just thought you'd cut your hair and grown a beard."

Cole was shaken by her touch. It was filled with the caring and tenderness he'd longed to feel from someone, from anyone, after the accident. Afraid of the feeling she'd aroused, Cole took her hand, gave it a comforting squeeze, and forced a smile. "This happened months ago. The doctors say I'm as good as new."

The anger in her eyes was gone, replaced with concern. "Oh yeah? Then what are you doing here?"

"For God's sake, Suzy," Buddy protested, "give the guy—"

"Leave her be," Cole said softly. Realizing the gesture would be welcome, finally, he brought Suzy to him and gave her a hug. Not until then was her softly rounding belly evident. She responded by wrapping her arms around his waist and holding him tight. "We all know subtlety has never been Suzy's strong suit."

Without letting go, she leaned her head back and looked up at him. "You don't have to answer. It doesn't matter why you came, just that you did."

"Careful, you're going to lose that tough-as-nails reputation."

She laid her head against his chest for several seconds before letting him go. "Pancakes all right?"

The thought of how heavily they would sit on his stomach

the rest of the day wasn't enough to make him chance offending her by turning down her offer. "Let me help."

One eyebrow went up in suspicion. "That smacks more of a plea than an offer."

A small boy appeared in the opposite doorway. He was wearing a shirt with the tag hanging out the front, Batman underwear, and bright red socks. "I can't find my shoes," he said. Although he'd directed the statement toward his mother, his gaze was locked on Cole.

"Where did you take them off last night?" Buddy asked.

"I don't remember." Still the boy stared at Cole.

Cole crossed the room and lowered himself on his haunches. "Hi, my name's Cole. What's yours?"

The boy blinked in surprise. "That's my name, too."

Cole felt the words in the pit of his stomach. He turned to look at Buddy and then at Suzy, seeking denial more than confirmation. His mind refused to let him believe what his heart wanted to be true.

Suzy smiled; Buddy nodded. "Why?" Cole asked, not knowing what else to say.

"I always liked the name, so I thought why not?" Buddy said.

"That's a bunch of crap," Suzy interjected. "He did it because you were the best friend he ever had, or so he thought."

"Why didn't you tell me?"

Suzy and Buddy exchanged confused looks. "We did," Suzy said. "We even asked you to be Cole's godfather."

Cole put a hand against the door frame to brace himself as he stood up again, ignoring the pain that shot up his leg and into his hip. "No one said anything to me."

Buddy turned to Suzy. "Didn't I tell you?"

She took a box of pancake mix out of the cupboard. "I even tried calling you a couple of times, but they said you were too busy to come to the phone."

And still Buddy had welcomed him into his home that morning. "I never got any of your messages."

"That's terrible. But it doesn't excuse you for not bothering to pick up the phone and call on your own," Suzy said.

One of the things Cole had admired as much as he'd disliked in Suzy was her tenacious adherence to the unvarnished truth. There was no defense for what he'd done, no one to blame but himself. Cole's silence and apathy had facilitated every roadblock Frank had constructed.

"He was busy," Buddy filled in for Cole.

It was obvious he'd provided excuses for Cole's behavior in the past and was simply continuing that pattern. And it was just as obvious Suzy wasn't buying what he was trying to sell. "No one is so busy they can't pick up a phone to call an old friend," Cole admitted.

A impatient wail came from the doorway. "I need somebody to help me find my shoes."

"You go," Suzy said to Buddy.

He gave her a pointed look. "You behave yourself while I'm gone."

She laughed. "Cole's a big boy now. He can take care of himself."

Six months ago, Cole would have agreed with her. He wasn't so sure anymore.

# 6

*Buddy Chapman propped his feet* up on the railing that ran around the deck at the back of the house. He was still reeling from the surprise of opening the door and finding Cole standing there. After years of hoping just that would happen, he'd given up thinking it ever would. And then there Cole was, big as day and, while not exactly good as new, still a damn fine sight.

After a couple of hours together, it was clear Cole hadn't come for old times' sake; he was looking for something. Buddy had danced around the subject, asking questions when it seemed Cole was slipping into one of his quiet moods and letting Cole take his own direction when it seemed he had something to say. Still he hadn't been able to get a handle on why Cole had really come. There was a sadness to it that left Buddy frustrated. Most of all he was angry at whatever or whoever it was that had stolen the joy from Cole's life.

Although only a dozen years separated Buddy and the Webster brothers, there was a time when he'd been more father to them than Frank. Buddy was the one they'd sought out when they needed someone to talk to, or someone to listen. They knew they could trust him to forget the embarrassing things they told him and remember the rest and never get the two mixed up.

Buddy hadn't realized how possessive he felt about Cole and Randy or how much he'd grown to love them until circumstance took them out of his daily life. He'd waited for years, with Suzy growing ever more impatient with the seeming rejection of the man she loved, for a sign the feeling had gone both ways. Finally Randy had reestablished contact, and now Cole.

The screen door opened behind Buddy. Cole came outside. He handed Buddy a beer, went over to the railing, and propped his hip against one of the posts. "I always thought New Mexico was desert," he said. "I never expected to find you living on the side of a mountain with a forest out back."

"You mean to tell me all the years you've been on the road you never once played New Mexico?"

He smiled and shook his head. "It doesn't seem possible, does it?"

"Every once in a while I get a wild hare and start thinking I'd like to go back out on the road again," Buddy said.

"And?"

He chuckled. "Suzy loads me in the car, drives down the road a piece, and checks us into some flea-bitten motel. It doesn't take more'n a night or two of that kind of livin' and I'm ready to go home again."

Cole didn't say anything right away. Then, in a quiet voice he asked, "What if the accommodations were better?"

Buddy took a swallow of beer. "You just makin' conversation or poking around with a purpose in mind?"

Cole turned and stared out into the surrounding forest, as if afraid to see as well as hear the answer. "Just for the heck of it let's say it was with a purpose."

A deep pleasure coursed through Buddy. He'd spent

his entire life in music, chasing a dream shared by every southern kid who ever picked up an instrument. His life would be a little sweeter from then on knowing that it wasn't because he'd never been asked that he'd stayed home from the dance, it was because he had declined the invitation.

"You don't need me," Buddy said. "Mark Stewart's a hell of a lot better mandolin player than I ever was." He couldn't let it go without adding, "Still, I appreciate the thought."

Cole turned back around and met Buddy's gaze. "Sometimes things like this aren't about who's the best."

Buddy couldn't look at Cole any longer, couldn't let himself see the loneliness in his eyes or allow himself to be pulled any deeper into Cole's problems. If he did, the temptation to break his promise to Suzy would be too great. "My giving up the road was more than I let on when we were talking about it before. Suzy followed me around all those years because she knew making a grab for the brass ring was something I had to get out of my system and that I wouldn't be much good to either one of us if I quit before I was ready. When that time came and I promised her I would never go back—at least not the way you're talking about—I let her believe it was safe to set root and start a family. She's found herself here. In all our married life, I've never seen her as happy."

"When she was traveling with us she never let on that she liked to paint." Drawn initially by the quality of the work, Cole had been startled to find Suzy's signature on paintings hung throughout the house.

"She kept it to herself so I wouldn't think she was making some big sacrifice to be with me. Said she knew who I was when we got married and wasn't about to try changing me." He came forward to set his beer on a small glass-topped table. "Now that she's free to do what makes her happy, her painting has come to mean as much to her as my playing ever did me. But there's more to it than that.

She likes running the gallery and meeting other artists almost as much as she likes selling one of her paintings."

"Where does that leave you?"

"I keep my hand in things. There's a group of us that plays the local clubs and another group that does some amateur stuff. I give lessons to some kids in town."

"And then there's your own kids," Cole said.

Buddy smiled. "I never thought I was the kind to be a stay-at-home daddy, but it seems to suit me fine."

"If you ever change your mind . . ."

"I won't, but I like knowing you made the offer."

They slipped into an easy silence. After several minutes, Cole asked, "Do you remember that summer we played the Twin City Roadhouse in Memphis?"

Buddy smiled. "You were seventeen and in love with a girl named Pansy. As I recall, she told you she was Elvis's illegitimate daughter."

"A couple of months ago, I asked Frank the same thing," Cole said. "Do you know what he remembered about that summer?"

Buddy could guess, but it was Cole's story. "What?" he prompted.

"I was having trouble hitting notes and the receipts were down fifteen percent over the last time we played the Roadhouse." Cole adjusted his glasses, pushing them farther up his nose. "All I've ever been to him is a paycheck."

It wasn't the statement as much as the acceptance in Cole's voice that startled Buddy. "Some people are better at showing how they feel than others."

"You've always defended him. Why?"

The question caught Buddy off guard. "I guess I thought since you and Randy didn't have anyone else, it was important that you thought Frank . . . I don't know, that you believed he—"

"Cared?"

"Of course he cared."

"You're doing it again, Buddy," he said softly. "I'm almost thirty-two years old and you're still trying to protect me from him. What do you think I would do if you finally admitted the only thing Frank ever gave a damn about was how far he could push me and how long he could stay on for the ride?"

So here it was at last, the search for the answers that had brought Cole all this way. "Maybe it's time I told you some things about my own father and how I feel about him. I don't know if it will, but it might help you understand what's going on in that head of yours.

"I don't talk about him much." Buddy sat forward, resting his elbows on his knees, holding the bottle of beer between both hands, slowly rolling it back and forth. "Suzy doesn't even know what I'm going to tell you. Thinking about him never did come easy and talking about him is a hundred times worse. But I believe what I've got to say is something you need to hear."

He put his beer back on the table, stood, and hiked himself up on the railing. When he was secure, he planted his hands on the smooth wood and hooked the heels of his boots on the crosspiece below. "My father was the champion drinker of all time and about the meanest drunk God ever put on this earth. He used to beat my mother and us kids as regular as Monday follows Sunday. Most of the time I was growing up, he wasn't working and my mother was. He'd pick up women, bring them home, and screw them right there with us kids in the house. That wasn't the worst of it. A couple of years ago I found out my sister's oldest girl belonged to my father.

"Still, even knowing all that I do, there's a part of me that can't let go of the belief that somewhere in that sorry alcoholic heart of his he loved me." It was the first time Buddy had ever admitted to anyone what he'd always considered a shameful secret. "I know it's sick, but there it is."

Cole let out a heavy sigh. "Do you suppose there's something wrong with us? I've known men who rejected their parents for sending one grandkid a better present than they sent the other. And here we are—"

"Looking for love from men who wouldn't know how to show it if they took a course in school. I don't mean to put Frank in the same league with my father—Frank's a saint in comparison. I only wanted you to know that you and Randy weren't hanging out there by yourselves. There's a lot of us never did make peace with the men who raised us."

"It's like a dirty secret passed from generation to generation," Cole said.

"You know, I always did think Frank was one of the loneliest men I ever met. In all the time I was around him, I never knew him to have a real friend." The telephone rang. Frustrated at the interruption, Buddy considered ignoring it but then remembered Suzy was still out with the kids and that their old reliable Ford was beginning to show a temperamental side. "I'll be right back," he told Cole.

"Take your time. You've given me some things to think about. While I'm at it, I'm going to take a walk to see if I can work some of the stiffness out of my leg."

Buddy opened the screen and stepped inside. "There's a decent path along the creek," he told Cole. "It goes about a half mile or so, then dead-ends by a waterfall."

"That's where I'll be if you need me."

By the time Buddy reached the phone, whoever had been trying to reach him hung up. He went into the kitchen to peel potatoes and cut up carrots to add to the roast he'd put in the oven earlier. That done, he was headed to find Cole when he saw Suzy pull into the driveway and went outside to help her with the groceries.

"I couldn't get anyone to cover for me at the gallery tonight so I dropped the kids off at Helen's." She opened the trunk and handed Buddy a bag. "I figured you'd want to take Cole with you."

He leaned forward and gave her a kiss. "You're the best." He shifted the bag to one side and held out his arm for another. "But you've really got to do something about this tendency you have to carry a grudge."

She smiled despite herself. "Stuff it."

"Help me out on this one. Wasn't it you who said you'd never forgive Cole Webster for treating me as though I were a pair of smelly socks?"

"If you're going to quote me, at least get it right. What I said was, throwing you away like yesterday's dirty laundry."

"I like my version better."

She propped the last bag on her hip and started toward the house. "Speaking of Cole, where is he?"

"His leg was bothering him so he went for a walk."

"Did you get a chance to talk? Is he as messed up as he seems?"

"He's got some problems," Buddy acknowledged.

"Anyone standing on the outside looking in would think Cole had it all." She opened the door and moved aside for Buddy to enter first. "He's changed so much. How did you ever recognize him?"

It was inconceivable to Buddy that anything could happen to Cole that could make him unrecognizable. "The same way I would our Cole and Darla."

"You're far too young to be Cole Webster's father," she chided him.

"Sometimes fatherhood is a state of mind, Suzy."

Cole returned from his walk and came inside through the sliding door. "I can see why you bought here," he said. "It's got the best of both worlds, civilized at the front door and wild out the back."

"I was sold the minute I saw the place," Suzy said.

Buddy put a carton of milk in the refrigerator. "She said it reminded her of her grandmother's house in the Smokies."

"The hills and trees, not the house itself," Suzy said. "Grandma lived in a split-rail cabin. She didn't get indoor plumbing until I was a freshman in high school."

Cole shifted his weight to his good leg and leaned his shoulder against the door frame. The walk had worked out some of the stiffness, but had done nothing for the pain. "I remember a club we played one summer in Gatlinburg. I was around ten or eleven and it was the first time I saw the Smoky Mountains." He hadn't thought about that summer for years. Now the memories beckoned him with the promise of forgotten treasures of his childhood.

"Randy and I took off exploring every morning and didn't come back until just before showtime." A private smile formed. "I was always Daniel Boone; he would be either Davy Crockett or the Indian chief, Tamtucket." The smile became a soft laugh. "One time we left earlier than usual so we could check out an abandoned cabin we'd found the day before. Randy spotted a bear and secretly began dropping pieces of the bread and cheese we'd stolen from the lodge kitchen."

"I remember when that happened," Buddy said. "You and Randy were holed up in that cabin for two days waiting for that bear to go away. The whole town was out looking for you."

"The lodge canceled our contract and we were out of work for almost two months. I don't think I ever saw Frank as mad before or since as he was that day."

"It must have been hard for Frank raising two boys all by himself," Suzy said.

Buddy laughed. "Especially the likes of Cole and Randy. What one didn't think of, the other would."

"You ever go back home?" Cole asked.

Buddy stopped to put some cans of soup in the cupboard. "You mean to Tennessee?"

What he'd meant was the South. When you moved around as much as he and Randy had, borders lost their meaning. Rather than try to explain, he simply said, "Yeah."

"Every spring," Suzy said.

Buddy emptied the bag he'd been working on, folded

it, and stuck it in a drawer. "She has it in her head that since we can't live there year round, she wants the kids to see it at its best."

"They only have a couple of weeks every year. I want them to love being there as much as I do."

Buddy moved her out of his way with a playful pat on the rear end. "I keep telling you, Tennessee is as much a state of mind as it is a state. You've got to live there to understand what it's all about."

The sentiment tapped something deep inside Cole. "I tried to explain that feeling to someone once. I don't think I succeeded."

"If you two don't get out of here and let me get dinner on the table, the show is going to go on without you."

"What show?" Cole asked.

Suzy looked from Cole to Buddy. "You didn't tell him?"

Buddy made a face. "I was working my way up to it."

"So tell me now," Cole said.

"There's a group of us that gets together to play every other week at the high school cafeteria. The money we earn goes to the music department."

Suzy gave Buddy a pointed look. "Don't be surprised if he asks you to join them."

A sick feeling hit the pit of Cole's stomach at the thought of performing again no matter how casually. "I couldn't," he said. "I didn't bring my guitar."

"You can borrow mine," Suzy said. "If I can find it under all the dust, that is."

"It's been months since I played," Cole stammered.

"You can practice on the way over," Buddy supplied.

"I don't think it's a very good idea."

Suzy planted her hands on her hips and pinned him with a stare. "I happen to think it's a terrific idea," she told him. "As a matter of fact, a night of pickin' and grinnin' with a bunch of wannabe musicians might be just what you need." She tilted her head toward Buddy. "Present company excluded on the wannabes, of course."

"They're not as bad as she makes them out," Buddy protested.

Cole could see it was useless to argue. Suzy believed every problem had a solution. It didn't slow her down in the least that she had no idea what Cole's problem might be. "I'll go," he relented, "but I don't know about playing."

Suzy turned to Buddy. "I've got ten bucks that says he'll be up on stage with you before the night's over."

Cole was tempted to take the bet but thought better of it. He preferred Suzy keep her illusions. There weren't that many optimists left in the world—at least not in his world.

When they arrived at the school, Buddy headed for the portable stage and Cole eased himself into a chair in the back corner of the cafeteria. He was surprised at the number of people who'd come out on a Wednesday night to listen to a group of amateur musicians play what almost passed for bluegrass. It wasn't that they were bad; it was more that they desperately needed to spend more time practicing together.

Buddy had warned him what was in store on the way there, not so much in apology, but in explanation. The banjo player was a firefighter, the guy on guitar taught math at the junior high school, the woman on fiddle managed a restaurant, and the bass player was a retired janitor. And then there was Buddy, light years ahead of the others in talent and as patient with the rest of them as he was with his own kids, as patient as he had been with Cole and Randy when they were kids themselves and he was trying to teach them a new song or guide them through yet another crisis.

No one could fault the group's enthusiasm, or the audience's. They'd all come for a good time and they'd be damned if a missed note or wrong key was going to get in their way.

Despite his conviction he'd only come there as a favor to Buddy, Cole found he was enjoying himself. His foot freely tapped with the music, his mind hummed along, his musical sensibilities corrected the mistakes, and frequent smiles worked the muscles around his mouth. As he listened, he was reminded of the small southern towns they'd played where men and women would come together on a lazy summer evening and communicate with their music. It might be the lawn in front of the courthouse, a campground, or a general store on a road that led to nowhere. The people might be there for a night or lifelong residents of the area; at times, they were both.

Cole had vivid memories of old men in overalls and women in calico, their instruments ancient pieces that had passed through generations, their smiles warm and welcoming and often gap-toothed. They were as much a part of his childhood as green beans cooked all day with a slab of bacon, lightning bugs, and jeans with holes in the knees.

Buddy announced the band would play one more song before taking a break and asked if there were any requests. Cole called out "Uncle Penn," one of the first songs Buddy had taught him when he joined the band.

Several people shifted to look at Cole. He ducked his head and stared at his shoes, glancing up again to see that there was only innocent curiosity on the faces turned his way. As much as he enjoyed his newfound anonymity, he still wasn't used to it. More to the point, he didn't trust it. Somewhere in his subconscious there was a loud, persistent voice telling him his days of freedom were, of necessity, numbered.

The audience gave their enthusiastic approval of the performance when the group finished Cole's request and laid down their instruments. Buddy picked up a cup of coffee and an assortment of homemade cookies and brought them with him when he joined Cole.

"Well, what do you think?"

"This is the way music should be played. The audience

doesn't have this much fun at one of my concerts." Cole rummaged through the cookies, settling on one that looked like oatmeal-raisin.

Buddy smiled at the compliment. "You're lying but it's nice to hear."

To be sure Buddy understood what Cole would say next wasn't along the same bullshit lines, he looked at him directly. "I don't know where you get off thinking you're not good enough to be in my band. You're every bit the mandolin player Mark Stewart is. I hate to admit it, but I actually forgot how talented you are."

"You never were a judge of musicians. I remember—"

"Cut it out, Buddy. I'm not trying to get you to give up what you've got here with Suzy and the kids, I'm just telling it like it is."

"You're not leaving me a whole lot of maneuvering room, so I better just say thanks and put an end to it."

The next and most obvious question was, how, with all of Buddy's talent, he could restrict his playing to Wednesday nights with marginal musicians and occasional club dates with his other group. At one time or another, he'd toured and recorded with the best in the business. They had a language that was all their own, sometimes spoken aloud, sometimes through their instruments.

"Suzy ever get a chance to hear you play anymore?" Cole asked. Surely she must see that Buddy's talent was being wasted. However peripherally she had been a part of his career, she had always understood how important his music was to him.

"If she finishes up at the gallery early, she stops by for a while."

"What does she think of the group?"

Buddy gave Cole a knowing look. "Other than telling me how wonderful I am, she never says much. But then she knows I'm doing exactly what I want."

"Ouch," Cole said, in acknowledgment of the gentle rebuke.

"I know it's hard for you to understand, but I really am happy here. All you hear are the mistakes; I hear the improvement." He chuckled. "You wouldn't believe how bad this group used to be. I discovered there's a real high that comes with teaching. Especially when the pupils are this eager."

"But don't you miss the learning? You were the one who told me always to find people who were better than I was."

"Do you remember every damn thing I ever told you?"

"You were the only one who ever cared enough to bother telling me anything," Cole said with brutal honesty.

Buddy dunked a cookie into his coffee and took a bite before he answered. "I promised myself I wouldn't go meddling in your life by giving you advice, but you just blew that notion all to hell. You know that old sayin' that you've got to stop to smell the roses once in a while? When I was caught up thinking fame and fortune was what life was all about, I told myself that rose wasn't going to smell one bit different if I smelled it while I was running. What I didn't realize was I could capture the smell all right, but I was missing out on some damn pretty scenery."

Listening to Buddy was like putting on an old pair of jeans: the thoughts were comfortable and unpretentious, the intent sincere.

"There's no way you could know what it feels like to watch your kids being born or understand what it does to your insides when one of them lights up with a smile because you walked into a room, but you can take it from me, I never got as much pleasure sittin' in a recording studio or on a stage. I'm not saying what I've got is for everyone. There's some who can only get those feelings when they're performing. I think you're one of them and that's all right. You just got to find some way of getting back to that place in your life."

"I'm not so sure that place exists for me anymore," Cole said.

"Oh, it's there all right. You might lose sight of it for a while, but things like that don't just disappear forever."

Cole wished he had a little of Buddy's confidence. "Any suggestions where I should look?"

"It'll come to you."

One by one the musicians began moving back toward the makeshift stage. "Looks like your break is over," Cole said.

"We'll talk some more on the way home," Buddy promised.

Cole nodded.

"Sure you don't want to sit in for a couple of songs?"

Cole was surprised that he was even tempted. "Maybe next time," he said.

"If it's the ten bucks—"

Cole laughed. "I'd forgotten about the bet, but now that you mention it, I should probably let her win."

Buddy picked up his mandolin. "You've got to stop doing things to please other people and learn to do them for yourself."

"And when I do?"

"I'm not saying it's the answer to all your problems, but it's going to give the people around you something to think about."

It gave Cole something to think about also. By the time they were on their way back to the Chapman house that night, he'd reached a decision.

Cole looked around the cab of Buddy's truck. "How much would you say this thing is worth?"

"What you mean is how much I think I'd have to pay someone to haul it away, don't you?"

"What is it, about a '72, '73 Chevy?"

"It's a '73 GMC."

"It seems to run all right."

Buddy cast a sideways glance in Cole's direction. "What possible interest is my truck to you?"

"I thought we might work out a trade. Your truck and a thousand dollars for my car."

"You're out of your mind. That car's worth more than my house."

"Weren't you the one who once told me the value of everything is subjective?"

"Yeah, but—"

"But nothing. Right now there is nothing more valuable to me than your truck and enough money to take me where I want to go."

"And where's that?"

"I'm not sure yet. The idea's still taking shape."

"Then how do you know a thousand is enough to get you there?"

"Instinct."

"That's a bunch of crap."

"I've got a little bit left from selling my watch, too. Now, will you do it?"

"What am I going to do with a Lotus?"

"Sell it. Put the thousand back in the bank, buy yourself a new truck, and put the rest of the money in a savings account for the kids."

"So that's what this is all about. You think I'm not—"

"What this is about is following a friend's advice and doing something for myself," Cole said. "There are places I want to go and I can't get there in that car."

Buddy didn't answer for a long time. Finally, he said, "Because people notice it."

"And they remember it."

"You're worried Frank will send someone after you?"

"Maybe not right away, but eventually."

"How long are you going to be gone?"

"All I know for sure is that I want to be the one who decides when it's time for me to go home."

"I understand why you want the truck, but I can't agree to something like this."

"Why is it so easy for you to give and so hard to take?" Cole asked. "It's only a car, Buddy. I didn't even pay for it myself; it was a gift from the record company when I signed the new contract with them last spring. Strip away all the pretentious garbage and what you wind up with is that your truck has all the same basic parts and does the same thing my car does. Which, as far as I'm concerned, makes it a fair trade."

"Then why am I paying you a thousand dollars on top of giving you my truck?"

Cole laughed. He took his cap off and ran his hand through his hair. "Because I always could talk you into a sucker deal."

Buddy left the main road and headed up the hill to his house. "I'm almost afraid to ask, but have you decided when you're leaving on this journey of discovery?"

"I figure I don't have much time."

"You didn't answer me."

"Tomorrow," Cole said.

"Suzy's not going to be happy about that."

"Once I get my life straightened out, she'll see so much of me she'll wonder how she ever thought to miss me."

"You're going to be so busy when you finally do get back home that—"

"It doesn't matter how busy I get once I've got my priorities in the right order again."

"That's easier said than done, Cole. Be careful you don't set yourself up for a fall."

Cole leaned his head against the back of the seat and closed his eyes. "I'm not going to worry about it anymore, because I know if something should happen to me, there's someone I can count on who will see that I get back up again."

The next morning, Cole pulled out of the service station where he had gone to fill up the truck before leaving Taos and spotted a music store across the street. On impulse, he parked and went inside. Ten minutes later he walked out four hundred dollars poorer, but the proud owner of a used Martin guitar just traded in that morning, in need of a little work, but basically sound.

As he walked back to the truck, he passed a pharmacy, and remembered he needed toothpaste. He was at the counter when he noticed a revolving stand with postcards and small, colorful cutouts in the shape of New Mexico. He picked up one of the state symbols, turned it over, and asked the clerk, "What do you do with these things?"

"Most people put them on their campers or motor homes." She held out her hand. "Here, let me show you."

Cole watched as she carefully peeled the backing off of one corner.

"You put this sticky part on your window, or anywhere you want, and everybody knows you've been to New Mexico. You must have seen them on motor homes."

"Yeah," Cole told her, making the connection, "lots of times." Because she'd taken the time and trouble to show him how they worked, he bought the one she'd shown him.

When he arrived back at what he'd already come to think of as his truck, he carefully propped the guitar on the passenger side floor, took out the New Mexico sticker, and put it in the back window. The action had a nice feel, as if it marked the beginning of something.

It was late afternoon when he stopped for gas again. On the way inside to pay he spotted a telephone and was struck with an urge to talk to Randy.

He paid for the fuel and traded the clerk a twenty-dollar bill for a roll of quarters. He was as likely to get Frank as Randy, but not even that was enough to put him off making the call. It was almost as if he needed Randy's absolution for taking off and leaving him behind.

Feeling better than he'd felt since leaving Cole at the restaurant, Randy knocked lightly on Belinda's door, waited, and then knocked again. She'd only spent one night with her mother, claiming even that had been too long. When she still didn't answer after his second knock, he went back down the hall and into the living room where the housekeeper was working. "Have you seen Belinda?" he asked.

"She was out by the pool a few minutes ago," she answered without looking up from her dusting.

Randy glanced at his watch. Had he checked the time earlier, he would have known where to look. It was her afternoon half hour in the sun. He thanked the housekeeper and went outside.

Belinda saw him coming. She brought the magazine she'd been reading up to shield her eyes. "Did Frank find you? He said he's been looking all over the place for you."

"Did he mention what he wanted?"

"Get real. Since when does he tell me anything?"

As Randy got closer, he saw that Belinda had untied the top of her suit, leaving two small triangles planted squarely in the middle of her breasts, the strings pulled to the side. It wouldn't take much of a wind to . . .

The thought left him both dizzy and irritated with her and with himself. Even if it seemed Cole didn't appreciate Belinda at times, she was his girlfriend. "I just thought you'd like to know I heard from Cole."

She placed one arm across her chest and the other behind her and came up to a sitting position. The strings meant to hold the top of her suit in place draped over her arm. "Where is he?"

"At a friend's house." Randy stood in the shade of an oak several feet from where Belinda lay exposed to the sun. Seeking a means to distract his thoughts, he lowered himself to his haunches and ran his hand over the just-mowed grass, plucking the blades the mower had missed.

She frowned. "He's still here? In Los Angeles?"

"What makes you say that?"

When she shrugged, the pressure of her arm against her breasts made them mound enticingly. "He doesn't have friends anywhere else."

Randy forced his gaze to the sprawling smog-filled Los

Angeles basin stretched out in the distance. Her statement didn't surprise him the way it would have a few days
ago. In the short time Cole had been gone, Randy had
learned more than he wanted to about the relationship
between his brother and the woman who had shared his
bed, and supposedly his life, for more than a year. The
most startling revelation had been how little Belinda knew
about Cole. Randy still hadn't figured out whether it was
Cole who had closed Belinda out, or if it was her lack of
interest in things that didn't directly involve her.

"These are people who knew Cole a long time ago,"
Randy said.

"Before he hit it big?"

"Before he was even close." Randy was about to tell
Belinda about Buddy and Suzy when something stopped
him. Perhaps it wasn't just an oversight on Cole's part that
he'd never mentioned them.

"I don't suppose he happened to say when he might be
coming home?"

"No, and I didn't ask."

"I can't believe how irresponsible Cole is being about
this. Someone should tell him Janet and Frank can't go on
protecting him forever."

"I don't think he cares."

Belinda swung her legs over the side of the lounge so
that she sat facing Randy. "Has it occurred to you yet that
Frank might be right about Cole?"

"In what way?" Randy asked carefully.

"Now don't take this wrong, but it seems to me that the
way Cole's been acting since the accident maybe he does
need to see a psychiatrist. It could be he should have been
seeing one all along."

Suddenly, with sickening clarity, Randy understood the
depth of Cole's loneliness. At a loss for words to answer
Belinda, Randy mumbled something about having work
to do, got to his feet, and walked back to the house. He
passed the track where Cole had run alone each morning

and thought about the number of times Cole had suggested they do something together and the number of times Randy had turned him down because he let whatever else he had to do take precedence.

Not even the accident had been enough to shake Randy's complacency where Cole was concerned. He never should have let Frank keep him from visiting Cole at the hospital.

Too bad he didn't believe in God. If he did, he would ask for a second chance to make things right with Cole. But even if there was a God, He wasn't the kind who listened to requests from the likes of Randolph Terrance Webster. Randy had discovered that fact when, as a kid, he'd spent night after night trying to convince God there were already enough mothers in heaven and that he should let Randy's come back home.

# 7

*After leaving Taos,* Cole charted a meandering course east, taking back roads instead of highways, stopping when the urge struck, eating fried chicken and biscuits and gravy and ham so salty it left him thirsty for days. He struck up conversations just to hear the local accents and got up early on Sunday mornings to attend as many church services as he could find just to hear the singing. Two weeks into the trip, he had added seven stickers to the original one from New Mexico.

He called Randy again when he hit Arkansas and when he crossed into Georgia. After he'd told him he was all right, and still hadn't decided when he would return, there wasn't much more to say, so the calls were brief and unsatisfying. Both times Cole had hung up with the feeling there was something Randy had wanted to tell him but didn't know how. Afraid it might be a plea for him to come home, Cole didn't push.

With the exception of a disconcerting episode in an Oklahoma store, no one had approached him with a look of recognition. In a way, the close call in the store had been his own fault.

Seeking more protection from the sun than Randy's baseball cap provided, Cole had gone into a boot and saddle store to look for a replacement. He took off his glasses while he tried on several Stetsons for size, not bothering to see how they looked. After a while he noticed a woman watching him. The intensity of her gaze became uncomfortably familiar. He turned his back to her and found himself facing a mirror. Even without his glasses, the impact of what he saw left him shaken.

For the first time in months he could see traces of the old Cole Webster. He shifted position to include the woman's reflection in the mirror. She was studying something on the wall above him. His gaze drifted upward and locked on a poster advertising Trail Rider boots. There was Cole Webster, life-size, in all of his old glory. Cole could hardly remember the photo session but couldn't complain about the results. He was positive he'd never looked that good in person. But then he'd discovered lots of things appeared better in soft focus.

He left without the new hat.

It was late afternoon when he arrived in Townsend, Tennessee, a resort community that stretched along a slow-moving river. Since he was only a few miles from the Great Smoky Mountains National Park, the main reason he'd come this way, he decided to stay the night and get an early start in the morning.

He turned into the first motel with a vacancy sign. It was perched on the side of a hill, nestled in a stand of pines. As he approached he could see it was a lot older and less well kept than it looked from the road. If experience held true, the rooms had walls of plywood, and no matter which one he was given, the one next door would have a couple on their honeymoon.

He was looking for a place to turn around when a man dressed in overalls and old enough to be his grandfather came out of the office and hailed him with a wave and a smile.

"Looking for a place to stay?" he asked as he ambled over to the truck.

Cole's doubts deepened. He'd seen greeters at Wal-Marts, but never at a motel. What kind of place was this? He mentally replayed the question and actually laughed out loud. He knew exactly what kind of place this was: the kind he'd stayed in the entire time he was growing up.

Cole leaned out his window. "Your sign said you had a vacancy."

The old man tucked his hands under the bib of his overalls. "Truth be told, we've got three. You can have your pick."

"I'll take the quietest one," Cole said.

"That would be the one that's around back. Don't hear any of the road noises from there. Or, if that's not to your liking, I could give you one up front here, right behind the office. I been told you can hear my TV. I play it kind of loud 'cause I don't hear as good as I used to, but I don't stay up as late as I used to either, so it probably wouldn't bother a young fella like yourself. Unless, of course, you were planning on going to bed right away so you could get an early start in the morning."

"You said there were three rooms," Cole prompted.

"The other'ns our honeymoon suite and kind of on the expensive side. It's got a king-sized bed and one of them bubbly baths. The wife talked me into puttin' the bath in when we was remodeling a few years back, but then she up and died before she could tell me what good it was."

"Sounds like the room in the back would suit me just fine," Cole said, unconsciously slipping into the man's rhythm of speech.

"Holly ain't been back there cleaning but a few min-utes—she was late coming to work today on account of a doctor's appointment—but she's a real fast worker, so it won't be long 'fore she's got the place good as new. Come on in the office and we'll get you a cup of coffee and registered while you're waiting."

"I might as well park this thing by the room first," Cole said. "What's the number?"

"Thirteen."

It was a good thing he wasn't superstitious. Cole put the truck in gear and pulled forward. There were only two cars in the main parking lot, and none in the back. From the looks of it, all the efforts at maintenance had been concentrated on whatever was visible from the main road. The rest was in desperate need of paint and repair.

The door to room 13 stood open, a maid's cart on the sidewalk out front. He parked so there was plenty of room for "Holly" to maneuver her cart past his truck, then got out and headed for the office.

"Aren't you going to lock it?" came a female voice from behind him.

Cole turned and saw a teenage girl standing in the doorway to his room. With no one else in sight, there was no question she was talking to him. She had a rag in one hand, a bottle of cleanser in the other. Her hair was short and dark and styled to look the same before or after a windstorm. Her eyes were an intense blue and flashed impatience. She wore no makeup.

Cole was tired and for some reason put off by her attitude. He slowly and purposely looked around before he again settled his gaze on her. "Are you telling me there's a need, or do folks around here just lock up their belongings on general principal?"

"On general principal, I suppose," she said. "That and the fact we get a lot of riffraff passing through these parts."

He had a peculiar feeling the riffraff part had been directed at him. "If you're the official welcoming party, I don't imagine they stay too long."

She smiled sweetly. "Just long enough to help themselves to what isn't locked up."

There was no way around it; she'd bested him. He pulled his keys out of his pocket, walked back to the truck, and made a point of locking it. "Satisfied?"

"It's not my guitar." She gave the rag she was holding several sharp shakes. "All I care about is keeping careless people from losing their belongings and going after Arnold."

"Arnold?"

"He's the owner."

"The old guy who stopped me on the way in," Cole supplied.

"It isn't unheard of for someone to say they lost a camera or some such thing when they really didn't just to get a free night's stay. Arnold figures if they're desperate enough to lie about something like that, he might as well go along with them."

"Obviously you don't agree."

"I'd have their asses in jail faster than—"

"I get the picture."

Again she smiled. "That was the whole idea."

Her eyes came alive with the smile. He was intrigued at the change. "Is there something special about me, or are you this friendly with all the guests?"

"I've been around too many musicians to put much trust in one," she stated, as if it were the key to understanding her aggressive protectiveness.

"You tagged me a musician just because I happen to have a guitar in the front seat of my truck?"

"Am I wrong?" she prodded.

"That's not the point."

"You have no point unless I'm wrong."

"All right, you're wrong."

Now her smile was annoyingly triumphant. "And you're a liar."

"How can you be so sure?"

"You're from out of state, which means you were probably either working your way toward Nashville to see about getting a recording contract or you were already there and they turned you down. You don't have a lot of money or you'd be driving a better truck. You're skinny and out of shape and your hands are too clean for you to be a laborer. It's obvious you don't spend a lot of time in the sun."

"What makes you think I'm not a banker on vacation?" Why was he wasting his time arguing with her? What possible difference did it make what she thought of him?

"The guitar."

"The guitar could be a gift for a brother who collects them."

"But it's not, is it?"

"No," he admitted.

"I rest my case." She gave her rag another shake. The end snapped as if on cue, punctuating her victory.

"You found me guilty with circumstantial evidence."

She studied him for several seconds. "I'll give you this, you're smarter than most of the musicians I've known."

"And you're smarter than most of the motel maids I've known," he fired back.

This time the smile was reluctant. With it, her entire demeanor changed. The aggressive girl with the chip on her shoulder was gone. In her place was a mischievous-looking tomboy, someone who gave the impression her life had held more delight than disaster. "I have to get back to work."

"Seeing how it's my room you're cleaning, I'm not about to stop you." He made a little bow before he left, but she was busy with the cart and missed his gesture.

She was gone by the time he came back. His twinge of disappointment puzzled him at first. And then he thought how long it had been since he'd had any but the most benign conversations and realized how much he missed the verbal sparring he and Randy engaged in when they were together. It was reassuring to know he missed something.

He took the guitar and his bag inside the room and laid

them on the bed. The place was old and dingy, but metic-
ulously clean. There were none of the amenities a newer
motel would offer, no stocked refrigerator or complimen-
tary coffee, not even an ice bucket. The glass in the bathroom had a small chip on the rim, and the soap wasn't big
enough to last more than a day. Which made sense. It was
unlikely many people stayed longer.

The price had been right, half of what he'd been paying. If he continued to be careful with his spending, he
could last another two weeks. Then he would have to call
it quits or have Randy wire him money.

He turned on the television to listen to the news and
shut it off again before the picture came into focus. There
was nothing happening in the world he could control or
influence, and he really didn't want to hear more about
the woman who'd dominated the news for days by setting
her own house on fire with her three children still inside.

After opening the curtain to let in light, Cole pulled the
pillows from under the bedspread, propped them against
the headboard, and opened the guitar case. He'd worked
on the old guitar more than he'd played it, cleaning years
of handprints off the lacquered wood and replacing the
tuning pegs and strings. He'd treated the instrument with
more care than the faithless lover it represented. The feeling was still there, the need was as strong as ever, but the
romance had a sordid feel to it.

Cole had a need for what he knew the music could give
him, the peace he'd once felt when it was just him and his
songs, when there had been no pressure to write something that would hit the top of the charts because the
possibility was so farfetched it was laughable. He wanted
to feel that rush of adrenaline that used to hit when he'd
walk out on a stage and see thousands of strangers he'd
make his friends before the night was over. If someone
didn't sing along on one of the rowdy songs that had
made him famous, he'd point them out, shake his head,
and hold up a cue card. They were there to party, he'd

tell them. By the time the night was over, he wanted everyone who left the concert to be convinced they hadn't spent near enough for their ticket.

He lovingly slid his hand under the neck of the Martin and lifted it out of its case. For now he would content himself with feeling the weight and shape of the guitar and the emotions that having it in his hands evoked.

He was learning patience.

When he awoke later, from a nap he'd had no idea he was going to take, the room had picked up an orange cast from the setting sun. A rumbling in his stomach reminded him that he hadn't eaten since breakfast.

It would be dark soon, and then in a few hours it would be morning and he'd be on the road again. He'd already faced several unsettling truths about distorted childhood memories on his trip. The towns his child's eyes had seen as rural paradises—filled with lots purposely left empty for baseball and abandoned houses left open for kids to explore—were in reality towns dying from poverty. Resorts that had been filled with the magic of lights and music and cotton candy stands, where he and Randy had wandered the streets in awe, now looked sordid and commercial. If he'd believed for one minute that it was possible to imagine the Smoky Mountains better than they were, he wouldn't go.

He laid the guitar back in its case. A feeling came over him that when he took the instrument out again, it would be to play. The idea didn't repel him the way it had in the beginning. Maybe it wasn't all he'd hoped for, but it was a beginning.

After checking out the restaurants along the main road in Townsend, Cole decided to go the few miles into Maryville for dinner. While he was eating he overheard a conversation in the next booth about a new singer working in one of the clubs in the neighboring town of Alcoa and decided to check him out before going back to the motel.

The guy was good, a little too eager, and not as familiar

with his arrangements as he should have been, but with a little work, Cole would have been willing to take him on tour with him as an opening act. If and when he ever went on tour again.

By the time Cole arrived back in Townsend, he had the road to himself. The parking lot at the motel had magically filled with cars, but the only lights that were on were the few outside the buildings. He pulled around back, got out, and walked over to his room. He had the key in the door when he realized he'd forgotten to lock the truck. It would be just his luck to have Holly arrive for work before he left the next morning and see the button riding high on the casing. He knew it was ridiculous to let himself feel intimidated by a wisp of a teenager he would never see again. Still, she'd had a point. Having someone steal his transportation now would really screw things up.

He headed back to the truck. The last thing he remembered was lifting his hand to put the key in the door.

# 8

*Holly paced back and forth* inside the curtained emergency room cubicle, trying to convince herself it was not only reasonable for her to leave, it was actually the right thing to do. She'd already done everything she could, everything that could possibly be expected of her. She had no business there. Not only wasn't she a relative, she wasn't even a friend. When the admitting nurse had questioned her, she couldn't give one answer. She'd even had to call Arnold to get the guy's name off the register. For some reason, Neal Chapman didn't seem to fit him. He seemed more the Jared or Dwight or Hank type.

If she could just get through the curtain without looking at him, she could make it. The instant the thought was formed, it was as if some perverse magnetic force took over and her gaze was drawn to his still form. He looked so awful with the blood all over his face and matting his hair. As she remembered from the day before, his hair had been light brown; now it seemed almost black. The nurse had told her head wounds often appeared worse than they were because they bled a lot.

Of course, she'd admitted, there was the little problem of the patient being unconscious for God knew how long.

It was a good thing Holly hadn't been able to sleep last night and had decided to come in early to do the book-keeping for Arnold. And it was a good thing the parking lot had been full and she'd had to go around back to find an empty spot. And it was good that Arnold was around to help her get Neal in her car. It was all good for Neal Chapman, not so good for her.

"Dammit," she groaned aloud. Anyone with the sense God gave a June bug would know they had to be on guard in a resort area. Tourists drew criminals. It was as natural and inevitable as the end result when you were stupid enough to try out for cheerleader with your best friend.

Holly crossed her arms and propped her backside against the edge of the gurney. She had a hundred things to do that day, not the least of which was cleaning twenty motel rooms. No one would blame her if she just quietly slipped out of the hospital and went about her business. She could always call later to see how he was doing. If he was awake by then she could even ask if he needed any-thing, and if he did, she could drop it off on her way home that afternoon.

All she had to do was put one foot in front of the other, not in little mincing steps, but nice long strides, and walk right out of Blount Memorial and into the sunshine.

She glanced at her watch. Sunshine would have to wait another twenty minutes.

*Damn, damn, damn.* She hated hospitals. People died in hospitals. Her mother and father had died in a hospital just like this. She knew because she'd been there when it happened.

She'd made it happen.

What a stupid expression—*Pull the plug.* No one had pulled any plugs, they'd simply shut off the machines because she'd told them it was all right to do so. The expression was almost as stupid as the way the two people she'd loved most in the world had died, using a kerosene heater to keep warm in the camper they'd saved for over five years to buy.

She could still hear the doctor telling her how lucky her parents were that she'd turned twenty-one the day before. As an only child and the closest relative, it fell to her to make the decision to end their lives. How fortunate for everyone, she'd gained her majority.

She'd buried her parents six years ago. It was the last time she'd celebrated her birthday.

The curtain parted. A short, harried-looking man, half glasses perched on the end of his nose, came in. He glanced up from the chart attached to the clipboard he was carrying and held out his hand. "Dr. Hardesty."

"Pleased to meet you," Holly said. She tried to step around him to leave, but it was impossible to maneuver in the cubicle.

"You're Mrs. Chapman?"

"Me?" The squeak in her voice made her sound like a 120-pound mouse. "No, I'm just the person who found him."

The doctor frowned. Plainly this was a wrinkle he hadn't anticipated and didn't want. He went on as if the information were of no consequence. "The injuries Mr. Chapman received several months ago make this a more difficult case than it would have been under normal circumstances. The X rays indicate the head wound he received last night isn't severe enough to have resulted in a prolonged loss of consciousness."

"What do you mean wasn't severe enough?" Holly said. "You haven't even looked at him."

He peered at her over his glasses. "If you're worried about the blood, that's normal."

"Normal?" There she went again. She cleared her throat and concentrated on lowering her voice. "I'm sorry but I don't see how you can use the word *normal* on anyone who looks the way this man—the way Neal—does."

"Head wounds are known to bleed profusely."

"And what did you mean about other injuries?"

"According to his chart, Mr. Chapman is still in the process of recovering from a severe head trauma. My guess would be an automobile accident. I had a case similar to his when I was an intern at—" He stopped. "Back to Mr. Chapman. He's going to need monitoring after he comes out of the coma and goes home. Not that I anticipate anything untoward happening, it's just that I feel it's better to err on the side of caution. Also, it would probably be better if he didn't climb stairs for a while. Is your home set up so that could be arranged?"

"Oh, he won't be coming home with me. Like I told you, I'm just the person who found him."

He tucked the clipboard under his arm, lowered his chin, and gave her a long-suffering look. "Have you notified his family then?"

Holly folded her arms across her chest, lowered her chin, and stared back at him. "Since no one, including me, knows who his family is, my guess would be they haven't been notified." Her patience growing thin, she told him, "Mr. Chapman checked into the Sleepytime Inn last night. He paid for one night's lodging, but due to an unfortunate run-in with the person who took his wallet and left him like this, he never got what he paid for."

Something brushed against her hip. She turned to see what it was and discovered Neal Chapman looking at her, his eyes narrowed in concentration.

"Molly?" he said.

"Holly," she corrected him and smiled in relief. It didn't matter that she hardly knew him; she was still grateful he hadn't died. "Welcome back."

The doctor nudged her aside. "How are you feeling?" he asked.

"Who are you?"

"Dr. Hardesty. You were brought into the hospital a couple of hours ago with a blow to the head. Do you know how it happened?" He took a penlight out of his breast pocket and flashed it in Neal's eyes.

"I was locking my truck. That's all I remember."

Holly winced at the revelation and backed toward the curtain. "Well, it's obvious you don't need me anymore, so I'll be taking off now."

Neal brought his hand up. "My glasses? Have you seen them?"

She'd known there was something missing, but every time she looked at him, she couldn't get past the blood. "You weren't wearing them when I found you."

"But I can't drive without them."

"They probably came off when you were hit," Holly suggested.

Dr. Hardesty shoved the penlight back in his pocket. He turned to Holly. "If you could step outside for a few minutes so I could examine Mr. Chapman?"

Holly leaned around the doctor to look at Neal. "I'm going back to the motel now. If I find your glasses, I'll drop them by on my way home from work."

Neal turned his head in her direction and squinted. "How long will that be?"

He sounded desperate. "I'll be back after lunch."

"That would be great."

She found the opening and pulled the curtain aside. "See you then."

Once outside the safety of the cubicle and exposed to the actual workings of the hospital, a new heaviness settled over Holly. Her gaze swept the dozen or more doorways, but none held the hoped-for Exit sign. Fighting the increasing sense of pressure, she laid her hand against her chest and forced herself to take a deep breath. Somehow, some way, she had to get over this feeling—and soon.

She didn't have all that much time before she would be the patient, not the visitor.

A woman with a tray of vials came up to her. "Can I help you?"

"How do I get out of here?"

The woman pointed back the way she'd come. "Down the hall and to your left."

With effort, Holly kept her pace unhurried. She nodded to the people she passed and even managed a smile for a woman holding a forlorn-looking toddler in pink-footed pajamas. And then she was outside again, back in the clean-smelling air, back where there were no cubicles with injured people or plugs to be pulled or life-and-death decisions to be made by terrified young women who until then had had trouble deciding which blouse to wear on a date.

Holly looked to the east as she got into her car. The sky was the deep purple of false dawn. People would be up and packing their cars by the time she arrived at the motel. The activity would bring a normality to the day, allowing her to lose herself in the mindless, repetitive motions of cleaning all those rooms.

With just a little luck, Arnold would have some reason to go into town that morning, and she could ask him to stop by the hospital to take Neal Chapman his glasses. Realizing how desperately she wanted Arnold to take the simple chore off her hands dismayed her. It wasn't so long ago Arnold had gone to Blount Memorial every day, a captive witness to the inexorable path of heart failure in a woman he'd loved and lived with for more than fifty years.

When had she turned into such a coward? At what point had she stopped doing battle with her past and allowed it to dictate and restrict her future? She couldn't let herself give in to feelings that would overwhelm her if given a chance, especially not now.


The afternoon sun sliced a path through Cole's hospital room. Without benefit of his glasses, the lines and angles and brightness and shadows created a surrealistic environment. It was strangely beautiful, but only tolerable for a few minutes before he would have to close his eyes to bring imagined images into focus.

Once the painkiller the doctor had prescribed kicked in, Cole had started feeling restless and eager to be on his way. He'd made an attempt to call Holly about his glasses but couldn't remember the name of the motel. When he tried describing the place to the operator, she told him it wouldn't do any good. She was from Alcoa and never got down Townsend way.

Reluctantly, with resignation, he came to the conclusion that he had another phone call to make. From the beginning he'd believed that when he finally decided to go home he would do so with answers to at least some of his questions. Lacking that, he would have the comfort of feeling at peace with himself.

He had neither. But then he'd thought he would be the one who decided to end his trip, not some nameless, faceless thug.

If there was something to be gained by waiting, he could understand why he still hadn't picked up the phone. But according to the policeman who'd come to the hospital that morning to take Cole's report, there was about as much chance of getting his money back as there was of a snake sprouting wings. From the looks of it, the hit had been random and the thief long gone.

Without money Cole couldn't go on. He supposed that in some ways it was easier this way. As with almost everything else in his life, the decision had been made for him. Maybe it wasn't such a bad way to live after all. Without the burden of decision making, he'd been allowed freedom to explore other things.

Jesus, who was he trying to kid?

He rolled onto his side and reached for the phone. He might have lost the opportunity to make the major decisions, but there were still some things he could control. He arranged with the hospital operator to have the call added to his bill. Then, without giving himself time to reconsider, he dialed the number.

Frank answered, his voice unnaturally cheerful. "Hello."

"It's Cole. Is Randy around?"

"I was beginning to worry something might have happened. It's been a week since we heard from you."

"I'm fine."

"When are you coming home?"

"Soon. Is Randy there?"

"I can't tell you how relieved I am to hear that. Janet's been run ragged these past two weeks with the press wondering what happened to the big announcement we promised. But she wants you to know she understands why you had to get away for a while and that she's not mad at you."

Subtle but effective. It hadn't even occurred to him Janet might be mad. It was her job to deal with the press, under all circumstances. "You can tell her I appreciate her understanding. Now about Randy?"

"One other thing. I wasn't happy with the last batch of shirts Crowell's sent over, so I sent them back. I hope that's all right."

What was going on here? Frank didn't give a damn what Cole thought about the shirts he'd contracted to wear onstage. "Dad, I'm not in the mood for this. I called to talk to Randy. Is he there or not?"

Several seconds passed before Frank said reluctantly, "I'll get him for you."

Cole rolled to his back, carefully adjusting his head to fit the indentation in the pillow. It wasn't that the bump hurt so much, but it did trigger memories of the last time he was in a hospital. He kept expecting the headaches to return and found that he was moving and holding himself to accommodate anticipated pain. The doctor had tried questioning him about the earlier accident. When Cole made it plain he didn't want to talk about it, the doctor made a bizarre attempt to appeal to his vanity, telling him how beautifully the bones in his face were mending, how masterful the treatment had been, and how fortunate he was to have escaped permanent damage or disfigurement.

Randy's voice, higher and louder than usual, broke the silence. "Hey, big brother, how's it hanging?"

"I need your help."

Randy hesitated before saying, "I don't want to hear about it. Not now."

Something was wrong. "When?"

Again he hesitated. "You can't call here anymore."

"What?"

Cole heard Frank in the background. "Give me that goddamned phone."

"Dad's recording everything you say." There was a scuffling sound. "He's had this thing called a trap put on the line. If you call here a couple more times, he's going to know right where to look for you. You're okay now, but if you stay where you are, you can't call here anymore. All it takes is three or four times."

Frank's voice overrode Randy's. "He's lyin' to you, Cole."

"Later, man," Randy said.

"Cole?" Frank shouted into the receiver. "Are you still there?"

Cole listened to Frank call his name several more times, then slowly replaced the receiver. He lay there for several minutes before he returned the phone to the nightstand, got out of bed, and went to the window. Everywhere he looked his world was in soft focus.

He blinked.

Nothing changed.

Nothing ever did.


Frank flung open the door to Randy's room. He had his mouth open to say something but stopped when he saw what his youngest son was doing. "Where the hell do you think you're going?" he asked.

Randy looked up from the suitcase he'd been packing. "What do you care?"

"I don't. It's Cole I'm thinking about. He's the one who insists you be here when he calls. As far as I'm concerned, life would be a lot easier if you weren't around."

"Brutal, but honest." Randy opened a drawer, scooped up everything inside, and dumped it in the already overloaded suitcase.

"You promised you would help us find him." Abruptly the combativeness left both Frank's voice and posture. He looked and sounded drained, the general turning over his sword at the end of a costly battle. "Why did you change your mind?"

Randy responded warily. He could handle an angry, aggressive Frank; the man talking to him now was unfamiliar and therefore not to be trusted. "Cole will come back when he's good and ready."

"You heard what the doctors said." Frank ran both hands across his face as if the motion could wipe the tiredness away. "Cole isn't himself anymore. He's suffering from that postshock thing. We've got to get him back here to help him. He can't do it on his own."

"That's a bunch of garbage. Cole's no crazier than I am."

"No one is saying he's crazy. He just needs help working things out. He needs to talk to people who have experience with this kind of thing."

Randy slammed down the lid to the suitcase. "He's doing just fine on his own."

Frank tensed. "How do you know that?"

Randy realized he'd already said too much. "Because I know Cole. He's always been able to take care of himself." He shifted his gaze to the dresser, making a show of searching for anything he might have missed the first time around.

"I don't understand you," Frank said.

Something snapped in Randy. "You're damn right

you don't understand me. You don't have any idea who I am." He leaned his weight on the top of the suitcase and tried to force the locks, but there was too much inside. "It's a good thing it wasn't me who disappeared and needed finding. You don't know enough about me to fill out a fuckin' missing person's report. I stopped counting on you the day Cole pulled down his first paycheck."

"That's not true."

He turned his back to his father. "What color are my eyes?"

"This is stupid. What possible difference does knowing the color of someone's eyes make? It doesn't prove anything."

Randy took no pleasure from Frank's evasion. It was an argument he hadn't wanted to win. Still, he couldn't back off. "*What color are they?*" he demanded.

Frank hesitated. "They're blue."

Randy turned and pinned his father with a withering look.

"So they're brown," Frank said. "Your mother's were blue. . . . You're so much like her. . . . I just thought . . ."

In all the years since her death, Randy couldn't remember ever hearing Frank talk about his mother. It disconcerted him to have her brought into the conversation now, especially in reference to him.

He made one more attempt to close the suitcase and then picked it up and dropped it on the floor beside the bed. The dramatic moment, the time for grand gestures had passed. The fire had gone out of him, its embers leaving him ambivalent and confused. Besides, there was no way he could move out of the house now without raising questions that would lead back to Cole. He glanced at the clock on the dresser. "When was I supposed to be at the studio?"

"Three o'clock."

"I'd better get out of here."

"There's still plenty of time."

Randy didn't understand Frank's seeming reluctance to have him leave. What he'd expected from his father was behavior true to past form, a bit of gloating or some other show of triumph over having gotten his way yet again. "What do you want from me?"

"I don't know," Frank admitted. "I thought I did, but I'm not so sure anymore."

At the admission, Randy's defenses slipped. A warning voice insisted he protect himself, but there was something more powerful urging him on, demanding he allow Frank one more chance to redeem himself, to listen when Randy wanted to talk, to prove there was room in his life for two sons. "Do you remember the year the band got hired to follow the rodeo circuit in East Texas?"

"Cole was ten—" He caught himself, but too late. "And you were . . ."

"Seven," Randy filled in for him.

"Yeah, that's right."

"You left me on a ranch with an old couple while you and Cole were on the road."

"The promoters wouldn't pay your expenses, so I couldn't see any sense in having you tag along."

After all this time, Frank's casual acceptance of the logic of the situation still had the power to hurt. Randy shoved the insult aside, relegating it to a place where there were a hundred other indignities and oversights too painful to forget. In reality, the break from traveling had been a godsend to a little boy who'd needed the warmth of welcoming laps and arms that were quick with hugs. "The man who ran the place"—how could he have forgotten his name?—"used to let me help him with the chores."

"You weren't put there to work," Frank said with a flash of anger, his protest a lifetime too late. "I paid those people good money to take care of you."

Randy went on as if Frank hadn't spoken. "When we fed the chickens, he would let me hold the babies, but they always fought to get away. Then one day he told me chicks were like people: the tighter you held on, the more they struggled to get free. He could see I didn't believe him so he made me sit perfectly still with my hand open while he put one of the chicks on my palm."

Randy locked eyes with his father. "The old man was right, the chick just sat there. After a while it hunkered down and fell asleep."

"So what are you saying?"

"You've got your hand wrapped so tight around Cole he can hardly breathe. If you don't loosen your grip, he isn't going to come back, ever."

"It's not the same. Cole is—"

Randy shook his head in defeat.

"He's sick," Frank insisted. "He needs our help."

"Cole's no sicker than any of the rest of us." Randy thought about what he'd said and let out a disparaging laugh. "Maybe I should find another way to put that."

"The doctors said—"

"Would you get off that doctor shit? They don't know Cole the way we do. Hell, two of them you called have never even talked to him. How can they know what's going on in his head?"

"Say we give him the time you say Cole needs. What happens if a month or two down the road he decides his life was pretty damn good the way it was, but it's too late to go back because while he was away everything went to hell in a hand basket? You know as well as I do we've been luckier than we've got any right to be. I never would've believed we could go all this time without one word leaking out that Cole hightailed it out of here. But just because we've gotten away with covering it up till now don't mean we're going to get away with it much longer."

"So what if we do get caught? What's the worst thing that can happen? Word leaks out that after living out here all this time Cole needed to go home again, to get back to his roots. His fans would eat it up."

"Is that where he is?" Frank asked carefully.

"Don't play that game with me, Frank. I didn't tell you anything you didn't already know or couldn't have figured out for yourself."

"If you know where he is and how to get in touch with him, why the big scene on the phone today?"

"He calls me, I don't call him. I know where he was a week ago, but he could be halfway across the country, moving in another direction since then."

"You asked about the studio. Does that mean you're going to do the shots after all?"

There was still some footage that needed finishing if the video for "A Walk on the Right Side of Town" was going to coincide with the release of the album. Frank and Janet were convinced they could reedit what they had, use Randy on a couple of long shots, and fill in the rest with news clips and concert footage. Randy's participation was minor but necessary if they were going to finish on time. "I wanted to talk to Cole about it first, but I guess there's not much chance of that now."

"Is that a yes or no?" Frank pushed.

"I'll do it."

"From where I stand, I don't see how we've got much choice how we go about things from now on." He gave the impression he was talking to himself as much as Randy. "We've all got to hold on to things as best we can. If luck's with us, when Cole decides to come back, he'll have something to come back to. If not . . ." He shrugged. "I guess we'll have to deal with that when the time comes."

Randy studied his father, suspicious at his sudden calm acceptance of something that had had him in a rage less than a half hour before. He didn't know this rational, caring man.

"You don't believe me, do you?" Frank said, as if he'd been able to read Randy's thoughts.

"Why should I? It isn't just Cole's life we're talking about, it's yours."

"And yours, too," Frank added. "We're as bound to each other now as we ever were."

"But I've got a lot of years ahead of me. I could go to college if I wanted."

"You never finished high school."

"And whose fault was that?" Randy threw back.

"If fixin' blame payed bills, this country wouldn't have a national debt." He ran his hand over his chin. "Look, I know you think I set this thing up today because I want Cole back for myself. I don't deny there's some truth to it. My life has been wound up with your brother's so tight for so long, sometimes it's hard to tell where I take off and he ends.

"But you're wrong if you think when Cole's career is over so is mine. There's one thing his leaving has done for me. It's made me realize that if this whole thing blows apart tomorrow, it might take me a year or two to get back up on my feet, but I'll be there. I'm damn good at what I do, Randy. This thing with Cole didn't just happen. There's not a day goes by someone at one of the record companies doesn't call the office or come knocking on my door askin' me to handle some hot new singer's career."

Randy didn't want to hear what Frank was telling him. They were thoughts and feelings he'd managed to put to the back of his mind, the way he did everything else that threatened him or demanded a piece of his freedom. For all of the seeming frustration that came with standing in his brother's shadow, there was something to be said for not being the one out there getting burned in the sun.

"But what will Cole do if he decides one day he was wrong and that he wants the career he threw away?" Frank questioned. "The minute he walks away from the spotlight, it will turn to someone else."

"Why didn't you tell me this before?" Randy asked.

"I thought you finally understood this wasn't some game you and Cole were playing to get back at me. You know your brother better than anyone. How could you believe he could find any real happiness if he lost what he valued most in this world? What would he do with himself? Where would he go? His entire life has revolved around his singing; he's not qualified to do one damn thing else. Cole's thirty-one years old, Randy, way too young to set himself down in a rocking chair to watch the world pass by."

"I guess I didn't think that far ahead," Randy reluctantly admitted.

"Cole hasn't done you any favors protecting you the way he has." It wasn't an accusation so much as a statement of fact. "You had more responsibility and more was expected of you when you were fifteen than you do now. Thanks to Cole, you've never had to grow up."

Randy had never wanted to do battle more than he did that moment, but he had no defense. "That's a hell of a thing to say to someone."

"It came harder than it sounded." There was apology and pain and understanding in the look he gave his youngest son. "One thing more . . ."

Randy sat down on the bed and put his hands out in surrender. "Go ahead. Lay it on me. How much worse can it get?"

Frank paused. "It can wait for another time."

"No, I want to get this over with."

"I'm not saying this because I think it's true, only because I think it's something you need to consider before—" He stopped and drew in a deep breath, plainly uncomfortable with what he would say next.

Randy tensed. In his entire life he'd never seen Frank hesitate to say something, whether it was mean or hurtful or an ass-backward compliment. "Whatever it is," Randy told him, "just say it."

"Why did you warn Cole away on the phone today?"

"I didn't want to be a part of lying to him. He trusts me. I'm probably the only one he does."

"That's the easy answer. It's the one underneath I'm

after. Are you sure there isn't something else going on with you, something you might not even have admitted to yourself yet?"

"What are you getting at?"

"All your life Cole's been the important one, the one who got the attention, the one standing center stage."

"So?"

Frank dropped his gaze to the toes of his lizard-skin boots. "If he doesn't come back until it's too late . . ." Slowly, his gaze came up until it was fixed on Randy's face. "If everything blows up in Cole's face . . ."

With a swift, violent movement, Randy came up off the bed. "How could you say something like that? Jesus, how could you even think it?"

But Frank would not be put off. In a voice filled with uncharacteristic empathy and understanding, he said, "The end of Cole's career is the one thing that could finally put you on equal footing with your brother— maybe the only thing."

Randy stood perfectly still for a long time, his hands curled into fists at his sides. He'd come through barroom fights feeling less battered. Over and over he told himself Frank's words had no merit; his father was merely striking out in retaliation, hitting where he knew Randy was most vulnerable, where he could draw the most blood. In desperation he looked into his father's eyes, seeking a glimmer of satisfaction that his attack had been successful. But there was only a naked sadness.

With slow, deliberate steps, Frank crossed the room. He stood poised in front of Randy, not saying anything, not doing anything, just standing there. Finally, he put his hand on Randy's shoulder and gently squeezed.

To his own surprise, Randy didn't pull away. It was the first time he could remember his father touching him in anything but anger. If he accepted the overture of peace, he would lose the focus of his anger.

The thought left him shaken.

# 9

*Holly pulled her Corsica* into the hospital parking lot, turned off the engine, and purposefully got out of the car. Her stride was long and determined as she hit the sidewalk and made her way through the front entrance. She was still able to smile when she stopped at the visitor's desk and asked where she would find Neal Chapman. It wasn't until she stepped into the elevator and the doors closed behind her that the smile faded.

She looked down at her hands. They were as still as the air on a lazy summer morning.

Not bad. Obviously the lecture she'd given herself on overcoming her fears and getting on with her life had done some good. Which wasn't surprising considering the monologue had gone on through the cleaning of twenty motel rooms.

She'd discovered early on that if she had something useful to think about or even a problem that required her undivided attention, the cleaning went twice as fast. Not literally, of course. Changing all those sheets and scrubbing toilets took a set amount of time no matter how consumed she was in her own thoughts.

Arnold had introduced her to books on tape. He had a whole library behind the desk in the office and had told her to help herself anytime she wanted. Reading was a passion in which she'd had little time to indulge since moving into her grandfather's old house in Maryville three months ago. Most nights she was too tired even to hold a book. She didn't enjoy the tapes as much as she did actually doing the reading herself, but it was a lot better than no books at all.

The elevator doors opened and started to close again before Holly realized she'd come to her floor. She broke the light beam with her hand and stepped into the corridor. A brass plate with room numbers and arrows pointing directions indicated she should go left.

As determined as she was not to look inside the rooms she passed, she found her gaze drifting from the numbers on the doors. Some of the men seemed desperately ill, others as fit as the people she passed in the hall.

There it was, room 436. The door was closed. She knocked lightly and waited. When there wasn't any answer, she knocked again, harder. When there still wasn't any answer, she pushed against the hand plate and peeked inside. The bed was empty. Confused, she opened the door farther and stepped into the room.

By the time she saw him standing at the window, his hospital gown open, his backside exposed, it was too late to get out without being caught.

"Nice view, huh?" she said.

His hand came up to close his gown as he turned to face her. "Holly?"

"Yeah, it's me." She dug in her pocket for his glasses. "I'm sorry I couldn't get here sooner, but it's been one of those days."

He took a hospital robe off the end of the bed and put it on. "I forgot you were coming," he said.

She handed him his glasses. "Something wrong?"

"Why do you ask?" he said as he settled the wire frames over his ears.

"I don't know. You seem different somehow."

"Maybe it's the clothes." He looked down at his bare feet and wiggled his toes. "Or should I say the lack of them."

"What did the police say?"

"Not much."

"I moved your things out of the room so you wouldn't be charged for another night."

He let out a humorless laugh. "It wouldn't matter much one way or another. In the corner I'm sitting in, it's a long way between being charged and paying."

"Actually, I was thinking as much about Arnold as I was you. He can't afford to let a room sit empty in August. It's the last big month of the season."

Cole sat down in the chair at the foot of the bed. "A woman from the hospital came by earlier and asked if the motel had insurance."

Holly flinched. "We did, up until last month." She'd done everything short of stand on her head to talk Arnold into keeping his policy, but the bill for his wife's headstone came in at the same time and he could only pay one.

"It doesn't matter. I told her I would take care of the bill myself."

"Did she say how much it would be?" It was more than idle curiosity that prompted her to ask. She'd been meaning to talk to her doctor about what charges to expect, but still hadn't broached the subject.

"No, and I didn't ask."

"You ever wonder who it was designed something so awful?" she asked, indicating his clothes.

He tilted his head to one side as if considering her question. What he said had nothing to do with what he had on, however. "You're a lot older than I thought."

Her hand went to her hair in a defensive gesture. "You make me sound ancient," she protested.

"That's not what I meant. It's just that when I first saw you, I thought you were a kid."

"I've got one of those faces, I guess." Cindy Crawford had nothing to fear from Holly Murdoch.

It was time to use her exit line and be on her way. When she'd called the restaurant to see if it was all right for her to be a little late for work that night, Linda Jeane had answered the phone and talked her into coming in three hours early to cover for her. It was hard to say no to someone who'd already agreed to take shifts for Holly when she needed time off that coming winter. "Are you sure there isn't anyone you want me to call for you? A friend? Relative?"

"There isn't anybody."

How could he not have anyone? She felt more than thought about what was coming next. "I know this isn't any of my business, but where are you going to go when you leave here? I mean without any money and all." Damn, damn, damn—just like that, she'd done what she'd sworn she wouldn't do. When she moved to Maryville she'd promised herself no more strays.

"I don't know yet."

"You want me to see if I can find someone who wants to buy a guitar? You won't get much—they're a dime a dozen around these parts—but if you're careful, it'll be enough to get you home."

"The guitar is all I've got," he said with an apologetic smile. "And home is wherever my truck's parked."

Oh, great. She'd been half a minute away from being out the door and she just had to open her mouth. Would she never learn? She stared at him. He wasn't much to look at with his hair going every which way from the bandage at the back and wearing a robe that was several sizes too big, but there was something familiar about him that engendered a comfortable kind of trust, as if he were a compilation of all the friends and neighbors and good old country boys she'd known all her life.

Sooner or later she was going to break down and take him in; it was as inevitable as her picking the one peach in the basket that had a worm in it. "There's a room over the garage at my place. You can stay there if you want. It's nothing fancy, mind you, but I can guarantee it'll be more comfortable than spending the night in your truck."

"Why are you doing this?"

"Probably because I don't have the good sense God gave a gnat. If I did, I would have left your glasses at the desk downstairs and been on my way. But no, I had to come all the way up here to see how you were doing. Stupid me, thinking you might be lonely and appreciate the company."

"I'm sorry. It's just that people who give me things usually want something in return."

If he was looking to have his ego stroked, he'd come to the wrong person. To make sure there was no misunderstanding about her intentions, she made a point of giving him the once-over. "For the life of me I can't think what you'd have that I could want."

"What you're saying is you don't think I'm much of a prize?"

"I don't want to hurt your feelings."

"It's okay. You don't have to say anything more. I have a pretty good idea what I must look like."

She *would not* feel sorry for him. "I suppose there are some ground rules we better go over now that you're going to be staying with me. First off, you've got a week to get back on your feet. If you decide you want to stay around after that, you're going to have to pay for your keep."

"And how much would that be?"

"Two hundred and fifty dollars a month for the room and board"—the figure just popped in her head—"or the equivalent in upkeep and repairs around the place." She was startled to realize she was developing an enthusiasm for the idea. She could use the money more than the labor, but it sure would be nice to have the house fixed up before January rolled around. "I'll credit you five dollars an hour for whatever work you do."

"And this is going to be all right with your grandfather?"

"What's my grandfather got to do with anything?"

"You said it was his place."

"It is, kind of. At least it used to be until he took off for Arizona to find himself a rich widow lady and learn to play golf."

Cole smiled. "Sounds like he got the calling."

"More like he woke up one morning and decided if he didn't use it, he was gonna lose it."

"What if I put in more than fifty hours a month? Are you going to pay me for the difference?"

"I can't. I'm scrambling for every dime I can get my hands on myself. Arnold has some work that needs doing up at the motel, though. You could probably collect a few dollars doing odd jobs for him. It wouldn't be much more than gas money to get you back on the road, but that's all you're looking for, isn't it?"

"I'm not sure what I'm looking for anymore."

It wasn't the answer she'd expected. There was something going on with Neal Chapman. Whatever it was, she didn't want to know. She had her own problems, enough to see her through this lifetime with some left over. To make sure there was no misunderstanding between them, she reiterated, "This is strictly a business deal we're talking about. I'm in the market for a handyman, nothing else."

"The thought didn't even cross my mind. Frankly, Holly, you're not my type."

She almost laughed aloud at the instant, defensive feeling his statement sparked. She should have been reassured that she held no appeal for him; instead she was annoyed. It seemed it was one thing to do the rejecting, quite another to be the one rejected. "Then we should get along fine."

"If you'll wait outside, it won't take me but a few minutes to get dressed."

What he said didn't make sense. She must have misheard him. "What are you talking about?"

"Getting out of here."

"You can't do that." The thought of having someone on her hands who might collapse and go back into a coma, or even worse, terrified her. "The nurse downstairs told me the doctor said you had to stay at least twenty-four hours."

"It was just a bump on the head." He went to the closet and picked up a plastic bag with his clothes in it. "I've had a lot worse."

"Here," she held out her hand, "you can't wear those, they've got blood all over them. I'll take them home and wash them and bring them back in the morning."

He opened the bag and looked inside. Reluctantly, he closed it again and said, "Did you bring the things I had at the motel? There's a change of clothes in the duffel bag."

"I took everything up to the office."

"Could you—"

"I can't go back there tonight. I'm already late for work as it is." Realizing he had no way of knowing what she was talking about, she added, "I work nights as a waitress."

He thought a minute. "All right, I can get there myself. If you'll give me your address, I'll take a cab back to the motel to get my truck and meet you at your house later."

"A cab?"

"Oh, yeah. I guess I would need to borrow a couple of dollars."

"I told you I—"

"Holly," he interjected, "I promise I'll pay you back, double if you want. Please don't fight me on this."

So it was going to be like that, was it? One pathetic little "please" and her resolve disappeared. She pulled the strap of her purse off her shoulder and dug inside for her wallet, took out several bills, handed them to him, and turned to leave.

"The address?" he reminded her.

When she couldn't find a piece of paper in her purse, Neal handed her a scratch pad. "Have Arnold tell you how to get there," she said after writing down the house number and street. She hiked the leather strap back over her shoulder. "If I think of something you need to know, I'll leave a note on the kitchen table."

"That's fine, but how am I supposed to get inside to read it?"

"The back door doesn't lock. It's one of the things I was talking about that need fixing."

"Before you go—"

"Now what?" she said with a show of impatience.

"I just wanted to say thanks."

She didn't want to smile; she felt put out and put upon and was going to have to drive faster than she liked or be late to work because of him, but there was no way she could resist the honesty or depth of feeling in the way he'd said that one magic word. The smile formed and there was nothing to do but add an equally sincere, "You're welcome."

Cole kept his eyes on the road as he passed the hospital on his way into Maryville. He was still a little bemused at how hard the woman in admissions had tried to keep him there knowing full well he couldn't immediately pay for the time he'd already stayed. She told him she'd never heard of anyone signing himself out against the doctor's advice and gave the impression she considered his behavior a personal affront.

He'd caught an image of himself in a glass door as he was on his way to call for a cab. What he saw wasn't impressive. The hour he spent in bureaucratic hell had left him haggard looking, with dark circles under his eyes. Of course the bloodstained clothes, the bandage on the back of his head, and his generally disheveled appearance hadn't helped. But then it was likely that if he'd looked better, the ambulance driver he stopped in the hall to ask about taxi service in Maryville probably wouldn't have taken pity on him and offered to drop him by the motel on his way back to Pigeon Forge. And he wouldn't still have the money Holly had given him.

The road curved. There was a grouping of stately old brick buildings to his left that he assumed was Maryville College. According to Arnold, it was one of the best private schools in the South. He was truly surprised that Cole had never heard of it and was about to recite a list of illustrious graduates when Cole deftly sidetracked him with a question about Holly.

Arnold's answer to Cole's query about how long she'd worked for him was brief and to the point." Two months." Cole waited, but the usually effusive old man showed no inclination to elaborate. Cole tried again, this time with an even more innocuous question about how Holly had come to work at the motel. Arnold said he couldn't rightly remember how their first meeting had come about.

Arnold was obviously protecting Holly. But whether the need was real or came from a feeling he should safeguard his young friend from inquisitive men, Cole couldn't tell. Either way, Arnold made it clear that should Cole's behavior be anything less than proper, he would have him to answer to.

Cole came to the parkway at the bottom of the hill where Arnold had told him to turn left. He entered a residential area with ancient trees that formed canopies over the houses and streets. There were children riding bikes and tricycles without regard to traffic and couples walking hand in hand on the sidewalks. Dogs sat on front porches and halfheartedly barked at passersby. Here and there lights came on behind windows that had been left open with the hope of catching an evening breeze.

The air was heavy and familiar and somehow uniquely southern. There was nothing to compare to it out west.

Tantalizingly elusive memories overwhelmed Cole. He was transported to his childhood, the journey meandering, more sensation than image. He'd never been in this place before and yet he knew it—the houses, the people, their expectations and dreams and hopes. This was a neighborhood where the lock on a back door could be broken an entire lifetime and nothing untoward would happen to the occupants. It was a place where a child was related to the neighborhood, watched and cared for by old and young alike, where wounded knees would be bandaged by a dozen mothers and hunger satisfied in as many kitchens.

Although Cole hadn't experienced such a childhood himself, he had observed others doing so in a hundred small towns throughout the South. What he didn't know for fact, he made up. And then at night he would put himself to sleep imagining he and Randy lived those wonderfully ordinary lives.

He came to the top of the hill where the road dead-ended and he was supposed to turn right. The houses here sat farther back from the road on lots large enough to hold several fruit trees and large detached garages. Holly had told him the house was on the left side of the road, white clapboard with green trim.

What she'd failed to tell him was that every house on the street was either white or cream or beige. Several sported green trim, in shades from apple to avocado, and all were surrounded by bushes and shrubs that were living testimonials to the fertilizer industry, hiding porches and windows and house numbers alike.

On top of everything else, the sun was doing a disappearing act.

After two more trips up and down the street, Cole settled on the house with a laundry line that held only women's clothing. He pulled into the gravel driveway and parked in front of the garage.

Out of habit, he knocked before trying the back door. When no one answered, he went inside, crossed an area that appeared to have been a back porch at one time but had been closed in and turned into a laundry room. He went through another unlocked door and wound up in the kitchen. Despite a large window over the sink, the room was too dark to see anything but shapes. He slid his hand along the wall until he found the light switch. A brass chandelier with three bare bulbs illuminated the spotlessly clean room.

Cole found Holly's note on the chrome kitchen table, sandwiched between milk-glass salt and pepper shakers.

*Neal,*

*We have a slight problem—I forgot the room over the garage is up a flight of stairs and doesn't have a bed. There's a sofa out there, but it's about two feet shorter than you are and you'd have to sleep with either your legs or your head hanging over the end. So, unless you have a thing about privacy and don't intend to follow any of your doctor's orders and would rather sleep on the floor up there (if so, there are sheets and blankets and an extra pillow in the hall closet), you might as well stay in the front bedroom. Actually, you can stay in any bedroom you want except mine.*

*I'll be home around twelve-thirty. Don't wait up for me. Sleep in tomorrow if you can, and we'll talk when I get back from the motel.*

*You can eat anything you can find, which isn't as generous as it sounds, I'm afraid. Like everything else around here, I'm behind on the grocery shopping, too.*

*Holly*

Cole shook his head in disbelief as he read the note. The only thing he could figure was Holly was either some kind of throwback to another era, or impossibly naive. What kind of woman invited a man she knew nothing about into her home to sleep in the bedroom next to hers? For all she knew he could be another Ted Bundy. Someone needed to teach her a thing or two about the real world.

The suggestion of food triggered a feeling of hunger. He'd skipped the hospital's offer of dinner in favor of getting to the motel and then to Holly's while it was still light outside. His gaze swept the kitchen as he tried to decide which cupboard was likely to hold canned goods. He settled on the one over the stove and crossed the worn linoleum to look inside. The knob came off in his hand. He put it on the windowsill and tried, without success, to pry the cupboard open with his fingers.

Cole moved to the next cupboard. There was only one shelf and it held plates and bowls. He peered inside and saw that the hangers for the other shelves had pulled loose.

He moved around the kitchen, opening and closing doors and drawers. Something was broken or missing everywhere he looked. He stood in the middle of the room with his hands shoved in his back pockets and slowly looked around. The place was a disaster. There was paint peeling from the ceiling and the linoleum had a hole worn all the way through in front of the sink.

He could work off a month's rent without ever leaving the kitchen.

# 10

*The smell of bacon drifted* into Cole's room and pushed its way into his subconscious. Not wanting to deal with the disappointment of waking, he put off the aroma to a dream and moved on to something else. But it followed him—through a concert, through New Mexico, and into the bedroom of a run-down white clapboard house with green trim.

As soon as his mind grounded him in the reality of where he was, his eyes came open. He stretched and yawned and reached for his glasses. When he'd settled on the room he would be using during his stay with Holly, he was convinced he was in for a miserable night. The old iron bed had been the better of the two he'd been offered. It had creaked when he sat on the edge and visibly sagged in the middle. But when he actually lay down, the feather pillow had cradled his sore head as if it had been made expressly for that purpose, and the covering sheet had settled around his body like a gentle lover. For the first time in recent memory, he'd found sleep a friend instead of a taunting enemy.

Feeling more rested than he had in weeks, he rolled to his back and was instantly reminded what had led to his being Holly Murdoch's guest. He groaned and sat up, gingerly feeling the back of his head. The amazing part was that he still hadn't developed a headache. As he sat there, he was enveloped by another wave of odors; this time fresh-brewed coffee and toast were in the mix.

He swung his legs over the side of the bed, parted the lace curtains that covered the window, and looked outside. The sun was long up. Holly should have left for work hours ago. He gingerly pulled his shirt over his head and slipped into his jeans, working the buttons as he crossed to the door.

There'd been no evidence of anyone else living in the house when Cole looked around the night before, but then he hadn't opened any of the closets or dresser drawers in the other bedrooms.

Cole reached for the door and pulled up short when another thought struck. What if she'd brought someone home last night? She wasn't his type, but that didn't mean she wasn't someone else's. He'd known lots of guys who went for the solidly built, outdoorsy types.

Now what? He could stay in his room until she left for work, or he could risk embarrassing her and himself by barging in on her company unannounced. Neither choice held much appeal.

His last meal had consisted of a can of ravioli and a diet soda. The promise laden in the smells that drifted through the door was simply too powerful to worry about being embarrassed. If she didn't want him around, he'd be happy to eat in his room.

He turned the knob at the same time a knock sounded.

"Oh," Holly said and took a step backward. "You surprised me."

Cole hiked up his pants. "I was on my way to the bathroom."

"Well, hurry. Breakfast is ready."

"I thought you left early for the motel."

She wiped her hands on the kitchen towel she was carrying. "I finished there an hour ago."

"What time is it?"

"Quarter to twelve."

"You're kidding."

"I was beginning to get a little worried," she admitted. "I figured you were tired, but you did get hit on the head pretty hard. I wasn't too surprised that you were still asleep when I came home from work, but when I got back from the grocery store, I was worried you might have up and died on me."

Cole laughed. "So you decided if the smell of bacon cooking didn't get me moving—"

"Nothing would," she finished for him.

"I'm sorry I scared you." Cole ran his hand through his hair. He was in desperate need of a shower. "I'll be there as soon as I've cleaned up a little."

"I'll give you two minutes and then I'm starting without you," she warned. "I hate cold eggs."

He didn't doubt the threat was real. "Did you make grits, too?"

"You like grits?"

"Hate them."

Finally he got a smile. "I wouldn't say that too loud around these parts if I were you. People have been run out of town for less."

He liked her smile. It was the kind that involved her whole face, not just her mouth. "Thanks for the warning. I'll be more careful from now on."

She started back toward the kitchen. "Just so you know, you've used up half a minute already."

Cole was still tucking in his shirt when he joined her at the table. He had no idea if he'd made the deadline, only that she'd waited. There were platters and bowls filled with scrambled eggs, bacon, fried potatoes, and toast in quantities enough to feed a half-dozen people. A glass of milk and another of orange juice sat in front of her plate. He'd been given the same in addition to a large mug of coffee.

"Dig in," she instructed, and handed him the eggs.

He didn't need a second invitation. Little conversation passed between them as they consumed the meal. Cole couldn't remember ever being as hungry or food ever tasting as good. The bacon was cooked just right, crisp without being burned. The potatoes had thin slices of sweet onion and the bite of pepper applied with a heavy hand. The eggs were fluffy and hot and cooked all the way through. There was real butter and what looked like homemade jam for the toast.

The coffee, however, tasted like hell.

Holly offered him the last piece of bacon.

He held up his hand to ward her off. "I already feel like that guy in *Alien.*"

"I never saw it. I don't like scary movies."

"He had this thing growing in his stomach—"

"I don't like hearing about them either." She got up to take the empty plates to the sink.

Cole helped her clear the table. "You cooked, I'll clean."

"Sounds good to me." She gathered the condiments and started putting them away in the cupboard beside the stove. When she finished, she turned to him. "I know it's not fair, but I can't seem to separate who you are from what you are. I've tried, but when I catch myself thinking you might be different, I start remembering all the guys I've met who were just like you and how wrong I was about them."

"Guys like me? What's that supposed to mean?"

She started to say something and then stopped, waited several seconds, and tried again. "I used to go with a guy named Troy Martin who was a wannabe singer who was convinced he was headed for the big time. When he went on tour he talked me into tagging along. Every town he played we met guys who were on the same road, playing the same fairs and honky-tonks.

"They looked and sounded different, but underneath they were the same. Every one of them was convinced that with the right break, they were going to be the next Cole Webster. I used to listen to them talk. They'd openly admit they would do anything, go anywhere, and step over or on anyone to get where they wanted to go. Their hunger didn't just drive them, it controlled them."

He wanted to tell her she was wrong, to tell her about Buddy and all the other friends he'd made along the way, friends he intended to work harder to keep from now on, but there was too much truth in what she said for him to convince her without telling her who he really was. He filled the sink with hot water and added a squirt of liquid soap. "You can't make it in the business without sacrifice," he said.

"I suppose that's understandable and even okay, as long as you're not the one who's being sacrificed. You can take it from someone who's been there, being tied down on some stone altar with a knife pointing at your chest gets old really fast."

"How do you know this Troy wasn't just your ordinary, everyday jerk? He could have been a mechanic or a grocery store clerk and treated you the same."

"I'd expect you to feel that way," she said without accusation. "After all—" She pulled up short. A strange look passed over her face. "Dammit," she said under her breath. To Cole she said, "I'll be right back."

Puzzled, Cole finished clearing the dishes. He was wiping off the table when he heard a noise coming from the hall bathroom that made him stop. Holly hadn't given any indication she wasn't feeling well, but there was no mistaking the sounds coming from the bathroom. Whatever was bothering her must have come on fast. The breakfast she'd eaten would have satisfied a small construction crew.

And then it hit him what was really going on. He'd seen it too many times to miss the signs.

Disappointment and a peculiar sadness took the bright edge off the morning. He returned to the sink, ran clean water over the dishes he'd already washed, and put them in the drainer.

Holly came back a shade paler and smelling of mouth-wash and toothpaste. Without saying anything, she picked up the towel and began drying a glass. When she reached overhead to put the glass away, her blouse rode up and exposed her waist. Cole saw that her jeans were unbuttoned and the zipper partially open. The sight confirmed his suspicions. He debated saying anything. After all, how she chose to control her weight was none of his business. But then she'd been willing to step in and help him.

"Holly, I know I don't have any right to interfere—"

"Oh, I really love sentences that start that way."

"I only wanted to tell you that I think you're pretty the way you are. Not everyone was meant to be five foot ten and ninety-eight pounds. I know a lot of guys who actually prefer women who have a little meat on their bones. Just because you got involved with someone who didn't, doesn't mean we're all like that."

She gave him a blank stare. "What in the world are you talking about?"

"I know what you just did in the bathroom."

"I'm sorry. I tried to be quiet."

He was taken aback at her ready admission. She couldn't know how serious it was. "What you're doing is stupid, not to mention dangerous. No man is worth it."

She propped her hands on her hips and glared at him. "You're crazy if you think I'm doing this for a man. This was my decision and mine alone. He doesn't know anything about it and I have no intention of ever telling him."

"Then why bother?"

"You think the only reason a woman would decide to keep her baby is to trap a man into marriage?"

"*Baby?*" Cole took a step backward. "You're pregnant? That's why you were throwing up?"

She frowned. "What other reason would I have for getting rid of the breakfast I spent the last half hour cooking and consuming, not to mention that I paid for?"

Cole felt more foolish by the second. "I thought you were trying to lose weight," he mumbled.

"I don't know what it's like where you come from, Neal, but around these parts, a thick waist and trips to the bathroom only mean one thing."

"You're pregnant?" Cole took another step backward.

"It isn't contagious."

"Shouldn't you be lying down or putting your feet up or something?"

She shook her head. "You can't possibly be that backward."

"I've never been around anyone who was pregnant."

"It happens all the time, to lots of people . . . well, women anyway. How is it possible that you've never been around one of us?" And then, as if she'd come up with her own answer, she tensed. This time it was her turn to back away. "Oh, God, I should have known. All the clues were there and I missed every single one. You just got out of jail, didn't you?"

He laughed. "No, at least not the kind you mean."

"There's more than one kind?"

"Those we make for ourselves."

"That's real pretty and would probably make a great song but you're going to have to come up with something better if you intend to stay with me. I have a baby to consider now, or at least I will have in another five and a half months."

She was going to find out about him sooner or later anyway, so he might as well get it over with. He had his mouth open to tell her when an intense feeling of impending loss came over him. The minute she discovered who he was, their relationship would change. She would look at him and talk to him differently. The openness would be gone. "The funny thing about all of this is that I was just thinking last night how crazy you were to let me stay without knowing anything about me."

"Then it shouldn't bother you to tell me now."

She wouldn't let it go until he came up with something. It would be easy to satisfy her with a lie, but he didn't want it between them. He settled for something in between. "I've been a loner most of my life. When I was growing up my father and brother and I moved around a lot. You don't make many close friends with that kind of life-style."

"How do you make a living?"

"With my guitar. You were right about that. I've learned I don't need much," he added with a self-deprecating smile.

"That's all you know how to do?"

"It's what I do best, but I've picked up a few other skills to carry me through."

"Like plumbing and painting and carpentry?"

"Some. I doubt there's anything around here I can't handle." It was close to the truth, if a little misleading.

"Well, you didn't seem all that upset that the police came to question you about the robbery, so I guess you're not some fugitive."

Cole went back to the dishes. He should have felt relief that his half-truths had reassured her, not guilt. After all, it wasn't a sordid past he was hiding. "I thought pregnant women were supposed to wear those T-shirts that had arrows pointing to their stomachs."

Holly picked up another glass from the drainer. "Why spend money on new clothes when I can still fit into the ones I have?"

"You can't be comfortable running around with your pants half undone."

Her hand went to her stomach. "I didn't think it showed."

"It probably wouldn't if you wore longer shirts."

"Could we talk about something else?"

"Sure." He fished the last fork out of the soapy water and pulled the plug. "Who's the father?" he asked.

"That's none of your business."

"The wannabe country music star, huh?"

"Like I said before, it's none of—"

"Did he want you to get rid of it?" Cole was surprised at his own persistence. It wasn't like him to push this way.

She tossed the fork in the drawer and turned on him. "I said I'm not going to talk to you about this."

"If nothing else, he should be helping you out with the bills, don't you think?"

With slow precise movements, Holly folded the towel and hung it over the oven handle. Without looking at him or saying another word, she walked out of the kitchen and into her bedroom.

Cole reached up to rub his neck and snagged the bandage, pulling it loose. Rather than try to get the adhesive to stick again, he took the gauze pad off. Frank would have a fit when he saw that the back half of Cole's head had been shaved again. At this rate, he was never going to get back to his trademark shoulder-length hair, the attribute one less-than-kind critic had declared was his sole claim to fame.

He went to the hallway and stared at Holly's door, trying to decide whether he should apologize for pressing her about something that was none of his business or let time do the apologizing for him. He'd never forced his way into anyone's life before and didn't understand why he'd done so with her.

Hell, there he went again, taking something simple and trying to make it complicated. His interest in Holly was undoubtedly nothing more than the satisfaction of finding someone whose life was as screwed up as his own.

✦　　✦　　✦

Holly rolled to her side, blinked her eyes open, and let out a groan. It was almost two o'clock. Half the day was gone and she still needed to wash her uniform for work that night.

The worst thing about taking a nap in the middle of the day was that no matter how long she slept, it was never long enough. She'd intended only to rest a few minutes while she waited for Neal to clear out of the kitchen, but it seemed that lately all she had to do was prop her head against something and she was out.

The sound of a guitar came to her, and for an instant her heart overruled her mind and she was convinced Troy had somehow found her. Then she realized who and what she was hearing and the hope died. She was angry at the feeling of disappointment. How long did she have to wait to be free of him?

She forced her mind to focus on the music. Neal was playing at songs, strumming chords, and laying out snatches of melodies. Some she recognized, others she was sure she'd never heard before. The unfamiliar ones were probably things he'd written himself. She'd never met a singer who didn't fancy himself a songwriter.

Thoughts of her dirty uniform still sitting on top of the washer intruded and provided the prod she needed to get out of bed. She stopped by the bathroom, then headed for the laundry room. A clicking noise greeted her as she stepped into the kitchen. It was the dryer. Curious, she looked inside and found her uniform, the plastic name tag still attached. After removing the tag, she restarted the dryer and then went to look for Neal.

She found him sitting under the beech tree, his back against the broad trunk, his head turned away from the house. He appeared lost in a world of his own making, bent over his guitar, deep in the music. She took the opportunity to study him unobserved. He wasn't the kind that could make her wish she hadn't gone to the dance with a date, but she would have remembered seeing him there. She'd had girlfriends who went for the moody silent types, mistaking taciturnity for intelligence and sensitivity. Bobbie Jeane Andrews would have locked her boyfriend in the bathroom if she thought it would get Neal to notice her.

Maybe it was the beard that made her wary. She recognized how she felt as a prejudice but couldn't help wondering if the wearer was trying to hide something. Still, she had to admit Neal's beard fit him somehow. It went with his melancholy eyes, made more so by his glasses, and a body so lean it hinted at self-denial. The only thing that didn't fit was the dumb baseball hat he'd had on when he checked into the motel. Why would someone from New Mexico wear a Los Angeles Dodger hat?

She approached slowly and waited for him to notice her before she spoke. "Not bad," she told him.

He lowered the guitar. "Thanks." The corner of his mouth came up in a half smile. "I'm assuming that was a compliment?"

"Actually, you're a lot better than I thought you'd be."

He ran the frets with quick, graceful movements before he gently set the guitar on the grass beside him. "Don't tell me I've been giving off amateur vibes again."

"You have to admit, you don't come across as the most successful musician around." She was glad to see he wasn't the kind who held a grudge. Most men she'd known would have reacted to her anger rather than realizing she had a right to demand her privacy.

"Do you want some help with dinner?" Neal asked.

"You cook, too?"

"Too?"

"I saw that you washed my uniform. Thanks."

"I figured you needed it for work," he said dismissively.

"How come you know how to do all these things?" There was as much unspoken in the query as spoken. In her experience, a man like Neal didn't have to do for himself. There were always plenty of women willing to do for him.

"Question time again, huh?"

"If you'd rather not, it's okay."

"I don't mind. If I do, I won't answer."

"Sounds fair," she said, and lowered herself to sit beside him. Again, a feeling lingered at the back of her mind that there was something familiar about this Neal Chapman. It was easy to imagine him the brother she'd never had, or at the very least, the male cousin she'd never known.

"My mother died when I was seven and my father never remarried. Someone had to learn to do the things she'd done." He plucked a piece of grass, bit off the tender white end, and stuck the blade in the corner of his mouth. "Since my brother was only four at the time, that someone turned out to be me."

"Gosh, seven, that's so young. I was twenty-one when my parents died. I felt so alone then. I can't imagine what it would have been like to lose one of them when I was only seven. It must have been terrible for you."

He studied her. "Twenty-one . . . that couldn't have been too long ago."

"Remember, I'm older than I look."

"Am I supposed to guess?"

She laughed. "Twenty-seven."

"I keep trying to fit you into some familiar corner of my mind," he admitted, "but you're not like any other women I've ever known."

She'd always considered herself painfully ordinary. "How am I different?"

"You know I'm a musician, you distrust me because of it, and yet you let me move into your house."

"That doesn't make me different, it makes me dumb."

"Why did you do it?"

He wasn't going to let it go until she gave him an answer he could live with. She settled on the easy, the obvious one. "I figured I either found a way to get this place fixed up or watched it fall down around me. You happened along at the right time."

Neal gave her a quick smile. "If you're not careful, I'm liable to think you were the one waiting for me outside my room."

Her first reaction was horror that he would suggest such a thing. On its heels came a burst of laughter. "What a great idea. Just think of the possibilities. If my car starts giving me trouble, I could have Arnold keep his eye out for a mechanic."

"I'd skip the mechanic and concentrate on a roofer, if I were you. There's a couple of places that look dicey up there. My guess is they won't make it through another winter. And you could always use—"

Holly heard a porch door slam at the neighbor's house. "Shhh," she told Neal. "I don't want Mrs. Stilltson to hear us talking like this."

It was Neal's turn to laugh. "Do you really think there's anything you could do or say that would sur- prise her?"

"What's that supposed to mean?"

"I picture you as the kind of person who would go walk- ing in the rain to see what it felt like, completely unaware of the uproar you were causing in the neighborhood with your wet T-shirt."

"You're not the first person who told me I can be a little oblivious to things," she admitted. Troy had ragged her about it the entire time they were together. "I really need to do something about it."

"Why?" There wasn't anything flippant or sarcastic in the way he asked; he seemed genuinely curious.

"Because I'm going to be a mother in a few months. Kids need normal mothers, not ones that have all the neighbors shaking their heads."

"Maybe," he said.

It wasn't the answer she'd expected. "Obviously you don't think so."

"It isn't the safe, ordinary things I remember about my mother. It's the time she took me to the beach when a storm was coming so I could feel the wind and see how it caught the tips of the waves. Summer nights we slept on the lawns at motels where we stayed so we could watch for satellites and shooting stars." He smiled. "Everyone thought she was crazy, including my father. He couldn't understand why anyone would pay for the use of a bed and then sleep on the ground. If I ever have a child . . ." He let the thought die unspoken.

"What was your mother's name?"

"Rose."

"That's pretty."

"She didn't like it, but I've always thought it was special."

"We were both named after plants," Holly said.

Cole smiled. "Plants with thorns."

"Maybe our mothers sensed we would need some kind of built-in protection." Holly didn't know what else to say, so she didn't say anything. Several minutes passed before she impulsively told him, "He doesn't know about the baby."

Neal turned to face her. "You just up and disappeared one day without saying anything? Do you think that was fair?"

She'd told Neal something she swore she wouldn't tell anyone and she had no idea why. "You were right about me and the rain and the T-shirt, but you left something out. I have this thing about bad timing. I'd forget that the day I went walking in the rain would be the one I was scheduled to meet someone about refinancing the house. He'd be waiting for me on the front porch when I came back and I'd never once think about how I looked."

Holly hesitated. Telling Neal what had happened between her and Troy wasn't the simple thing it seemed. It was opening a door and giving him access to who and what she was. That kind of friendship carried its own burdens and complications.

But then he would be out of her life in a few weeks and

she would have her privacy back again. In reality, if she was ever going to talk about Troy to anyone, Neal was the perfect someone.

"The day I picked to tell Troy about the baby," she went on, "I was all powdered and perfumed and standing at the door in a skirt that wasn't as long as my heels were high. I'd decided to wine and dine and seduce him before I gave my speech about the joys of fatherhood. What I didn't know was that he'd been working on a speech of his own. His manager had decided that in order to give Troy's career a boost they were going to repackage him in the country hunk mold. Overnight I'd become a liability. He said he was heartbroken about having to give me up, but knew I would understand that his first responsibility was to the people who'd worked so hard to get him where he was."

"That's bullshit," Neal said. "Half the men who hit the charts are husbands and fathers."

"But those weren't the ones Troy and his manager were chasing; it was Cole Webster." A woodpecker's rhythmic beat sounded in the distance. Holly turned to the sound and saw a stricken expression pass over Neal's face. It was gone so quickly she wondered if she'd imagined it. "I heard Troy talk about Cole Webster and how brilliantly he'd been managed and how much he'd done for country music and how talented he was so many times I could mouth the words right along with him." She brought her legs up and put her arms around them, but her burgeoning stomach made the position too uncomfortable to maintain for long.

"I take it you didn't share his feelings?"

"Oh, I suppose Webster's no better or worse than any of the rest. I just got sick to death of hearing about him."

"Damned with faint praise."

"Don't tell me you're after that same brass ring."

"I never have understood why anyone would pattern himself after someone else," Neal said. "Why buy a copy when you can have the original?"

She stretched her legs out and leaned back on her hands. "I don't want you to take this the wrong way, but now that I've gotten to know you a little better, I think I've figured out why you've never made it big."

An amused smile crossed his face. "Oh? And why is that?"

"You're not self-centered enough. In the beginning I thought it was just an excuse Troy used for the things he did, but the longer I was around the business and the more wannabe singers I met, the more I realized that overblown egos were as much a part of them as their guitars."

"Were you this"—he struggled to find a word—"negative the whole time you were with Troy?" he asked carefully.

"No," she admitted. "When we first got together, I was as caught up in Troy's career as he was." The good times were as painful to remember as the bad. "Something magical happens when it all comes together," she said wistfully. "Even for the people who wait backstage. But then I'm not telling you anything you don't already know."

"It's been a long time since I was on a stage."

"The accident?"

He visibly drew into himself, giving the appearance of a startled animal preparing to defend itself. "How did you know about that?"

She was confused by his reaction. "The doctor told me you had some broken bones in your face. He said the scar over your eye wasn't very old." Her explanation seemed to reassure him. "The nurse figured it was a car wreck and that you'd hit the windshield," she went on. "Was that what happened?"

"It was a motorcycle. A tree kept me from going down a canyon."

She winced. "Kind of a mixed blessing."

"I guess you could say that."

"Good thing the guy who stole your wallet hit you on the back of the head."

"Another one of those mixed blessings, I guess."

Holly smiled. "I can see where you might not want too many more. I forgot to ask how you were feeling today."

"Better."

She braced her hand against the tree and got up. "Soup and corn bread okay for dinner?"

He stood next to her and reached for his guitar. "I'll help."

"Don't take what I said about singers personally. It's only my experience and how I feel about things."

"I'm sure you have every right to feel the way you do, Holly."

"But not about you. I wasn't being fair. I can see you're different." A hummingbird swooped past them on its way to the begonia basket hanging on the back porch. Holly had always held a special place in her heart for the tiny birds. As a child she'd secretly believed that seeing one would bring her something wonderful. Now, she had sense enough to enjoy them for what they were.

# 11

*Belinda pulled her Corvette* into her mother's driveway, anxious to drop Rhonda off and be on her way again but knowing better than to let it show.

"Remember, you've only talked to him twice the whole time he's been gone and the second time was an accident. He really called to talk to Randy," Rhonda said, stopping to take a drag of her cigarette. "That has to mean something."

"Thanks for pointing that out to me, Mother." As if she needed someone else around to state the obvious. "But I'm not worried. As soon as Cole is home and I can get him alone, we'll be right back where we were."

"Four weeks is a long time."

"Gee, has it been that long?" Belinda snapped irritably.

"Don't go getting nasty, now. I was simply trying to—"

"I know what you were trying to do, Mother, but you're just going to have to trust me on this one. I've talked to Randy every time he's talked to Cole, and I'm convinced that Cole's leaving had nothing to do with me."

"Don't be so sure, sweetheart. From everything

you've told me, my guess is that when Cole comes back, he's bringing a new broom. You'd better watch yourself when he starts cleaning up around there or you're going to find yourself swept out right along with all the others."

"I might have agreed with you last week, but something's happened since then. I think Cole is going to be surprised by what he finds when he gets here."

"In what way?"

"It's kind of weird. Randy and Frank are actually talking to each other."

"I didn't know they'd stopped."

"I mean really talking. They hardly fight anymore."

Rhonda didn't say anything right away. "Do you know what brought about this change?"

"No."

"I would suggest you find out."

"Why?"

"Think about it, Belinda. With Randy out of the way, who is Frank going to use for target practice?"

"Randy would never let that happen. He's always taken my side over Frank's."

"That was before the rules changed. If you know what's good for you, you'll do whatever you can to get things back the way they were."

"I wouldn't if I could. It's been too nice around there without the constant bickering between those two."

"I'm going to remind you of this conversation when you're back living in a one-room apartment in Burbank."

"You worry too much." Belinda shifted in her seat, as if preparing to leave, hoping her mother would take the hint.

"And I'll keep on worrying until you get Cole to make some kind of a commitment." She took another drag of her cigarette.

"Mother, please. You know how I feel about your smoking in the car."

"I forgot," Rhonda said unconvincingly. She hit the

switch to roll down the window and tossed the cigarette out on the lawn.

"As soon as Cole gets back I'm going to suggest we—"

"You don't want to push too soon," Rhonda said. "The timing has to be just right."

Would her mother never give her credit for knowing what she was doing? "I've got to go, Mom. I'll be late for dinner if I don't get out of here right now."

"Let me know if you hear anything."

"I will."

"Love you." She leaned forward to kiss her daughter's cheek.

"Love you, too," Belinda said, executing a well-practiced air kiss.

An hour and a half later, she was finished with her shower and in the process of hooking the front clasp on her bra when someone knocked on her door. "Belinda, it's Randy. Can I come in?"

"Just a minute." She slipped into her robe as she crossed the room, not bothering with the sash. "As you can see, I'm running late," she said.

"I can come back later," Randy offered.

"What's up?" He seemed uncomfortable at her appearance, which was puzzling considering the number of times he'd seen her sunbathing wearing far less. Still, sensitive to giving the wrong impression, she drew the robe closed and held it in place with her hand.

"Buddy just called. He's heard from Cole."

Randy had broken down the week before and admitted to her and Frank that he'd been in contact with Cole through Buddy Chapman. She'd resented being excluded, but hadn't confronted him. Now she put on her best smile, the one she didn't use very often because it created wrinkles around her eyes, and asked, "So when can we expect him?"

"That's what I wanted to talk to you about."

Her smiled faded at the seriousness of his voice. "Did something happen? Is he all right?"

"As far as I know, he's fine. He's just not coming home as soon as we'd hoped."

"This is starting to get a little old," she said, making no attempt to hide her anger. "Someone needs to tell Cole he's made his point."

"I know you're disappointed, so am I, but there's not much we can do about it."

"I told you once before that I thought Frank might have been right about Cole needing to see a doctor. Now I'm convinced. He isn't acting like someone who's got it together." She was as scared as she was pissed off, and the combination made her indiscreet. "Does he have any idea how hard you and Frank and Janet have been working to save his ass?"

"I've never said anything to him about it, but I'm sure he knows."

"His whole career is going to blow up in his face."

"Obviously he's willing to take that chance."

"And what about all the rest of us—I mean, the rest of you," she amended quickly. "You and Frank have put as much time and energy into Cole's career as he has. How can he be so irresponsible? How can you let him?"

Randy took her arm and gently guided her back into the bedroom, closing the door behind them. "It's okay," he said. "I don't blame you for being scared. I am too. If screaming helps, then go ahead and scream, but not here. You never know who might be listening."

He was right. How could she have been so stupid? Frank screened the hired help and made them all sign agreements that they wouldn't talk to the press, but that didn't mean a thing when money was being waved around. There was too much at stake for her to be so careless. "I just miss him so much there are times I think I'll go out of my mind with worry. My heart would break if Cole were to lose the thing he loves the most because we didn't try hard enough to make him see what he was doing."

"That isn't going to happen. Frank and Janet and I have

been working on something I think will help us pull this off. It's so damn simple, it's brilliant."

"Are you going to let me in on it, or is this something else I can't be trusted to keep secret?" She hadn't meant to sound so bitchy. There was no advantage to alienating Randy. She put her hand on his arm, determined to keep their relationship on firm ground. "I'm sorry. You're the last person I should be taking this out on. Forgive me?"

He put his hand over hers. "There's nothing to forgive."

At the point where the contact would have become intimate instead of friendly, she withdrew and sat on the edge of the bed, patting the spot beside her. "Tell me about your plan."

Instead of sitting next to her, Randy went to the Queen Anne chair in the corner and lowered himself to the footstool, bracing his arms on his knees. "Janet is going to arrange a press conference."

"Another one?"

"This time we're going to go with the truth, or as much of it as we can. The press release will read that after putting twenty-seven years into his career, Cole has become concerned that if he doesn't take some time off just to kick back and relax, he's going to lose his edge. Therefore, while he'll be continuing the behind-the-scenes work on the next album, he will not be touring, doing television or radio shows, or giving print interviews in the immediate future. The official word is that in order to keep lines of communication open between Cole and the press, he's asked me to represent him."

Randy paused as if waiting for her to respond. When she didn't, he added, "We're lucky he's not the first entertainer to suffer burnout and disappear for a while."

"Why you and not Frank?" she asked.

"Dad seems to think they'll accept me more readily than they would him."

"'Dad?' You must be getting along even better than I thought."

"Every once in a while we do some backsliding," he admitted, "but not as much as I would have expected, considering where we were before."

"How nice—for you both."

"A month ago I wouldn't have believed it was possible."

"I guess something positive has come out of Cole's being gone, after all." The words almost stuck in her throat. "Maybe when he hears what you've done and knows he isn't going to be hounded to go on the talk-show circuit when he comes home, it will make it easier for him."

"You really miss him, don't you?" Randy said.

"He's the air I breathe," she told him, not caring how melodramatic it sounded, going for all the effect she could muster.

He got up and put his hand on her shoulder. "Cole's got to have an idea how you feel. I can't imagine he'll stay away much longer."

"I don't know what I'll do with myself if he does."

"Maybe if you keep busy, the time will pass faster."

"It's not that." She dropped her gaze to her lap and stared at the point where the robe opened to expose the top of her thigh. "I didn't want to say anything, but I've run out of money and without Cole here, I don't feel right going to the office and asking them to write a check." Actually, Rhonda had warned her off doing any such thing, saying Frank would be inclined to scrutinize every action and it was important she appear above reproach. But four weeks without any spending money was getting a little ridiculous. She'd had to use her credit card for everything, including the gratuity for the woman who washed her hair at the salon.

"Do you want me to ask for you?" Randy questioned.

It was on the tip of her tongue to tell him yes when she realized in order to do so, he would have to know how much she received. To someone like Randy who thought

Levi's were the ultimate fashion statement and his pickup a financial drain, the five thousand she spent on incidentals every month would seem incredibly irresponsible. "I don't want to add to everything you're already doing for Cole. As long as you think it's all right, I could take care of this myself."

"I don't mind, Belinda. As a matter of fact, I'd like to help you. I know how hard it can be asking other people for money. How much do you need?"

Damn him. He'd put her in a corner. It would be a tactical error to insist she go to the accountant herself after complaining the idea made her uncomfortable.

"Five hundred dollars?" She looked up to catch his reaction. He seemed surprised, but made an effort to hide it.

"I'm going into town in the morning. I'll take care of it then."

"I wouldn't have asked except—"

"You don't have to explain," he said.

She stood to walk him to the door. "I'll be down as soon as I get dressed." He turned to leave. She put her hand on his arm to stop him. "I wish you were my brother."

He touched her cheek with the back of his fingers. "It would never have worked."

She felt a familiar shiver race down her spine. With everything else that was going on in his life, it was nice to know she could still get to Randy. It wasn't fair, she supposed, but then there wasn't anyone else she could practice on without repercussions. Randy liked her, a hell of a lot more than he should, but he would never do anything about it. His loyalty to Cole bordered on the fanatic.

Randy took the back stairs to the kitchen, not wanting to run into his father until he had time to think about the conversation with Belinda. He was having trouble getting a handle on her lately, especially the subtle ways she'd begun coming on to him. She wasn't stupid. She knew his feelings for her went into areas they had no business being. So why the game playing?

She was using him, that much was sure. But to what end? Was she indulging in a little fun at his expense or did she think he would push Cole harder to come home if he thought things were getting out of hand between the two of them? Neither option held much appeal.

And the money thing. She had to think him dim-witted not to see how much she spent on herself every month. Was he supposed to be such a hillbilly that he didn't know the scraps of cloth she called swimming suits cost hundreds of dollars, or that a normal family could have lived comfortably for a year on what she paid for the shoes and purses in her closet? He never shopped in Beverly Hills himself, but he knew enough people who did.

Until now he'd been inclined to give Belinda the benefit of the doubt and blame Cole for her extravagances. God knew Cole was insistently generous with the people he cared about; Randy had been the recipient often enough himself. So why was Belinda being coy and asking for five hundred when that wouldn't see her through one trip into town let alone an entire month?

Randy didn't need, and he sure as hell didn't want, more questions without answers cluttering his life. Not now. If the truth be known, not ever. He wasn't even sure he wanted to keep the jobs he'd taken on recently. Having people come to him to solve their problems or make decisions for them was a lot more work and headache than he'd ever imagined. Randy was a long way from admitting it out loud, but he could feel a begrudging respect growing for his father.

When there were quiet times, which seemed to come less often of late, Randy's thoughts invariably went to Cole and the downside of fame—the work, the expectations, the demands, the crazies that appeared as predictably as the phases of the moon, the larcenous with their extortion schemes, the good charities that wanted his time and money, the bad ones that simply wanted to use him, the merchandizing problems that came with discovering that a hundred thousand coffee cups sold the previous year had tested too high for lead, dealing with the guilt that came with turning down requests to visit dying cancer patients—the list went on and on and on.

Randy no longer wondered why Cole wanted to escape. The question had become why he hadn't gone sooner.

# 12

"*What does it feel like* to be pregnant?" Cole asked. He sent a quick look in Holly's direction before focusing on the hairpin turn ahead.

She stuck her arm out the window and cupped her hand to trap the wind. "Strange."

"How so?" he prodded. She'd fallen asleep soon after they left Townsend, missing most of the trip through the Smoky Mountains. They were on their way to Asheville to clear out a storage unit she'd maintained for the past three years and could no longer afford. He'd been amazed at how soundly she slept curled up on the seat beside him, her head resting against his leg. Every once in a while she would shift position and make soft, unconscious groans of protest over the cramped quarters. But for the most part, she seemed as content as if she were in her own bed. Cole had spent the time remembering and going over the song Randy had left in his truck. Mentally he'd worked out several arrangements but wasn't satisfied with any of them. Even so, it felt surprisingly good to be thinking about music again.

She ran her hand through her tousled hair and turned to look at him. "You want details, or the *Reader's Digest* version?"

"We've got another hour before we get to Asheville, you might as well stretch it out."

"It's pretty boring."

"I don't believe you."

"Now if that isn't a typical male reaction. I'll bet you think I have this inner glow that makes me feel all benevolent and maternal."

"Remember I've been living with you for a week now. If you glow, you save it for when you're at work."

She chuckled. "Actually, I'm worse there. Not at the motel, but at the restaurant. There are times the smell of food makes me so sick to my stomach I feel as green as the stripe on my uniform."

"How long is that supposed to last?" He slowed as he crested a hill, letting his gaze sweep the horizon. The mountains appeared an endless rolling wave cloaked in a mantle of blue-gray mist; their beauty was intoxicating.

"Everyone's different." She pointed to a grassy turnout farther up the road. "Let's stop for a minute so I can get out and stretch."

Cole hit the turn signal, pulled over, and shut off the engine. Because the handle was missing on the passenger side, he got out and came around the truck to open the door for Holly. "It seems a little dumb to put yourself through something like that every night," he said, picking up their conversation again. "Why don't you quit until you're past this stage and then go back?"

"I need the money," she said patiently, as if he were one of the slower pupils in the class. She took his hand but let go the second she was safely on the ground. "I realize there's no reason you should know this, but babies are expensive."

"You mean cribs and clothes and things like that."

"I mean doctors and hospitals and food. The rest is

nice, but not necessary." She pressed her hands to the small of her back and walked over to a low railing.

"What about your insurance?"

She turned, her expression incredulous. "There are times I really wonder about you."

"Now what?"

"Where would somebody like me get insurance?"

It had been a pretty stupid question, considering her circumstances. As kids, whenever he and Randy took off somewhere, they were warned to be careful. In the same breath would come, "Remember, we don't have any insurance. You get hurt and there's no one gonna fix you up." He followed her to the edge of the turnout. "The state?" he suggested.

"You mean welfare."

"Isn't that what it's there for?"

"I pay my own way or I don't go."

It seemed a peculiar sentiment for someone in her position, but Cole didn't think it wise to point out that once she decided to have the baby, she'd given up the option of "not going."

"What do you plan to do when the baby's born? I realize you're as tough and stubborn as they come, but if you're paying for the hospital, that must mean you're planning to take time off to deliver."

"I want to have enough money by then that I can afford to stay home a couple of weeks. After that I'll take the baby to the motel with me. It will be off season so the work won't be more than I can handle right away. I haven't talked to Arnold about it yet, but I don't think he'll mind."

She'd obviously planned for everything, except for the unexpected, like a bout of the flu, a baby that needed special care, clothes for them both, or new tires for her car.

"You thought I was just being nice when I said you could stay at the house with me, didn't you?" Holly continued.

"Actually, it wasn't your handyman abilities I was after, it was your truck. I've been trying to figure a way to get my stuff out of that storage place since I moved into my grandfather's house, and then you came along. Do you know how much they want to rent a truck, not to mention a big burly guy to do the loading and unloading?"

"I hesitate to point this out, but you're still missing the big burly guy."

"You're not so bad. The two of us will have that place cleaned out in no time."

She was determined he see how capable she was, or more to the point, how capable she wanted him to think she was. "How am I supposed to earn my keep if I let you do half the work?"

"You've got plenty of time to do that. Remember you're still on your free week."

"Is Asheville where you and Troy lived?" It was hardly the hotbed of country music, but when you were starting out, you took jobs when and where you could.

"We met there. I was working for the booking agent who handled Troy. We'd been going together for a couple of months when the agent cut a deal for him to open a show for Mandy Lewis after her regular guy got sick. Mandy liked what she saw and decided to take Troy on tour. He asked me to go with him, so I packed up everything I owned and put it in storage. After that he went from one job to another, always hooking up with a bigger star. He was with Emily Thomas when we split."

"Is he any good?"

"You're asking the wrong person." She hedged. "I didn't go to work for the booking agent because I knew anything about music. It was just a part-time job that turned permanent."

"Where is Troy now?"

"He was headed for Nashville last I heard."

Cole figured he'd gone this far, he might as well go all the way. "Did you love him?"

"That's kind of personal, don't you think?"

"Only if you didn't. Then it becomes a question of why you decided to have the baby."

"It wasn't that simple."

"I imagine something like that never is," he said.

"You're forgetting this baby is mine, too."

"Maybe so, but it could have come at a more convenient time. Seems to me you're walking a mighty fine line between making it and ending up on the street."

"What business is it of yours anyway?" He'd plainly hit a tender spot. "Why do you care?"

She had him. How could he explain something to her that didn't make sense to him? "I'm curious why people do things."

"God, you music people are all the same. The only reason you're interested in me is because you think my story might be fodder for a song someday."

Her accusation held enough truth to sting. "If you ever find yourself in one of my songs, I give you permission to sue."

She sat on the railing and looked up at him, a smile playing at the corners of her mouth. Her anger was like lightning, quick and explosive, but short-lived. "All you have is your truck. If I took that, you'd never leave."

"I was thinking more along the lines of my spare T-shirt."

"I'm worth a lot more than a T-shirt," she protested.

"Oh, hell yes." He liked that she didn't back down. "Anyone on the verge of multiplying and dividing has got to be worth twice the normal person."

"That's good," she said.

"Feel free to use it whenever you want."

"And in exchange?"

He grinned. "I get to put you in a song."

"Do you always get what you want?"

Cole thought about her question. "There are some people who probably think so."

"But you don't?"

He tried to brush her off. "Yeah, I guess I do."

"You guess?" She shifted position on the railing.

He hesitated. "I've had a lot of trouble lately figuring just what it is I want."

"That's a luxury I don't have anymore."

Her statement caught him by surprise and made him see how self-centered he'd become. Placed on opposite sides of a scale, his problems wouldn't lift hers off the platform. "I'm sorry."

"I'm not. At least not anymore." She pushed herself up. "As much as I'm enjoying this, if we don't get going, you'll be driving back over these mountains in the dark."

Cole held her door while she climbed in the truck, then he went around to the driver's side. He slid behind the wheel and saw that she was going through the grocery bag that held their lunch. "Hungry?"

"All the time lately."

"I suppose that means you're going to eat something now, in the truck, while we're still on this narrow winding road?"

"I'll just have a banana."

He turned the key and waited while the truck completed its familiar sputtering start. "How far should I go before I start looking for another place to pull over?"

"I'm getting a lot better," she assured him.

After checking behind him, Cole eased onto the road. "Better than what?" he muttered.

"I heard that."

Ten minutes later they stopped again. Holly was bent over beside a stand of mountain laurel, holding her stomach while Cole held her shoulders. He had a roll of paper towels tucked under his arm. Several yards away a cedar waxwing watched them, its head cocked in curiosity.

Standing around while someone emptied their stomach wasn't a new experience for Cole or a particularly off-putting one. Randy's drinking years had left Cole both experienced and immune.

Holly straightened slowly. "I don't want to hear it," she said and held out her hand.

Cole tore off a section of towels and gave it to her. "You never did finish telling me what it's like to be pregnant."

She gave him a scathing look. "It's charming. Can't you tell?"

Cole smiled as he put his arm around her, pulled her into his side, and walked back to the truck. "Maybe we should save it for later."

The sun rode low in the sky by the time they reached the laurel thicket the second time that day. Cole had cut his speed considerably, hoping it would lessen the strain on the old truck from the weight they carried.

Holly had gone at the packing as if it were a puzzle, fitting each box and piece of furniture into the next, building a solid, compact unit. What she couldn't fit in was stacked to the side for pickup by a local charity.

"Have you figured out what you're going to do with all this stuff when we get home?" Cole asked.

She finished a yawn before answering. "Store it in the garage until I can go through it and mark prices for the sale."

"How much do you think you'll make?" Most of the furniture was secondhand, things she'd picked up at garage sales and flea markets; the rest had come from discount stores. The boxes were filled with kitchen and bathroom supplies.

"I'm hoping for five hundred, but I'll be happy with half that."

Randy carried more in pocket change; Frank paid more for his shirts. And Belinda . . . "That's a month's rent for me," he said. It was the only contributing comment he could make.

"Not this month. What you did today knocked at least a week off your rent."

Cole did some quick calculations. They'd left Maryville at five that morning. He glanced at the dashboard clock. It was closing on nine—they'd be lucky to be home by midnight. Another hour or so to unload—roughly twenty hours. At five dollars an hour, she owed him more than a week. If there were any way to point out her miscalculation without seeming as if he was complaining, he would have teased her about it.

As if she could read his mind, Holly broke in with, "Maybe we should make it two weeks."

"Whatever you say."

"I'm not being generous." It was said as if she were making a confession. "I like having you around a lot more than I thought I would."

He gave her a quick smile. "And you figure I'm not going to leave as long as I've got room and board paid ahead?"

"Something like that."

He reached down and caught her hand in his and gave it a squeeze. "I like you, too."

She didn't say anything for a long time, then looked at him and said self-consciously, "I guess I needed a friend. I just didn't know that I did until you came along."

It was so damn tempting to have Randy send the money Holly needed. She could stop work and stop the constant worry about whether she was going to be able to pay the bills. She could get whatever she needed for herself and for the baby and maybe even enjoy what was left of her pregnancy.

But if he'd learned nothing else about Holly, he'd learned he had about as much chance getting her take unearned money as he did convincing her that her life would be easier if she gave the baby up for adoption. She was as passionate about controlling her own life as she was possessive about her unborn child. He innately knew that for him even to mention either possibility would shake their newfound friendship.

Someday—his big fear was that it would be sooner than their fledgling relationship could handle—he was going to have to tell her who he was. Frank and Janet weren't going to be able to keep the press at bay forever. When the news finally did break, he was either going to have to go back and try to pick up the pieces or knowingly and consciously let his career die an inglorious death.

Cole rounded a curve and caught his breath at the sight that greeted him. He slowed and pulled off the road. "Have you ever seen anything as beautiful?" he said to Holly.

A break in the trees formed a window to let them see the sun bleeding into the horizon. The smoky mist that lay blanketed between the rolling mountains looked like glowing embers in an enormous fireplace. The near hillside reflected brilliant orange, the next copper, the next a dark gold. At their back and sides the forest was green and lush and alive with the sounds of birds and insects.

"It's been a long time since I stopped to look at a sunset," Holly told him.

"How could that happen?" It wasn't an idle question; he really wanted to know.

"I've been so busy—"

"It has to be more than that," he insisted. "How long does it take to look at a sunset?"

Her eyes mirrored an inner effort to find an answer. "I don't know. Maybe it was that I didn't want to see."

"Why?"

"There are some things that are meant to be shared."

Cole felt like kicking himself. Without saying anything more, he got out of the truck and freed the blanket they'd wrapped around the coffee table.

Curious, Holly stuck her head out the window to see what he was doing.

"It's time you started watching sunsets again," he said and opened her door. "That kid of yours needs a mother who pays attention to such things." He tucked the blanket under his arm and reached for her hand. When they'd made their way across the roadway to the grassy area, he gave a disapproving sound. "I can see I've got my work cut out for me."

"Now what?"

"You didn't look both ways." Cole felt a swell of pleasure when the teasing reprimand elicited a laugh.

"I thought you said you didn't have any kids of your own."

He spread the blanket on the embankment. "My brother became my responsibility when my mother died."

"Where was your father?"

"Mentally or physically?" The question hung between them until Cole added, "At least he stuck around. I have to give him that much."

"Some men don't know how to be fathers." She sat down and motioned for him to sit next to her.

Cole lowered himself to his haunches and gazed at the setting sun. "Men like Troy?"

"Blaming him for the way he is makes about as much sense as yelling at a bull for not giving milk."

"He might have surprised you," Cole said.

She leaned back on her elbows. "That will forever be one of the great mysteries of my life."

"It doesn't have to be. Nashville isn't that far away."

"I'm ancient history to him, a closed book, a canceled sitcom."

"Why are you so damn stubborn when it comes to him?"

"Why are you so damn pushy?"

"If it were my baby, I'd want to know."

"Even if you had someone new on your arm?"

"What makes you think—"

"The Sunday supplement in *The Tennessean*. According to their 'inside sources,' Troy Martin and Emily Thomas have become an item."

A stabbing pain shot up Cole's leg. He rocked off his

haunches and settled beside her. "That didn't take long."

"My first mistake was taking up with Troy. I'm not about to make the second by letting him know I'm going to have his baby. What if he did hit it big one day and decided he liked the idea of being a daddy? Can you imagine the custody battle? There I would be in one corner with one of those lawyers who advertise on late-night television while he was in the other corner with some hotshot who looked down on people like me from penthouse offices. No, thank you. I have nothing to gain by telling him and everything to lose."

"What gives you the idea Troy's going to make it big?"

"His singing might not be anything special, but he has a knack for picking hit songs. He can buy a CD the day it's launched and tell which songs should be released as singles, which ones will most likely be released, and which ones will make it to the top."

"That's quite a skill."

"But that's not the main thing he has going for him. He's as thirsty as a man a week lost in a desert. He'll go right over anyone or anything in his way and never feel the bump."

"But you stayed with him." He didn't ask why, leaving that to her.

"What can I say? You make excuses for people when you think you're in love."

Cole had known a lot of people in the music business like Troy Martin. They confused the necessity for a thick skin and tenacity with ruthlessness and egotism. "I have a feeling Troy's going to find the going a little tougher in Nashville. Those people can take care of themselves."

"It's an ugly business with mean-spirited people and I don't want my baby anywhere around it."

"You're painting with a mighty broad brush."

"I'm sorry, I know I'm probably stepping all over your dreams, but someone like you doesn't stand a chance with those people, Neal. Country music has this squeaky-clean image, but it's a lie. I've seen performers high on everything from alcohol to crack cocaine. And even with all that's been written about AIDS, there are still some of them crazy enough to sleep with any female who can make it backstage. For every musician who gets a recording contract there are a thousand just as talented who—"

"Why should the people in country music be any different from the rest of the population? I'll give you there might be a few more who go off the deep end," Cole said.

She turned to look at him. "But it doesn't make one lick of difference to you when you're around them, does it?"

"Watch the sunset, Holly."

"If my kid ever so much as brings a guitar in the house I'm going to ground him for a year."

"That's probably the one sure way to have him grow up wanting to be just like his father."

She collapsed backward and let out a frustrated groan. "This parenting stuff is hard."

"Especially, I would think, when you're trying to do it alone."

"One thing for sure, I'm going to make sure he sees lots of sunsets."

Cole lay down beside her on the blanket. Their arms and hands touched. Holly's fingers closed around his. They were friends sharing a quiet moment. "Just give him lots of love and attention. It's got to be more important than being right all the time."

"Is that what your mother was like?"

"It's the way I remember her."

"I know my mom and dad loved me, but they weren't the kind to show it." She moved her head so that it was leaning against his shoulder. "I don't care if it spoils my baby rotten, I'm going to pick him up every time he cries."

"What if you get one who never cries?"

"Then I guess I'll just have to give him a pinch now and then."

"Sounds like good solid parenting to me."

Holly's hand tightened around Cole's; her nails dug into his palm.

"What's wrong?" he asked.

"There's something crawling on my foot. Please, get it." She shuddered. "And don't tell me what it is."

Cole sat up, spotted a quarter-sized beetle making its way across her ankle, plucked it off, and tossed it down the hill. "It was a butterfly looking for a place to bed down for the night," he told her.

She worked her way up to a sitting position. "Thanks, but I can always tell when someone's lying to me. I have this built-in thing that goes off like an alarm clock."

He shook off a twinge of guilt as he stood and held out his hand. "I appreciate the warning."

Holly brought the blanket up front with her when she got in the truck. They hadn't gone five miles and she was sound asleep again.

Cole turned on the radio for company and was startled to hear a song from *Silver Linings*. Obviously they'd gone ahead with the release plans despite the furor the record company must have created when they discovered their top producer wasn't going to be making the prescribed publicity rounds. Yet more guilt hit Cole when he thought what it must have been like for Frank and Janet to launch *Silver Linings* without his help.

For the next ten miles Cole tried to convince himself Frank had gone ahead with the release for self-serving reasons. But no matter which direction he chose to come at it, he reached the same conclusion. It was Cole's career Frank was trying to save, not his own. If Webster Enterprises fell apart tomorrow, there would always be someone willing to hire a behind-the-scenes man like his father. Hell, they would be lining up for the opportunity.

Cole rhythmically tapped the heel of his hand against the steering wheel in frustration. He didn't want to think about how irresponsibly he was behaving or that the people he'd left behind in California were worrying about him or that dozens of employees counted on him.

What he did want was a little more time, a few days, a week at the outside. Maybe by then he would find a way to help Holly, a way to sidestep her stubborn insistence on making it alone.

# 13

*Because of the time* difference between Tennessee and California, Cole had to wait until Holly left for work at the restaurant the next day before placing his call to Randy. He'd called Buddy collect from phone booths twice in the past week, but it was the first time he'd tried to call the house since the robbery. As luck would have it, Frank answered.

"Hello," Frank said, his tone uncharacteristically pleasant.

"Do you still have the phone trap on the line?" Cole asked, fighting the old anger.

"I had a feeling it was you."

"Is the trap still there?" Cole persisted.

"No, I had it taken off after your last call."

Frank was eminently capable of doing something behind his sons' backs, but as far as Cole knew, he had never lied to either of them when asked a direct question. "Is there anything else going on that I should know about?"

"I take it you want to know if I'm still trying to find you?"

"Are you?"

"No."

The news didn't bring the reaction Cole would have expected. "Is Randy there?"

"Hold on, I'll get him for you."

"Wait," he said. There really wasn't any reason he couldn't tell Frank what he was going to do.

"I'm still here."

"I heard the single on the radio."

"I'm sorry. I wanted to talk to you before we released it, but there was no way I could put it off any longer."

"I figured as much."

"The video launches next Wednesday."

The conversation had taken on a surreal quality, as though everything was normal between them. There was no hostility or anger in their voices, nothing to indicate the intense pressure they were both under. "I've reached a decision."

There was a long pause. "So that's the reason you called?"

"I want you to announce I'm suffering from exhaustion and that I'm going to take some time off."

The air between them almost crackled with tension. "How long?"

"Six months," Cole said.

Frank gasped but refrained from saying anything. Cole was as surprised by his announcement as his father obviously was. He had no idea where the figure had come from. When he'd picked up the phone, he'd been thinking two weeks.

"Does that include the time you've already been gone, or are you talking six months more?"

"More."

"All right," Frank said after a long silence. "If that's what you want, I'll do what I can at this end. It fits in with the plan we've already been tossing around here. You do realize you're talking about being gone from your music almost a year, Cole. Maybe it'll work, maybe it won't."

It was not the reaction Cole had expected. A cold chill crept up his spine. "Are you all right?"

"Me? I'm fine. What makes you think I'm not?"

"Because you should be fighting me on this."

"Is that the reason you're not coming back?" Frank asked. "Because of me?"

"You know it's more complicated than that."

"Well then, would my fighting you do any good? Would it make you come home any sooner?"

"No," Cole told him.

"Maybe I'm just tired of doing battle with you, Cole. If you haven't figured out yet what you're doing and you aren't scared shitless over the chances you're taking with your career, I don't know what more I can say or do to get through to you."

Cole took his glasses off and laid them on the table. He rubbed his eyes and the bridge of his nose, then pressed his palm against his forehead. He was so goddamned tired of being tired. "I do know what I'm doing, Frank. I think about it all the time. The trouble is I can't seem to find it in me to care if everything falls apart."

"I don't want you to wake up one morning and decide you want what you let slip away," Frank said.

The statement was charged with emotion, but Frank's voice was flat, as if he truly had given up the fight. Cole didn't recognize this defeated man masquerading as his father, and he didn't trust him. While the sentiment was laudable, lions only lay down with lambs on Christmas cards; in the real world, the lamb was lunch.

"I'll get Randy for you," Frank said.

Before Cole had a chance to reply, his father was gone. Randy came on the line a few minutes later.

"Dad told me the news," he said, skipping the greeting. "Jesus, Cole, why six months?"

"I don't know. It just seems like a good round number, I guess."

"Belinda's going to throw a fit when she finds out. Or were you planning to have her join you?"

A weight descended on Cole. He'd forgotten all about Belinda. How was that possible? "She wouldn't like where I am."

"Are you still in Tennessee?"

"Yes."

"Nashville?"

"God, no. I'm staying away from places anyone might expect to see me. The only time I had any trouble on the road was when I went into a record store that had this stupid life-size cutout of me by the register and a boot store that had my picture hanging all over the walls."

"You keeping your hair short?" Randy asked.

Cole touched the back of his head. "Yeah. As a matter of fact, I got it chopped off again about a week ago."

"Cole, have you thought about what you're doing? Are you sure what you've got here is so bad that you don't ever want to come back to it?"

"Sounds as though you've been talking to Dad."

"Yeah, a little."

"Since when?" Cole had meant the statement as a joke.

"I think your leaving did something to him. He's changed."

"Come on, Randy. People don't change, at least not people like Frank. He didn't get what he wanted one way, so he's just trying another."

"I don't know. Maybe you're right. But that's not why you called. What do you want me to do? Send money? You don't have to tell me where you are. I could send it to Buddy and he could see you get it."

The idea had appeal. "Maybe it would be better if we kept Buddy the middleman. That way Dad couldn't pressure you to tell him where I am."

"He won't do that. Not anymore. But I think you're right about it being better if I don't know myself. It makes things with Belinda easier."

Cole felt as though he and Randy no longer formed a united front where Frank was concerned. It wasn't that he believed Randy now sided with their father. It was more a feeling that the three of them had shifted into a triangle. "I've been meaning to talk to you about the demo tape you left in your truck. Did you ever get hold of the writer for me?"

"He was really excited that you liked his stuff."

"I don't feel right asking him to hang fire while I'm out here screwing around, but I hate to give up that song."

"Don't worry about it," Randy assured him. "There isn't a songwriter I know who wouldn't be willing to wait six months to have you record one of his songs."

"Assuming I'm still in the business by then."

"You will be. It's in your blood. Besides, you don't have the training to do anything else."

"Now you sound like Frank again."

"You can't ignore everything he says just because he's the one saying it."

"I can't believe what I'm hearing," Cole said. "Has he been brainwashing you?"

Randy's answering laugh was laced with irony. "Now you're beginning to sound like me."

"I'm serious about the song, Randy. It means a lot to me."

"Stop worrying, this guy is as anxious to work with you as you are him. He even sent another demo tape the other day."

"Good." As much as he disliked bringing up what he would say next, it had to be faced. "I don't know what to do about Belinda."

"I guess you have to just tell her the way it is and then stand back. She's not going to be thrilled at the news, but she'll come around. She knows how unhappy you've been."

Randy had misinterpreted Cole's concern. He assumed Cole was afraid of losing Belinda when in reality Cole felt he had no right to ask her to wait for him the six months he would be gone. To do so implied a commitment he wasn't ready to make, to her or to himself. Cole decided to let it go. "Is Belinda there now?"

"She met Rhonda for lunch and was going to do some shopping afterward. She said something about the fall styles coming out weeks ago and how far behind she was."

It was the first time Cole had heard Randy say anything approaching disapproval where Belinda was concerned. "Tell her I'll call again in a couple of days."

"How much money should I send through Buddy?"

"Five, six hundred."

"Why so little?"

"I'm going to have trouble explaining that much if I get caught with it."

"What in the hell does that mean?" Randy asked. "Are you in some kind of trouble?"

"Only the kind I made for myself. The people here think I'm a drifter who's down on his luck."

"It'll be interesting to see how they react when they find out the truth."

It wasn't something Cole wanted to think about right then. "Don't give up on me, Randy," he said impulsively.

"Now why would I do that?"

"I don't know. I just don't want things to change between us. This trip has brought back a lot of memories about the things we went through when we were growing up. It's made me realize how important you are to me."

Randy made a gagging sound.

Cole laughed.

"That's better," Randy said. "You were beginning to worry me." And then more seriously, "Change isn't always bad, Cole."

"Why don't you tell that to Frank?"

They'd said their good-byes when Cole remembered one more thing he wanted Randy to do for him. "When you send the money . . ."

"Yeah?" Randy said.

"Send the tape with the new songs, too." He could almost feel Randy's smile over the phone.

"You can't wire packages, Cole."

"Then have Buddy send it general delivery."

"Boy, you really do like this guy's work."

Cole didn't answer right away. "I have a feeling he could be the key, Randy."

This time there was no addendum to the good-bye. Cole hung up and still had his hand on the receiver when the phone rang. "Hello?"

"Neal, it's Holly. I've been trying to get you for the last half hour."

"A friend was expecting me. I had to let him know I wouldn't be coming his way after all." He'd hoped to "earn" enough money to cover the call before having to tell her about it. "Why have you been trying to reach me? Has something happened?"

She ignored his question and asked one of her own. "What are you doing?"

"I'm—"

"Never mind. I want you to get down here as fast as you can. And bring your guitar."

"Why?" he asked cautiously.

"I just found out Leroy fired the singer who's been working here. Frankly I don't blame him. I would have fired the guy a long time ago. Anyway, I said I had a friend who played fantastic guitar who desperately needed a job. I told him you could sing, too. Can you?"

"A little," he hedged. "Holly, I don't think this is a very good idea."

"For heaven's sake, this could be the break you've been looking for."

"Meaning people in the music business scout your restaurant?" Hard to believe, but then Maryville was on the way to one of the largest resort areas in the state.

"No, it's mostly locals," she admitted. "But that doesn't

mean it couldn't happen. Remember, success is where preparation meets opportunity."

Cole almost laughed out loud. "Where did you hear that?"

"Troy's manager used to say it all the time. He was one of those people who have a cliché to cover every occasion. But just because it came from him doesn't mean it isn't true."

"I haven't done a live performance in a long time, Holly. I'm not sure—"

"Don't give me that. I've heard you play and you were fine. Besides, you're not following much of an act."

He'd carried the humble part as far as it would go. To continue would only make her suspicious. "I'll be there as quick as I can."

"Just so you know, your meal's included and you don't have to pool your tips."

"It sounds great," he said.

"See, I told you things would work out."

"It's a little early to start celebrating. I don't have the job yet." And he would do whatever it took to make sure he didn't get it.

The restaurant, Leroy's World Famous Barbecue, was located across the street from Foothills Mall, the city's main shopping area. Cole pulled into the parking lot and felt a peculiar knotting in his stomach. The idea he could be feeling stage fright was so bizarre, he dismissed it out of hand.

Holly must have been watching for him because she met him at the door, taking his arm and steering him around tables. Finally she stopped and pointed.

"Over there." She indicated a small platform, raised about a foot off the floor. A backless stool, an artificial plant, a tip jar, and a microphone were sitting on the platform; a recessed ceiling light illuminated the corner.

"Where's Leroy?"

"In his office."

"Is that where he wants me to audition?"

She grinned. "You don't have to audition. You've already got the job. Leroy said if you were good enough for me, you were good enough for him."

Now what? He either walked out and left Holly to explain his strange behavior to Leroy, or he got up on the makeshift stage and gambled that someone would recognize his voice and then him.

"What's wrong?" Holly asked. "I thought you'd be excited about the chance to earn some money."

He had a hollow feeling in the pit of his stomach. "It's been a long time."

"Just play the same songs you were playing in the backyard the other day, and you'll do fine. This is a real forgiving crowd."

He glanced around the room. Only two tables held families and the rest were couples, most of them under thirty-five—men and women who knew and liked "new" country, who could easily have come to this particular restaurant as much for the entertainment as the food. The hollow feeling spread; his heart beat faster.

Holly put her hand on his arm. "Neal?"

And then he knew what it was. "Unbelievable," he said softly to himself.

"What?" Holly questioned.

"It's really happening. I've got a case of stage fright."

"Is that all?"

"It's been so long I nearly forgot what it was like."

She sent a glance back toward the kitchen and gave him a not-so-gentle nudge toward the stage. "It'll go away as soon as you start playing."

But he didn't want it to go away. The nervousness, the anticipation, made him feel alive. He ran his thumb across his palm. It was damp. He looked at Holly and smiled. There was no way she could comprehend how special the gift was that she'd given him. The possibility of being discovered was nothing in comparison. "Thanks," he said simply.

She gave him another push. "Thank me later, Neal. I've got to get back to work."

Impulsively, he bent and kissed her cheek.

Her hand came up and touched where his lips had been. She flushed and looked unsure what to do next. "I just got you a job," she told him, "not a winning lottery ticket."

"And I was just thanking you." The last thing he wanted was to screw up their friendship with anything personal.

"Break a leg."

He laughed. "I already did."

"Well then, break the other one." She turned and took off at a near run toward the kitchen.

Cole removed his guitar from its case, checked the tuning, then adjusted the microphone and the stool. Finally, he took Randy's cap from his back pocket, put it on, and pulled the bill down to throw a concealing shadow over his face. Physically, he'd come to rely on the scars, the altered shape of his nose, the haircut that had turned his hair from sun-bleached blond to dark brown, the glasses, and a week-old beard to protect him from discovery. There was nothing he could do to disguise his voice without being obvious.

If this was to be the end of his anonymity, at least he could go back to Los Angeles knowing it was still possible to feel a sense of anticipation over a live performance. It wasn't everything he'd hoped for, but it was something.

He hiked himself up on the stool, nervously cleared his throat, and started playing "When I Think of Yesterday," a song he'd written for his third album. It had been dropped in favor of a rodeo song that Frank and the A & R people at the record company thought would give the release a better balance. The cut had been floating around ever since, always in the running to be included when they were putting together one of the new albums, always losing out to something more commercial.

He'd played the guitar twice since the accident, but his singing had been limited to accompanying songs on the radio. A shiver of fear splayed goose bumps over his arms as he opened his mouth and began.

Not bad. He wasn't at his peak, but he'd done worse, like the night they were on the bill with three other bands at a honky-tonk on the Texas Panhandle. To kill time between sets, Randy challenged him to a drinking contest. When it was their turn to go on for the last set, the microphone was the only thing that had kept him upright.

Cole neared the end of the first chorus and was tempted to gauge the crowd's reaction, but changed his mind at the last second. The longer he kept himself closed off from them, even if only in his own mind, the longer he remained free. He ended the song with a short riff, looked up, and almost fell off the stool in surprise.

No one was looking back. They were cutting meat and eating potatoes and drinking coffee and talking to each other, but they weren't clapping and they sure as hell weren't caught up in having a celebrity in their midst. He might as well have been invisible, the source of piped-in music, a jukebox in the corner. He tapped the microphone with the tip of his finger to make sure it was working. It was. He scanned the room and saw Holly standing beside one of the tables, a pencil in one hand, a pad of paper in the other. She was as oblivious to him as everyone else.

Finally she glanced in his direction, smiled, and gave him a quick thumbs-up signal. If she'd heard him, everyone else must have, too. For cryin' out loud, what was it with these people? Were they so far out of step they didn't recognize Cole Webster when they heard him?

The thought had the same effect as dunking his head in a watering trough. Cole smiled. The smile became a chuckle and then a laugh. Now he had people staring at him. Still, he couldn't stop.

Holly came over, maneuvering around the tables with

sure, quick steps. She put her hand over the microphone and asked, "Are you all right?"

Cole nodded and tried to look serious, but it was useless. Another wave of laughter hit and he was off.

"Is it your head . . . where the guy hit you?" Holly whispered.

Finally it was the flash of fear he saw in her eyes that sobered him. "Something just struck me funny."

"Maybe it was too soon for you to go back to work. Do you want to take a break?"

"I'm okay . . . really."

"Are you sure?"

He gave her his best attempt at an Italian accent. "What'sa matter? You never heard no one laugh before?"

She took a step backward. "I won't be far."

He liked that she was concerned about him. He adjusted the guitar and strummed a soft chord. "I'll call if I need you."

Her smile was quick and perfunctory and never reached her eyes.

Cole looked at all the people who weren't looking at him. One way or another, he was going to make them sit up and take notice.

It was ten minutes after midnight when Cole put his guitar in its case and called it a night. He'd played every song he'd ever recorded, several of Garth Brooks's, ten vintage Vince Gill, three Kathy Mattea, and four Mary Chapin-Carpenter. None brought more than a smattering of applause. Leroy's World Famous Barbecue was the hardest room he'd ever worked and he couldn't remember the last time he'd had as much fun.

Leroy Higgins signaled to him from across the room where he was talking to one of the waitresses. "Wait up a minute," he said.

Cole climbed back up on the stool and folded his arms over the top of the guitar case. From what Cole had seen that night, Leroy had taken it on himself to personally dispel the notion that all fat men were jolly. It wasn't that smiles didn't come easily to him, it was just that they were an affront to his sensibilities.

The conversation ended and Leroy walked the woman to the front door, his arm resting lightly across her shoulders. He held the door for her and watched while she walked to her car, then headed toward Cole. "Got a minute to talk?" he asked as he neared.

"Sure," Cole told him.

Leroy pulled out a chair and sat down. "You're a hell of a guitar player."

"Thank you."

"But—I hope you don't mind some advice."

"No, go ahead." Cole could feel a smile coming on. He reached up to scratch his stubbly beard, then propped his chin on his hand, covering his mouth with his fingers.

"I know it's tempting to give a crowd what you think they want, but playing songs someone else made famous ain't doin' you one lick of good. You need to work on a style of your own, and stop tryin' so hard to sound like Cole Webster. You ain't as pretty and you don't sing as good, but you play the guitar a hell of a lot better. It's something worth buildin' on. I know it probably don't seem fair, especially with you lookin' a little like him and all, but Webster got there before you, kid, and he ain't about to move over to give you his space. You're gonna have to find one all your own if you want to make it in this business."

How strange to have his own words used against him. "Does this mean I'm fired?"

Leroy brushed something white off his dark blue slacks. "Hell no. Like I said, I think you've got talent. You just need to figure out what to do with it." He pointed to the jar at Cole's feet. "How much you make tonight?"

Cole didn't want to tell him.

Leroy read his reluctance correctly. "It ain't no big secret it wasn't much."

"Three dollars and fifty-seven cents."

"Who was the cheap screw that stuck you with the pennies?"

"I don't know."

"Well, don't you worry about it none." He reached in his pants pocket, brought out a wad of money, peeled off several bills, and handed them to Cole.

"You don't have to do that," Cole told him.

"You tellin' me you're willin' to work for nothin'?" Leroy said gruffly. "Holly thinks you're a whole lot smarter than that."

"Who's talking about me?" Holly demanded.

Cole glanced up and saw her heading their way. She looked tired. After the night she'd put in, he was surprised she was still upright. "Shouldn't you be on your way home?" he gently chided.

"I will be as soon as I finish."

"There ain't nothin' needs doin' around here I can't take care of," Leroy told her. "Now you do what Neal says and get on home."

Holly propped her hands on her hips and looked from Leroy to Cole and back again. She tried to appear mean but couldn't keep the impish challenge from her eyes. "Get this straight you two, no one tells Holly Marie Murdoch what to do."

"I wouldn't dream of it," Cole said.

She reached for the tie on her apron. "As long as we've got that worked out, I think *I'll* call it a night."

"Good idea," said Cole. "Glad you thought of it." Her answering smile was warm and intimate and made him feel a part of something special.

"Good night, Leroy," she said.

"Drive careful, Holly." Leroy stood and held out his hand to Cole. "See you tomorrow night?"

"I'll be here," Cole said.

# 14

*Cole took a step back* to study the cupboard with a critical eye. The door still wasn't square. Worse yet, he didn't think the plug he'd fashioned to reinforce the wood was going to hold the weight long. It looked as if he'd have to move the hinge after all. Which meant the cupboard on the other side of the sink wouldn't match if he didn't move its hinges, too. Both would look like hell unless he stripped and sanded the finish and started all over with a primer and a couple of coats of paint. What had begun as a simple project to get the door to close properly was becoming a major renovation.

Holly opened the back door and stuck her head inside. She wiped the perspiration from her temple with the back of her hand and said, "Are you at a stopping place?"

"What do you need?"

"Your help for a couple of minutes. I can't get the dresser on the truck by myself."

"What dresser? And what truck?"

"Whose truck do you think?" she countered. Before he could say anything, she went on, "A couple of days ago a guy who runs a secondhand store in Alcoa came into the restaurant. He said he was interested in my furniture. I thought since both of us had the day off, we could take some of the things over and see what he's willing to give me for them. I know I'd probably get more selling it myself, but then that's what I thought when I sold my CD collection and found out later that I could have made twice as much if I'd gone to a music store where they handle used CDs."

He considered giving her his speech about the resale of CDs and how it was hurting the music industry, but decided to save it for another time. "It sure would be a lot easier if you could unload everything at once."

"Best of all, I could pay the rest of what I owe to the hospital."

Cole slipped the screwdriver he'd been using into his back pocket and followed her out of the house. Thoughts of cannibals and big metal cooking pots hit as he stepped into the backyard. For days he'd told himself it wasn't the heat but the humidity. He was convinced he'd been in more comfortable saunas.

Holly got to the garage door and had it open before he could tell her that if she didn't stop lifting things, she was going to hurt herself. She didn't, of course, and wouldn't have listened to him even if he'd managed the warning.

Until then, other than unloading the things they'd retrieved from Asheville and rummaging through the workbench for tools, he'd paid little attention to the contents of the garage. Now, as he looked around, he could see that between the piles of junk, there was a promise of treasure.

An ornate iron bed frame stood behind discarded gardening tools, an ancient horse collar hung on the wall, and a stack of Burma Shave signs were propped between two wall studs. Furniture her grandparents must have considered outdated but too good to throw away sat tucked in a corner, the covering dust as thick as the cherry veneer on the end tables.

"Your grandfather must not have spent much time out here," Cole said. "This place looks like a tomb."

"When my grandmother was alive he was always out here puttering around on something for her." Holly stepped around a stack of fence posts and looked up at the open trusses. "After she died, he told me he thought it would be easier if he cleared her things out of the house and put them in the garage. Then he could go through them and sort everything out later, when it didn't hurt so much. He never did."

Cole stuck his hands in his back pockets and slowly turned in a circle. "What's he planning to do with the rest of this stuff?"

Holly let loose with a disparaging laugh. "He's already done it. He gave it to me."

"Everything?"

"He said if he was going to make new memories and leave the hurting behind, he had to start over with new people and new things."

"Your grandmother must have left a big hole in his life."

"Grandpa always said she was his reason he got up in the morning. I think he would have been okay eventually if my mother and father hadn't died so soon after Grandma. At their funeral he told me that he knew eventually he could accept losing Grandma because it was the natural order of things, but that it was wrong for a son to die before his father and he would never get past it. He wouldn't go home until I promised him I'd do everything possible to see that natural order wasn't broken again."

"Does he know about the baby?"

"Not yet." Holly bent and brushed the dust off the top of a box. "I decided to wait until I was further along."

"How do you think he'll react?"

She tugged on the tape that held the top closed. "A year ago he would have been a nervous wreck and beside himself with excitement at the same time. He'd have insisted I move in with him and would have driven me crazy hoverin' and watchin' and fussin'."

"But now?"

"He's making a new life for himself in Arizona. I'm not sure how I'll fit in."

The catch in her voice told him she wasn't as detached as she wanted him to believe. "So all this junk is yours," he said, taking another look around.

"Yeah. It's kinda like being dumped in the jungle without a guide. I have no idea what comes with memories and what came from someone else's garage sale."

"Maybe you could write your grandfather and ask him."

She shook her head. "I would never do that."

"All right. What about other relatives?"

"My dad was an only child."

"Then it's simple. You keep what you like and sell the rest." He swung his arm wide. "There's enough out here to pay for two babies."

He'd struck a responsive chord. "You really think so?"

"I've never done something like this before," he admitted, "but it seems to me—"

"I couldn't," she said, her excitement fading. "What if Grandpa changed his mind?"

"Then you tell him why you sold everything and what you did with the money. I'm willing to bet there's nothing in this garage that means more to him than you."

"Still, it's not like I'm starving."

Cole threw his hands up in frustration. "I'll never understand how you women think."

She gave him a dirty look. "Keep that up and you're going to have me wondering how I could have thought I liked you."

"You'd look more intimidating if you wiped the dust off your nose."

She passed her sleeve across her face and kept her arm there far longer than necessary, trying to hide the grin that had already reached her eyes. "I guess we could take that old chrome kitchen set with us. I don't see how it could have much sentimental value when my grandmother used to tell me she thought it was the ugliest thing in Christendom." She shrugged. "And I suppose if we looked, we might find one or two other things."

"Then let's get started before it gets any hotter."

Nothing was written on the outside to indicate the contents of any of the boxes, so the search became an adventure, a treasure hunt of sorts. They discovered old linens that had become feasts for families of enterprising mice and sets of multicolored curtains, orange, brown, turquoise, and yellow made of fiberglass and ignored even by time.

The suitcases held clothes, musty, but undamaged. Most were women's from the thirties and forties, made for someone taller and thinner than Holly's grandmother. She said she couldn't imagine who they'd belonged to but wanted to keep them because they were so beautiful.

Next they tried a trunk and found the small treasures that Millie Murdoch had chosen to accompany her through life. Holly lifted each item with the reverence afforded ancient parchment. Some things triggered memories; others she wondered that she'd never seen. It was an eclectic assortment: gaudy rhinestone pins, a hand-tooled leather purse from a trip to Mexico, a pencil caddy made by loving five-year-old hands. A lifetime's worth of greeting cards were held together with a lavender ribbon. A heart-shaped candy box was filled with photographs.

Holly sat the box on her lap and started going through the pictures. She handed one to Cole. "This was taken on my first day of high school. I was so scared that morning."

"You don't look old enough to be in high school," Cole said.

"The bane of my life. I have this crazy dream that when I'm sixty I'll go to bed one night looking like a kid and wake up looking like an old woman." She handed him another picture. "This is when I graduated."

"You look the same."

"Thanks for pointing that out."

"I know a lot of women who would give—"

"I don't want to hear about it." She put the photographs back in the box. "I'll bet you were the kind of kid who ran for student council when you were in high school."

"You'd lose. I never stayed in any school long enough to run for anything. Frank had me take a high-school equivalency test when I turned sixteen. That was the end of my formal schooling."

"Who's Frank?"

Only then did Cole realize how careless he'd been. "My father," he said without elaboration.

"You call your father Frank?"

"It was easier that way."

"He didn't want people to know you were his son?"

"It was more complicated than that." Somehow he had to get her off the subject. "Where did you go to high school?"

"Memphis. Except for crossing the river to Arkansas to visit my mother's friend, I never left Tennessee until I went away to college." She turned her attention back to the trunk. Tucked in the corner, halfway down, she found her grandmother's recipe box and let out a squeal of delight. "I've wanted to ask Grandpa about this for years but didn't have the nerve." She looked at Cole and grinned. "Tonight I'm going to fix you the best pecan waffles you ever ate."

"It seems like forever since I had a pecan waffle," he said. Probably because he didn't like them, never had. But there was no way he'd tell Holly that. He'd eat pecan waffles for a week if it would make her happy.

When the trunk was empty and the treasures were scattered all around her, she sat back on her heels. "I was so lucky," she said. "The whole time I was growing up I was surrounded by people who loved me unconditionally. They truly believed I was the smartest and prettiest and most talented child ever born." As she spoke, she traced the embroidery on a checkered apron with the tip of her finger. "I want that for my baby."

From everything she'd already told him, what she wanted was going to be hard to pull off. She only had her grandfather to give such love, and he was two thousand miles away. Cole didn't know what to say.

After several minutes Holly began filling the trunk again. "This one we keep," she said as she closed the lid.

"We don't have to take everything in at the same time. As a matter of fact, we'd probably get a better price if we didn't. Why don't we start with the things we brought back from Asheville and see how that works out?"

A slow smile spread across her face. "I like you, Neal Chapman."

A flush of pleasure left a sense of well-being. "I like you, too."

"Why don't you start loading the truck and I'll go inside and get us something to drink."

"Before you go . . ." He could already hear her answer. "First, I want you to know what I'm going to tell you isn't up for debate."

"All right, you've got my attention."

"I've pulled in some really good tips these past few days and I'm going to use some of that money to take you out to lunch. I saw an interesting place when I was in Alcoa the other day."

"Okay."

He blinked in surprise. "Just what is that supposed to mean?"

She smiled. "What part didn't you understand?"

"The easy acquiescence."

"Acquiescence?" she mimicked with a show of surprise. "Just what kind of country singer are you?"

He gave her a hard look. "Was that a personal slam or just another dig at what I do for a living?"

An immediate, repentant expression came over her

face. "I didn't mean anything. It was reflex." When he didn't answer, she added, "I really am sorry."

He knew she thought he was upset because he'd told her how little schooling he'd had and wanted to make it clear that that wasn't the reason. What he wanted her to acknowledge was her tendency to put words between them whenever she got it in her head that they were enjoying each other's company too much. "How long is it going to take for you to stop seeing Troy when you look at me?"

"That's not what I'm doing."

"The hell it isn't. You're as wrapped up in him now as the day he walked out."

Her eyes locked on his. "Then why am I glad he's gone?"

"Are you?"

"I'll admit there's a hard fact sitting in the middle of my throat that chokes me every time I think about him. I stayed with Troy long past the time I stopped loving him, but I was too blind to see it until I got away. It near drives me crazy to think I could have actually married him." She wiped her hands down the front of her jeans. "How can I ever trust my feelings again?"

"You had the baby to consider."

"That's an easy out, and don't think I haven't tried to make it work. But if I'd really been thinking about the baby, I would have hightailed it out of there the second that dot turned pink and I knew I was pregnant."

Unbidden, an image of Belinda came to Cole. "Sometimes you have a need to believe things that aren't true." He was talking to himself as much as Holly. "If you're lucky, the need passes before you've done too much damage."

"So you don't think there's something innately wrong with me?"

"Innately?" he mimicked with a show of surprise. "Just what kind of waitress are you?"

She laughed. "That's what I like about you, Chapman. You give as good as you get."

"Now about lunch . . ."

"Before you say anything more, I've got a deal for you."

"Dammit, Holly, you said you weren't going to do that."

"That was before. Besides, what's it going to hurt to listen?"

"Do I have a choice?"

"No." Her eyes grew animated. "There's no way we could have lunch at a nice walk-in, sit-down place for less than twenty dollars. But if you gave that money to me instead, I could make you the most incredible dinner you've ever eaten."

There was something going on; he just didn't know what. He guessed. "You remembered one of your grandmother's recipes, didn't you?"

"Am I that easy to read?"

"I'm that good."

"Do we have a deal?"

"It depends." He didn't want to give in too easily. "First tell me what you're planning to serve."

"Something I've been craving for weeks."

Damn, she was better at this than he was. How could he possibly refuse her now?

"Pork chops slow cooked in apples and sauerkraut."

He almost gagged. "You made that up."

"No, I didn't. It's wonderful, I promise."

The better part of their afternoon was spent with the thrift-store owner. The pattern was set immediately; Cole would unload an item, the owner would put a price on it, and Holly would try to talk him into upping it. Cole could almost hear her mind working as she added the price of each piece to the last, calculating how close she was to paying off the hospital.

When they left, she made a point of telling Cole loud enough for the store owner to hear that she hadn't gotten near what she'd expected. As soon as they were down the street she let out a squeal of delight and said, "Wow, I never thought I'd get that much for all that junk, did you?"

"But I thought you said—"

"I didn't want him to think he might have paid more than he had to," she said reasonably.

Cole saw the sign of the restaurant where he'd planned to take Holly for lunch. He cast a longing look in its direction as they drove by.

"Stop pouting," she said. "You're going to love my dinner."

Later, much to his surprise, he found that the pork chops and apples and sauerkraut were every bit as good as she'd promised.

They were clearing the table when she turned to Cole and, with obvious difficulty, said, "I've changed my mind about the crib. You can buy it for me—for the baby—if you still want to. If you don't," she added in a rush, "that's okay. I understand. After all, there's no reason you should become involved in his life, too."

She was talking about the crib he'd found at the thrift store. "I haven't changed my mind, Holly," he told her. "As soon as I get the money together, I'll go over and pick it up."

"I'll pay you back as soon as I can."

It was useless to argue money with her. "Why don't I take it out in rent?"

"I owe you two months already."

"Are you beginning to worry I might never leave?" He didn't realize until he asked the question how anxious he was to hear the answer.

She thought for a while before she said, "I didn't know how much I missed having someone to talk to around here until you came along."

When the dishes were done, Holly put the movie Cole had rented into her grandfather's old VCR. She spent several minutes trying to adjust the color before giving Cole an apologetic smile. "I'm afraid this is as good as it gets."

Cole patted the cushion beside him, giving her the better end of the sofa. "It looks fine to me."

She settled next to him. "So you're color-blind, too."

"Too?" he questioned.

She laughed. "It was just an expression."

Fifteen minutes into the movie Holly claimed she'd been dying to see since its release three years earlier, she was sound asleep. With each deep, rhythmic breath she tilted a little closer. Finally, Cole guided her to his lap, propping one of the needlepoint pillows under her head. He swept the hair off her forehead, then rested his hand at her waist and went back to watching the movie.

He probably should have helped her to bed before she fell into such a deep sleep, but he liked having her with him. He'd never felt as comfortable with a woman so near his own age, but then he couldn't ever remember having one for a friend before. At least not a real friend, not the kind you shared your life's stories with. In the short time he'd been with her, Holly already knew more about him than Belinda did after a year. Only a gnawing, persistent fear kept him from telling her everything.

# 15

That Friday, while Holly was at the motel, Cole went to the Western Union office in Alcoa to pick up the money Randy had sent through Buddy. Including what he had left from the crib he picked up the day before, Cole had a grand total of $540 and an odd amount of change in his pocket when he walked back out onto the sidewalk. He stood and watched the gathering clouds for several minutes, hungry for a change, but knowing the rain they would bring would only add to the humidity.

Never had he felt as rich or wanted to celebrate more. Even if his debut week hadn't been a wild success, he had a strong sense of actually having earned a portion of the money in his pocket, a feeling he hadn't experienced in years. It felt good. Almost as good as the second time he'd had a woman and the first time he'd known what to do with one.

He got in his truck and headed for the hardware store to pick up the paint for the crib. Along with white, he chose the five brightest colors he could find. When

Holly's baby woke up every morning Cole wanted him to see balloons floating in the clouds and to feel their freedom.

Three days had passed since she told him he could buy the crib for her. She hadn't mentioned it again and he purposely let her think he'd forgotten. He wanted to give her the present when it looked new again, as if it had been made especially for her baby.

Normally, it was easy for him to keep a secret, but this one sat on the end of his tongue like a bewitching gremlin.

Two hours and several stops later, he pulled into the driveway at Holly's house, both disappointed and glad that she hadn't beaten him home. He was anxious to see her but couldn't help thinking how much fun it would be to have everything set up as a surprise when she walked into the kitchen.

He stuffed the smaller packages he'd bought at the mall into a larger bag and propped the daisies he'd picked up at the grocery store on top. His first choice had been a bouquet of multicolored roses, but then it occurred to him how difficult it would be to explain how he'd spent more money than he should have. Holly could figure prices better and faster than a scanner. The two times Cole had gone grocery shopping with her she'd had the total figured before she put her cart in the checkout line. And she had it figured to the penny.

The sky changed from dove to gunmetal gray as darker clouds moved in and cast the kitchen in deep shadow. Cole turned the light on before he went to the sink to fill a glass with water. He propped the daisies inside, put them on the table, then started breakfast. The blueberry muffins he made from a mix but couldn't find muffin tins, so he baked them in a pie plate. Next came a fruit salad. When he was finished he folded the bags around the presents he'd bought, trying to make them look as if they'd been wrapped. He found some string in a drawer and made makeshift bows, finishing them off with daisies propped in the middle.

An image of one of the stylishly wrapped presents Belinda always brought him after a shopping spree flashed in his mind. In comparison, his efforts looked pathetic. With his string and flower it was almost as if he were purposely drawing attention to the paltriness of the offering. Maybe it would be better just to give her the bags without any trimming. He was about to do just that when he heard Holly's car pull into the driveway. He stood at the window and saw her get out and press her hands to the small of her back. Slowly, she stretched backward.

Cole opened the door. "Rough morning?"

A smile wiped the tiredness from her face. "I think everybody who rented a room from Arnold last night had a half-dozen kids with them. There were cookie and cracker crumbs from one end of the motel to the other."

"A preview of coming attractions?"

"Not mine. I never did understand why a two-year-old couldn't sit down to eat a cookie, or, for that matter, a man sit down to go to the bathroom."

There was no way he wanted to tackle that one. "You can take a nap after breakfast. It's almost ready."

"I'm not very hungry," she said apologetically.

"That's okay," he said. He worked to hide his disappointment. "It'll keep."

When she was through the mud room and at the kitchen door, she stopped abruptly. "What is that smell?"

Cole came up behind her. "Blueberry muffins. Well, not muffins exactly, more like a cake. Same thing, different shape."

She twisted to look at him over her shoulder. "You baked?"

"I told you I could cook."

"Cook, but not bake. There's a difference."

"It wasn't any big deal. I opened a box and followed the directions."

"How long before we eat?"

He gently moved her forward, out of the doorway. "I thought you said you weren't hungry."

"I changed my mind."

"There's fruit salad in the refrigerator. You can start on that."

"I'll wait for the blueberry . . . whatever."

"You have to eat some fruit salad first."

"I have to do what?"

"According to that baby book you left on the sofa the other night, you're not eating enough of the right kinds of foods. The chart said you should have a lot more fruits and vegetables and less meat."

"I don't believe this. Who made you—"

He put a hand on each shoulder and guided her to the table. "Save your energy. I'm in too good a mood to fight with you."

"Neal, we need to talk about this. I told you in the beginning I . . ." She was distracted when she noticed the packages on the table. "What's this?"

"It's nothing special," he said dismissively. "Just something I picked up when I went out this morning."

"Before I make a fool of myself, am I right in assuming they're for me?"

"Who else?"

"Why?"

Her question confused him. "It's nothing complicated, Holly. You've done so much for me, taking me in and all, I wanted to do something in return."

She seemed to relax a little. "No other reason?"

"What other reason could there be?"

In a strangely self-protective gesture, Holly's hand went to her stomach. "None, I guess." Her other hand came up to cover the first. "I feel like an idiot. It's just that I forget sometimes."

"Forget what?"

Her cheeks colored. "About being pregnant."

Cole dug a frying pan out of the cupboard. "I can't imagine ever forgetting something like that."

"I've had a lot on my mind lately."

"Anything I can help you with?" He took the eggs out of the refrigerator.

She frowned. "You've got to stop doing that, Neal. You're a nice guy and I don't want to hurt your feelings, but I'm not your responsibility and I don't want to be. You should be concentrating on your own problems. God knows you've got enough of them."

He put the eggs on the counter and sat down opposite her. "We're friends, remember?"

"Please try to understand," she said. "I have to think of myself and my baby first. I can't let myself get any more attached to you than I already am. The kind of friendship you're talking about takes energy I don't have. I don't want to miss you when you leave."

Cole sat back in his chair and stared at Holly. She wanted him to believe he was a temporarily useful drifter to her, nothing more. He had no problem with that. But what was she to him?

"I think I know what's going on here," she said. "It's been so long since I've been around anyone like you I didn't see it at first. My grandmother used to divide the people she knew into givers and takers and believed that in order to be truly happy you had to find someone who was your opposite or have a helping of both inside yourself."

Cole folded his arms across his chest and settled deeper into his chair, stretching his legs out in front of him.

"It's hard to live with someone who has too much of one or the other in them, but if two of the same kind wind up together, they'll drive each other nuts."

He waited for her to go on. When she didn't he asked, "If you were trying to make a point, I missed it."

"I understand now that you didn't spend your money on me because of some ulterior motive; you did it because it's the kind of person you are—a giver. You need to do nice things for people, to take care of them."

Cole unfolded his arms and shoved his hands in his pockets. "Let me see if I'm following you on this. If I'm the giver you say I am, then it follows that in order for me to be happy, I need to hook up with a taker?"

She nodded. "You got it."

"So, as I see it, it's your job to act surprised and happy over the presents I give you and not turn a simple thank-you into something complicated."

She reached across the table and tried to touch his arm. "Now you're mad at me."

He pulled away. For some bizarre reason, he didn't want the intimacy between them. The buzzer sounded on the stove. He slid his chair back and stood. "I'm not mad at you."

"Then why are you acting this way?"

He grabbed a towel and took the pie plate out of the oven. "You still haven't explained why you thought I was coming on to you."

"I feel stupid about that, okay? It was a knee-jerk reaction. For a minute I forgot about being pregnant and that there wasn't a man in his right mind who would be interested in me."

"Do you want me to take the presents back?"

The question brought a sheepish grin. "No."

"Then either open them now or get them off the table so we can eat." The words were harsh, the tone less so.

"Am I to assume the flowers are for me, too?"

"No, they're for me. I've always been partial to daisies."

"Liar." She slipped the string from the first bag and looked inside. "What is it?"

"I don't remember." He didn't want her to see how anxious he was to have her like what he'd bought.

Holly laid the tissue-wrapped garment on her lap. She caught her breath when she saw what it was. "Oh," she said softly. "It's so beautiful." She brought the infant sleeper to her cheek.

"The clerk said white wasn't practical, but I liked this one the best. You can take it back and get one of the other colors if you want."

"This is what he's going to wear when he comes home from the hospital," Holly announced.

"You didn't tell me you were having a boy."

"I don't know if it's a boy for sure. I just don't like saying 'it' or 'the baby' all the time."

"When do you find out?"

"Not until he's born. I'm not having an ultrasound."

"I thought the book said it was a pretty standard test nowadays."

"There isn't any need. The doctor tells me I'm doing fine." She refolded the sleeper and put it back in the bag. "And it's money I can use for other things."

"What if I paid for it?" Whatever their relationship, he couldn't stand by and let her cut corners where her or the baby's health was concerned. "And don't lay any of that 'giver' crap on me or think I'm trying to buy my way into your life."

"I'm not going to worry about that stuff anymore. Even if you were attracted to me, in another month you'd change your mind."

"Why should another month make any difference?"

"There's going to be a lot more of me. You'd be so turned off you wouldn't be able to get out the door fast enough." She picked up the second package. "I appreciate the offer to pay for the ultrasound. If something happens that the doctor thinks I need one and you're still around, I just might take you up on your offer."

He tried to picture her with an obviously rounded stomach. No matter how large he made her, she was still Holly, not the grotesquely misshapen thing she seemed intent on convincing him she would be.

She pulled the daisy from under the string on the second package and put it in the glass with the others. "I know you want to help out, but you're being impractical.

The main tourist season will be over in another month. Places around here will be closing, not hiring. You're going to need every dollar you've earned when you decide to go back out on the road."

"Open your present," he said, uncomfortable with discussing the future with her.

"I wish you wouldn't have done this."

"We've already been over that, Holly."

She untied the string and laid it aside. "I'm not very good at this kind of thing."

"All you have to do is open the bag, look inside, act surprised, and say you love whatever it is."

When she saw what he'd given her, she laughed. It was a bright pink T-shirt emblazoned with the words Baby on Board.

"Now you don't have to worry about people thinking you're putting on weight," Cole told her.

She was still smiling when she leaned back and stared up at the ceiling. "I appreciate the thought, Neal. But considering I've been doing everything I can to keep anyone from finding out I'm pregnant, I hope you understand if I don't wear this for a while."

"No one knows? Not even Arnold and Leroy?"

"They're the last people I want to find out. I've been with both of them long enough to know how old-fashioned they are about having a pregnant woman work for them. I'll be lucky if I don't have my hours cut in half when they find out."

"Aren't there laws about things like that?"

"Get real. What am I supposed to do, sue? A lot of good that would do me when I need money now."

"So I guess it wasn't the best present I could have gotten you."

"Maybe not the best," she agreed. "At least not right now. But I'm not going to be able to hide behind baggy shirts forever."

"Let's eat," he said, anxious to have the meal behind them.

"I've ruined this for you, haven't I, Neal?" she said softly. "I know what it feels like to be where you are. I'm sorry."

"It's okay."

"I'm not used to having someone do nice things for me. It's a lame excuse, but it's the only one I have."

"I guess we'll have to keep practicing until you get it right." He didn't want to be pulled any deeper into her life than he already was, but he didn't know how to keep it from happening.

"Be careful. I have a feeling I could take to this kind of treatment. You could wind up with a spoiled, demanding monster on your hands."

"I think I can handle it." He cut a wedge of blueberry "muffin" and put it on her plate.

"Does this mean I don't have to eat the fruit salad first?"

"No, it just means I'm trying to find a way to shut you up so I can eat."

She had her mouth open to answer him but no words came out. Instead, she put her hand on her side and sat perfectly still.

"Is something wrong?" Cole asked.

"I'm not sure."

"Are you in pain?"

"No. It was a weird kind of fluttery feeling, like there was a butterfly trapped inside me." She blinked. "Oh my God, do you suppose it was the baby?"

"You've never felt it before?"

She shook her head as she moved her hand more toward the middle of her stomach. A smile of wonder made her eyes sparkle when she looked up at Cole. "There it is again."

"Was it the same?" He felt left out, the way he had when he was twelve and came back from a summer on the rodeo circuit in Texas to discover Randy had found a new best friend.

"Come here," she said, and moved her hand again. "You can feel for yourself."

He held back, not understanding why. "According to the book, you're right on schedule. Around four months is when the baby's big enough for the movements to be felt."

"He stopped," Holly said.

"According to the book, you'll start feeling—" He didn't finish.

"What?" she prodded.

"I don't want to spoil it for you."

"Very clever, Mr. Chapman."

"How else am I going to get you to read this stuff for yourself?" Unwilling to do anything to dampen her mood, he decided to skip cooking the eggs and stabbed a strawberry with his fork. He reached across the table and held it in front of her.

"I'm not real crazy about—"

"I don't care. It's good for you."

She leaned forward and let him put the strawberry in her mouth. "Someday I'm going to have to meet your little brother and ask him if you were like this with him, too." She pulled her chair closer to the table and picked up her own fork. "If you were, you must have driven the poor kid crazy."

"He turned out okay." She'd hit a tender spot, one Randy had pounded so often when they were growing up, it was still sore.

Lightning flashed at the window; thunder rattled the panes. A gust of wind slapped branches against the house and sent a curling cloud of dust across the yard.

"Looks like the storm is getting close," Holly said.

He was grateful she didn't prod him about Randy. "How long is it supposed to last?"

"Couple of days. At least that's what the guy on the radio said."

"I was going to start painting the trim on the house, but I guess it'll have to wait."

"If you're planning to use that paint out in the garage, you better check it first. I have a feeling it's pretty old."

"Did your grandfather just turn the place over to you?"

"Physically, but not legally. Neither of us had the money for that."

"But you can stay here as long as you want?"

"Until the place falls down around me."

Cole chased a grape around the bottom of his bowl and thought how unalike he and Holly were and yet how much they had in common. "How long do you figure you'll have to work to pay for the baby?"

"Through Christmas."

"When are you due?"

"Around the first of January."

"And you think you're going to keep it a secret until then?"

"That's not what you asked me."

"How much money do you need?"

She gathered the dishes and stood. "What is it with you and my finances? Why are you so interested?"

"I'm just curious."

"Well, don't be. It's my problem and I'll take care of it my own way."

"Why are you so goddamned stubborn about this?" He knew he had no business pushing her but was too caught up in what was happening between them to back off.

"Why do you care?" she shot at him. "It's my baby and my life, neither of which are your concern."

Cole threw his hands up in defeat. They'd been sharing a pleasant meal only minutes ago. What the hell happened? "Forgive me. I had no idea my interest would be so offensive."

She dumped the dishes in the sink and turned on him. "I knew it was a mistake to let you stay here."

Another log for his fire. "Since when are you 'letting' me stay here? I thought I was paying for the privilege."

She was quiet for a long time after that. "It's against my

nature to let people do things for me. I don't want to feel as if I owe them something."

"*People*? Since when did I become people again? I thought we'd moved beyond that."

"How am I supposed to make special rules for you and not everyone else?"

"That's not up to me to figure out."

"You can be a real hard-ass, Neal Chapman."

"Look who's talking." What was going on here? What were they fighting about? And why? "I'm going to get out of here for a while."

"Have a hot date waiting for you?" she baited.

"A lot you'd care if I did."

"You're right. I wouldn't. Why should I?" She tucked a dishtowel in her waistband. "I never should have gone to the hospital with you."

"I'm beginning to wish you hadn't. We'd both be better off."

She stared at him in silent fury, then pointedly turned and started the water in the sink.

Cole stormed out of the kitchen, down the hall, and onto the front porch, closing the door behind him with a satisfying slam.

He walked over to the porch steps, leaned his shoulder into the pillar, and stared blindly into the distance. His heart thundered in his chest; he drew in a deep breath and let it out slowly.

He had no right to be mad at her, but reason eluded him. She'd made him see what an ass he'd been making of himself and it was embarrassing. He'd thought he was over his compulsion to mother people, but obviously the childhood habit still lingered.

Jesus H. Christ, had he really told Frank he wasn't coming back for six months? Maybe his dad had been right about seeing a psychiatrist.

Well, it was over. As soon as Holly left for work that afternoon, he was going to call the office and have

Denise—assuming she was still Frank's secretary—hire a plane to meet him in Knoxville. The next time he went on the road, it would be in a half-million-dollar bus, not a broken-down pickup truck.

The idea was sounding better all the time.

# 16

By the time Holly finished in the kitchen she was suffering pangs of guilt over the stupid argument she'd had with Neal. She was confused about why it had happened. It was almost as if she'd purposely set out to punish him for being nice to her, as if some part of her was intent on driving him away. Imagining him gone left a hollow feeling inside. She'd done precisely what she promised herself she would never do again, at least not until she was emotionally stronger. Worst of all, it had taken less than three weeks for Neal to get close enough that she would miss him when he was gone.

She folded the towel and hung it over the oven handle. She couldn't give him an explanation—what she was feeling was far too complicated and private—but she could give him the apology he deserved.

Holly found Neal sitting on the front porch swing, his elbows on his knees, his head between his hands. "Is it all right if I come out there with you?" she asked.

He looked up. "You can do whatever you want, it's your house."

"I just want to apologize and then I'll leave you alone."

"That isn't necessary."

"What?—that I tell you I'm sorry, or leave you alone?"

"Either one."

She sat on the railing in front of him, bracing herself with her hands. Behind her the clouds finally let go of their burden; the rain came down in rhythmic, noisy waves, hitting the pavement and bouncing in the air again before finally settling into miniature ponds and rivers. The overhang kept all but an occasional ricocheting drop from hitting her. "Did that book you were reading say anything about pregnant women being moody? It would be nice if I had a legitimate excuse for acting the way I did."

"If it did, it was in one of the chapters I skipped."

She didn't say anything. The silence grew awkward between them, and she could see the breach the argument had created was not going to be closed as easily as she had hoped. A simple "I'm sorry," no matter how sincere, wasn't enough.

She'd been too wrapped up in her own feelings to understand how vulnerable Neal was when he'd reached out to her. Living alone for those two and a half months with only her own thoughts and problems for company had made her focus on what was wrong with her life rather than what was right. It was almost as if she'd bought into the idea that she would be punished in some way if she dared to smile or laugh or find pleasure in a shared moment with a new friend. Maybe it was that somewhere deep inside she could still hear the tent preacher who came to town every summer talking about the price God extracted from sinners. Maybe she was scared that if she didn't pay that price now, she would be forced to settle up after the baby was born. And maybe the thought that terrified her and kept her from sleeping at night was the possibility it would be her baby who had to pay.

Neal shifted forward on the swing and started to stand. "Don't go," she said.

He sat back down. "Sorry. I thought you were through."

"As much as I'd like to put the blame on screwed-up hormones, that's not why I picked a fight." The admission came hard, but she owed him. "I was mad at you."

"Why? What did I do?"

She couldn't hesitate. If she did, she would change her mind about telling him. "I was doing fine before you came," she said in a rush. "I'd convinced myself I liked living alone, that I didn't need anybody, not even a friend. Then you moved in and I couldn't pretend anymore. You haven't even been here a month and I can't stop thinking what it's going to be like when you're gone." She shot a glance in his direction. "Pretty stupid, huh?"

An inner voice told her not to go any further, but she couldn't stop. "But that's not the worst part. All this time I thought I was so brave, but I'm not. I'm terrified. I don't have a clue what to do with a baby. Now, all of a sudden, I'm starting to have these thoughts that if I really loved him I'd give him up for adoption. But I can't, Neal. It breaks my heart just thinking about it." She expected to find him put off or overwhelmed at her revelations, but his face was unreadable.

"Isn't there somewhere you could go, a class you could take that would help you?" he asked.

"I shouldn't have dumped on you like this." She stood and brushed off the back of her jeans. The air smelled sweet and clean; she pulled it deep into her lungs. "It wasn't fair. I'm sorry. I promise I won't do it again." *Just don't leave me.* She had to get out of there before she made an even bigger fool of herself and actually said the words aloud.

Neal reached for her hand and prevented her from going. "I know what it's like to be lonely, Holly."

"I didn't tell you what I've been going through because I wanted you to feel sorry for me." She couldn't stand the thought that he might see her as some pathetic little waif who would fall apart in a strong wind.

"God forbid I should ever do that." He gently gathered her into his arms and held her the way a parent would a grown child who needed comforting.

She fought the urge to run and instead held herself still, not struggling, but not returning his embrace either. "I think I'll go in now. I'm a little tired. I should probably take a nap."

Neal's hands came up and cupped the sides of her face. He looked into her eyes for a long time, telling her without words that he understood. Unexpectedly, he gave her a kiss, touching his lips to her forehead.

When he released her Holly was too shaken to move away. She stood with her head tilted back, her eyes locked on his, transfixed by something she didn't understand. All she knew was that her need to be connected to someone, no matter how tenuous or short-lived, overruled every other consideration. She desperately didn't want the moment to end. Her heart willed him to kiss her again.

A spark of comprehension and then ambiguity flashed in his eyes. He lowered his head slowly. She felt his breath first, hot and sensual and intoxicatingly intimate. Then came the soft caress of his beard on her chin. Then their lips touched. The meeting was tentative and over too soon, the fleeting detour of an autumn leaf on its way to earth. He stayed close and waited. She held her breath, filled with anticipation, afraid to withdraw or make a sound that would break the spell.

As if whatever affirmation he'd sought had been granted, he kissed her again. This time he parted his lips, giving and inviting at the same time. She tasted blueberries and melon and coffee. How familiar and comfortable it was to share breakfast with him. How alone she would feel in her own kitchen when he was gone.

The kiss deepened. Neal put his hands on her waist and drew her closer. Her pregnancy-swollen breasts felt on fire where they pressed against his chest. A new hunger rose inside her, one she had no business feeling.

Dear God, what was she doing? How could she have let this happen? She turned from his kiss and pressed her face against his shirt. "This is insanity. I'm sorry, Neal. It's my fault. I never should . . ."

"I thought—never mind. It isn't important." He didn't finish.

She could just imagine what he thought.

"You should go inside, Holly. It's late."

"I'm not tired anymore."

"Then I'll go in. I need some time to think."

He hadn't said "alone" but it couldn't have been plainer. Her heart raced. She'd done it now, scared him away with her neediness. She couldn't blame him. What man in his right mind would let himself get involved with a pregnant woman? She brought her head up from his chest and forced a smile. "It's those damn hormones again. They just won't leave me alone."

"Give them a couple more months."

"You can stay out here," she told him. "I'll go inside." Holly congratulated herself on how normal she sounded. "I should probably take a nap."

"Do you want me to wake you?"

It would be easier than resetting the alarm, but she didn't want him to feel he had to stick around the house because of her. "I'll take care of it."

She couldn't think of anything else to say, so she went inside. When she was where Neal couldn't see her, the stiffness left her spine. She leaned heavily against the smooth oak door that separated them. Why couldn't she have met him six months ago or even six months from now?

Again, her timing was terrible. She must have been born short a battery in whatever internal clock regulated such things.

When she was in high school she agreed to go to the

prom with an old friend five minutes before the guy she'd been praying would ask her finally did. Five years ago, a month after she moved to Asheville, on an impulse she decided to take her shower before she went to bed instead of in the morning. She was turning her bed down when she saw the light blinking on the answering machine and found the message from the radio station telling her she'd missed winning seven thousand dollars in prizes.

And if she'd counted the number of birth control pills she had remaining before, instead of after, she and Troy made love that last time, she would have noticed there were too many and she wouldn't be pregnant.

And she wouldn't have moved back to Maryville.

And she wouldn't have met Neal Chapman.


Cole arrived at the restaurant an hour early that night. He'd been in his room when Holly left for work. She hadn't bothered to say good-bye or leave a note, which didn't surprise him considering how insistent he'd been about wanting to be alone. He couldn't stop thinking about what had happened between them and how it had ended. He had to talk to her, to make sure she understood that when he told her he wanted time to think, he wasn't trying to shine her off.

He scanned the main room for Holly but couldn't find her. Seconds later she came out of the kitchen, rows of plates balanced on both arms. He sat at an out-of-the-way table and waited to catch her in a quiet moment, but she was either unusually busy, or purposely avoiding him.

To kill time, he picked up a newspaper and automatically turned to the entertainment news. He was struck by an unexpected flush of pleasure when he saw *Silver Linings* had debuted at number one on both the country and pop charts. Plainly old habits and old ambitions died hard. An article about the album filled half the opposite page.

Cole skimmed the first column. Randy's name was scattered throughout the piece. Normally Frank or Janet or "an informed source at Webster Enterprises" would be the ones quoted for the requisite interviews that accompanied the launch of an album. The article closed with a reference to Cole's six-month hiatus and a quote from Randy.

WHEN ASKED ABOUT THE SPECULATION BY SEVERAL CRITICS THAT HIS BROTHER WENT INTO SECLUSION TO AVOID FALLOUT FROM HIS LATEST ALBUM, WEBSTER HAD THIS TO SAY: "THE ONLY FALLOUT COLE CARES ABOUT IS FROM HIS FANS. THEY SAID ALL THERE IS TO SAY ABOUT SILVER LINING WHEN THEY PULLED THEIR WALLETS OUT OF THEIR POCKETS AND PURSES AND MADE THIS ALBUM THE TOP SELLER IN THE COUNTRY TWO WEEKS RUNNING."

Cole found it disconcerting to have his brother defending him. Randy had stood in the background his entire life, while the spotlight focused on Cole. The few times he'd been interviewed had been as background for an article on Cole. This time, Cole might be the subject, but it was Randy's piece. Cole was proud of him, but puzzled, too. This was a Randy he didn't know.

He started to turn the page when something caught his eye. Buried in the middle of a celebrity gossip column, in bold print, was the name Troy Martin. The blurb was a publicity plant, announcing Martin's appearance at a benefit concert. Meaningless really, but an indication there was a buzz around town that Troy was someone to watch. At the level Troy was now he could stumble and disappear far more easily than he could rise. It was more tempting than Cole would want to openly admit to arrange for a "foot in the aisle," but Cole had a feeling the effort would be redundant. Troy would take care of his fall himself.

After returning the paper, Cole glanced at the clock over the cash register. He started work in ten minutes. He saw Holly head back to the kitchen and moved to intercept her.

"I have an order that's up," she said.

"It can wait."

She moved to go around him. "No, it can't. They've already waited too long."

"I only want a minute." He pulled her into the hallway that led to the bathrooms. "Here." He dug in his shirt pocket and pulled out a worse-for-the-wear yellow carnation.

She looked at the flower and then at him. "What's this?"

"I want you to get used to me giving you things."

After several tense moments, she asked, "Does that mean you're staying?"

"Until you throw me out."

"I thought maybe I had—"

"What? Scared me off?"

She took the carnation from him and wove it into the buttonhole on the front of her uniform. "Something like that."

"I don't know what happened between us today, Holly, or if it means anything." He brought his hand up to touch her arm. She backed away as if operating on reflex. "But I'd like to stick around for a while to find out."

Before she answered, she widened the space between them even more. "For a while?" she shot at him. She was suddenly, inexplicably angry. "Is staying with me like playing house for you? What do you think I am, a stopping-off place where you can find shelter and companionship and pretend you're part of something you miss when you're on the road? Then when it stops being fun, you pack your suitcase and take off?"

She'd done it again, attacked just when he thought everything was going great for them. "Do you honestly believe that's what I'll do?"

"Why shouldn't I? You're an itinerant musician." She stopped. Plainly realizing how accusatory she sounded, she added in a more reasonable tone, "You go where the work is and you dream of the day you'll be discovered so you can have your own bus and be on the road even more. I'm not saying there's anything wrong with that. I believe in dreams and the people who dream them, but what you're after has nothing to do with me. I got left behind once. I won't let it happen to me again."

"What do I have to do to get you to stop seeing Troy Martin when you look at me?"

"We wouldn't even be having this discussion if you hadn't caught me at a bad time today." Now she was talking to him in an irritatingly reasonable way, a teacher explaining to one of her pupils why he couldn't pound erasers. "You were nice to listen, but I had no right to unload on you the way I did. I promise it will never happen again."

"So that's it? I can hang around on the fringe, but anything personal is off limits?"

"Goddammit, you act like it's a matter of choice." Her voice broke and she stopped to clear her throat. "I can't afford to count on you, Neal. If it were just me, I might take the chance." She ran her hand along the side of her face and across her eyes, then turned to cast a nervous look at the doorway. She finished in a whisper. "But it's not."

"So what you're saying is I can stay and fix the place up, and pay a little rent, and be your friend when and if you decide it's all right?" They were engaged in some bizarre dance, one step forward, three back. "Well, it's not good enough, Holly. I won't let you keep me at arm's length. What happened between us this afternoon wasn't because you were feeling sorry for yourself or because it was raining. It happened because we feel something for each other. I don't know what, but it's there."

She brought her chin up a notch. "Don't you dare say something you don't mean, just because you think it'll get you what you want."

"Is that what Troy did?" He had to be careful what he said so it wouldn't come back to haunt him later. "We have to talk, Holly . . . about a lot of things. And we have to do it over a lot more meals and another rainstorm and while watching at least a dozen more sunsets."

"My mother warned me about poets."

He smiled in relief that she was no longer on the attack. "What did she tell you?"

"That they would either break my heart," she said softly, "or make it soar."

"Your mother sounds as if she was a bit of a poet herself."

"She had enough in her to know what she was talking about."

"I can't promise I won't ever hurt you," he said. "There are too many things in my life that are beyond my control."

She didn't ask him to explain. Instead, she said, "I shouldn't admit this, but that fruit salad you made me eat this morning actually stayed down."

She'd confused him and then he understood that in her own screwy way, she was letting him back in her life. "It probably has more to do with how far along you are in the pregnancy than what I fed you, but I'd be happy to take the credit."

"Been doing more reading, I see," she said.

"I'm just about through with the first half of the book. There're some interesting things in there. I'd tell you about them, but I might forget something important."

"What makes you think I haven't already read about them myself?"

"If you did, you skipped a lot. There were pages stuck together all through the book."

"All right, so I haven't read the thing cover to cover," she admitted. She came up on her toes and gave him a kiss on the cheek. "Friends?"

He looked deeply into her eyes before slowly bending

to return her kiss, his aim more direct. "Friends it is," he said.

When he released her she pressed the tips of her fingers to her lips and swayed backward. "You don't have the first clue what you're doing."

"Why don't I?"

A tall, blond woman in a waitress uniform leaned into the hallway. "You want me to take care of table six for you?"

"I'll be right there," Holly told her. To Cole, she said, "We'll finish this later." She was at the doorway when she turned and flashed a smile that lit up her face. "I almost forgot—thanks for the flower."

# 17

*Randy walked through the glass doors* into the reception area of Webster Enterprises. A lot had changed at the office in the time Cole had been gone, some of it good, all of it surprising. Denise was still in place as his father's secretary, but there was a new face at the receptionist's desk. The bookkeeping department had taken over Janet's old suite, and she'd moved into a larger room with a window that looked west toward the Pacific instead of north toward the Hollywood Hills. The young and enthusiastic crew that took care of Cole's fan mail and put together the quarterly magazine that went out to over a half-million fans had expanded and moved their operation down the hall, leaving the main office as quiet as a church on a Monday morning.

Randy wasn't sure how he felt about the changes. It was one of those cases where you didn't realize you missed something until it was gone.

After dropping a packet of receipts off at bookkeeping, Randy swung by Frank's office to tell him Buddy had called that morning with word from Cole. Frank wasn't in and Denise was away from her desk. Randy thought about leaving a note but decided to go inside and wait instead.

His father's cluttered desk gave Randy pause. Disorder was as alien to Frank as spontaneity. Randy's gaze swept the room. There were stacks of papers everywhere, as if Frank hadn't been there for months. But that didn't make sense. His father missed birthdays, not work. Whenever he spent a day at home waiting for Cole to call, he spent that night at the office.

Janet appeared in the doorway. "Quite a mess, isn't it?"

He turned to her. "What is all this stuff?"

"With everything else that's been going on lately, Frank's gotten a little backlogged."

"This is more than a little backlogged." Randy went to the desk, picked up a folder, and glanced inside.

Janet came up behind him and peered over his shoulder. "That's an adoption group that's after Cole to be in their ad campaign. They're convinced all their financial problems would disappear if he would agree to be their poster boy."

Randy scanned the letter dated a week earlier. "They make it sound as if hundreds of kids' lives depend on Cole giving his permission to use his picture." He shot a glance over his shoulder at Janet. "They're good. They make him sound like an uncaring SOB if he refuses."

"It's their business to know how to push all the right buttons," she said. "And it's Frank's to refuse in such a way a story can't be sold to the tabloids painting Cole as an uncaring celebrity."

Cole was known as a soft touch in the industry. He routinely gave a percentage of his concert grosses to some charity. "How does Cole pick the ones he wants to support?"

"Cole doesn't see any of the letters until Frank has checked them out. If he did, he wouldn't have the time to make the money everyone wants from him."

"Then how does Dad decide which ones to show to Cole?" He held up the folder. "Why not the orphans?"

Janet frowned in concentration. "As I recall, this is the one where the directors' salaries and operating expenses totaled more than ninety percent of the money they took in last year."

"You've gotta be kidding."

Janet smiled. "Welcome to the real world, Randy."

"What made them think Cole would be interested in helping them? He was never an orphan."

"What possible difference would that make?"

"You would think if they really wanted to suck him in, they'd come after him with some personal angle."

She patted him on the arm. "They do, sweetheart. It's called guilt. How can Cole justify keeping all his money for himself when there are so many in this world with so little?"

"Seems to me they should turn some of that reasoning on themselves."

"Precisely what your father told them."

Randy looked at the stacks of correspondence sitting around the office. The implication was staggering. And even though it was reasonable and understandable, Frank's insulating Cole the way he did was still a form of censorship, and Randy didn't like it. "I understand why Frank thinks he has to shelter Cole from all this, but who's protecting Cole from his protector?"

"There's nothing secret about what's in here," she said, showing a flash of irritation.

"Why are you so quick to defend Frank? You know as well as I do that he can take care of himself."

"Since the day I started working here I've listened to you and Cole complain about your father." She moved around the desk and sat down. "I've kept my mouth shut because I didn't think it was my place to be putting the two of you in yours, but I can see I should have said something a long time ago." She pointed to a chair on the other side of the room. "Bring that over here. It's time you learned what your father does for this business."

He brought the chair over and sat next to her. "Are you sure this is all right with Dad?"

"What?"

"Going through his papers."

"Didn't you just insist they weren't his?"

Still he hesitated.

"Trust me, Randy. Your father is not going to consider this an invasion of privacy. If he wasn't so paranoid about overseeing every aspect of Cole's career, he'd turn this stuff over to the first person he could find willing to take it on. Do you really think he needs to worry about the fabric content of the T-shirts sold at Cole's concerts at the same time he's trying to find ways to keep Cole's career from disintegrating?"

"Frank doesn't turn decisions over to someone else because he wants to be in control."

Janet picked up a pencil and held it suspended between both hands. She didn't lift her gaze when she said, "I've been with this operation for four years now and I still don't know what makes you guys tick." She looked at him. "How can you live with someone your entire life and not know anything about him?"

"Where are you going with this, Janet?"

"You've got it in your head that Frank gets involved in everything you and Cole do because he's some kind of control freak but—"

Randy held his hands up to stop her. "I like you, Janet, and I know you're one smart lady about a lot of things, but when it comes to figuring what Frank is or isn't, I've got time and experience on you. Being in control is as much a part of my father as his curly hair and bad temper."

She leaned forward in her chair. "Frank is scared to death that if he lets himself slow down or if his control slips, everything good that's happened these past seven years will go away. He's like a man trapped inside a water wheel not knowing whether it's the water or his running that's keeping the wheel turning. What he does know is that if he stops, and it was him and not the water, he'll never get it going again."

"That's crazy." Randy pushed his chair back and stood. He didn't like hearing Frank shared a vulnerability with Cole. It was as if the doubts and fears they had in common bracketed the two of them and left him on the outside. "It's no mystery how Cole got where he is and why he stays there—hard work and talent."

"Anyone in this business who's halfway honest will tell you they don't have the first idea why someone like Cole or Garth Brooks or the Beatles or Elvis become superstars." She reached for his hand and gave it a tug. "Now sit back down and stop acting like I'm saying mean things about the runt of the litter. Cole doesn't need you to defend him; his success speaks for itself."

He collapsed as much as sat in the chair. "I'm tired," he admitted. "And strung out farther than I ever thought I'd reach."

"You're entitled. It's been rough going around here for a long time now."

"Why do you think Cole really left?" he asked. The question had haunted him for weeks.

"Because he doesn't drink or do drugs and he likes his women one at a time. Leaving was the only escape open to him." She paused. "You and Frank were too busy trying to deal with your own problems to see what was happening to Cole and he didn't know how to tell you. I wish to hell I'd seen it coming. I should have. I've seen it a dozen times before. But Cole took me by surprise."

"Cole's good at hiding how he feels. It comes from all those years of going out onstage and making the audience believe he liked being in the business," Randy said.

"How can you be so sure he didn't?"

"Because I didn't," he admitted.

"And it follows that Cole would feel the same?"

There was no challenge in her question, only curiosity. "We always have." A knot formed in Randy's stomach as his thoughts progressed to a place he'd avoided until then. "You don't suppose Cole going over that cliff wasn't—"

"An accident?" she finished for him. "I've wondered about that myself, but it doesn't fit. If suicide was Cole's intent, why pick a place with so many trees to block the fall?"

"Dad must have wondered about this, too."

"He's done more than wonder about it, Randy. He's agonized over it. It's been all I could do not to . . . Never mind. I shouldn't have brought it up."

There was a peculiar tone in Janet's voice. It would seem her feelings for Frank went deeper than she'd let on in the past. It was inconceivable to Randy that someone of Janet's sensitivity and sophistication could let herself get emotionally involved with his father.

"Are you sure you know what you're doing?"

"Randy, I never meant for you or anyone else to find out how I feel about Frank. It isn't something I ever intend to do anything about so I would appreciate it if you would forget what you heard today."

"But—"

"Please, Randy, just let it go."

He didn't know what to say, and then, "Did you know Cole has moved in with someone?"

"I didn't, but I'm not surprised. I'm assuming the reason you're telling me is that this person is a woman."

He hadn't been so quick to reach the same conclusion. "Cole said she was the kind who picked up strays."

"Obviously she doesn't know who he is."

"He's going to tell her eventually, but he has to straighten some things out first."

"Things like Belinda?" Janet asked.

"That would be my guess," he said.

"How do you feel about them breaking up?"

Randy shifted in his chair. "If you had asked me that two months ago, I'd have said Cole was making the biggest mistake of his life. Now I'm not so sure."

"I'm surprised to hear you say that."

"Why? Because I spent the last year thinking I was in love with her myself?"

"Whew. When did this monumental piece of self-discovery take place?"

"I used to try and convince myself I liked being around her because we had so much in common. I had this romantic notion that we were both outsiders. I was the hanger-on brother of a famous singer and she was the girl who took the centerfold road to reflected glory." He grinned self-consciously. "Sounds like I just laid the groundwork for a real tearjerker song."

"It must have been hard on you when you realized what you were really feeling."

He put his hand on the desk and pushed and then pulled, setting the swivel chair in a gentle rocking motion. "It would have been a hell of a lot harder if I hadn't had my eyes opened about her and Cole. I used to think they had this big love thing going." He stopped rocking. "I'm not putting this very well."

"You're doing just fine," Janet assured him. "Belinda believes sex originates with the body and with Cole it's in the mind. You get good entertainment combining the two philosophies, but you never get anything lasting." She sagely added, "A dark bedroom is a great equalizer."

"There are a hell of a lot of daylight hours," Randy countered.

Janet gave him a motherly pat on the knee. "Come back and talk to me when you're a little older and your testosterone is in balance with your brain cells."

"What's this about testosterone?" Frank said from the doorway.

"Don't worry, Dad," Randy said. "We weren't talking about you this time." He stood. "Janet was trying to convince me there's life outside the bedroom."

Frank gave Janet a questioning look. "I thought you had a meeting this morning."

"It was canceled."

Randy's gaze shifted from Janet to his father and back again. What did she see in him that the rest of them didn't? He realized as soon as he'd asked himself the almost rhetorical question, the answer wasn't as clear in his mind as it had been several months ago.

"I'm outta here," Randy said and started for the door. "If you need me, I'll be with Bob Mathews. I told Cole I'd have the figures on *Silver Linings* the next time he called."

"He asked for them?" Frank said.

"Not exactly." He should have known how excited Frank would get hearing something like that.

"Then what exactly did he ask?"

"Nothing," Randy admitted. "I was the one who brought it up. I figured it couldn't hurt to keep him informed."

Frank nodded. "You're right. It was a good idea."

Randy didn't take in the compliment at first; he wasn't used to his father giving them. Hell, he couldn't remember Frank ever telling him he'd done something right. He didn't know what to think or how to react. "Like I said, I've got things to do." He looked at Janet. "See you later."

"Take care, Randy." Janet made a move to get up from her chair.

When Randy was gone, Frank said, "I don't know how to get through to that kid."

Surprised at the admission, especially considering how well Frank and Randy had been getting along lately, Janet sat back down and waited to see what would come next.

"I've tried everything," Frank went on. "Randy just won't let me in."

"Maybe he doesn't hear you knocking." She'd been raised with two brothers, had gone through a dozen or more boyfriends, had been married for six years, and had worked around men all her life, and she still didn't understand them. Faced with the same situation, a woman would simply tackle it head-on. There wouldn't be the subtleties, the beating around the bush, the belief that one or two attempts at normal conversation was enough to set aside a lifetime of animosity. Frank and Randy needed to talk to each other, really talk, the way women did when something was bothering them. But how to convince Frank.

"I don't know what else I can do," he said.

Frustration bubbled inside her. "Why are you telling me how you feel and not him?"

"He wouldn't listen."

"How do you know?"

"I just do."

Their conversation had an artificial, scripted air about it. She could imagine the same thing happening when Frank and Randy tried to talk to each other. "Then maybe you need to show him."

He gave her a guarded look. "What do you mean?"

She almost laughed out loud. "Don't worry, I'm not suggesting you throw your arms around him every time he walks into a room."

He relaxed a little. "All right, then what did you have in mind?"

"Give him some responsibility." It sounded so clichéd she hesitated elaborating. But clichéd or not, it was precisely what the two of them needed. "Show Randy you trust his judgment and that you have confidence in his ability to get things done."

"And how am I supposed to do that?"

She didn't answer right away. "The same way you would if it were Cole." If she gave him a detailed outline, she would become his crutch. She didn't want that kind of relationship with Frank.

He leaned his shoulder into the door frame and ran his hand across his chin. "You think he's ever going to come back?"

For an instant she saw the father, not the manager. "I don't know," she told him honestly.

"I miss having him around." He hesitated. "But then if he hadn't gone . . ."

"What?" she prompted.

He visibly struggled with the answer. "I'm not sure I would have ever seen to give Randy more than a passing thought."

She was too stunned at the admission to say anything in reply. What came next surprised her even more.

"You had lunch?" Frank asked, making an obvious attempt to sound casual.

"No." It wasn't even eleven o'clock yet. How could she possibly have had lunch?

"Any plans?"

"For lunch, you mean?"

"Yeah." He straightened and shoved his hands in his pockets.

She was scheduled to meet the marketing director of the Laid Back shirt company. It could wait. "Believe it or not, you caught me on my one free day this week."

Frank seemed unsure what to do next.

This time Janet had no qualms about getting involved. "I know a great Chinese restaurant not far from here."

"Great. I love Chinese."

She smiled. "I know."

# 18

*The tires of Belinda's Corvette* screeched in protest as she turned into the driveway of her mother's house. She got out of the car and ran up the sidewalk, using her key and going inside without ringing the bell, slamming the door behind her. "Mother," she shouted. And again, only louder, *"Mother, where are you?"*

Rhonda came down the hallway, drying her hands on a kitchen towel. "I'm right here," she said in a disapproving tone. "You really shouldn't shout that way, Belinda. It makes you sound common."

"Fuck common," Belinda said, but lowered her voice anyway.

Rhonda shuddered at the crude language. And then, as if realizing Belinda's outburst went deeper than the ongoing frustration over Cole's absence, a frown appeared. "Something happened. What is it?"

Belinda's anger crowded her throat and made speech difficult. "You'll be happy to know, Cole finally called me." Her hands drew into fists at her sides. "He said—" she stopped to take a breath, "he said he wanted me—"

Again she stopped. Not wanting to see the look in her mother's eyes when she found out what Cole had said, Belinda shifted her gaze to the ceiling and stared at the hairline crack left by the last earthquake. "Cole has decided that he's been unfair to me by taking off the way he did."

"It's about time he apologized for what he's put you through. I hope you didn't let him off too easily. You have a tendency to do that, you know."

How like her mother to manage the truth by creating her own version. "He didn't call to apologize, Mother. He's decided I should be free to pursue my own life rather than waiting around for him to decide what he wants to do with his."

Rhonda moved leadenly to the sofa and collapsed, sinking deep into the cushion. "How could he do that to you? How could you let him? What did you say?"

"What could I say? I told him there was nowhere I wanted to be except by his side, that I had no life without him. Which is a hell of a lot closer to the truth than he'll ever know." She let out a quick, bitter laugh. "I have a closet full of clothes from Rodeo Drive, a safe full of jewelry, and a car that cost more money than I earned my entire acting career. If I let Cole get away with this, not only won't I have any place to wear my clothes and jewelry, I won't be able to fill the car with gas. Yesterday I spent the last of this month's allowance on a present for Randy. I'm broke, Mom." Finally she met Rhonda's gaze. There wasn't the belittling look she'd anticipated; there was fear.

"Cole can't just brush you off like you were a piece of lint. You've been with him over a year now. Surely that counts for something. We'll get a lawyer, one who specializes in cases like this."

Belinda didn't want to admit she'd quietly checked into the possibility of a palimony suit two weeks ago, just in case. She'd used phony names of course, but the situation she'd described was her own. Both attorneys had suggested her "friend" come in to discuss her case in further detail, but neither had sounded eager enough for her to feel encouraged. It was better to let Rhonda think Cole's phone call and suggestion they go their separate ways had come as a complete surprise. Otherwise, Belinda would have to explain why she'd done nothing to protect herself financially.

"You can't let him just dump you like this, Belinda." Rhonda ran her hand through her hair, leaving the dry, bleached strands standing on end. "You've been out of circulation too long. You're too old to start over." Her voice broke. "Where will you go? What will you do?" She sent her daughter a pleading look. "What will *I* do? I count on the money you give me every month." She glanced around the room. "I'll lose this house without it."

Belinda had never seen this side of Rhonda. It was disconcerting to see a chink in her mother's defensive barrier, but discovering the weakness gave Belinda a heady sense of superiority. After years of waiting, she sensed an opportunity to wrest emotional control from her mother. The success of one would depend on the other. Suddenly the stakes were doubled. "I don't intend to give up without a fight," she said with renewed conviction.

Rhonda perked up at the statement. "Of course you don't. My girl isn't the kind who lets herself get pushed around." She held out her hand. "Now come over here and tell me what you intend to do and how I can help."

Belinda sat beside her mother on the avocado-green sofa. "I haven't decided yet."

"Then we'll work on it together. Two heads are better than one, especially when they're ours."

"Think about what you just said, Mother." Their lives had turned upside down. It was as if she and Rhonda had traded places and Belinda had become the mother, the care giver, the one who reassured and comforted.

"You know what I mean. We've always been able to figure

things out when we worked on them together." She smiled and reached for Belinda's hand. "It'll be just like old times."

Only it wasn't old times. Her mother was right. Good old Belinda Sue Hanover had been out of circulation too long. The centerfold spread that once had been her ticket to the in parties around town was ancient history. There were a hundred younger, firmer, prettier girls who'd scrambled past her while she took time off to concentrate on Cole.

Rhonda gave Belinda's hand a reassuring squeeze. "Don't go drifting off on me, sweetie. We've got our work cut out for us. Now tell me exactly what Cole said when he called."

"He said he'd been doing a lot of thinking while he was on the road and that he'd decided it wasn't fair to leave me hanging while he tried to make up his mind what he wanted to do. He said I needed someone who could be here for me, someone who knew what he wanted and could appreciate what I had to give."

"And what did you say?"

"At first I was too stunned to say anything. Naturally he assumed I was crying."

"Naturally," Rhonda echoed.

"I sniffed a couple of times and told him I was willing to wait as long as it took for him to decide. I said his being gone had only made me realize how much I love him."

"Perfect," Rhonda said. "Unless . . ."

"Unless what?" Belinda challenged. She wasn't about to let her mother shake her newfound confidence with niggling doubts.

"There's another woman."

Belinda's throat went dry. "That's impossible. He hasn't been gone long enough to have found anyone else."

"How long does something like that take?"

"It's just not possible. I've been everything Cole could want in a woman." If only she felt as confident as she sounded.

"I'm not saying he *has* found someone else, just that it's something we have to consider."

Belinda felt herself slipping. "I've got to find a way to get him back here."

"As far as I'm concerned there's only one word that counts for anything when it comes to situations like this, and that's money. Lots of it. He didn't happen to mention how much he was going to give you, did he?"

"Cole would never offer me money to leave. He'd consider something like that demeaning for both of us. What he said was that he would make sure I was all right until I found a job and could take care of myself." She shook her head. "He even offered to have Frank put in a good word for me with some casting directors so I could get going on my career again. Can you imagine?"

"Did he happen to say what you were supposed to do while you wait around for him to come back?"

"He said I could live at the house until I found someplace else to stay. He even had the nerve to tell me about some apartments he'd seen in Laguna. Can you imagine?" It was a given that Belinda would sleep in her car before she moved back in with her mother. The one night they stayed together when Cole first left, they'd been at each other by breakfast the next morning. "I figure as long as no one else knows about our conversation I can continue drawing my allowance. It isn't a lot but I'll put aside what I can."

"Surely Cole must have said something about how much money he'd give you to see you through."

"Not enough." She wasn't about to give Rhonda ammunition for future arguments.

"When you turned down this 'not enough,' what did you say?"

"That I wanted him, not his money."

"Clever girl," Rhonda said. "I assume he upped the offer then?"

"I told you, Cole would never do something like that.

It's not the way his mind works. And, believe me, I'm not about to suggest it. The minute I do, there'll be no turning back. Besides, it's not a settlement I'm after, at least not right away." She needed a plan, something to guide her, to give direction. Now she was like a goldfish in a carnival bowl, swimming like crazy and not going anywhere. Finally, an idea began to form. With it came a smile.

Rhonda recognized the look and came forward in her seat. "I can't tell you how happy you just made me." She was grinning with excitement. "There for a while I was afraid you were going to let that bastard get away with dumping you."

"Careful, Mother, that *bastard* is going to be your son-in-law."

Rhonda clapped her hands and let out a squeal of delight. "That's my girl."

"Now all I have to do is figure out a way to get him back here, and as soon as possible—just in case there is another woman."

They lapsed into a thoughtful silence. Several minutes passed before Rhonda said slyly, "He'd be here in a flash if he thought you were pregnant. We could make up something to cover your keeping it a secret till now. Then, with all the stress he's put you under by being gone so long and calling and wanting to end the relationship . . . well, it certainly wouldn't be unheard of for the strain to cause you to lose the baby."

"I couldn't do that to Cole," Belinda said with finality. It was better her mother think her virtuous than know the truth. Rhonda was fanatical in her belief that should a marriage fail, children were the one sure way a woman had to get a judge to rule in her favor. She would not be happy to learn her daughter had ignored her advice and that she would never be the grandmother she envisioned. Rhonda wasn't hesitant to tell anyone who would listen that she lived for the day she could join the beauty pageant circuit again with a grandchild.

"That's okay," Rhonda said. "I understand. Don't worry, sweetie, we'll think of something else just as good. There's no one can beat us when we work together."

"I love you, Mom," Belinda said. It felt wonderful to be with someone and not have to pretend. It would be even better if she could be completely honest, too. But you couldn't have everything.

# 19

*Something woke Cole* from a sound sleep. He turned to his back and listened, but as far as he could tell, nothing out of the ordinary had disturbed the night. He tried to remember if he'd been dreaming, but if he had, the images were lost. With the confidence of someone who spent countless nights staring into the darkness, Cole knew he would not be going back to sleep. He turned to look at the clock and saw that it was four-thirty, too early to get up and move around the house. Holly was even a lighter sleeper than he was.

Holly—of course. The sound he'd heard must have been her using the bathroom.

Cole got out of bed and slipped into his jeans. He shivered and rubbed his arms to warm them against the cool air. Autumn had settled in with gentle persistence, stealing summer's warmth a degree at a time until one morning Cole had gotten out of bed and was surprised to find the polished oak floor cold against his bare feet.

He reached for the shirt he'd left on the bedpost the night before. It wasn't just cold, it was damp. The house was in desperate need of major weatherproofing, not the Band-Aid work he'd done last weekend. But Cole couldn't think of any way to sneak the materials into the budget before winter was on them. He kept looking for an opportunity to tell Holly who he was, knowing if he picked the wrong time, the trust she'd begrudgingly given him would disappear as quickly as a pond full of ducks on opening day of hunting season. As they'd come to know each other better, their relationship had grown more complicated.

Holly had a deep-seated hunger for stability and a need for a conventional, secure environment. She'd convinced herself there were emotional dragons she would have to slay to protect her baby and that she was destined to handle them alone. No man could be trusted to love both her and her child the way they needed to be loved, and she would never settle for less. He'd come to understand that the reasons she would use to reject "Cole Webster" were as valid and compelling as those he'd used to run away from him.

Cole made his way across the room, feeling for landmarks that had become familiar in the two months he'd been there. He eased the door open and allowed himself a sense of satisfaction that his efforts the day before had made the operation silent. The floorboards were another matter. There was no way to get down the hall without announcing he was coming, so he didn't even try.

He neared Holly's room and saw she'd left the light on. He glanced inside to check on her. She wasn't there. Worse yet, her bed was made. "Dammit, Holly," he said to the empty room.

He went to the kitchen and looked out the back door. As he'd suspected, her car was gone. Cole gave his anger free reign. It was either that or admit how much it scared him to think of her running around alone in the early morning hours. He felt double-crossed. She'd promised him that if he found a way to cut expenses to equal what she earned doing Arnold's bookkeeping she would quit.

Even that was a compromise. He'd wanted her to give up cleaning the rooms. He'd spent last Saturday caulking the windows and putting weatherstripping around the doors to lower the heating bill, knowing his efforts wouldn't make any real difference in the drafty old house, but convincing her the savings would be substantial.

He'd kept his end of the bargain even if he had told a small lie to get what he wanted. By God, he would see she held up her end, too.

Cole's anger flared anew as he pulled into the motel driveway and saw the office light burning, confirming his suspicions. He drove his truck around back and pulled in next to Holly's Corsica. She hadn't even taken the precaution to park in the front, completely ignoring what had happened to him and what could just as easily happen to her.

He made no attempt to muffle his footsteps as he stormed up to the office and threw open the door. What he found inside stopped him cold. Holly was at the desk, slumped forward, motionless.

"Holly?" he questioned. She didn't respond. His heart in his throat, he crossed the room and knelt beside her. "Holly?" She made a soft, protesting groan and turned her head. Several seconds later, she turned back again, facing him.

Cole rocked back on his heels, flooded with relief and fury. She hadn't been hit over the head—she'd fallen asleep. He didn't know whether to laugh or throw something. For long seconds he stared at her. The dark circles under her eyes looked as if they'd been put there with a marking pen. She wasn't pushing her limits anymore; she'd passed them. If she tried to keep going at the pace she'd set when she first came to Maryville, she could end up damaging herself or the baby. But how was he supposed to convince her?

And what gave him the right to interfere? As she constantly pointed out, they were only friends; their lives, their problems, were their own.

In the past month he'd thought a hundred times about all the ways he could have missed meeting her. Simple things like if he'd stayed at another motel or skipped coming to Tennessee or hadn't gone back to lock his truck that night. Any one of them and he would never have known she existed. Without him she would hold down her three jobs until she was satisfied she had enough money set aside to see her through her pregnancy and the weeks after. She would live in a house in desperate need of repair, she would wear clothes made from curtains, and her baby would sleep in a dresser drawer lined with blankets that she had lovingly cut down to size from her own bed.

As much as he wished it weren't so, Holly could get along without him.

She didn't need him.

But he needed her. Sometimes it frightened him how much.

He brushed the hair from her temple, leaned forward, and touched his lips to her forehead. There was a proprietary intimacy in the gesture. He liked the way it made him feel, but it confused him, too. He didn't understand what was going on inside him. Until now, in the quiet and solitude of this moment, it had been easy to put what he was feeling down to his lifelong attraction to the underdog. But there was more to it than that.

He couldn't leave her crumpled over the desk but didn't want to wake her and have her miss the sleep she so obviously needed. His only choice was to chance moving her to the sofa Arnold used for his afternoon naps.

She didn't make a sound when he picked her up, but slipped her arms around his neck as if he had carried her this way a dozen times before. Considering her rounding middle and voracious appetite, she was lighter than he'd expected, and warmer. Her hair smelled sweet and clean and wonderfully enticing. He took a deep breath and closed his eyes and tried to imagine what it would be like to bury his face in her hair and have her in his arms conscious and willing.

He felt a loss when he laid her on the sofa and stayed crouched beside her for a long time, taking in the minute details that only came with close, unhurried examination. Her eyelashes were long and thick and blond at the ends. She had a small mole behind her ear. He could see her pulse at the base of her neck and how red and rough her hands were, the nails broken, the cuticles ragged. She had a scattering of freckles across her nose. Her lips were full and slightly parted.

The memory of how those lips had felt touching his own returned and consumed him. Heat spread through his midsection and into his groin. He caught his breath at the intensity of his longing.

He had to get out of there before he did something stupid. With a quick, fluid movement he stood and looked around the room for something to cover Holly. When he couldn't find anything he took off his jacket and laid it across her shoulders.

He glanced at the window and saw that the sun would be up soon. A car drove past on its way out. A guest leaving, a room that needed cleaning. Something to do to kill time while he waited for Holly to wake up. Cole went outside to look for Arnold and found him already up, cleaning crimson and yellow leaves out of the swimming pool.

Holly's arm ached where she'd been lying on it. After trying to turn over, she realized there was something wrong with her bed. She opened her eyes, looked around, and frowned. As soon as she saw where she was, she remembered coming to work but couldn't think how she'd gotten from the desk to the couch.

Her arm tingled. She sat up and tried to work out the needlelike sensation. Something slipped from her shoulders. It was Neal's jacket.

What was . . . oh, no. He must have heard her leave, figured where she'd gone, and followed her. She scooted to the edge of the cushion and pushed herself up. Automatically she laid the flat of her hand on her stomach in what she'd come to think of as the pregnant woman's salute. Realizing what she'd done, she dropped her hand to her side. Her pregnancy would be obvious soon enough. She didn't have to announce it prematurely by constantly patting her stomach.

Holly shivered as she made her way to the window. Either it was unseasonably cold for the middle of October or she was coming down with something. She slipped her arms into Neal's jacket and told herself firmly it was the weather. She didn't have time to get sick.

Wondering how long she'd been sleeping and where Neal had gone, she stuck her finger in the miniblind and gently lifted the slat to see what was going on outside. Neal and Arnold were sitting on the edge of the brick planter box talking. She could just imagine what, or more to the point *who,* they were talking about.

She went outside to join them. "Morning," she said, only then realizing how deep into the morning it was.

"We were beginning to think you might sleep straight through to tomorrow," Arnold said.

Neal didn't say anything; he just looked at her, his expression unfathomable.

"I guess when you burn the candle at both ends one day the flame's going to meet in the middle," she said. "But I feel great now. I'll have those rooms done up in no time."

"No need," Arnold told her.

She was too late. He knew all about her and she was fired. She sent an accusing glare at Neal. "You just had to tell him, didn't you?"

"Holly, shame on you," Arnold injected. "That's no way for you to be talkin' to a man who spent his mornin' doing your work."

"You cleaned the rooms?" she said to Neal.

"There were only ten of them," he told her.

"What time is it?" she asked.

Neal shrugged. "Remember, I don't wear a watch."

Arnold glanced up at the sun. "I'd say it's movin' on twelve." He chuckled. "That's accordin' to my stomach, not any great skill as an outdoorsman."

Without conscious thought, Holly's hand went to her own stomach.

"Hungry?" Neal asked.

Only then did she realize what she'd done. She dropped her hand to her side. "As a matter of fact, I am."

"I figured you might be so I went to the store and picked up some things. I thought we might go on a picnic if you felt okay."

"Why wouldn't I?" she said too quickly.

"You sure you ain't comin' down with somethin'?" Arnold asked. "You seem a mite short today."

"I guess I just don't feel right having someone do my work for me." Actually, it was everything she could do to keep from checking the rooms to make sure they were done the way she liked them. About all the motel had to offer was cleanliness.

As if he could read her mind, Neal said, "Is there something you want to do before we take off?"

"No. Unless—"

"Yes?" Neal prompted.

"Nothing." To question his work would be tantamount to passing judgment on his gift. If he had left something undone, she would take care of it tomorrow.

Neal turned to Arnold. "I'll see you get your blankets back."

"No rush," he said. "They're pert near as old as I am."

"I'll get the truck," Neal said to Holly.

"I'm sorry, Arnold, but it looks like I took on too much when I agreed to handle your books," she said when Neal was gone. "I hate to give up the job, but I guess I'm going to have to. I'll stay on until you can find someone else, but you should probably start looking pretty soon."

He seemed confused. "But Neal just got through tellin' me you was givin' up the cleanin' so you could keep on doin' the books."

"He what?" she questioned.

"I got to admit I was a little surprised when he said he would be doin' the cleanin' from now on, but I figured what with you expectin' it was only a matter of time before you—"

"He told you?" She felt betrayed.

Arnold's bushy eyebrows drew together in a puzzled frown. "Told me what?"

"That I was going to have a baby."

"Lordy, Holly. You ain't sayin' you think he don't know, are you?" He scratched his head. "I suppose that's possible. I've been around men who were as thick as a post when it come to things like that. Sad thing is those kind are the ones who take the longest to get used to the idea. If'n I was you, Holly girl, I wouldn't be puttin' off tellin' Neal he was gonna be a daddy much longer."

Holly was speechless. Talk about being thick. It had never occurred to her that people would assume Neal was her baby's father. But it made sense. Neal was the only man Arnold had ever seen her with, the only man she ever talked about. Who could blame him for jumping to the wrong conclusion?

"If Neal didn't tell you about the baby, how did you find out?"

"You must of forgot about me and June havin' six of our own." He shoved his hands under the bib of his overalls. "I wasn't foolin' about you lettin' Neal in on your secret. Could be he's blind about seeing how much you're fillin' out 'cause he's so head-over-heels crazy about you."

"We're just friends," Holly automatically protested.

Arnold chuckled. "So that's what you young people are callin' it nowadays."

Neal pulled up beside her in the truck before she had a chance to answer. He was smiling. She sent him a foreboding look. The smile faded.

Arnold opened the door and gave her a hand up. "Now don't you forget what I told you."

"I won't," she promised.

They were halfway down the driveway when Neal asked, "What was that all about?"

"Oh, nothing special. Arnold was just filling me in on how I'd lost my job."

"I was going to tell you—"

"Stop. I don't want to hear it." She swallowed her feeling of impending loss that made her feel as if she were choking. "This isn't working, Neal. I think it's time you moved on."

# 20

*Cole waited until they were* at the end of the driveway before he said anything. He stopped the truck, laid his arm across the back of the seat, and focused his attention on Holly. "Am I supposed to guess what brought this on or are you going to tell me?"

"You had no right to tell Arnold you were taking over my job. What am I going to do when you decide you're bored and want to take off and I'm as big as a house? There's no way Arnold's going to give me my job back in that condition. Thanks to you he thinks I'm incapable of handling the work." She propped her elbow against the window and leaned her chin into her fist. "I know you think you were doing me a favor, but now I'm dependent on you. I can't afford to let that happen."

"You know whatever I make is yours. I owe you back rent anyway."

"Don't patronize me. The deal was either you worked or you paid. You've already put in enough hours to pay your rent through the next two months."

He slipped his hand over his mouth to cover his grin.

The last thing he needed was for her to think he didn't take her seriously. "You've been keeping track of my hours?"

"I told you I would. It's only fair."

"And I've really worked that many?"

She eyed him suspiciously. "Give or take."

"Seems to me I'd be an idiot not to stick around and collect. Unless you want to pay me the equivalent in salary."

"You know I can't do that."

"Then it looks as if I'm staying." He thought a minute. "Let's see, two months from now—you wouldn't throw me out just weeks before Christmas, would you?"

She smiled despite herself. "Don't count on it. Obviously I didn't tell you dear old Scrooge was a close relative."

Cole touched her shoulder. He meant the caress to be a simple, reassuring gesture, but it seemed he was incapable of thinking of her in strictly friendly terms anymore. His hand lingered as he battled a desire to touch her more intimately, to kiss the hollow at the base of her throat and to feel her response in the quickening of her heartbeat. What surprised him was his need to have her want him as much as he wanted her. The force of it lay against his chest until he had to concentrate to draw a breath.

Afraid he would scare her if she looked at him and saw in his eyes what was going on in his head, Cole withdrew his hand and concentrated on merging into the oncoming traffic. "You know this country better than I do," he said. "Where's a good place to have a picnic?"

"You mean after we finish talking about getting my job back."

"It's settled, Holly. I should have made you quit weeks ago."

"There you go again acting like a Neanderthal." She threw her hands up. "What is it going to take to convince you that you have no right to tell me what I can and can't do?"

"A Neanderthal?"

"I'm serious, Neal. If our friendship is going to have any chance at all, you have got to stop interfering in my life."

It pained him that she thought his concern interference. "I don't know any other way to be," he admitted. "When I care for someone, I just naturally want what's best for them."

"That's okay," she said. "As long as you realize what's best for me is for you to let me make my own decisions."

"How can you make rational decisions in your condition?"

She folded her arms across her stomach. "I'm pregnant," she said with a show of irritation, "not mentally impaired."

"I meant your financial condition. And while we're at it, would you mind telling me what's so wrong with letting me help out? You keep insisting we're friends. Isn't that what friends do for each other?"

She was quiet for a long time. "Turn around," she finally said.

He gave her a questioning look.

"You asked me if I knew a good place for a picnic. I do, but it's the other way."

Plainly she either didn't know how to answer him or she didn't like the answer that had occurred to her. Their skirmish had settled nothing. He checked his rearview mirror, slowed, and made a U-turn. "Compromise?"

"I'd like to hear the terms first."

"I'll stop trying to run your life."

"And in exchange?"

He looked straight ahead, not wanting to see her expression when he told her, "You have to admit I'm more than a friend to you."

"You're asking a lot," she said softly.

"If you say it once, I promise the second time will be easier." There was a lump in his throat the size of a baseball.

"Can I think about it?"

"What are you afraid of, Holly?"

"Me. You. A hundred things." She turned away from him. "Goddammit, would you take the blinders off, Neal?" She took his hand and pressed it against her stomach. "Feel that? I'm not just fat, *I'm pregnant*. Do you have any idea what I'm going to look like a month from now? Two months?"

"Like you swallowed a basketball. So what?"

"There are husbands who can't . . ." She stumbled over the words. "Husbands who are turned off by their own wives the last months of pregnancy, even when it's their baby she's carrying. Did you see that picture of Demi Moore on the front of that magazine?"

"Yes?"

"And it turned you off, right?"

A slow smile was his only answer.

She groaned. "Please tell me you're not some pervert who goes around looking for pregnant women to—" She groaned again.

"Holly, you've convinced yourself you're unlovable and there's nothing I can say that will change your mind, so I'm not even going to try."

"What's that supposed to mean?"

"You leave me no choice. If you won't listen to words, I guess I'm just going to have to stick around and prove you wrong." It was everything he could do to back off. He wanted them to move past where they were. He couldn't tell her the things he needed to tell her until then. "How far are we from this picnic place of yours?"

She let out an audible sigh, visibly relieved that he had given her the time she'd asked for. "A half hour." She looked around. "Maybe forty-five minutes?"

"There's an apple in the bag if you're too hungry to wait that long."

"Something tells me this isn't going to be a cold fried chicken and potato salad picnic."

He laughed. "Maybe after the baby's born." The instant the words were out of his mouth he realized what he'd done. He tried to downplay his assumption she would still want him to be a part of her life then. "Of course whatever and whenever you eat is completely up to you."

This time it was her turn to laugh. "I like you, Neal," she said. "A lot."

"I like you, too, Holly." It wasn't everything he'd hoped, but it was a start.

At Holly's direction, Cole parked in a wide spot in the narrow one-way road that made a circle of Cades Cove. "Why here?" he asked.

"That house over there"—she waited for him to look in the direction she was pointing—"is where my grandfather and his father were born." She had indicated a log cabin with a wide front porch and no windows. "The land it's on belonged to his family for over a hundred years."

Cole couldn't imagine such a thing. If there was history to be proud of in his family, no one had ever told him. "What happened?" he asked. "Why did they sell?"

"Everyone around here did. They didn't have a choice. The entire cove belongs to the park system now. Considering how long it's been since any of my relatives lived in this house, it doesn't make sense, but I get a feeling of family when I'm here."

A gust of wind stripped a palette of leaves from the nearby trees and scattered them on the road. One landed on the truck, came up on end and spun across the hood, then disappeared over the side. "It looks cold out there. Would you rather eat inside?" Cole asked.

"You're letting me decide?"

He grinned. "Just keeping my end of the bargain."

"Then we eat outside."

Later, as Holly stuffed the wrapper from her sandwich into the grocery bag, she said, "I wish you'd brought your guitar."

"Serenading you wasn't what I had in mind when I left the house this morning." He closed the bag and tucked it behind his head as an impromptu pillow. He'd been wrong about it being cold. The wind was warm with the promise of a long Indian summer.

Holly scooted back on the blanket to prop herself against a tree. "Leroy thinks you have talent. He says you could go somewhere with the proper handling."

"When did he say that?"

"Last night. He really liked those new songs you did."

She was talking about the ones Randy had sent him. He'd hesitated about singing them in public without a contract with the writer, but Randy had assured him it was being taken care of. "I like them, too," he said.

"I was watching the crowd, and people actually stopped eating to listen to you."

He rolled to his side to look at her. "Can't ask more than that."

"Are they yours? Did you write them?"

"I wish I had. Actually, it was my brother who put me on to the guy."

"Your brother's a singer, too?"

He was getting sloppy. It was time to change the subject. "Tell me about Troy."

"I already told you everything there is to tell."

"Did you love him?"

She looked uncomfortable. "I thought I did."

"But now?" he prodded.

"I was lonely, and—"

"He was a warm body."

"You sound as though you've been there," she said carefully.

"More than once," he admitted.

"That's what scares me, Neal."

"I know. It scares me, too." But not in the same way. He had no doubts about his feelings for her but was sick with worry that her feelings weren't strong enough yet to keep her from walking when she finally learned the truth about him.

A private smile stole over her lips. She pressed her hand to her stomach. "I guess nap time is over."

Cole watched her, caught up in the expression on her face. He tried to imagine what she was feeling. Did the emotion go beyond the sensation of having your insides used for a punching bag?

She looked up and caught him staring at her. "Come here," she said. When he was beside her she took his hand and laid it where hers had been.

"I can't—"

"Wait a minute. It isn't as if he's doing a jig in there."

"Will you be disappointed if it's a girl?"

Her mouth drew up in a sheepish grin. "I had a dream the other night that I had a girl and she didn't talk to me until she was five because I had called her a boy for nine months."

He tried to concentrate on why he was touching her and not how much he liked it. "I've been setting money aside for an ultrasound. But you can use it for something else if you want," he added quickly.

"I talked to the doctor and he said he didn't think I needed one. And I saw an article the other day about a study that showed some women who had the test gave birth to smaller babies."

"Didn't it say they were women who'd had the test five times or more?"

"I can't believe I'm doing this," she said. She ran her hand through his hair in an impulsive, tender gesture. "I spent the first three and a half months of this pregnancy dying for someone to talk to about what was happening to me and it turns out to be you."

Was he so hungry to be touched that his insides knotted at a casual gesture? "I'm glad to see you're reading."

"You lied about the pages of the book being stuck together. I checked and there weren't any ragged edges."

"It was—" He felt a gentle rolling motion under his hand. His mouth opened in surprise. "Was that it?"

"Uh-huh."

"Incredible." He mentally urged the baby to move again. "Wow."

"The last time I was in the office the doctor let me listen to his heartbeat."

"What did it sound like?"

"A hummingbird."

"According to the book—"

"A hundred and fifty is normal," she finished for him.

A long time passed before either of them said anything. Finally it was Holly who broke the silence with a quiet "Thank you, Neal."

"What for?"

"Sharing this time with me."

He came up on his knees and stared at her long and hard. "I'm going to kiss you, Holly."

She flushed. "What am I supposed to say to that?"

He came forward. "Nothing. I just didn't want to take you by surprise or scare you or"—he was close enough to feel her breath against his lips—"or make you think . . ." The rest was lost as their mouths melded.

Cole had never felt such strong desire. Instead of a liability or a weakness, his need for her became empowering. He tried to restrain the kiss, to make it gentle and inviting, but when she opened her mouth and eagerly touched his tongue with her own, he was lost. He ran his hands down her arms and brought her closer, wanting to feel her against him. The position was awkward and he was afraid of hurting her. Reluctantly, he let her go.

"I'm sorry," she said. "It was reflex."

His answer was physical and unmistakable. He put his hand at the back of her head and brought her forward again. This time he was the aggressor, eagerly exploring her mouth. He cupped her breast and for a glorious second she pressed herself against his hand. But then she pulled away.

"We shouldn't be doing this," she said in a breathless

whisper. She touched her stomach in a brief, but to Cole, unmistakable gesture. They weren't the words he wanted to hear, but he knew she was right. As much as he wanted to make love to her, he could understand why she wouldn't feel the same about him. Her body wasn't hers alone anymore. She had the baby to think about. He would have to be patient. Still, reason could only take him so far. It was going to take some doing to put his hunger for her on hold. "Want to go to a movie?"

"Not really, but it's probably a good idea." When she looked at him there was naked acknowledgment of what had just happened between them. "Wherever we go, I think it better be public."

On the way back to town what had almost happened between him and Holly played itself over and over in Cole's mind. As much as he'd wanted to make love to her, there was something nagging at him, a voice that insisted they weren't ready—*no, that he wasn't ready.*

When the answer came, it hit with sickening force. He'd never believed his life-style had made him vulnerable to the HIV virus, but who could be sure anymore? He'd slept with more than one woman in the past five years and, foolishly, done so at times without protection. Even though the test he'd had at the hospital after the accident had been negative, the doctor had warned him that, to be sure, he would have to be tested again in six months.

How could something so fundamental have slipped his mind?

"Would you mind if we skipped the movie?" he asked. "I forgot that there was something I had to do this afternoon."

"I don't have any plans. Would you like me to go with you?"

He shook his head. For all her show of worldliness, Holly was still a country girl ready to bestow her trust like a gift. "This is something I have to do alone."

"Okay," she said a little too brightly.

"I'll tell you about it someday," he promised.

Holly spotted a tape sticking out of the tape player and reached over to push it into the machine. Seconds later the cab was filled with music.

The words reached out to Cole as if they had been written especially for him. All his life he had sung love songs and never really understood them.

Until now.

# 21

"*I have a collect call* for anyone from Neal Chapman," the operator said. "Will you accept the charges?"

"Yes, I will," Buddy replied. To Cole he said, "Why collect? How come you're not using the credit card?" Before Cole could answer, he added, "Never mind. It's not important. I'm just glad you decided to call."

The concern in Buddy's voice put Cole on edge. "What's up?"

"I heard from Eric George a couple of days ago. He said someone had been to his house asking questions about you. And then Mike called this morning and told me the same thing had happened to him. Do you have any idea what's going on?"

"Have you talked to Randy about this?"

"I called the house about a half hour ago. They said he was on his way to the office and that he was going to be there all afternoon."

"What office?" Cole asked, momentarily distracted.

"Yours."

"What's he doing there?" It was a stupid question to ask Buddy. Why should he be expected to know Randy's comings and goings?

"According to what he told me last week, he'll be spending a lot of time behind a desk from now on," Buddy said. "He's taking over the merchandizing department."

Cole was dumbfounded at the news. In the past whenever he brought up anything to do with the business end of Webster Enterprises, Randy had pointedly yawned or rushed to change the subject. If Cole had persisted because he wanted another opinion about something, Randy would leave the room. And now he was taking over the merchandizing department? It didn't make sense. He was going to have to call Randy himself and find out what was going on.

"When you talked to him last week," Cole said, going back to the original subject, "did he mention anything about Frank trying to find me again?"

"The only thing he said about Frank was that he was on vacation."

As far as Cole knew, Frank Webster had never taken a vacation in his life. "Are we talking about the same Frank here? My father?"

"I know, it blew me away, too. But wait until you hear the rest. He didn't go alone. He took some woman named Janet Reynolds with him."

With that everything fell into place. Frank wasn't on vacation; he'd merely gone somewhere else to work. "Where did they go, Nashville?"

"Hawaii."

Frank would never pick a place like Hawaii to conduct business. He had a thing about paying for long-distance calls and when he was working he was on the phone more than he was off. "Well, I'll be dammed," Cole said more to himself than Buddy. Cole needed time to absorb something this out of the ordinary. "Back to Mike."

"Oh, yeah. He said he tried to pump information from

the guy who came to see him, but he was real close-mouthed and wouldn't give out."

"How did Mike think to tell you about it?"

"He'd been talking to Eric and they started comparing notes. They decided that with both of them involved, it wasn't a coincidence and that you should know what was going down. Since I still kept in touch with Randy, they thought I was the best way to get the information to you."

"Neither of them thought to get in touch with me themselves?"

"I told you when you were here, Cole, the people who knew you in the old days feel the ties between you and them were cut when you hit it big."

"Did you set them straight?"

"I didn't feel it was my business. If you want to hear from those people, it's up to you to tell them."

Since he'd been gone, Cole had had to face some truths about himself that weren't particularly flattering or appealing. For all of his complaining that he had no control over his own life, he'd discovered he liked having things done for him.

It was a hell of a lot easier for Cole to sit back and let someone else, usually Frank, make his decisions, especially the ones that were uncomfortable or required personal attention. The more isolated and insulated Cole was, the less guilt he felt over things he couldn't control. In reality, he'd abused old friendships because he had no other choice. When there were thirty hours' worth of work that had to be squeezed into a twenty-four-hour day, some things, and a lot of someones, were bound to be left behind.

As much as the realization sickened him, he had to admit not only had it been convenient, it had been expedient to have Frank to blame for all the mistakes and hurt feelings of the past five years.

Cole cleared his throat, trying to dislodge the bad taste his flirtation with honesty had produced. "I'm sorry," he told Buddy. "I had no right to expect you to smooth the waters for me with Mike and Eric."

"Times change, Cole, and people change along with them. There's nothing saying you gotta bust your butt to hang on to every friend you ever made just because you feel guilty that you succeeded and they didn't. It drives me crazy just thinking about it, but it's a whole lot easier for some people to stick with you through the bad than the good. You just have to—" He stopped. "My God, would you listen to me? Tell me I don't sound as dumb to you as I do myself."

"Not dumb, Buddy, just a little preachy. But what you're saying is something I needed to hear. When I get back—"

"It's about time," Buddy injected, plainly pleased about something. "I'd about given up hope I was ever going to hear that from you."

"I don't know what you're talking about," Cole said, honestly confused.

"You turned the corner, kid. This is the first time I've heard you say 'when' you come back. Till now it's always been 'if.' Did something happen you haven't told me about?"

Only at that moment did Cole realize that somewhere, somehow, he'd reached a decision about what he wanted to do with his life. He'd expected something cataclysmic, a moment of revelation arriving on a clap of thunder. Instead, the resolution had been carried on a breeze so soft it had disturbed neither thought nor emotion.

"There's something else I discovered about myself a couple of weeks ago," Cole said in wonder. "I get off on the feeling that comes when I'm in front of an audience, especially when I can make them stop what they're doing to listen to me sing."

"You're singing?" Buddy was incredulous. "In public? And no one has recognized you?"

Cole chuckled. "Ain't it grand?"

"How in the hell did you pull that off?"

"People see what they expect to see. The Cole Webster the public knows lives in California in a great big house behind a great big fence. He sings with a ten-piece band in front of thousands of people. He has long hair, is clean shaven, and doesn't wear glasses. And he sings Cole Webster songs. Why in the world would anyone mistake me for him?"

"No one—not one single person—has figured it out?" Buddy questioned. "You're in Tennessee, for Christ's sake. Nashville isn't five hours away."

"Exactly. What would a celebrity like me be doing in a town like Maryville when the city that's the heart and soul of country music is right up the road?" Cole ran his hand across his beard. "The doctor was right, by the way. The swelling has gone down and the scars have faded. That face staring back at me in the mirror each morning is beginning to look more and more familiar."

"Then I'd say your days of living the quiet life are numbered. I don't care how small the town is that you're in, someone's going to look up one day and see past the disguise. I just hope you've told Holly who you are before that happens. It would be a hell of a thing for her to have to learn from someone else."

There wasn't anything Buddy could say to Cole that he hadn't already said to himself. Rather than get into it again, Cole changed the subject, turning the focus back on Buddy. "By the way, you forgot to take the telephone bill out of that last money order you sent me."

"It wasn't enough to bother with."

"We had a deal, Buddy."

"Oh, so it's all right for you to trade your Lotus for my truck, but you get all bent out of shape if I eat a fifty-dollar phone bill?"

"If it'll make you any happier, I'll give you back your friggin' truck when this is over."

"You think I want that piece of junk cluttering up my driveway?"

Cole laughed. "Get off the phone, Buddy, and let me talk to the brains in the family."

"Hang on a minute. I'll get her for you."

Several seconds later, Suzy came on the line. "Did you get her to quit?" she asked.

"She wasn't very happy about the idea."

"But you convinced her, right?"

"In a way."

"What's that supposed to mean? I wasn't kidding when I told you it was dangerous for Holly to be working as hard as she is," Suzy said, her speech impassioned. "Doing waitress work is hard enough; add everything else she does and it's just too much."

"She isn't working at the motel anymore, at least not as a maid. Arnold fired her. Now I've got her job."

"You're doing maid's work?" Suzy said carefully.

"I knew I could count on you to understand, what with you hating sexism as much as you do." Sometimes it just all came together. He wished she could see his self-satisfied grin.

"So what's the latest?" she quizzed him.

"Holly let me feel the baby moving," Cole said, making no attempt to hide how much it had meant to him.

Suzy's voice softened. "I remember when Buddy felt Cole move for the first time. It was very special, for both of us."

"I'm in love with her, Suzy," he admitted, liking the way it sounded.

"Of course you are. I've known that for weeks. You're going to make a terrific daddy for that baby."

Her words and the confident way she said them made Cole's chest swell with pleasure. "There's something I need to ask you, but I—"

"I don't know why I'm letting you off the hook so easy, but I have a feeling what you want to know is whether it's all right to have sex with a pregnant woman. Am I right?"

Suzy was never going to win an award for subtlety. "That pretty much sums it up," he admitted.

"Every woman is different, of course, but there are some of us who have this screwy hormone thing that turns us into maniacs the second trimester. If Holly is anything like I am, the two of you are going to have a terrific time."

Cole could hear Buddy in the background groaning in embarrassment. "And if she's not like you?"

"Don't push her. The wait will be worth it."

"Thanks," Cole said.

"Anytime. By the way, did you find out when she's due?"

"Three days before you are."

"Wouldn't it be neat if I was early or she was late? The kids could celebrate their birthdays together." She laughed. "At *your* house."

Cole liked that Suzy had already included Holly and her baby in her and Buddy's lives. It made his own dream all the more real. Someday he was going to have to tell Holly how he'd really become an expert on pregnancy. It was either confess his source of information or have Suzy do it for him the first time she and Holly got together.

They talked for another five minutes, until Suzy had to leave for work. After telling her good-bye, Cole said, "Put Buddy back on the phone, would you?"

He was on the defensive when he returned. "If you're going to rag on me again about that bill, I don't want to hear it."

"It's not about the bill," Cole assured him. "I just wanted your gut instinct on this business with Mike and Eric. My inclination is to go with Frank, but then I've noticed I have a tendency to blame him for everything."

"You've started seeing that in yourself, have you?"

"Yeah, and I can't say I like it much."

"Well, as tempting as it is to lay this on his doorstep, I don't think he's involved."

"Why tempting?" Cole asked.

"Because then we wouldn't have to look someplace else for an answer. Or did you have someone in mind?"

"The only thing I can come up with is that there's a reporter who figured there was more of a story than we were letting out and decided to start snooping around."

"Makes sense to me."

"I'm going to give Randy a call and see what he thinks," Cole said.

"Let me know if you find out anything."

"I will," Cole promised. He hung up and immediately dialed the office number in Los Angeles.

"Webster Enterprises," a softly southern voice answered. "How can I help you?"

"I'd like to speak to Randy Webster."

"And who shall I say is callin'?"

The question gave Cole pause. "Tell him it's Buddy Chapman."

"Please hold."

Randy picked up immediately. "Have you heard from Cole? Did you tell him about—"

"He told me," Cole said. A smile formed. It was good to hear Randy's voice.

"How's it going?"

There were a dozen ways he could answer, all shades and variations of the truth. "I'll deny this if you repeat it, but I think I'm starting to feel a little homesick."

"For *California?*"

"For my old life. Or at least the updated version, which is the way I want my old life to be when I come back."

"I'd given up ever hearing those words from you," Randy said.

"I decided I like singin' for my supper. Good thing, too, since it's all I know how to do."

"Dad said something along those lines just after you left."

"Speaking of Dad, I understand he's in Hawaii."

Randy snorted. "*Was* in Hawaii. He didn't last three days."

"But he went," Cole said. "You had to be as surprised as I was."

"That trip is all he can talk about since he came back. You'd think he invented vacations."

"You're leaving something out," Cole prodded.

"Buddy told you, huh?"

"It's true then? Janet really did go with him?"

"Talk about an odd couple," Randy said. "I still haven't figured what she sees in him, but then I never have been very good at things like that."

"What about Dad?" Cole asked, bracing himself for the answer. A lot of women had come and gone in Frank's life the years they were on the road. They were all short-term, temporary diversions for a man on a mission, or so it had seemed to his sons. It had never occurred to Cole and Randy that Frank might be lonely, that he might want someone besides his sons to share his life, or how hard it would be to find a woman willing to step in and become mother to two boys hell-bent on making their father's life as difficult as their own.

"He's worse than Janet," Randy told him. "I damn near had to tie him down to get him to listen to me about her, but as soon as he opened his eyes, there was no stopping him."

Cole was hit with the sobering reality of being on the outside. He didn't like the feeling. "How did you get involved in this thing?"

"Janet and I were working at the office one day when she let it slip how she felt about Dad. She was really upset that I'd found out and made me promise I wouldn't say anything, but—"

"You couldn't resist playing matchmaker." More than anything else that had happened since Cole left, Randy's involvement in Frank's private life told him how dramatically their relationship had changed. Cole was pleased for them, but he was disappointed he hadn't been there to share in the healing.

"I think it's going to work out for them," Randy said.

Picturing Frank and Janet as anything but sparring partners was more than Cole could manage without actually seeing the two of them together. "I have a feeling I already know the answer to this, but what do you think the chances are that Frank is behind whoever's out beating the bushes and asking questions about me?"

Several seconds passed before Randy said, "I don't know what you're talking about."

"I'm sorry, I thought maybe Mike and Eric might have called you, too." Cole filled him in on the information Buddy had relayed earlier.

"Frank's not involved," Randy said without hesitation.

"What makes you so sure?" Cole had to know whether the answer was based on Randy's newfound feelings for Frank or something he knew for fact.

"He and Janet have worked their asses off setting it up for you to be gone the six months you wanted. Why would they do that and then ruin it all by trying to get you to come back early? Besides, Frank thinks if he's not careful, you might decide to stay away permanently. He's not about to do something that could come back on him the way this could."

Randy's assurances helped ease Cole's mind. Even if some reporter had decided to start snooping around on his own, the only people who could tell him anything wouldn't. "You should probably fill Dad in on this, just in case."

"I don't see any reason you couldn't tell him yourself."

"Because you'll be seeing him and can do it for me," Cole snapped, making no attempt to hide his irritation. "It's not that big a deal."

Randy gave as good as he got. "I'm through being your errand boy, Cole. From now on, if you want Dad to know something, you're going to have to take care of it yourself."

Cole flinched. They were the very words he'd wanted to say to Frank and Randy all of his life, only he'd never had the guts. "I'll call him later."

"I'm sorry, Cole. I shouldn't have come on so strong to you."

"Don't apologize. You were right to say what you did. There's just one thing."

"What's that?"

"I want you to remember this conversation." He prayed it would never come up between them, that the gains he and Randy and Frank had made in the past months wouldn't vanish when he went home, but it never hurt to have something in reserve.

"If you catch me backsliding," Randy said, "I hope to hell you hit me with something harder than this."

It was that simple. Randy understood precisely where Cole's thoughts had led. It had always been that way between them. He was struck with how deeply he missed being with Randy and how anxious he was for Holly to meet him. But the overriding emotion Cole felt was fear. His newfound enthusiasm, all that he dreamed for the future, would disappear if he screwed up and lost Holly.

He needed time to be sure that didn't happen.

"Cole?"

Cole mentally shook himself. "Yeah?"

"Do you want me to do some checking around to see if I can get a fix on who's trying to find you?"

"I want you to do more than that. Talk to Marshall and have him put some people on it." Marshall Thompson, a retired FBI agent, handled security for them when the band was on the road.

"What are you going to do if it is a reporter?"

"A lot depends on who he works for. If it's someone legit, we find out how much he knows and if it's enough to cause problems, we buy him off with an exclusive."

"And if he's a free-lancer?"

"I'm screwed." In this case, free-lancer was a kind-hearted

euphemism for someone working to sell the story to the highest bidder. The more sensational the writer could make the piece, the more a tabloid would pay. Cole didn't stand a chance trying to reason with them, and as far as he was concerned, offering money was tantamount to paying blackmail.

"As soon as I hear something I'll leave word with Buddy."

The reasons Cole had set up the now awkward communication system no longer seemed valid. "Got a pencil?"

"Hang on a minute," Randy told him. "Okay, I'm ready."

Cole gave him Holly's telephone number. "Just remember to ask for Neal Chapman."

"Interesting choice of names."

"The Chapman part was a good trigger when I came out of the coma. It helped me to remember—" He caught himself, but it was too late.

"What coma?" Randy demanded.

"It's a long story. I'll tell you about it when I get back."

"You had a relapse?"

He wasn't going to let it go. "I got hit on the head, but it was months ago," Cole said. "I'm fine now."

"Goddammit, when are you coming home?"

"As soon as I can work things out with Holly."

"What's to work out? I don't understand this big fear you have that she's going to dump you the minute she finds out you're Cole Webster. It doesn't matter what name you go by, you're the same person."

"It's a little more complicated than that. Holly has this thing about trust and country singers. If it weren't for the baby—" Damn, he'd done it again.

"*Baby?*" Randy yelled. "You're going to be a father— I'm going to be an uncle—and you've waited all this time to tell me?"

"It's not as simple as it seems," Cole said slowly.

"How can—oh, you mean because of Belinda?"

Cole groaned. Somehow he'd managed to put her out of his mind yet again. "She's still staying at the house?"

There was a long pause before Randy said, "Of course she's still here. Why wouldn't she be?"

"I told her weeks ago it was over between us. She was supposed to be looking for someplace else to live."

"Are you sure she understood you? She never said anything about it to me."

"I'm sure. But it's not your problem, it's mine." With Belinda still living in his house how would he ever convince Holly he wasn't just like Troy?

"I wouldn't mind helping you out on this one," Randy said. "Especially if it'll get you and Holly and that nephew or niece of mine back here any sooner."

"What if I told you the baby wasn't mine?"

"You mean biologically?"

"Yes."

"I'm assumin' it's a package deal with Holly?"

"Yes."

"Then as far as I'm concerned that makes you the daddy and me the uncle."

Only then did the far-reaching implications hit Cole. "And Frank the grandpa."

Randy laughed. "Just don't let him put a guitar in the kid's hands. Look how you turned out."

Cole heard Holly's car pull into the driveway. "I've got to go," he said. "Call me as soon as you hear anything from Marshall."

"What about Belinda?"

"I don't know. Before I do anything, I have to figure a way to keep her from being hurt any more than she already has been."

"Maybe I could—"

"I've really got to go, Randy." Holly was coming up the back step.

"Can I tell Dad about the baby?"

"*No.*" That was the last thing he needed.

"Just testing." Randy chuckled. "See ya."

"Soon, I hope," Cole said to himself as he replaced the receiver.

Although Cole had had only two rooms to clean that morning and had finished his work long before Holly, she seemed surprised to see him standing in the middle of the kitchen. "Have you been waiting for me?"

"I couldn't find anything for lunch so I thought we'd go out for a hamburger."

She put her purse on the table, shrugged out of her coat, and hung it on the back of the chair. "There's tuna fish in the cupboard."

"We've already had tuna four times this week. I don't know about you, but I'm getting a little tired of it." Since their picnic in Cades Cove three days ago, they'd been like wary prizefighters, never coming close enough to touch, forever circling. The hunger inside Cole was matched only by his fear. He'd never wanted anything as much as he wanted a life with Holly.

"Arnold isn't going to be able to keep us on much longer if things don't pick up at the motel and I don't see that happening with the rain ruining what little fall color is left."

"It'll be all right, Holly. We'll get by."

She ran her hand through hair desperately in need of a trim. "I wish I could be as—"

"Trust me on this." She looked so dejected he went to her and took her in his arms.

She laid her head against his chest. "It's just that—"

He touched his chin to the top of her head and drew her in closer. "Holly, you're not listening to me. I said we'd get through this and we will."

"I want to believe you. I really do."

"But?"

It was a long time before she answered. "I love that you see magic in sunsets, but only one of us can be a dreamer, Neal."

"You're wrong, Holly. There's room for both of us and I'm going to prove it to you."

Her arms tightened around his waist. "That would be the best present you could ever give me."

# 22

*Holly waited for the traffic* light to change, her thoughts, as usual, focused on Neal. A week had gone by since their picnic, a week that ranked right up there with the best in her life. She was learning to laugh again, at silly things that would have been the source of frustration a couple of months ago. When she poked a hole in the rotted screen door with her elbow, she hadn't automatically thought how much it would cost to have it fixed, but how lucky they were summer was over. Neal had given her a ten on the idiotic happiness scoring system he created. She'd tried to scowl at his impromtu award ceremony but couldn't pull it off. Especially when he insisted on taking her in his arms and giving her a congratulatory kiss.

For all of Neal's protestations that her bulk wasn't a turnoff, she was beginning to wonder if the message had reached his subconscious. Which was okay if it hadn't. At least for now. She could understand his hesitation—she had a mirror.

The light changed and she started toward home again, stopping for the mail as she turned into the driveway. She took a minute to sort through the flyers, stopping when she saw an envelope with her doctor's return address on it. Curious, she tore it open as soon as she parked her car behind Neal's truck.

She was confused when she saw the letter was addressed to Neal, glanced at the envelope and saw that it had been, too. What was her doctor doing writing to Neal? She hesitated. One of the things she'd learned at her mother's knee was that a lady never snooped.

But then no one had ever accused her of being a lady.

*Dear Mr. Chapman:*

*I am pleased to inform you that all the blood pathogen tests you requested have come back negative. Your concern over possible harm to Ms. Murdock or her baby should you engage in intimate relations was admirable, but unfounded.*

*The information you requested on the Lamaze classes is enclosed. If I can be of any more assistance to you on this or any other medical matter, please let me know.*

*Sincerely,*
*Patrick Sidney, M.D.*

At first Holly was confused why Neal would go for blood tests and then it came to her. He could give her gifts for the rest of their lives; none would be as special as this. She got out of the car and went to look for him. She found him taking a shower.

She considered knocking on the door to let him know she was home and that she'd intercepted the letter and that she loved him more with every breath she took. She had her hand raised when it came to her that there was a better, far less wordy way to let him know how she felt.

Before she could reason out the sanity of what she was

doing, Holly had her clothes off. The door she tapped against wasn't to the bathroom itself, but to the shower.

Cole noticed a shadowed form outside the glass enclosure. He stepped from the spray, cracked open the door, and saw Holly. She had a towel draped across her middle; her legs and arms were bare. A bolt of heat shot through him; he let out a groan. "Do you have any idea what you just did to me?"

"No."

He glanced in the mirror and saw her bare backside, confirming his suspicion she wasn't wearing anything underneath the towel. "What's this about, Holly?"

"I accidentally opened your mail."

"What's that got—"

"From Doctor Sidney."

"Oh."

"He said you passed your test."

"I just thought—"

"You don't have to explain."

Cole let the door swing open. "Are you sure about this?"

She nodded.

His finger dipped into the hollow between her breasts. He gently tugged the towel from her grasp and let it fall to the floor. For long seconds he stared at her, his eyes filled with longing. "Do you want to come in or do you want me to come out?"

The look on his face told Holly everything she needed to know. She was beautiful to him. Her burgeoning waist was as inconsequential as the mole on her shoulder. She stepped into the warm spray and his eager arms.

Water cascaded over them creating a slick, sensual coat where their bodies touched. Cole lowered his head, meeting her upturned mouth and covering it with his own. The kiss was explosive, sending shock waves throughout his body.

"It's time I told you something," he said and then hesitated. It was only weeks ago that he'd made a big deal out of saying what was happening between them needed time to grow and develop. Would she be suspicious of any declaration he made now, under these circumstances? He considered waiting until later, then decided he was tired of erring on the side of reason.

"I love you, Holly," he said.

She looked at him. "I know." She smiled. "I think I love you, too."

He backed away from her, as far as the confined space would let him. "Think?"

"All right, I know I love you."

"What are we going to do about it?" He wanted her to be the one to say they belonged together, hoping it would make her commitment deeper.

A spark of mischief lit her eyes. "Now or later?"

She'd purposely misinterpreted him, but it didn't matter. For now, her being there was enough. Cole's restraint joined the water sheeting off his back and disappeared as effortlessly. He moved toward her, anticipating the feel of her body before the actual contact, experiencing the moment in waves. His hands cupped her buttocks. He pulled her tight against him, pressing the heat of his erection into the softness of her belly.

A deep moan rose from her as she rocked her hips in unmistakable invitation. "If what I'm feeling has anything to do with messed-up hormones, I hope it never goes away."

Cole laughed. This moment, standing in a shower barely big enough for one, in Maryville, Tennessee, about to make love to the woman he loved more than anything or anyone else on earth, was the most perfect he'd ever known.

Holly touched the side of his face. "What are you thinking?"

"How much I love you."

Her finger traced the scar on his temple and the one over his eyebrow. "I wish I'd been there for you."

He took her hand and pressed a kiss to the palm. "So do I," he told her softly. More than she would ever know.

She looked into his eyes for long, intense seconds. "Touch me," she whispered.

He needed no further invitation or encouragement. His hands slid over her body, exploring the curve of her neck, the slope of her shoulder, and the small hollow at the base of her spine, always gentle, infinitely thorough. When she tried to hurry him, he held her hands at her sides and continued the exploration with his mouth and tongue.

At last his finger found the swollen nub between her legs. She gasped at the intense, raw hunger that stole her reasoning. Her body was no longer hers to control. One emotion, a single need, drove her. She moved to his rhythm, pressing against his hand. Neal bent and licked the water from her nipple, then brought the rigid tip into his mouth, stroking it with his tongue. Holly pressed her back against the tile and dug her hands into Neal's shoulders, her eyes closed, her mouth slightly open as she caught her breath in a gasp. Cole felt her rhythmic contractions beneath his hand and thrust his finger inside to hold her.

Holly opened her eyes and met his gaze. A slow, seductive smile crossed her lips. She came forward, ran her tongue around the curve of his ear, her hand around his erection, and whispered, "Could we move this to the bedroom?"

Cole's midsection tightened. It was going to be an afternoon to remember.

Light from a full moon spilled through the bedroom window and lay across the queen-sized bed like a celestial quilt. Cole tucked his hand under his pillow and stared at Holly, careful that his movements didn't disturb her sleep.

He ached to touch her, to feel the softness of her lips and the supple feel of her skin. The memory of doing so still echoed in his senses; the fire that burned inside her still warmed him.

When finally their passion had been sated and they lay in each other's arms it was time for yet a new intimacy. Holly asked about the scar on his leg and he told her how it had gotten there, liking that it was the truth and that there would soon be no more lies between them.

As he watched her, Holly stirred and rolled to her side, facing away from him. He moved to cradle her, gently laying his arm across her swollen waist, his hand on her belly.

The baby moved. A feeling of well-being and love washed over Cole. "Your life will be filled with satellites and sunsets and trips to the ocean," he whispered to the child he would raise as his own.

As if in response to his promise, the baby moved again. At that moment something mystical happened between them. Cole knew with unshakable certainty that Holly was having a girl and that it didn't matter who had provided the sperm that sparked her life; he was her father.


"Good morning," Holly said.

Neal blinked his eyes open and smiled. "You're beautiful," he told her.

She laughed softly. "Where did you leave your glasses? I'll get them for you."

He propped himself up on his elbow and kissed the end of her nose. "I don't need them."

"If you want me to believe you, first you're going to have to tell me where you intended that kiss to land."

"Exactly where it did—on your chin." He put his hand at the back of her neck and drew her to him. This time, as his mouth closed over hers, there was no mistaking his aim or intention.

She moved closer, fitting her ample curves into his accommodating body. Incredibly, with only a kiss, she was ready for him. Somehow during their lovemaking the night before, he'd convinced her she was the sexiest woman alive and she reveled in that knowledge. She felt no shyness with him, no need to hold her shoulders back to make her breasts ride high, and no need to hide who and what she was to try to please him.

He liked her just the way she was. Her heart skipped a beat. He *loved* her just the way she was. She knew that because he'd told her last night, over and over again, until she had no choice but to believe him.

Neal kissed the sensitive hollow behind her ear. Holly moved her head to one side and sighed. "If we keep this up, we're going to be late for work," she said, trying hard to make it sound as if she cared.

He reared back, eyed her, and grinned. "I told Arnold not to expect us before noon today."

"You were pretty sure of yourself."

He cupped her breast with his hand and made slow sweeps across the nipple with his thumb. "This was too important not to be."

"You're crazy."

"No, I'm just a man who's finally found what he's been looking for all his life."

She traced the outline of his chin with the back of her fingers, lightly touching his neatly trimmed beard. "What's so remarkable is that I believe you."

"I don't want you to ever doubt how I feel about you, Holly. No matter what happens."

A warning sounded in Holly's mind. "You make it sound as if you're expecting something."

"Do I?" he asked with too much enthusiasm. "I didn't mean to."

He was scaring her. "Neal, if there's something I should know, just tell me."

He stopped her with a kiss. "If you want to talk," he murmured against her lips, "we can talk. But not like this. There's no way I can stay in this bed and concentrate on anything but making love to you."

His words aroused her as effectively as his hands. "Whatever it was," she said, "it'll keep."

An hour later Cole was back in the shower when Holly came into the bathroom. "I'm going to the store for eggs," she said.

He propped the door open several inches and peered out at her. "If you wait a minute, I'll go with you."

"I can be there and back by the time you get out."

"I take it you're hungry?"

"Starved."

"Go on then. I'll see you when you get back."

She came forward for a kiss and almost forgot about breakfast. It was as if she weren't the master of her body anymore. A look, a touch, a kiss, and she was lost. She brushed a drop of water from her nose. "If you want breakfast, be dressed when I get back," she warned him.

The left side of his mouth came up in an enticing, lustful grin. "What do you think Leroy and Arnold would say if we asked for a couple of days off?"

She pushed a dripping strand of hair back from his face. "How Leroy and Arnold feel doesn't concern me." God, how she hated being practical. "It's what the electric company will say when we try to explain why we can't pay them next month."

Cole grew serious. "There are some things we have to talk about when you get back."

She knew what he was getting at and had already decided to stop fighting him. He could help her pay the bills from then on. "I love you."

"Keep that thought," he said.

It wasn't what she wanted to hear. She tried again. "I love you, Neal Chapman."

"And I love you, Holly Murdoch."

She smiled. "That's what I was after."

"I'll tell you a hundred times a day if you promise me something."

"Bargaining for my affection?" she teased. "Shame on you."

"If you truly believe I love you, Holly, we can get through anything."

"Why wouldn't I believe you?"

He waited a long time to answer her. "I don't know."

She cupped the sides of his face; water dripped on her arm. "Don't look so sad. We're going to be fine. There isn't anything the two of us can't handle together."

"I love you."

She kissed him, thoughtfully and tenderly. "Ninety-eight more to go, Chapman."

"Hurry back," he murmured.

"As fast as my Corsica will go."

By the time Holly pulled into the parking lot at the grocery store her plans for breakfast had undergone a radical change. The bacon and eggs and pancakes she'd planned seemed impossibly time-consuming, both to prepare and eat. A good whole-grain cereal was not only healthier, it was a lot faster.

She caught a glimpse of herself in the plate-glass window as she neared the store entrance and was so startled, she stopped for a closer look. Her self-satisfied grin might as well have been a flashing neon sign announcing the previous night's activities. She tried for a serious expression and was willing to settle for pleasant, but no amount of coaxing herself could wipe the grin off her face.

The only thing to do was get in and out of the store as fast as possible and hope she didn't run into anyone she knew. With a hurried step and downcast eyes, she went inside.

No one stopped her; no one even looked her way. She gathered her groceries and headed for the checkout stand. The woman in front of her suddenly remembered she had coupons in her purse. While Holly waited for the checker to sort them out, she glanced at the magazines and tabloid papers lined up on both sides. Halfway through her perusal she froze. Her heart leaped to her throat; her hands locked on the cart. For long seconds she stared at the man on the cover of *The World Reporter,* trying to deny and then rationalize something she couldn't comprehend.

"I can take you now," the checker said.

Holly looked up to see the man motioning her forward.

"Ma'am, if you'll push your cart up, I can take you now."

Woodenly she did what he asked. He was ready to ring the total when she told him, "Wait." She reached for a copy of the tabloid.

"Some story, huh?" the checker said. "They couldn't find Elvis, so now they've got a reward out for Cole Webster."

She frowned. "Cole Webster?"

He turned the paper around so she could see the picture. "This is what he's supposed to look like now accordin' to his girlfriend. Ain't it somethin' what they'll print in these things?"

Neal was Cole Webster? He had a girlfriend? Holly put her hand to her mouth. She felt as though she was going to be sick.

Cole was out of the shower and getting dressed when he decided he didn't want to wait for Christmas to give Holly the crib. He wanted to give her something to celebrate the change in their relationship, but more importantly, he wanted her to know that he thought of the three of them as a family. Trailing in importance, but still in the running, was how pleased he was with the way the crib had turned out. He'd been dying to show Holly the transformation the painting had accomplished, and there would never be a better time.

He brought the pieces in from the garage and began assembling them in the kitchen, periodically stopping his humming to listen for her car. Despite his determination to meet her at the door, he became so absorbed in what he was doing, he missed hearing her return, not realizing she was standing in the kitchen watching him until he got up to move to the opposite side of the crib.

His greeting caught in his throat when he saw the stricken look on her face. He laid the screwdriver on the table. "What's wrong?"

She held her hand up to stop him when he made a move toward her. "Don't touch me."

"Holly, what is it?" Sudden and intense fear made Cole go cold.

"How could you do this? Why would you?" She shook her head, as if trying to deny something too painful to acknowledge.

"Tell me what you're talking about." Only one thing could have shaken her this badly, but he couldn't accept the obvious. After all the time they'd been together, how could she suddenly have figured out who he was? And on this morning of all mornings.

She brought her hand up and he saw she was holding *The World Reporter*. With her eyes locked on his face, she turned the paper over to the front page. Cole didn't have to look to know what was there, but almost as if he didn't have any choice, his gaze was pulled to the drawing. What he saw knocked the wind out of him.

The picture wasn't a sloppy composite put together by someone who'd picked up a piece of gossip at the hospital and imagined what Cole Webster would look like after having his face smashed; it was a perfect likeness.

A knife would have caused less pain than the sense of betrayal that swept through him. Not a dozen people knew how the accident had changed him. Only two of the doctors who'd taken care of Cole knew who he really was; the rest of the hospital people knew him under an assumed name.

It made him sick to think someone he trusted could have done this to him, but the picture was so detailed, right down to the length of his beard and the location and shape of his scars. Beneath the picture was something he hadn't noticed before, a ten-thousand-dollar reward for the first person who called in with information on the whereabouts of Cole Webster. He didn't have to look inside to know what was there. Along with a wrap-up of his career would be a listing of the women he'd known, more damning, the woman who was waiting for him to return.

He didn't have much time.

"You lied to me. All this time you lied to me," Holly said.

Cole held his hand out to her. She backed away. "I'm sorry," was all he could think to say. Where were the words that would make her understand?

"Damn you." She threw the paper at him. "You had no right to make love to me last night."

He was quicker when he reached for her this time, bringing her into his arms before she had a chance to react. He held on to her despite her struggle to free herself. "Are you mad because we made love, Holly? Or because you fell in love?"

"I trusted you." Her accusation was filled with pain. "I didn't want to." She stopped fighting and stood perfectly still. "God, I'm so stupid."

"Except for my name, I never lied to you, Holly."

"Maybe not openly, but you left a hell of a lot out. Including a woman who thinks you're coming back to her. And dumb Holly went along for the ride."

The phone rang, momentarily distracting Cole. Holly slipped from his grasp and headed across the room. "Don't answer it," Cole commanded.

"I'll do what I damn well please," she shot back. "This is still my house and my telephone." She jerked the receiver off its hook. "Hello." The word was more accusation than greeting. A second later, she shot a disgusted look in Cole's direction. "Just a minute," she said to whoever was on the line. To Cole she said, "It's for you."

He hesitated. His old life, where answering or not answering a telephone could be fodder for an article, had come thundering back. "Did they give a name?"

"It's some guy named Frank."

Cole took the phone. "If you're calling to tell me about the piece in *The World Reporter*, you're too late." Holly started to move away. Cole grabbed her hand. This time she didn't fight him.

"I'm sorry, Cole. The thing caught us completely off guard. Janet said her spy at the paper didn't even know they were working on something about you, that everything was done behind closed doors because they were afraid of being scooped."

Cole desperately needed someone to vent on. With a jolt, he realized that six months ago, it would automatically have been Frank, whether he deserved it or not. Even more startling was the realization that Frank would have taken the abuse in stride. "Obviously they knew we wouldn't let them have an exclusive if we found out what they were up to."

"What do you want me to do?"

It was on the tip of Cole's tongue to tell his father that he was perfectly capable of taking care of himself, when it struck him how petulant the reply sounded. Had he learned nothing the past half year? It was time Cole recognized his father's strengths instead of looking for his weaknesses. Frank was at his best managing a crisis.

Before Cole could answer, there was a loud, insistent knock on the front door. Holly jumped at the sound, then tried to move around Cole. He blocked her path. "Hang on a minute," he said to Frank, and then to Holly, "Don't follow me."

She glared at him. "I'm through listening to you, Neal, or Cole, or whatever the hell your name is."

"Goddammit, this isn't a game, Holly. You either do what I tell you or I'll find a way to make you." He moved even closer, purposely intruding on her space to make his point. "Do you understand?"

The fire drained from her. "Yes."

Cole went to the front bedroom window and carefully drew the curtain aside. He spotted a woman dressed in a gray suit standing on the porch and then a man half hidden behind the spicebush, camera poised. As he watched, another car drove up and stopped. The two people who got out were duplicates of the first.

How had they found him so quickly? Almost as soon as the question arose, a dozen possibilities presented themselves. He'd done nothing to hide or disguise himself while living in Maryville. Whoever had called the paper could be anyone, from the woman next door who'd loaned him a cup of sugar to one of the waitresses at the restaurant. Ten thousand dollars was a hell of an enticement.

Cole went back into the kitchen and picked up the phone. "Do whatever it takes to get us out of here, Frank, and make it fast."

# 23

By the time Frank called back to tell him everything had been arranged, so many reporters and photographers had gathered around the house they were spilling into the neighbors' yards. The noise from shouted questions and requests for pictures made it impossible for Holly to finish her phone call to her grandfather. She hung up with the promise to fill him in on the details when he met her at the airport in Phoenix. Outside, before the police arrived to clear everyone off the property, plants had been trampled, Holly's and Cole's laundry had been stripped from the clothesline, her car and his truck had been rummaged through, and by design or accident, the living-room window had been broken.

They were sitting at the kitchen table, Holly with her hands wrapped around the cup of hot chocolate Cole had fixed for her, Cole with a cup of coffee, when she told him, "I think you should know the only reason I'm going with you is because of the baby. If it wasn't for him—"

"*Her,*" Cole said softly but emphatically.

She sent him a withering look. "If it wasn't for *him,* I wouldn't walk outside with you."

Cole decided it wasn't the time or place to tell Holly how he knew her baby was a girl. He would save it for later when she could look back on the first time they'd made love and remember there had been magic on that night. He refused to consider the possibility there would never be another night like it. She undoubtedly believed that now, but he'd find a way to get her to change her mind. Whatever it took, he would do.

A half hour later, when the limo arrived and the bodyguards were in place, Cole and Holly made a dash from the house to the car. They were accompanied by the sounds of automatic cameras and flashing lights. A caravan of police and reporters followed them from Maryville to the Alcoa airport where Frank had arranged a private jet to meet them.

The limo drove onto the tarmac, the driver positioning the car beside the plane to allow Cole and Holly to step from one to the other. Cole tried to shield Holly from the photographers who lined the chain-link fence, their long-range lenses focused on the steps of the plane, but he knew from past experience it didn't matter how poor the photograph on a story as hot as this one; there would be something on the front page with the next edition.

"I've never been in a plane before," Holly said woodenly as she sat in the seat Cole indicated.

He took the seat opposite her, his back to the cockpit. "Are you afraid of flying?"

"Even if I were, nothing could scare me as much as what's outside."

"It won't take long before flying seems as natural to you as walking and the reporters become background."

"That's not going to happen, Neal."

He didn't correct her. "If flying bothers you, we can use one of the buses," he said, being deliberately obtuse, hoping she would go along with him. "We take them out on tour all the time. You wouldn't believe how comfortable they are."

"Don't do that," she said.

"How can you give up on us so easily, Holly?"

"I can't live like this. And even if I wanted to try and talk myself into believing I could, I don't want my baby to have this kind of life. It isn't natural. You know as well as I do, I didn't come with you today because I wanted to, Neal . . . Cole." She turned to look out the window. "The man I fell in love with was named Neal Chapman. I don't even know Cole Webster. Why would I want to spend the rest of my life with him?"

He didn't know how to answer her, which words would make a difference. Finally, they were cleared for takeoff and the plane began to move. Cole rebuckled his seat belt.

"It will never be the same for me in Maryville," she said. "Knowing you has changed my life forever. I can never just be me again. I'm going to always be that 'Cole Webster woman.' Dammit, I liked who I was. I hate that it's been taken away from me and there's nothing I can do about it."

"I'm sorry." To say more, to try to deny what they both knew to be the truth, would trivialize her pain.

"Look at that," she said, and pointed out the window. "They can't even see us, but they're still taking pictures." There was a hysterical catch in her voice. "Do you suppose they're hanging around because they think the plane might crash and they'd miss it if they went home to their families?" When she looked at him, there were tears in her eyes. "I can't live like this." The words sounded like a mantra to a new religion, one created just that morning.

"I know how ugly all this looks and how frightening it seems." Actually, it was seeing it through her eyes that reminded him how he had felt when he first became the focus of a media frenzy. The contrast made him aware of how habituated he'd become. "I won't lie to you—it's not a once-in-a-lifetime thing. This is a part of who I am. I don't like it. I wish there was a way to keep it from happening, just like I wish there was a way to keep the trash newspapers from printing the half-truths and outright lies that are going to be there tomorrow. What you saw today is the kind of thing I've been running from, Holly—why I was in Maryville, why I met you."

"Are you telling me you did this whole Neal Chapman thing just to get away from reporters?"

"It's more complicated than that," he admitted. "The accident I told you about left me questioning everything I was and everyone I knew. It wasn't until you coerced me into singing again that I remembered why I used to love it and realized that, for good or bad, it's what I am.

"The downside to finally accepting myself is knowing how you feel about people like me. It's what stopped me every time I thought about telling you who I really was. I kept thinking if I just gave you a little more time, you'd see I was different. And then this happened."

"You're not different, you just think you are. How could you tell me you loved me when you knew there was someone waiting for you back in California?"

The catch in her voice belied her clear eyes. How was he going to explain Belinda to her without sounding as cavalier as he seemed? He unbuckled his seat belt and came forward to take Holly's hand. As if sensing his intention, she folded her arms across her chest and turned to stare out the window.

Cole leaned back in his seat. "I'm not going to let you off this plane until you've heard me out."

She was quiet for a long time after that. When she looked at him, she said, "You have from here to Phoenix to convince me."


It was late afternoon in Phoenix when the plane touched down. Holly looked more tired than Cole had ever seen her. Still, she managed an encouraging smile when she caught him staring at her. He'd been using the telephone in the forward section of the cabin, arranging several last-minute details of his homecoming, and at Holly's request, informing Arnold and Leroy that they were short two employees. Cole was confident the two men had already figured out as much for themselves, but was willing to do anything to ease Holly's mind.

"I'm fine," she said, plainly responding to his worried expression.

"I don't want to leave you here." It was more than knowing how much he would miss her. He had an unshakable feeling that no matter how intelligent the reasoning for keeping her isolated from the media circus he would face when he got home, it was a mistake for them to separate.

"We need some time away from each other," she said reasonably. "I have thinking to do and you have . . . I can only imagine all you have to do."

"You're not changing your mind already, are you?" The transition from hostility to understanding had been hard won. She'd held on to her protective anger until he was afraid nothing he could say would make her let go.

"Right now, all I know for sure is that I love you."

"Promise me you'll hang on to that. And if it turns out that it's not enough, you'll give me a chance to make it right."

"I won't do anything without talking to you first." She took his hand and gave it a reassuring squeeze.

The plane made a tight turn and headed toward a small private terminal. Cole looked out the window and scanned the area for anyone carrying a camera. "It looks as though we pulled it off," he announced. "You should be safe at your grandfather's house for a few days at least. By then everything will have settled down enough to get you to LA without going through another scene like the one we just left."

"You sound so sure of yourself."

"There's not enough story in this to last more than a

week. As soon as they've had a chance at me in a press conference and see that I'm basically the same person I was this time last year, they'll move on to something or someone else." Out of the corner of his eye, Cole spotted a man wildly waving at their plane. He was wearing a blue golf shirt and khaki slacks and looked as if he were about to burst with excitement. Cole directed Holly to look out the window. "That wouldn't be your grandfather, would it?"

She spotted him immediately. Her smile was warm and filled with pleasure. "Grandpa doesn't do anything half-heartedly."

Cole was glad to see a spark in her eyes again. Selfishly, he wished that he'd been the one to put it there. His gaze swept the terminal, settling on a woman dressed in a dark blue suit and carrying a briefcase. It gave him an unfamiliar sense of satisfaction to see that Frank had come through for him yet again.

As the plane moved closer to the awaiting people, Holly put her hand to the window and returned her grandfather's wave. With her fingers pressed against the glass, she said, "Isn't it amazing the way your mind protects you and lets you forget how much you miss someone?"

"Is that an observation or a prophecy?"

The question made her think. "I don't know." She turned to look at him. "Maybe both."

Again Cole was hit with the gut feeling that it was a mistake to leave Phoenix without Holly. If only Frank hadn't told him Belinda was already on the way to the airport with Randy.

The pilot's voice came from the overhead speaker. "The truck we ordered to refuel is standing by, Mr. Webster. As soon as we're loaded, we can request clearance for takeoff."

Cole pressed the intercom switch. "Thank you." When he glanced back to Holly, it seemed as if a veil had been pulled over her eyes. "What's wrong?"

"I can't believe I'm seeing you like this. To me, all of this is new and strange, but you just take everything in stride. I've never even been on a plane before and you know how to use all the buttons. Last night you were a good old country boy who—" She stopped and drew in a deep breath, then put her hand to her mouth and blinked against a sudden onrush of tears. "Who bought a crib in a secondhand store and turned it into—"

"I didn't think you noticed," he said.

"What if it's not there anymore?"

He shifted to the seat beside her and took her into his arms. "It's all right, Holly. I'll get another one."

"I don't want another one."

"Then I'll have someone go to the house and get it and send it to us."

She was frowning when she looked up at him. "It's so easy for you. Is that what it's like to be rich?"

Before Cole had a chance to answer, the plane stopped and the copilot came out of the cabin to help with the door. Holly sat up and combed her hands through her hair.

Seconds later a booming voice filled the cabin. "Holly girl, where they hidin' you?"

"I'm over here, Grandpa."

Cole stood and moved out of the way. Instead of immediately going to his granddaughter, Horace Murdoch approached Cole. He studied the younger man for several seconds. "You must be the fella that got my Holly in this mess."

The statement caught Cole off guard. He didn't know whether he should stand firm and admit his guilt or get out of the way. And then it occured to him that Horace might be referring to Holly's burgeoning stomach. She'd told him about the pregnancy over the phone, but actually seeing her for the first time was undoubtedly a shock. "I'm aware how bad this looks, but I want you to know—"

"You don't owe me any explanations, son. I was only

commentin' on what I been told. If you're good enough for Holly, you're good enough for me." He took his hands off his hips and extended them to Cole in a hearty, two-handed greeting.

"I love your granddaughter, Mr. Murdoch." He found he liked saying the words out loud.

"'Course you do." He looked at Holly and smiled. "What's not to love?"

"You look wonderful, Grandpa," Holly told him. "This place must be good for you."

"And you look like one of them tea roses Grandma used to grow, blossomin' to beat the band." He gathered Holly in his arms.

A movement at the door drew Cole's attention. The woman in the suit had come inside and was discreetly waiting for him. Cole excused himself and went to her.

"I have the money and cashier's check you requested," she said, and handed him an envelope.

"Thank you." Cole glanced inside to be sure there had been no miscommunication and that the full amount was there.

She nodded. "We were pleased to be of service to you. If there is nothing else . . ."

"No, this takes care of it."

"Then I'll just wish you a pleasant flight and be on my way."

Cole returned to Holly and her grandfather. He handed the envelope to Horace. "If I gave this to Holly, it would take me the rest of the night to talk her into keeping it."

Rather than look inside, Horace felt the weight. His eyes narrowed in suspicion. "You think she's gonna need so much the short time she'll be here? It was my understandin' she wasn't gonna be stayin' with me but a couple of days."

Only then did Cole realize the money could be construed as a payoff. "There are some hospitals that won't take you in if you don't have insurance or can't prove you have money to take care of the bill. I don't expect anything to happen, but until Holly's covered under my policy, I don't want to take any chances."

"He's right, Grandpa, as much as I hate to admit it." To Cole, Holly said, "Don't ever try going around me again."

"I was only thinking about the baby, and how stubborn you can be about taking money."

"You don't know me as well as you think you do, Cole Webster. If need be, I'd steal the change out of a Salvation Army bucket to protect this baby."

"And you'd work your fingers to bloody stumps to pay it back," he countered.

Horace chuckled at the exchange. "So that's the way it is between you two. I always did wonder what kind of man Holly would end up with." He looked from Holly to Cole and back again. "This baby of yours is gonna be a real handful."

Holly flinched.

Cole smiled. "Especially if she's anything like her mother."

*"He,"* Holly said.

"We best be headin' out if we're gonna beat the traffic," Horace said to Holly. He clasped Cole's shoulder. "I'm lookin' forward to gettin' to know you better, son."

"Thank you, Mr. Murdoch."

"I like that you haven't forgotten the manners your mama taught you, but we're family now, and Horace is good enough." He moved toward the door. "Holly explained why you couldn't get off the plane on account of someone seein' you and then followin' her, so I'll just wait outside so you can say your good-byes in private."

"You have the number at the house?" Cole asked when Horace was gone. "And the one for the car phone?"

"I thought you said your brother didn't have a phone in his truck."

"He doesn't, but—"

"I'm kidding."

"Well, don't. This is too serious. I want to know you can reach me no matter where I am or what I'm doing."

"It's only for a couple of days," she protested.

"Is it?"

"I love you, Neal . . . Cole. I'll get it right one of these times."

"But is loving me enough?" He knew it was a mistake, but he couldn't let it go.

She waited a long time to answer him. Finally, in stark honesty, she said, "I don't know."

It wasn't what he wanted to hear. He kissed her, long and hard and deep. There was a desperate quality to the kiss as he tried to imprint himself into her mind and body. He couldn't lose her.

The first thing Cole heard when he emerged from the plane two hours later was an indiscreet whoop of joy from Randy as he came charging across the tarmac. He was unprepared for the impact when his brother picked him up and swung him around and was gasping for breath when he finally put him down again.

"Hot damn it's good to see you," Randy told him, grabbing him again, this time in a bear hug.

Cole laughed at the exuberant greeting. "It's good to see you, too." It was better than good; it was a lifeline. He'd learned home wasn't a place so much as it was the people who lived there.

"How's Holly?" Randy asked. "Is she getting through all this okay?" Before Cole could answer, Randy added, "Her being upset won't hurt the baby, will it? Does she know a doctor in Phoenix? Not that I think she's going to need one, but it wouldn't hurt to be prepared."

Cole pulled back to study Randy. "Are you on something?"

"Screw you." Randy laughed. "I'm just so damn glad to have you home. Now are you going to answer me or am I going to have to throw you down and beat it out of you?"

"Holly's doing all right." He pushed his glasses higher on his nose. It would be good to have his contacts back again. Actually, as the plane neared Los Angeles, he'd been surprised to discover there were a lot of things he was looking forward to. "At least she was when I left her. She handled finding out who I am better than I would have if I'd been in her position. But then that's the way she is. She let that son of a bitch Troy Martin walk out on her without so much as—" Cole stopped, realizing it wasn't the time or place to get into Troy Martin with Randy. "It really sticks in my throat that he's moving up as fast as he is."

Randy threw his arm across Cole's shoulders and started walking toward the hangar. "And he'll probably make it if he doesn't do something to self-destruct first."

A plane took off behind them and Cole had to shout his next question. "Have you heard anything from Marshall?"

"He traced the man who was snooping around with Mike and Eric back to a private detective here in LA. The guy's done work for Marshall in the past. Supposedly, he's really good, and he doesn't come cheap."

"Something tells me whoever hired the detective also gave the picture to *The World Reporter*. It's the why I can't figure out."

"You wouldn't believe the shit that's hit the fan around here since that rag came out this morning. There's so many reporters up at the house it took Frank fifteen minutes to get through the crush."

"How come no one followed you?"

"Frank sent me packing as soon as we got your call this morning. Belinda and I stayed at a motel in El Monte and waited for his call about where and when to pick you up."

"Where's Frank now?"

"He and Janet are leading a bunch of reporters on a chase out to LAX." Randy directed Cole around the building.

They had started across the parking lot to Randy's truck

when Cole looked up and saw Belinda. She was provocatively posed against the front fender, wearing a white Lycra jumpsuit that seemed almost transparent in the overhead streetlights. He'd never seen her look better.

Randy followed Cole's gaze. "Frank told her to dress inconspicuously."

"This is bound to be awkward. I'm sorry you had to be dragged into it," Cole told him. "I understand Frank tried to talk her into waiting for me at the house."

"And she tried to talk me into staying home and letting her pick you up alone."

Belinda started toward them with the practiced walk of a runway model. As she drew close she flashed a brilliant, triumphant smile. "You look fantastic," she said in a husky voice. "Good enough to eat. Which is exactly what I have in mind the minute I get you alone."

Cole cast an embarrassed glance at Randy. This was a Belinda he didn't know. The woman he left six months ago would never have come on to him in public. It wasn't that she didn't talk this way, but that she saved it for the bedroom.

Belinda picked up on his discomfort and said, "Randy knows how long it's been for us. He doesn't mind." She pushed herself between them, put her arms around Cole's neck, and kissed him, her tongue reaching for the back of his throat.

The depth of his revulsion at the kiss startled Cole. He'd expected to feel compassion or even guilt when he saw Belinda again, not enmity. He untangled himself from her grasp. "Remember, we're trying not to draw attention," he told her.

"Oh, it's all right for Randy to go running across the—" She caught herself. "You're right. I'm sorry. There'll be plenty of time for us later." She took his arm and pressed her breast against him as they moved toward the truck.

The few, brief conversations they'd had since he tried to end things between them had made it plain that she wasn't going to let go of their relationship without a fight.

But this went beyond anything Cole had imagined. There was a feel of desperation in Belinda's actions.

They arrived at the truck. Cole absently gave Belinda a hand up as he tried to reason through the new set of questions swirling through his mind. And then, with a sinking clarity, he realized what was bothering him.

It was her smile when she first saw him.

She hadn't looked pleased that he was there or even relieved; she'd looked victorious.

He put his foot on the running board and pinned her with a cold, hard stare. "How much did they pay you for the picture, Belinda?"

The color drained from her face. "I don't know what you're talking about," she stammered.

"You better hope it was enough to keep you until you can find someone else to take over the job, because I'm through."

"How could you accuse me of doing something like that?" She put her hand on his arm. "It's been a long trip," she said reasonably. "You're tired. Once we get back to the house and you've had a chance to rest, you'll see things differently."

"Why did you do it, Belinda?" Cole asked, his anger mixed with genuine curiosity. "Was it the money?"

Her eyes flicked from side to side, and she ran her tongue across her lips. "I didn't . . . I wouldn't . . . ." Her hand tightened on his arm. "Cole, please, think of all we've meant to each other."

He almost laughed. "Have I always been that easy to manipulate?"

"You've got to understand." She'd broken and said too much. She tried another tack. "I was desperate to have you home again. And I was scared. Yes, that's it, I was scared out of my mind. And I was lonely. You can't imagine what it was like here without you." She cast a frantic look in Randy's direction. "Tell him the hell I went through, Randy. You saw me. *Tell him.*"

"Leave Randy out of this," Cole said.

"Look at me, Cole," she commanded. "Think of the nights we've shared. I'm the fulfillment of every erotic dream you ever had. It can be that way for us again."

"Save it for a singles' ad, Belinda." He took her hand from his arm. "Who knows, after what you did for them, maybe the people at *The World Reporter* would be willing to give you a discount."

# 24

"*How did you know?*" Randy asked as he pulled up to a stop sign.

"It just all kind of fell into place," Cole said.

"Do you think she called the papers after we left the airport?"

"I'd put money on it."

"You were kind of hard on her," Randy said, "especially when she asked you for cab fare."

"For the fifty thousand she got for my picture she can *buy* herself a cab." He was more disappointed than angry, but anger was easier to deal with.

"Do you believe her?" Randy asked a short time later.

"You mean about why she did it?"

"Yeah."

Cole rolled down the window and let the cool evening air wash over him. "Oh, I think love was probably what drove her, but it wasn't love for me, it was for what I could give her. There's only one way for someone like Belinda to achieve the life-style she thinks she deserves, and that's by attaching herself to someone like me. In a way, it's her career, it's what she trained herself to do."

"Have you known this all along?"

"Probably. I just didn't want to admit it. When you go somewhere with a woman like Belinda on your arm it shows everyone how successful you are."

"And what does going somewhere with someone like Holly say?" Randy prompted.

Cole smiled. "How lucky I am."

"It looks like I'm going to have to get me one of them. Holly have any sisters?"

"I've never noticed you lacking in the female companionship department."

"I've been looking, but I can't seem to find that special one," Randy said with unusual candor. "I keep letting myself get sidetracked by butterflies with broken wings."

"And something tells me it's only going to get worse."

Randy shot Cole a questioning look. "What's that supposed to mean?"

"As soon as word gets around about that sensitive side of yours, women are going to be beating down your door."

"What sensitive side?" Randy asked warily.

Cole became serious. "The side that writes songs."

"What makes you think I do that?"

"Don't even try to deny it," Cole said. "If I hadn't had my head stuck where it didn't belong, I'd have seen your hand all over that music a long time ago." Several seconds passed before he added, "Why didn't you want me to know?"

"I was looking for an honest opinion."

"Well, now that you've got one, what do you intend to do?" Cole asked.

"That all depends."

"On?"

"Whether you're interested in—"

"Goddammit, Randy, you better not be thinking about selling those songs to someone else."

"Well, I'll be. It looks like I finally got the upper hand on something in this family."

"Don't go getting cocky on me."

Randy looked at Cole and grinned. "It's too late. I intend to milk this cow until the bucket's overflowing."

Cole leaned his head back against the seat and closed his eyes. A contented smile formed. Randy was entitled to his bucketful and several more besides.

"Don't get too comfortable," Randy warned. "As soon as we hit Dellwood Boulevard, I'm pulling over and you're getting in the back."

Cole couldn't help but smile. What a great homecoming, hiding in the back of a pickup truck to get through the crowds of reporters. Ah, the glories of fame.

The sky had turned purple with the promise of dawn when Cole finally gave up on the idea of sleep the next morning and went downstairs to fix himself a cup of coffee. Frank was already in the kitchen, dressed in an old plaid bathrobe and the slippers Randy had given him for Christmas almost fifteen years earlier.

"Welcome home," Frank told him.

It was the first they'd seen of each other since Cole's return. "Thank you." Feeling generous, he added, "It's good to be here."

"Are you up because you couldn't sleep, or because you're still operating on Tennessee time?"

"Probably a combination of both."

"It appears the months you were away were what you needed. I haven't seen you look this good in a long time."

Cole ran his hand over his freshly shaven chin. He'd had the beard so long it was going to take a while to get used to having it gone. "I had trouble getting my contacts in this morning." He blinked several times in reflex. "They still feel a little strange."

"Maybe you need a new pair."

"Maybe." A stranger listening to their conversation would think they had simply picked up talking where they'd left off the night before.

"How's Holly?" Frank asked with seemingly genuine interest.

It was a question Cole hadn't expected. He was surprised Frank would willingly bring up something so potentially divisive. "She was asleep when I called last night. Horace, that's her grandfather, said she was tired, but other than that, she seemed okay to him."

Frank poured another cup of coffee and handed it to Cole, then walked over to the table and sat down. "When I got home last night Randy told me what happened with Belinda. I was so mad I said I was going to pile her stuff out on the tennis court and have a barbecue for the reporters hanging around out front. Janet talked me out of it."

Cole laughed. "Too bad. It sounds like a great idea to me."

Neither man said anything after that. Soon an expectant silence hung heavy between them. Cole tried to cover the awkwardness by rummaging through the refrigerator. Frank nervously stirred sugar in his coffee. It was as if the years of antagonism that had brought them to this time and place could not be put aside until they were acknowledged.

Frank stopped stirring and took a sip of the thick black liquid he called coffee and everyone else called syrup. "Did you find what you were looking for, Cole?" he asked in a quiet voice.

Cole put bagels and cream cheese on the counter and sat down opposite his father. "I don't know that they were the ones I set out to find, but I came home with a few answers."

"I don't want to make more of it than you mean it to be, but you said 'home.' Was that just an expression, or . . ."

"I've changed since the accident. From the looks of it we all have. I'm hoping it's permanent, because there's no way in hell I'll go back to the way it was around here before I left." He paused to let the threat settle in and be accepted, then realized he'd left out the most important part. "I know now that being a singer is what I want to do and that right here is where I belong."

"I've been thinking along those same lines, Cole, and believe it or not, I don't want things going back the way they were any more than you and Randy do. In order to keep that from happening, I've come up with an idea that I want to tell you about." Frank stuck the spoon back in his cup and started stirring. "You know how record people are always bringin' me singers and asking me to take them on? Well, I decided it might do all of us good if I had a couple of other people to manage." He was stirring so fast the clanging coming from the cup made it sound like a bell. "That doesn't mean I'll be slackin' off around here or down at the office. And if the time ever comes that you start thinking I'm too busy to do right by you, I'll pull back till we've got it worked out. But I won't ever go back to having nothing but your business to keep me busy. Hell, with Randy taking over as much as he has I don't know that it would even be possible anymore. There's hardly anything left for me to do at the office."

"I know how hard this has been for you." It had taken thirty-two years for Cole to see his father as human and fallible and not an invincible enemy.

"It's been hard on all of us," Frank said, the noise from his stirring as loud as his voice.

Cole reached across the table and took the spoon away from his father. "You asked me earlier if I found what I was looking for when I left."

"I didn't mean to pry or to make it seem as if you had to tell me if you didn't want to."

"Do you remember when I was eighteen and we spent those six months straight in Nashville? My voice had finally settled down and you were convinced I was ready for my big break."

"I knocked on the doors along Music Row every day of every week that we were there," Frank said. "There wasn't a record company anywhere in that city I didn't hit at least twice."

"While you were inside talking business I would go over to the university and walk around the campus. I'd talk to the kids I met and pretend I belonged. At night I'd think about someone I'd seen that day and try to imagine what it felt like to be him. I wanted it so bad it hurt."

Frank combed his hands through his hair and looked up at the ceiling. "And here I thought I was giving you and Randy this amazin' childhood. You were living the life and doing the things other people were always sayin' they wished they had the guts to do. Every time you went out on a stage, there wasn't a man in the audience that wasn't secretly wishing he was you—then and now."

"I guess it was something I couldn't be told but had to find out for myself."

"The sorry thing is that you didn't get to pick your time to come back, that it was done for you. And you shouldn't have had to leave Holly behind the way you did."

"We'll get through it," Cole said.

"Damn straight we will." Frank grinned. "Now that we're on the subject, I think it's time you told me about this grandson of mine."

"Grand*daughter*," Cole corrected. "There's really not much to tell other than Holly's going to be making her own changes around here and I don't think any of us is man enough to stop her."

"I was just wonderin', not that I'm going to do anything about it real soon, but I've been thinking . . . well, I've been doing more than thinking if the truth be known, it's more like—"

"Jesus, Dad, would you just spit it out?"

Frank took a drink of coffee and cleared his throat.

"What would you say if I told you I've been considering giving that little girl you and Holly got coming a grand-mother?"

A slow smile spread across Cole's face. "I'd say it would be just about the best present she's going to get from any-one."

Later that morning Cole was swimming laps with Randy when Janet came out of the house and walked across the lawn toward them. "Anyone want to see today's papers?" she asked, waving a copy of a tabloid over her head.

Cole swam to the end of the pool and hiked himself out of the water. "I take it you already know what's there?"

"Other than a lot of creative speculation about your rea-sons for being in Tennessee, they're all frantic for details about the pregnant mystery woman. I should warn you that whatever facts they couldn't get from Holly's friends and neighbors, they made up."

Randy joined them. "What do they say about Cole?"

"That he's been sequestered in an undisclosed loca-tion," Janet said.

"Why do they say I'm hiding now?" Cole asked.

"You're going to love this one—the majority of the tabloids are saying that the plastic surgery you had after the accident wasn't successful and you've turned into a pathetic monster." Randy started to say something. Janet held up her hand. "Wait, there's more. According to unnamed sources, Cole was suicidal when he saw his face so Frank arranged for him to impregnate Holly to give him a reason to live."

"And do they say how Frank went about arranging this?" Randy asked.

Cole groaned as he scanned the paper Janet held. "I hope Horace keeps this crap away from Holly."

"I can hardly wait to parade you out at the press confer-ence," she said to Cole with a wicked grin. "After we stick a hat on you to cover the short hair, no one is going to be able to tell you were ever in an accident." She tossed the stack of papers on a nearby table and began sorting through them. "There's a particular one in here I thought you might want to see."

She handed Cole a copy of the mainstream Nashville newspaper. Unlike the others that had blurred photographs of him and Holly, taken as they made their frantic dashes to and from the limo, these showed her clearly. The pictures were several years old. Holly's hair was longer and she was bone-rattling skinny, but the facial difference was so slight a child could make the connection.

"Where do you suppose they got them?" Janet asked.

"I don't know," Cole said, staring at the paper. It was inevitable that a good picture of Holly would surface eventually, but Cole had hoped it wouldn't happen until after they were together again.

Randy came up beside Cole and peered over his shoulder. "I like this woman. She looks feisty, like she's got a mind of her own." He chuckled and gave Cole a playful punch on the arm. "Something tells me we're going to get along just fine."

Cole had a gut feeling that he should do whatever it took to clear the path for Holly to join him as soon as possible. "Can you move the press conference up?" he asked Janet.

The depth of his unspoken fear was communicated to her in the single question. Her smile faded. "You want it as soon as possible, I assume?"

He nodded.

"I'll see what I can do."

The next day Cole was talking to Buddy when Janet came into the living room. He motioned that he would be off the phone in a minute, then glanced up and saw the look on her face. "Buddy, I'm going to have to call you back."

"Be sure and tell Holly that we've got the spare room fixed up for your visit."

"I'll do that," Cole said, his eyes locked on the woman who looked as though she'd rather be anyplace but there, "just as soon as I find her." He hung up. "What's happened?" he asked Janet.

"I take it you haven't seen *The Tennessean* yet?"

"No."

"Have you ever heard of a man named Troy Martin?"

The question hit him like a gut punch. He reached for the newspaper she was holding. He didn't have to look past the headline—"WEBSTER'S FATHERHOOD QUESTIONED"—to know what was going on. Troy Martin had seen an opportunity to get his name in the paper and had grabbed it. "No wonder she wasn't answering the phone this morning," Cole said.

"You mean Holly?"

"If she's seen this . . ." But then reason prevailed. Unless Horace lived near a large bookstore or frequented someplace where they sold out-of-state newspapers, there was no way Holly could have read that morning's *Tennessean*.

"She wouldn't have to see this," Janet said softly. "From what I've been able to find out, the story's been picked up by damn near every newspaper in the country. I should have come to you last night when I was called for a statement, but I thought the story was so asinine it wasn't worth waking you."

"I assumed Frank or Randy would have told you the baby wasn't mine."

"They don't think that way, Cole." She paused, as if gathering strength for the battle ahead. "What do you want me to do about this?"

Frank came into the room. "You told him?" he asked Janet.

She nodded. "Now we're trying to decide the best way to handle it."

Cole stood and walked to the window. He stared outside for several minutes before he turned and said, "I want you to find out whether Troy Martin is doing this because he cares about the baby or the publicity."

"And if it's the baby?" Janet asked.

"Then we'll have to work something out," Cole said.

"And if it's for the publicity?" Frank asked.

"I'll make him the sorriest son of a bitch who ever lived. He used Holly and got away with it. I'll be damned if I'll let him use her baby."

"Maybe you should call Holly to warn her this is coming," Frank said.

"I've tried to reach her all morning."

"I think we should have someone fly down there to pick her up." Janet crossed the room and gently laid her hand on Cole's arm. "She's got to know you're going to stick with her through this. If it were me, I'd be out of my mind with worry by now."

"You're right, but I can't do anything like that until I can get her on the phone," Cole admitted reluctantly.

"Why not?" Frank and Janet asked at the same time.

"I don't know where Horace lives." The truth of it was, he hadn't even thought to ask. Holly was only supposed to stay in Phoenix for a couple of days. He had her phone number. Why would he need anything else?

Frank let out a frustrated groan. Janet gave him a silencing look. "It's not as bad as it seems," she said. "We have the phone number; we can check the reverse directory. If I leave for the airport now I can be in Phoenix in a couple of hours. I'll call when I get there, and if you've heard from Holly in the meantime I'll drive out and pick her up. The two of us can be back here by tonight."

The waiting would be excruciating. Cole hated staying behind but knew he wouldn't even be able to get through the Phoenix airport if someone in LA discovered him. "I'd send Marshall, but I think you're going to have your work cut out for you as it is. She'd never agree to leave with a great big lumbering detective."

Janet gave him a reassuring smile. "She may be tough, but I'm tougher."

"God, I hope so," Cole said.

When Janet and Frank were gone, Cole went to the phone and tried Holly again. He let the phone ring a dozen times before he finally gave up. As he returned the receiver to its cradle, he checked the time. He would try again in ten minutes.

He was back at the phone in five.

Cole was alone when the call came from Janet later that night. She'd found a note with Cole's name on it attached to the front door of Horace Murdoch's duplex.

"Open it," Cole told her.

"Are you sure?" Janet said gently. "Wouldn't you rather read it yourself?"

"I don't want to wait that long."

There was a tearing sound and then:

*Dear Cole,*

*One of the things I love best about you is that you've always understood why I had to put my baby before anything or anyone else. I know that he was almost your baby too, and that your love for me included him, but I can't let that get in the way of what I have to do. I can't let Troy take my baby. I've thought about this, Cole, and it scares the hell out of me. There are a lot of judges in this country who would claim I wasn't fair to Troy because I never told him about the baby and that I was unfit to be a mother because of what happened with you. What if I got one of those judges?*

*Grandpa is going to stay with me until after the baby is born. He's confused about Troy and how he fits into my life and keeps telling me I should just tell him to go to hell, that my baby already has a father.*

*I love you and I'm sorrier than I know how to say*

*for hurting you. I'll never stop wondering what our
lives together would have been like, but right now
leaving is all I can see to do. Please forgive me.*

*Holly*

There was a catch in Janet's voice as she finished. "Do
you want me to read it again?"

"No," he said.

"I'm so sorry, Cole."

"I'll find her, Janet," he said with conviction. "I don't
care how long it takes, I'll find her."

Randy came in a short time later. He started to say
something, stopped, and stared at Cole. "Jesus, what happened to you?"

"Holly's gone." It was everything he could do to say the
words out loud. "She found out about Troy and took off."

"You couldn't talk her out of it?"

"I didn't get a chance."

Randy sat down across from Cole. "She must really be
scared."

"That baby is everything to her."

"What can I do?"

Cole didn't have an answer; he didn't know what he was
going to do himself yet. And then, "You can call the airport and have a plane ready as soon as possible."

"You think you know where she might have gone?"

"No." His fear and anger had found a target. "But I
know where Troy Martin is."

The plane Randy hired landed in Nashville an hour
ahead of the sun the next morning. Cole gave the limo
driver directions to Emily Thomas's house and sat back
for the ride.

Randy had offered to come with him. When Cole
refused, he'd insisted. But this was something Cole had to
do alone. He'd left Randy at the airport, off on a wild

goose chase looking for a pilot who was already in the cockpit. Fifteen minutes into the flight, Randy was on the phone complaining. It wasn't until Cole convinced him that he had no intention of taking Troy on physically that Randy agreed not to follow.

A black eye wasn't what he wanted to give Troy Martin. Cole had something more permanent in mind.

The limo driver stopped outside the gated entrance and sent word that Cole Webster was there to see Troy Martin. The iron barrier swung open immediately, almost as if he'd been expected.

Troy met Cole at the door. Displaying a wide grin, he stepped aside to let Cole enter the expansive, marble tile foyer. Troy was tall and muscular, his hair expertly and expensively cut to cover a thinning pate. He was dressed in a dark blue silk bathrobe, open to his waist to expose a thick mat of chest hair. His legs were bare, his feet in slippers. The projected image was proprietary, as if he were the owner of the sprawling home instead of merely a temporary guest.

Troy smiled and held out his hand. "It's a real honor to have you here. I've been a fan of yours for years."

"Save it," Cole said, ignoring Troy's outstretched hand. "You know why I've come. Let's get on with it."

"I'll have some coffee brought into the living room."

"I won't be here that long."

"Now there's no reason this can't be handled in a civilized manner."

Cole studied him. "I can assure you my lawyers are as civilized as they come," he said coolly. "Until they get into a courtroom, that is."

The smile left Troy's face. "Now why would you want to bring lawyers into something that could just as well be handled between friends?"

Cole had the answer he'd come for. It wasn't Holly's baby Troy was after. "I just assumed you would want your parental rights protected."

Troy picked up on the change in Cole and was visibly shaken. "Well, I wasn't thinkin' of doing anything on a legal level, if that's what you mean."

Cole shoved his hands in his pockets to keep them still. "What level was it you had in mind?"

"I just figured that since the two of us have something in common, it would be natural to want to help each other out every now and then."

"I see. And how did you figure you would help me out?"

Troy ran his hand across his chest in an agitated gesture, then pulled the robe closed and retied the sash. "I thought you might want a clear road with Holly, that's all."

"And the baby?"

He put his hand to his mouth to cover a nervous cough. "You get one, you get 'em both."

"And in exchange?" Cole pushed.

"You could introduce me around. You know, put a good word in with the people who count."

Cole paused, giving the impression he was considering Troy's proposal. "Kind of a gentleman's agreement, is that what you had in mind?"

"That's it," Troy said eagerly.

"I don't know," Cole said. "My attorneys seem to think it would be a lot better for Holly and the baby to establish legal ties with you." He was taking a hell of a chance Troy wasn't smart enough to call his bluff. "That way they'd have financial security for the next twenty years no matter what happened with me."

"Legal ties?" Troy repeated, his eyes wide.

"You know—alimony, child support, that kind of thing. I should tell you, Troy, my attorneys are good at what they do. When they get through with you, you'll be lucky to keep half of what you make for the next couple of decades."

"Not if I say I made a mistake and the baby's not mine."

"There are blood tests that—"

"You son of a bitch—why'd you really come here?"

"To find out what kind of person you are."

"That's it?"

"There's one other thing. You know all those people you wanted me to put in a good word with for you?"

"What about them?" Troy asked warily.

Cole's voice became menacing. "I don't think you want me to mention your name at all."

"Are you threatenin' me?"

"I'm just saying you want to stay as far away from me and the people I care about as you can—out of sight, out of mind."

"What if those lawyers of yours did up some papers that said I don't want anything to do with that baby?"

"Is that what you want?"

"If it'll get you off my back."

"I'm afraid that won't work, Troy. Anything you do has to be strictly voluntary. Otherwise you might come back later and say I coerced you into giving up your rights."

"It's what I want."

Cole nodded, acknowledging Troy's capitulation. "Have your lawyer send a copy of the papers to my office."

"I don't have a lawyer."

"Would you like me to recommend one?"

"I'd like you to go to hell."

For the first time since arriving, Cole smiled. "Good luck on your career, Troy."

# 25

**Ten months later**

*Cole climbed the ladder* at the back of the stage to check the rigging on the aerial pulley system that would carry him across the stadium for the opening of the show. It was the most ambitious stunt he'd ever tried and the most dangerous. So far they'd played three cities on the tour and he'd made his flashy entrance without mishap an even dozen times. Frank swore he aged another year with each show but couldn't argue with the crowd's reaction.

Four wires led from the stage into the audience and no one outside of the crew and band knew ahead of time which one Cole would slide down that night. So far the reviews on the show were mixed, which surprised none of them. The critics who were purists hated the theatrics, claiming special effects weren't what country music was all about; the more open-minded critics liked the lights and smoke but complained that all the "bells and whistles" carried over to the ballads and were intrusive even when absent. Frank had made small adjustments as they moved from city to city, and all were confident they finally had it together for this, their opening night in Dallas.

"Did you try the hand brake?" Cole asked the man working with him. "It seemed a little mushy this morning."

The man nodded. "Randy said it was just the way you like it."

"Randy?" Cole questioned.

"He was sliding down all morning. You'd think this was his private amusement park."

Randy came strolling across the stage. "Not true," he protested. "I'm only checking things out to be sure the star doesn't fall on his ass and embarrass the band."

Cole threw a wad of silver tape at his brother. "Where'd you take off to? Frank's been looking everywhere for you."

Randy waved the question aside. "I've been around."

Sensing there was something wrong, Cole pushed. "Around where?"

Randy hesitated before he said reluctantly, "Janet needed some help checking out the Hollys."

As if sensing the conversation was about to turn personal, the stagehand wandered away.

Cole hated that he couldn't just leave what had happened outside alone but had to ask, "And?" Ever since he appeared on the *Barbara Walters Special* and pleaded for Holly to contact him, he'd been inundated with women pretending to be her. The wannabes called and wrote by the hundreds. They stood outside his office, his home, and the stage door of every concert. Even after all the disappointments, Cole held on to the hope that the real Holly would write or call or simply show up one day.

"There were a couple that looked pretty close, but they couldn't answer any of the questions about Phoenix."

Cole straddled the top of the ladder and wrapped his feet around the second rung. There were times when thoughts of what he'd lost with Holly would hit him so hard he could barely function. Frank and Janet had damn near killed themselves putting the tour together to get him back onstage again. But more important, to get him out of the house and to keep him from going into the room he'd had decorated for a little girl, to keep him from staring at the crib he'd brought back from Tennessee and, in his darkest moments, had begun to think would never be used.

"It would hurt Buddy and Suzy to know this, but I can hardly stand to be around David," Cole said. "Every time I look at that baby I think about Holly and . . ." Cole reached up to rub the back of his neck. "God, you must get tired of listening to me go on about this."

"Sometimes," Randy said, "but then there's other times you make me wonder what it would be like to love someone as much as you love that woman, and I feel jealous."

"Has it changed me so much?" Cole asked.

"You look at things differently now. It's as if you walked through a door when you met Holly and now you can never go back. What you learned, you can never unlearn."

Cole smiled. "Sounds like you're working on a new song."

"It's a theme I've been thinking about lately," Randy admitted.

Cole looked around the stage, at the crew engaged in last-minute preparations and at the empty stadium that would be filled with sixty thousand people in less than five hours. "Thank God for all of this," he said to himself as much as to Randy. "It's what keeps me going. I don't know what I'd do without it."


Holly checked the number on her ticket against the number on the seat and then turned to the stage to see how far back she was. Her heart sank. With all the paraphernalia between the front of the stage and the first row, she was a lot farther away than she'd counted on being.

Three hundred dollars. It was a lot of money to hear someone sing, but she had no doubt if she hadn't paid the scalper's price, someone else would have. She'd started combing the concert ticket ads in the newspaper the day she arrived in Dallas and the eighteenth row was the best she'd been able to do.

A month ago she thought reaching the decision to see Cole again had been the real battle, that once it was behind her all she'd have to do was write or pick up the phone. It had taken months for her fears about Troy to shrink to a manageable size, and even more months of her grandfather's loving attention and the growing joy of being a mother, to help her recover from a crippling case of postpartum depression.

In the back of her mind she'd accepted the possibility that Cole had moved on without her; it was the chance she'd taken when she left. With Troy barging back in her life, she was trouble for Cole and God knew he already had enough of his own. The one thing she'd never imagined was that coming to the decision to see him again was nothing compared to how hard it would be to pull it off.

In a stupid gesture used to finalize her decision to leave Phoenix, she'd thrown away the unlisted phone numbers Cole gave her. So instead of calling, her initial attempt to contact him had been through a letter. The response had come from his fan club and had consisted of a mass-produced 8-by-10 photograph with a machine-stamped autograph and a newsletter telling about the current concert tour.

Her second attempt had been to call Webster Enterprises. The woman who answered the phone hadn't actually laughed at Holly when she told her who she was, but she'd come close. When Holly persisted, telling the woman Cole would be extremely unhappy when he found out she'd called and couldn't get through to him, she learned she was the hundredth "Holly" to call that day. Confused, Holly had done some research and discovered what was going on and why so many women were trying to pass themselves off as her.

She and Horace agreed it was useless to write or phone again; she would have to go wherever Cole was. According to the newsletter the fan club had sent, that meant Kansas City. She'd arrived several hours before Cole's last show was to begin and had the cab driver drop her off at the performers' entrance. The months she'd spent on the road with Troy had given her a familiarity with backstage operations and she was confident, given the chance, she'd be able to talk her way inside.

She wasn't even able to get close enough to try. The "Hollys" waiting for Cole were hundreds deep.

She wasn't discouraged when she left Kansas City: she was determined. She was going to see Cole again if she had to follow him to every concert date in the country. Which she sincerely hoped wouldn't be necessary, considering that the money Cole had given her in Phoenix, and that she'd tried to use as sparingly as possible, was running low. She and Horace had lived frugally in the small Louisiana town where they'd settled, and the hospital and doctor had cost less than she expected, but no matter how hard they tried, they always wound up spending more money each month than she earned working part-time at the restaurant.

A woman moved past Holly and sat in the seat next to her. She was wearing a black Stetson, bright red shirt with silver buttons, black jeans with a silver belt buckle, and red-and-black boots with silver toes. Her smile was as flashy as her outfit. "Is this your first time seein' one of Cole Webster's concerts?" she asked conversationally.

"I've heard him sing, but it wasn't in a place like this." The size of the stadium and the number of people who'd come to see Cole awed Holly. It was one thing to read about Cole's popularity, another entirely to actually see it for herself. Even with the evidence all around her, it was hard to make the mental transition between the man she'd known who had sung to a roomful of people more interested in studying their menus than listening to him and this megastar with thousands of fans buying everything from T-shirts to coffee cups just because they had Cole Webster's picture on them.

"Don't tell me you're one of the people who heard him play in that restaurant in Tennessee. There's gotta be a couple thousand of you at last count."

"I don't understand what you mean," Holly said.

"I'm sorry to sound so disbelievin', but it seems like everything written about Cole Webster since all that business of him showin' up in Tennessee has another person claimin' they recognized him when he was there but didn't tell no one because they didn't want to disturb his privacy. You gotta admit it gets a little hard to swallow after a while, kind of like all those people who say they saw Elvis down at the local McDonald's."

"I guess when you're as famous as Cole Webster is, everybody wants a piece of you," Holly said. "Even if it's in the telling of an embellished story."

"Personally, I don't blame him for taking off the way he did." The woman smiled. "I'm just real glad he didn't stay."

"I take it you're a longtime fan?"

"I go all the way back to when he was playing the honky-tonks in these parts. The first time I saw him standing up onstage I told Skeeter—he was my husband at the time—to mark my word, Cole Webster was gonna be somebody someday." She talked with a proprietary pride, as if her prediction had somehow had a hand in making Cole the star he'd become. "What about you?" she asked.

"I don't go back nearly so far," Holly said.

Members of the opening band walked out onstage and took their positions. The show was about to begin. A nervous excitement came over Holly, a cold fear gripped her insides, her skin felt on fire. After all these months, in less than an hour, she would see the man she'd decided she wanted to spend the rest of her life with, the man who would be the father to her baby, the man she loved beyond reason and beyond her fear of Troy Martin and his power over her.

The time passed with the speed of a cloud floating across a summer sky. Holly uncharitably prayed for the warm-up singer to trip on something or to develop laryngitis. And then finally, Cole's band was in place and the house lights were dimmed. An expectant hush fell over the stadium; the cumulative anticipation of sixty thousand people became a living, breathing thing. Her eyes were fixed on the dark stage when a dozen searchlights began sweeping the audience. She was confused and looked to the woman beside her.

"What's going on?"

"Shhhh," she harshly admonished, and then excitedly pointed. "There."

Holly looked toward the back of the stadium where she'd been directed. Just then the lights converged and someone leaped in the air and came flying in their direction. A deafening roar swept the audience as they came to their feet. It seemed impossible, but the cheering increased as the figure came closer. Holly could see that it was a man, and that he had a guitar strapped to his back, and that he looked a lot like . . . oh, dear God, it didn't just look like Cole, it was Cole.

He hit the stage at a run, turned to face the crowd, and threw his fist in the air in triumph. The band broke into his signature song, a hard-driving, this-is-who-I-am, take-it-or-leave-it country rock piece that shook the cheap seats with the foot-stomping that accompanied the dominant bass. Cole approached the edge of the stage, swung his guitar across his hips, and let go of the first stanza in a deep-throated roar. Sixty thousand voices joined in.

Holly stood frozen, her mouth open in surprise. She tried to fit the man onstage into the nice, tidy mold her mind had reserved for Neal Chapman. But the mold was a triangle, and Cole Webster was a sparkling, spinning cube. His talent electrified her. The air crackled with the force of his personality.

The song ended; the applause went on and on until Cole held up his hand to quiet the crowd. Laughing, he told them they were going to have to show some restraint, that he had a set number of songs to sing and he wasn't about to let them go home until he'd finished. They shouted their approval.

When he got them quiet again, he introduced the band, telling short intimate stories that changed the men and women who surrounded him from nameless musicians into individuals. Only the bass player remained.

"And now I want you to meet the real talent in the Webster family," Cole said, "my brother, Randy. A few months back, while I was out wandering around this fantastic country of ours, he was home writing the songs for the album we'll be releasing in the fall. I don't want to say too much about how good he is—he is my *little* brother, after all, and I wouldn't want to be the one responsible for him getting a big head—but the songs Randy wrote for this album are the best I've ever recorded." Cole waited for the applause to die down before he added with a grin, "Each and every day I say a prayer of thanks that God gave me a brother who can write like a poet and sing like a lovesick tomcat."

Randy laughed along with everyone else. Cole walked back to center stage and strummed the opening chords to a ballad. When he started to sing, his voice was clear and pure. He told about a farmer too long in the fields, his wife too long in the kitchen, their dreams and hearts too long on hold.

Tears filled Holly's eyes as she listened. Cole didn't just tell the story about the farmer and his wife; he felt it. And in the process, he made everyone else feel it, too.

The third song was another ballad. This time, to reach the audience on a more elemental level, the house lights were turned on. Cole came to the edge of the stage and looked into the faces of the people who had come to share their evening with him.

It was the moment Holly had been waiting for. Her hands trembling, she dug into the oversized purse tucked between her feet and took out a folded piece of canvas. She only had a minute, two at the outside, for him to notice her, the approximate time she figured it would take for the people sitting behind her to call the security guards to complain.

She struggled getting her sign open and almost raised it upside down, but finally she held her message aloft . . . and waited. Her eyes were closed and she could hardly breathe.

The band didn't miss a beat.

Neither did Cole.

And then, abruptly, Cole stopped singing while the band played on.

Onstage Cole stared at the four words written in red; the words to the song he'd barely begun to sing froze in his throat. The message he read could only have come from one person. His mind wouldn't let him believe what he was seeing. He'd been disappointed too many times. But his body refused to listen to his mind. His heart beat so loudly it drowned out the music.

As a prompt, the band started the song over. When Cole didn't pick up the cue, they tried again. Still he stood rooted and silent and staring out into the crowd.

At last he found his voice. "It's about time you got here," he said with an aching tenderness, making no effort to hide the pain he'd suffered waiting for her.

Holly slowly lowered the canvas and peered over the top, saying a fervent prayer that she would find herself looking into Cole's eyes. All around her she heard whispered questions that rode the crowd like ocean swells. When she saw that Cole was indeed talking to her, she could hardly contain her joy.

The message in his eyes, the words he'd spoken, were as private as they were personal, yet it was as if there were only the two of them in the enormous stadium. "It took me a while to find the way," she called back.

Cole unsnapped his guitar, laid it on the stage, and hopped down to the floor.

Holly dropped her sign and moved past her confused seatmates.

Impatient to touch her, to prove to himself she was real, Cole reached for Holly before she came to the end of the aisle. She leaned forward and threw her arms around his neck. He swept her off her feet; they turned in slow, joyous circles, the force of their embrace seemingly melding them into one.

Their coming together sent a new ripple of confusion through the audience. And then the softly spoken words, "I love you, Holly," were picked up on Cole's cordless microphone and carried throughout the stadium. A new wave, one of excited understanding, followed.

Someone clapped; someone else joined in. Seconds later, as Cole bent to give Holly a heartbreakingly tender kiss, a thundering sound of approval and of vicariously shared happiness surrounded them.

Back at Holly's empty seat, the woman in red and black bent to retrieve the sign that had started all the commotion. She held it up to read the message.

I NAMED HER ROSE.

The woman frowned. Why in the world would anyone get excited about something like that?

# Author's Note

*I'm often asked* where I get my ideas for books and always feel a little guilty when the answer isn't at least as interesting as the story. By necessity, a writer's life, at least this writer's life, is pretty ordinary—when I'm working, it's just me in my office at the computer, my cat asleep on my lap or on top of the file cabinet. *Alone in a Crowd* was an exception, however, and just for fun, I thought I would share the story behind the story with you.

Four years ago I was completing work on *The Way It Should Have Been* when my husband, John, called from the firehouse and casually asked how I'd like to drive the support vehicle for a group of fire fighters who were thinking about bicycling across the United States. Never believing for a minute the trip would take place—John's bike had more cobwebs than the Addams family attic—I said, "Sure, why not?" and went back to work. What he failed to mention was that they were making the trip to benefit the Firefighters Pacific Burn Institute, a charity set up by local fire fighters to support the burn unit at the University of California, Davis, Medical Center. Had I known this, I would have realized the trip, no matter how arduous or improbable, was a done deal.

Six months later, I was in Santa Monica, California, sitting behind the wheel of a thirty-five-foot motor home asking myself how on earth I'd gotten there.

The trip started out rocky but turned into the adventure of a lifetime. The back roads and byways we traveled took us through spectacular country I'm convinced I would never have seen any other way. The men and women in the volunteer and paid firehouses where we stayed were, without exception, warm, generous, and welcoming.

By Memphis, Tennessee, we were ready for a break. Our day off turned serendipitous when John and I decided to visit Elvis Presley's Graceland. Extraordinary fame and its consequences have always fascinated me. I'd wanted to write about the subject for years, but the characters who could tell such a story kept eluding me. Then, as I walked through the rooms of Graceland, it wasn't the incredibly famous and wealthy entertainer who intrigued me; it was the desperately lonely man. "What would it feel like" and "what if" questions filled my mind.

When we left Memphis the next morning, there was another passenger in the motor home, Cole Webster. By the time we reached Virginia Beach, Virginia, Holly and Frank and Randy had all climbed on board. Over the following two years there were countless changes and adjustments to the story. For me, this fine-tuning is the fun part of my job. The hard part comes when I've finished the writing and have to let the story go. The most rewarding is still a year or two away, when readers tell me they were as caught up with the characters as I was. I hope this happened to you.

For their parts in the serendipitous creation of *Alone in a Crowd,* a tip of my hat goes to my traveling companions—Phil Reif, Don Hartwick, Dave Clifton, Dennis O'Sullivan, Dave Saylors, Erik Naisbitt, Dan Magaw,

Nancy Elliott, and most of all, my very special husband, John Bockoven. A loving and heartfelt thank-you goes to Cliff Haskill and Caryl Henderson, directors of the Firefighters Pacific Burn Institute, who were with us in spirit all the way.

### *Alone in a Crowd* by Georgia Bockoven

After a terrible accident, country music sensation Cole Webster must undergo reconstructive surgery which gives him temporary anonymity. Before he can reveal his true identity, Cole loses his heart to Holly, a beautiful woman who values her privacy above all else. Cole must come to terms with who he is and what he's looking for in life before he can find love and true happiness.

### *Destiny Awaits* by Suzanne Elizabeth

When wealthy and spoiled Tess Harper was transported back in time to Kansas, 1885, it didn't take her long to find trouble. Captivating farmer Joseph Maguire agreed to bail her out on one condition–that she live with him and care for his two orphaned nieces. Despite the hardships of prairie life, Tess soon realized that this love of a lifetime was to be her destiny.

### *Broken Vows* by Donna Grove

To Rachel Girard, nothing was more important than her family's cattle ranch, which would one day be hers. But when her father declared she must take a husband or lose her birthright, Rachel offered footloose bounty hunter Caleb Delaney a fortune if he'd marry her–then leave her! Cal knew he'd be a fool to refuse, but he would soon wonder if a life without Rachel was worth anything at all.

### *Lady in Blue* by Lynn Kerstan

A delightful, sexy romance set in the Regency period. Wealthy and powerful Brynmore Talgarth never wanted a wife, despite pressure to restore the family's reputation by marrying well. But once he met young, destitute, and beautiful Clare Easton, an indecent proposal led the way to a love neither knew could exist.

### *The Long Road Home* by Mary Alice Monroe

Bankrupt and alone after her financier husband dies, Nora MacKenzie's life is shattered. After fleeing to a sheep farm in Vermont, she meets up with the mysterious C. W. Friendship soon blossoms into love, but C. W. is keeping some dangerous secrets that could destroy them both.

### *Winter Bride* by Teresa Southwick

Wyoming rancher Matt Decker needed a wife. His mother sent him Eliza Jones, the young woman who had adored Matt when they were children. Eliza was anxious to start a new life out west, but the last thing Matt wanted was to marry someone to whom he might become emotionally attached.

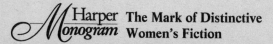